DATE DUE

DATE DUE	
MAR 2 7 1997	
[MAY 0 5 1997	
JUN 1 8 1999	
AUG 0 8 2001	
DEC 1 3 2004	
JAN 2 9 2009	
WITHDRAWN	

Family Fortunes

Also by
ELAINE BISSELL

Women Who Wait
As Time Goes By

Family Fortunes

Elaine Bissell

St. Martin's Press
New York

Design by Doris Borowsky

Library of Congress Cataloging in Publication Data

Bissell, Elaine.
    Family fortunes.

    I. Title.
PS3552.I7728F3   1985   813'.54   85-12530
ISBN 0-312-28050-5

First Edition
10 9 8 7 6 5 4 3 2 1

This is a work of fiction. Any resemblance of characters to actual persons, living or dead, except for public figures, is purely coincidental.

For my daughters, Mary Jane,
Kathleen, and Susan

Family Fortunes

Prologue

The sun burst over the walls of the mosque that soared just above them and spilled from its minaret in a shower of gold into the narrow street, already filled with honking taxicabs, small dusty automobiles, little boys pulling goat carts, and the singsong whine of peddlers. He gazed at the moving mosaic of color, the sea of people, women with children straddling each hip, men with worry beads sitting on stools near doorways, donkey carts and battered bicycles, narrow shops selling everything from caftans to copperware and fake antiquities.

As he slid down lower onto the base of his spine in the rear seat of the tiny Fiat, he put on his sunglasses. It was always a matter of compromise for him, trying to see through the windows of a small automobile like the Fiat. He had to hunch up his long legs and slide into a half-lounging position.

"Not that it matters," he muttered, while pulling out a cigarette.

Alerted by the tone to some kind of ribbing, Alec Harwood glanced at him in the rear-view mirror and saw his slightly crooked grin. "Not that *what* matters?"

"Seeing what it is that you're almost running into every thirty seconds or so. All goats or donkeys look the same, alive or dead. But do me a favor and just warn me, if you can, when you're about to hit one. I realize you feel that Beirut is overpopulated . . ."

"That bloody goat I hit yesterday ran directly in front of the car before I could put on the bloody brakes."

"Excuses, excuses." Steve grinned as he tapped the shoulder of the stocky man sitting next to Harwood. "Keep an eye on him, will you, Carmine? He has tunnel vision and slow reactions."

"Go back to your blasted tape recorder, will you," Alec mumbled, but with a smile nudging the corner of his mouth. "Or to sleep, which would be greatly preferred." The good-natured raillery was a large part of their strong friendship. And although it had taken some getting used to, Carmine now smiled.

"Sleep? With you behind the wheel?" Steve grinned through the mirror again, but picked up the small microphone and began recording in a low droning tone. ". . . which should make us ask, what is at the core of the intra-Lebanese conflict, what is the basis of the violence? A crisis of loyalty? Of identity? The Maronites believe this. They think of themselves as forming a religious, cultural, and distinctive ethnic group—" He cut it off for a moment and tapped Carmine on the shoulder again. "Give me a light, will you, Carmine?"

He was leaning forward, the cigarette clenched between his teeth. As he remembered, his jaw tightened. *Just like the Marlboro man,* she had always teased him, her lovely smile widening. He puffed hard, then slowly leaned back again, letting the cigarette dangle from the corner of his mouth. As always, when she suddenly came into his thoughts, she lingered there and the longing flared anew. He always thought of her the way she was when he first saw her, sitting there at the typewriter in the huge, deserted newsroom, pounding at the keys in that funny hunt-and-peck manner, concentrating so hard, she wasn't even aware he was watching her. The dark hair was long and touched with reddish lights. Her profile was like an etching, the skin almost translucent.

He had been dozing, feet up, swivel chair pushed way back, hat over his eyes, just back from his first assignment in Vietnam. He had wakened and was peering at her from beneath the hat, immediately wondering what it would be like to make love to her, and then, surprisingly, he had chided himself. There was a quality about her . . . a difference . . . no one-night stand here. This was no quick conquest. She made him think of roses and candlelight and the elusive fragrance of expensive perfume.

He squinted his eyes as the smoke curled upward and the little Fiat bumped over the cobblestones. Suddenly his mouth tightened and the jaw tensed, drawing bronzed skin tautly over the high cheekbones. Hard to believe she had been such a fraud . . . still hard to believe . . . all that time she had fooled him. Let him believe she was someone different from the person she really was. He took a deep breath and let it out slowly, then looked out through the window, letting the swirl of color and motion sink into his senses again, pushing past the memory of her face, of her voice, husky and low, making himself hear the sounds of the street again, the barking dogs and screaming children, the erratic chorus of Arabic splashing across the early-morning air.

Sometimes he could go for days without thinking about her by pushing himself for long hours from dawn until night and then falling into bed in exhaustion. But suddenly, with the fragment of a song, or a glimpse of sunset, or just the way a woman might suddenly turn her head at the table next to his in a café, his mind would be filled with her once more. It never failed, the torture beginning again.

"Watch that goat, Alec!" he called out, forcing the mock alarm into his voice. "He's got a small boy attached to him. And yesterday's goat brings the score to three this month."

The knot in his stomach was uncurling, and he could feel the tension in his shoulders receding. He picked up the microphone again.

Carmine looked around at him with a wide grin on his swarthy face. His two colleagues argued about everything, about the sun coming up, the moon going down, the number of Islamic mosques or Greek Orthodox churches in Beirut, the weather, how many words each of them had filed to their wire services that day, anything and everything. Harwood was running his hand through his spiky red hair, which meant the argument was just getting under way.

"Well, I paid the fellow for his bloody dead goat and even he seemed to be admitting that the blasted creature swerved in front of the car before I could make a move—" The words froze.

Carmine had seen the swift shadow of motion first and slammed his hands flat on the narrow dashboard, while shouting, "On my right!" Alec swung the steering wheel wildly.

But it was too late. A ramshackle-looking van with dust and mud-encrusted windscreen and windows cut in front of the little red Fiat. It seemed to come from nowhere. At first the three men thought it was just another of the many collisions that occurred daily in the narrow streets of the ancient sections of Beirut, and they cursed as the fenders meshed with a grind of metal and broken headlights, while people and goats and carts scattered.

Steve lunged forward in the rear seat, his hand on the door handle, ready to leap out and start cursing at the other driver, but he quickly grasped Harwood's shoulder instead. Men with submachine guns were tumbling from the van.

3

"Christ! It's an ambush!" he said, his voice low. Then he shouted. *"Move this crate!"*

He heard the grind of gears, saw Harwood's hand whip the gear-shift forward; at the same moment his door was ripped open and hands pulled him out to the street. From the corner of his eye, in that split second, he had seen Harwood and Carmine both being dragged from the car, and heard the sudden shrieking and babble of voices as people fled in all directions. He lunged forward, lashing out with his free arm, and then he felt a sharp, excruciating blow at the back of his head. He slumped over, gasping with the pain, light flashing behind his eyes while everything blurred in front of him. Half-carried, half-dragged, he felt himself being heaved into the van, then someone tying his ankles and his wrists behind him. A blindfold was wrenched over his eyes.

He heard voices, shouts, and knew that Alec and Carmine were somewhere in the back of the van with him, along with two or three other men who uttered quick, gutteral, Arabic oaths. He felt the sudden motion of the van's wheels underneath as his face ground into the rusted metal flooring and something sharp cut into his cheek. The pain at the back of his head was throbbing into a dull ache. He tried to arrange his thoughts, fighting through the jumble to reorient himself. *The date . . . start with the date . . . November fourth. . . .* He tried to move, but his head was jammed into a corner, then someone kicked at him and pushed him hard against the side of the van. Holding himself rigid, he inched his head around so that the pressure against the sharp object eased on his cheek.

It was sorting out now, thoughts falling into place. Her face . . . always her lovely face. Floating there somewhere. Just out of reach. The eyes filled with hurt, large and dark-lashed. Watching him. And the terrible, deep hurt. She had been standing in the lobby of the hotel in Saigon. His second assignment in Vietnam. He was with the Senator, who was there on a fact-finding tour. As he walked toward her, the Senator's voice boomed out in surprise, "Why, Caroline! Caroline Kendall! What are you doing here, of all places?"

Caroline Kendall? He had paused in confusion, then walked slowly on, watching her, his eyes never leaving her face as it grew pale, the happiness and excitement at seeing him slipping from her eyes. *Caroline Kendall?* All that time he had known her as Carol Kramer. Carol Kramer . . . a reporter on the *World Inquirer* in Boston.

It had ended in that moment. She knew it almost as quickly as he

4

did. Knew it when he stopped and stared at her, while the Senator bumbled on. "Why, Caroline," he had said as he kissed her cheek. "I just had lunch with your father at the Union Club last week." He had looked around at Steve. "We've just been on an inspection tour at Hué and some members of the press came along. This is Steve—"

"I *know* Steve, Senator." She had spoken quickly when the Senator tried to introduce them, and he had turned to Steve with new respect in his eyes and said, "Well, then, you must know Lawrence Kendall as well, Caroline's father."

"Lawrence Kendall? *The* Lawrence Kendall?" Steve heard his own voice saying the name with a remote, cold anger. It had all ended there. They had walked away from the Senator, into the bar of the Continentale Palace Hotel, and there in the dimly lit room it had ended. He had walked out of her life. But in all the years that had passed, she had still been a part of him . . . deep inside. It was something that had never changed . . . never would change.

Carol . . . Caroline. He formed the name on his lips . . . *Caroline* . . . and as he did, he suddenly heaved upward, a shout roaring from his throat. When a blow stung the back of his head again, he slumped down and everything began to slip away from him . . . far, far away, until there was nothing. Just her face as his body floated down into a deeper and deeper darkness . . . and then . . . nothing.

BOOK
I

1
1979

"Excuse me, Miss, but—can I help you?"

She turned and looked at him, her movements calculatedly slow and measured. He was stocky, medium height. The sleeves of his white shirt were rolled up into tight wedges high on his arms. He had a pencil stuck behind his ear and wiry graying hair that stood up from his forehead in tiny waves like an old-fashioned marcel. His face was seamed, eyebrows bushy, eyes cynical.

"No, thanks," she said with a cool expression. "I'm just waiting for someone. And looking."

She had been gazing around at the sea of desks—circa 1930, she estimated with a quick glance—and the years of accumulated litter, piles of newspapers, discarded coffee containers, books, and unreturned file envelopes. The tall windows obviously hadn't been washed in years.

"It's certainly a mess, isn't it?" she said with a critical edge, glancing at him from beneath the shadowy brim of her hat. "And the desks should be in an antique show."

He looked her over, the brown lizard shoes and purse, rich dark brown fur coat, chunky gold necklace and earrings, a hint of expensive perfume. Junior Leaguer, he thought, with some do-gooder article for the Living section.

"Look, Miss, I'm sorry," he said brusquely. "We don't permit the public to come in here. But I'd be glad to direct you to wherever it is in the building you're going." He was talking loudly to be heard over the drone of teletype machines and typewriters. "To the Women's Department or back to the security desk."

"What's your name?" she asked and saw his face redden.

"Y'know, I don't want to be rude, but it's against all regulations—"

"I asked for your name." Her voice was cool and there was a small smile on her face, a face one was not likely to forget, with its exquisite bone structure and hauntingly beautiful eyes that shaded from blue to violet.

"It's Harry Drummond and I happen to be the editor of the international desk here and—"

"I thought so," she said, her smile widening enchantingly to reveal two even rows of perfectly formed teeth. "Ed Pinckney said to look for a bull-voiced man with gray hair like wire wool and blue eyes that could cut you to ribbons." She was laughing softly.

"Ed? Ed Pinckney? You know Ed—?" They both turned as a man's voice called to her.

"Sorry, Miss Kendall, my secretary just told me you'd come on up here." He was smiling warmly. "I was tied up with the circulation people."

Drummond's head was whipping confusedly back and forth between them as he murmured the name *Kendall.*

"Oh, I see you've met Harry," the tall white-haired man said, as he came up to them.

"Well, she's met me, but I haven't met her," Drummond said, still confused, but the old spark returning.

"Caroline Kendall, Harry," Walter Fairfield said with a smile. Then he looked at Caroline. "Don't pay any attention to Harry. He's the fourth-floor grouch."

"Oh, but I *do* pay attention," she said, as Drummond's mouth dropped a little and he stared at her, while mouthing the words *Well, I'll be damned!*

She grinned. "I was completely out of line, coming up here on my own when I already knew what the rules and regulations were, and I apologize." She put her hand in Drummond's while he still watched her with a kind of astonishment. "Mr. Drummond is to be commended for telling me off."

"And how is old Ed Pinckney?" he murmured, slowly dropping her hand.

"Still making trouble in Boston." She grinned wider. "Writing a political column now, as you probably know, for the *Inquirer.*"

Drummond was finally smiling. "He always was a maverick."

"As most good reporters are." She turned then and gazed down the length of the block-long city room, Drummond walking away somewhat dazedly, muttering how nice it was to have met her. She was slowly shaking her head back and forth. "I never get over it," she said in a low voice, and Walter Fairfield understood what she meant. A familiar lump was filling her throat as she felt the same thrill and excitement she had known as a child when she saw the vast city room of a newspaper for the first time. She had been standing with her father in a doorway, her hand clutching his. It was the day he had bought the paper in Newark, New Jersey, for Kendall, Inc. Although she had been only eleven years old, she had somehow sensed the power and force that seeped through the excitement and dust and crowded clutter of that sprawling city room.

And now, just as on that day almost thirty years ago, agile young copy boys—one a girl, she noted—were stripping copy from the wire machines and rushing it to one or the other of the eight news desks —international, national, city or state, and sports, business and finance, and the cultural desk—where each editor sat in the slot, his ten or twelve copy editors sitting around the rim. Some editors and reporters, a small group in one area, were working on the new word processors, lines of words spilling onto the green electronic screens.

"I know, I know," the editor-in-chief was saying. He was rangy and tall beside her, with amused brown eyes and an almost soldierly bearing. "We were slow to start as far as computerizing and electronic newsrooms go. We're probably at the bottom of the list and just beginning to experiment with it. But at least it's a start."

She moved with a quick grace as they walked along the side of the long room. He had helped her off with her coat and she was carrying it over one arm while gesturing with the other, a slender, eager woman in a blue silk suit, her words falling on his ears in a soft, husky rush. Men would stare at her even if she weren't Caroline Kendall, he thought.

"Well, it's one we can certainly start building on," she said. She looked at him with curiosity. "Why did they begin it in such a half-baked way?"

"Money was getting scarce, which was why we were for sale."

"I knew that." She smiled at him again. "A reason we got it at the price we did. Well, by spring we'll have video terminals at almost every desk and at the news slots as well." She looked out across the sea of desks, more than half of the hundred or so empty. The beat reporters were off at the courts or City Hall or the Municipal Building, while others, those on general assignment or on special beats, were out covering or looking for stories. Some of them were beginning to hurry in now as night started to fall. One older man sat down at his desk without removing his coat or hat and was pounding his typewriter. A young woman with long auburn hair and knee-high boots pulled up over her blue jeans sat on the corner of another woman's desk and started reading to her from a notebook, while the older woman listened and nodded, then began typing.

Caroline felt a bittersweet twinge of recognition. The girl reminded her of herself years before. "We weren't permitted to dress like that," she murmured, then smiled. "And that was when blue jeans first became the uniform." She looked up at Walter Fairfield. "But our editor-in-chief hated the Sixties and everything about it." She laughed softly. "It was skirts for the women, and ties and jackets for the men. So Ed Pinckney came to work one morning with a carefully knotted tie over a T-shirt that said MAKE LOVE, NOT WAR on it."

As Fairfield chuckled, she looked overhead and then around at the walls and floors. "We also need to do some face-lifting here, Walter. The place needs to be brought into the twentieth century." She was raising her voice to be heard over the jangle and clatter of wire machines and typewriters, the ringing telephones and shouts of reporters as they called back and forth. "It's terribly primitive."

So it was to be first names right from the start, was it? All right, he thought, and looked down at her with a smile.

"I'd heard you were a stickler for modernization, for upgrading of working conditions," he said, a note of caution in his voice, startled all over again as he gazed at her. He had been told Caroline Kendall was good-looking and of course the pictures of her that the *Morning Journal* had published over the years confirmed that fact. But he had been unprepared for *how* good-looking, for how really beautiful she was. Deep-lashed blue eyes that shaded to violet had a compelling intensity in them, and there was passion in that full-lipped mouth, passion for all things in life. She was sleekly elegant, with narrow, aristocratic hands and feet and high cheekbones beneath a cloud of dark hair that turned under and fell almost to her shoulders.

His laugh was more a chuckle. "But may I suggest that you proceed slowly. Too much sudden luxury and comfort might have a reverse effect on the staff and make them less eager and willing. It was bad enough we went from hot lead in the composing room to cold type almost overnight. That caused a trauma we're still experiencing." He was laughing softly and she suddenly grinned at him, the large wide-set eyes dancing with lights.

"I *do* bash my way through, I guess. Once I started working for Kendall Newspapers at the *World Inquirer,* my father always groaned when he heard my voice on the long-distance phone. 'Now what!' he would always say." Her smile seemed conspiratorial.

"Shall we continue?" Walter Fairfield was laughing. Walking along the side of the cavernous room, she breathed in the dust as another woman would breathe perfume. Twilight outlined the tall, soot-grimed windows and beyond she could see snow falling again, a resumption of the storm that had delayed her arrival from Boston for several hours. The evening staff was still coming in, some sitting, some standing about in small clusters drinking coffee, one largish group dividing a big, round, redolent pizza that someone had brought in from down on Forty-second Street, another pulling hamburgers and sandwiches from several big bags that one of the copy boys had just dumped on a desk.

She saw the tempo quickening as she and the newspaper's editor-in-chief slowly made their way toward the corridor. Morley Harris, the drama critic, was sitting at his desk going through the day's mail, a white silk scarf draped over tuxedoed shoulders, his black chesterfield within arm's reach so that he could grab it and dash out to his opening night. The men on the national desk were wandering back and forth between their desk and the clattering high-speed transmitter that connected the *Journal* wire room with the bureau in Washington. The other ticker machines were pouring thousands of words from throughout the world into the city room. Her fingers literally itched as she watched them. It had been years since she had sat beneath the bright lights at a desk in a city room pouring her heart and her energies into a story. Oh, she still wrote an editorial on occasion. But it wasn't the same. Nothing would ever be the same, she thought, as memories of those days flooded through her with the suddenness of a summer storm.

She looked around as the editors sitting in the bull pen walked back toward the managing editor's office. That would be the final news meeting of the day, when decisions would be made for the page-one stories to run in the next morning's editions. She smiled, a certain sadness in that smile, remembering how Steve and Ab Streitner had sometimes sat at their desks, watching the parade into the managing editor's glass-walled office at the Boston *Inquirer,* and laid bets that a local story about political graft would again take precedence over a national or international story that was shaking the foundations of governments all across the planet.

"He's a provincial ass," Steve would always say of the managing editor. It had been the time when Americans were first going into Vietnam in large numbers. "He doesn't know Saigon from Stalingrad."

"Now see here, McCallum!" Ed Pinckney would usually say, imitating the managing editor's irritatingly nasal voice. "Everytime the Chinese or Russians jump, it isn't always front-page news."

"Coming, Miss Kendall?" Fairfield called out from several feet ahead of her as he turned and watched her, a curious expression on his face. She hesitated for a moment, recalling Steve's slow grin, the way he let the match burn down almost to his fingers. Sometimes, with a maddening innocence on his ruggedly handsome face, he would walk into the managing editor's office without knocking during these sessions to announce with a perfectly straight face that a reader had just phoned in to say she had seen the first robin of spring or that kids had opened a water hydrant on Summer Street, and the whole block was flooded and freezing over. He had gotten away with it because of who he was, a Pulitzer Prize-winning reporter, a foreign correspondent with two tours to Vietnam, three to Israel and Egypt, and now Beirut. . . .

"Yes," she said with a vague sort of smile as she followed Walter Fairfield toward the corridor, away from the warming familiarity of the city room. It was larger than most, but like all city rooms, the wastebaskets and ashtrays overflowed, and desks were stacked high with files and papers, copy boys dashed along between the battered desks, and piles of newspapers cluttered the narrow aisles; there was the jangle of voices and wire machines and typewriters, the sobering presence of scarred, mustard-colored walls and the blue light of early evening filling the tall windows.

"Call composing!" a voice suddenly shouted above the drone of noise. "We've got a makeover for page one." Caroline Kendall and Walter Fairfield stopped dead in their tracks just as they were turning into the corridor. One of the editors at a wire machine ripped a piece of copy off, shouting, "Students in Teheran have stormed the American embassy and taken 90 people hostage. They're demanding that the United States turn over the Shah to them."

14

They watched as the usual pandemonium broke loose, assignment editors shouting orders at reporters, four men and a woman running out of the managing editor's office. Someone turned a television screen on and she saw the big bold letters SPECIAL BULLETIN.

"Fullerton," a voice called out. "The Shah's here—having a gall bladder operation. Check on it. Have someone get the story, reactions, the works. Keyes, get over to the consulate. McBain, get up to the library for clips on the background." As the reporter ran, he shouted, "And I want a map of the city with the location of the embassy!"

"Good Lord! Do you realize what this could mean?" Fairfield said.

"It's terrifying." She closed her eyes for a moment. Always in moments like these, she thought of Steve, no matter where he was. And now in Beirut . . . She turned her face away to hide the sudden fear.

Fairfield led her toward the elevators in the corridor. The old-fashioned clanging cages of iron were still manned by gray- and white-haired attendants whom Caroline felt certain must have been there for forty and fifty years, from the days when the *Morning Journal* had been a young and feisty voice on the New York newspaper scene. No longer young, and struggling to survive with the decrease in newspaper readers, it was still feisty and that was why Caroline Kendall had bought it. That and the price, and because she felt she and the newspapers needed a new challenge.

They stepped into the elevator and were silent as the wizened attendant sent it to the fifth floor, where they got off. As she walked beside Fairfield, she saw how tense he was, how he ached to be back in the charged-up city room.

"Please," she said, pausing, her hand on his arm. "You should probably go back down."

But he smiled and took her arm again. "I'll catch up with it later."

"The editorial board room and the library," Fairfield said, leading her from the marble-floored corridor into the deep hush of two long connected rooms. She saw paneled walls and long walnut conference tables gleaming in the dim light; her feet sank into dark red carpeting. *Oh, my God, Steve, please leave that insane place and come back.*

She simply nodded, not trusting herself yet to speak. Just the morning before, she had checked the wire copy when she first arrived for the day at the *Inquirer.* Another raid on the Lebanon-Israel border near Safad had meant forty-two more dead. The raids were occurring almost daily, the death rate horrifying, the terrorism growing.

Like a sleepwalker, she followed the editor-in-chief into another wide corridor. This one was carpeted and lined with wallpaper in a fine colonial print on each side; small brass light fixtures with tiny silk shades glowed on the walls. Two secretaries sat at the far end in front of two office doors. They entered the one at the corner, and Caroline found herself gazing around a spacious room. She managed to smile at Walter Fairfield, who stood near one of the long windows with its heavy silk drapes in gold. Softly burning lamps illuminated the pale gold carpeting and shone on the highly polished desk.

"The publisher's office," he said with a gracious smile.

"It's more than I expected," she said, attempting a laugh and feeling grateful that it came out sounding normal.

"Well, Phil Cunningham's wife, Vera, had it decorated it to suit *her* tastes. Old Cunningham himself wouldn't have cared if it had looked like a prize fighter's locker room. Probably would have preferred it." Fairfield was grinning, relieved that the stricken look had left her face. "He must be miserable, retired to Florida and living in that pile of glass and redwood she made him build on the beach." What was it that had upset her so? he wondered.

"I met him once with my father," Caroline said, while wandering to one of the other windows and looking down onto Forty-second Street. "He was one of the last *originals*, wasn't he, a roll-your-sleeves-up publisher who still wrote his own editorials and cursed the day they invented electric typewriters?" She smiled at the editor-in-chief, a man who wore soft shetland sweaters beneath his sport jacket.

"A hard man," Fairfield mused softly. "A cigar-smoking, tobacco-chewing, whiskey-drinking old buzzard who, oddly enough, was one of the first to let women in the newsroom. He said, 'If she's as good as a man at reporting the news, then why stop her?' He would have liked you, Miss Kendall."

"Caroline," she said quickly with a smile.

"I've heard you did it the hard way, working as a reporter in Boston for several years, with no one knowing who you were, then out of the Rome bureau before you were discovered to be Caroline Kendall."

She bit her lip, then quickly turned and walked toward the door. He watched her admiringly. She was like a racehorse, slender, almost boyishly so, with a willowy grace and long, slim legs that made her walk firm and purposeful. A nose that was a centimeter too long and too narrow, and eyes that sat almost too widely apart beneath her brow, kept her just short of what was considered traditionally beauti-ful. The cheekbones were too high, the mouth too generous. And yet, other women who were more typically attractive felt threatened by her looks. She was on the tall side, about five-seven or -eight. Fairfield could see that she took daring risks with her clothes, without knowing they were risks. A slouchy, deep-brimmed hat enhanced her classic features and long, leggy slenderness. She wore big chunky pieces of gold jewelry and a distinctive perfume that had been concocted for her alone by a leading parfumière in Paris. There was an elusive sensuality about Caroline Kendall.

"It's hard to believe," Walter Fairfield had said to his wife two weeks earlier when Caroline had come to the *Journal* to sign the contracts. "Here she is, one of the richest women in the world. Yet she's very real. Nice. And down-to-earth and hard working, I'm told."

Caroline was turning at the door. "I've kept you from getting home. . . ."

"Not at all." He smiled as he crossed to her. "I'm here until after the final news meeting. In case something earth-shaking happens."

"Like today?" she said quietly.

"Like today." He took her hand. "I'm glad that someone like you bought the *Morning Journal.* It means a great deal to me—"

"You'll stay on, I hope."

The smile crept to his warm hazel eyes. He had liked her father, Lawrence Kendall, the few times he had met him. And now he liked her. And although Kendall Newspapers represented just a small frac-tion of Caroline Kendall's holdings, he felt certain they were the most important to her. For that he admired her even more.

"I'll be staying," he said. "And with pleasure."

They both turned as one of the secretaries spoke. "A call for you, Miss Kendall," she said, holding the phone out and handing it to her. Fairfield stood at a discreet distance while Caroline spoke quietly into the phone, her face paling a little. When she put it down, she looked around at him. He could see she'd had bad news.

"It's my mother." He could hear the tension and fear in her voice. "She's been in the hospital. She seemed to be . . . holding her own. But that was one of her doctors. He said she suddenly took a turn for the worse." She shook Fairfield's hand again. "Just about an hour ago."

"Yes, we had a brief story about Mrs. Kendall going into the hospital. I'm terribly sorry," he said. "Is there anything I can do?"

She nodded and tried to smile at the two secretaries, then walked with Fairfield toward the door at the far end of the private corridor. "Just play it as quietly as possible." She was pulling on her gloves, her motions tense and erratic. "Everything has been done that can be. She's been in remission this last time for months. We—I even had hope . . ." She was shaking her head, and he could see the sorrow in her face, hear it in her voice. "But now the cancer has spread to other areas." She turned at the door and put out her hand again. He shook it slowly.

"I am here if you need me," he said simply.

"Thank you." Her voice was almost a whisper and the smile was fleeting. But he saw in it the grain of friendship and clasped her hand with both of his before letting go. Then he watched as she went swiftly through the door and down the gray marble hallway toward the elevators.

When Gail Halloran stepped off the curb in front of the Shubert Theatre on Forty-fourth Street, two taxis skidded to a stop, one cutting in front of the other. Just to be obstinate, she climbed into the second one, relieved to be leaving the snowy night outside.

"Columbia-Presbyterian Hospital," she said as the taxi shot out into the traffic. "Hey! Hey, guess what?" the driver yelled back over his shoulder when recognizing her. "I saw your movie just last night." She looked at his squat neck and forced a smile. *One of those.*

"Well, I'll be damned!" Gail said, balancing a mug of coffee she had brought with her. She felt slightly disoriented as the taxi went northward. Ordinarily, she and Jack would be heading for Sardi's or "21" or to one of the little Italian places in the neighborhood. But she'd gotten the call from Caroline. And Jack was in San Francisco, listening to a male rock singer with the idea of signing him and his band. Whenever he went himself instead of sending someone else from his agency, that meant the singer was really hot.

The taxi driver had no intention of giving up. "What a coincidence. Hey, lady, you are good! I mean, *you are really good.* You know that?" he demanded, looking over his shoulder with a nerve-wracking frequency instead of ahead of him at the madly wheeling vehicles.

"Well, thank you. That's very nice—"

"Yeah, you are somethin'. In that scene where you an' the guy you finally fall in love with are singin' an' dancin' your way across the damned Brooklyn Bridge, boy, I thought I'd croak. How d'ya like that? The damned Brooklyn Bridge that I've drove across maybe a thousand times. Man, oh man, you are somethin'."

She closed her eyes and only half-listened as his voice droned on and on. What had Jack said, that last minute at the airport the day before? "I'll try to get back, honey, by day after tomorrow. I hate leaving you at a time like this, knowing how upset you are about Elizabeth, but with Caroline coming down from Boston tomorrow and—"

"I'll be all right, darling," she had insisted. But he had known she wouldn't be all right, that she was never all right when he was away from her, that she needed him like she needed water and food and breath and sleep. She had lived without him for so many years, but now . . . She had put her hands beneath his trench coat and wound them around him tightly while he held her, his chin just touching the top of her blonde head, both oblivious to the bright lights and pushing crowds, the clamorous noise. There was the familiar aroma of his shaving lotion, the lean, tall elegance of his body, his arms holding her hard. She had looked up into his face, eyes caressing the sharp, handsome contours, the dark eyes that told her so much. He was her strength. "A little toughy like you?" he always laughed teasingly when she told him that. "You have the strength of ten. I'd hate to get in a fight with you." But he knew what she meant. She'd been a fighter, a survivor for so long. After years, she had leaned against him, finally saying, "Love me. Care for me. I need you."

The taxi screeched around a corner and Gail called out, "Hey, could you take it a little slower, pal? You're spilling my coffee."

He laughed loudly, turning to look at her again, his narrow ferret eyes and bulging cheeks making him resemble a fat Central Park squirrel. "Wait'll I tell the ole girl about this one," he said with a chortle. "I'll be damned. Gail Halloran in my taxi!"

"If you live to tell it," she muttered, holding onto the strap and trying to balance the coffee mug out in front of her over the jump seat, away from her clothes, just as he dove into the middle lane, narrowly missing a brown Mercedes and a bus that was spewing clouds of black smoke from its exhaust.

When they pulled up at the entrance of the hospital, Gail finished the last drop of coffee, stuck a five- and a ten-dollar bill through the handle, and handed it up to the driver. "Keep the change," she said. "And the mug."

"Hey, thanks," he grinned, looking at the meter. He was way ahead for the night. Then he shouted out the window as she walked beneath the canopy toward the revolving glass doors where light spilled onto the sidewalk. "Hey! It was a pleasure, Gail."

"Oh, don't stand on formality," she shouted back. "Call me Gail anytime."

But her face was set in grim lines as she ducked it into the collar of her coat.

"That's Gail Halloran," she heard a voice call out. From the corner of her eye, as she stepped out of the taxi, she had seen a cluster of men and women, some with cameras in their hands, over at the side, looking cold in the light but wet snowfall. Of course, there *would* be reporters here. The day before the newspapers had run a brief story saying that Mrs. Lawrence Kendall's condition was considered critical, that she was failing rapidly. She kept a grim expression on her face as she hurried past. Some of the reporters were probably Caroline's own employees, not even aware yet that she had acquired the *Journal.*

"Miss Halloran—" It was a chorus of voices as they surged toward her.

But she ran on, shielding her face with her collar. "Sorry! Later, perhaps," she called out as she hurried through the revolving doors.

When she felt the clasp on her shoulder, she knew it was Gail's hand even before turning her head and looking up at her in the shadowy room.

"Thank you for coming," she whispered, as Gail knelt down beside her and held her for a moment. When they pulled back a little and looked at each other, Caroline saw tears on Gail's lashes.

"Don't say that," Gail said, her voice low and trembling. "I love her, too, you know"—her voice caught and broke a little—"even more than I realized."

Caroline nodded, her hands holding Gail's, and she almost smiled. Two nurses on the opposite side of the room, one bending over Elizabeth in the high white bed adjusting one of the tubes running to her nose, were staring at Gail. One nudged the other with her elbow and whispered something. They recognized the blonde hair, piled high in the artfully messy crush that drifted about her face and neck in wistful little wisps that gave her wide-set green eyes and generous flash of mouth a tempting, teasing, gamine look. She had the appearance of being tall. Her long, leggy grace was a considerable part of her charm. But it was her green long-lashed eyes and flashing smile, the high-piled golden hair and upturned nose that people recognized.

Her name had blazed in two- and three-foot-tall lights on most of the marquees in the theatre district. She had starred in numerous musical comedies over the past decade and longer. The last three were made into films and Gail had made the transition easily into movie theatres.

"Mama's flying from Zurich tonight," Gail whispered. "She'll be here in the morning." In her big white Krizia overcoat with creamy wool slacks underneath, the flamboyant Gail managed somehow to look understated. Caroline slowly shook her head and tears came to her eyes. She tiptoed to the bed and bent down close to Elizabeth's ear. Gail stood beside her, clasping Elizabeth's limp hand.

"Ellie's coming from Bellone, Mummy," Caroline said in a soft voice, unaware that she had reverted to the childhood term. Elizabeth's eyes were closed. The doctor had said earlier she was in a semi-coma. But Gail thought she felt a slight motion in her hand as Caroline repeated it over and over, marveling at the remnants of beauty that remained in Elizabeth's pale ravaged face.

"Come outside," Caroline whispered to Gail and they left the room swiftly, walking on their toes until they were in the corridor with the door closed. They stood by one of the wide windows, looking down into the street, now lightly mantled with snow. It was past midnight, and the street seemed deserted except for the dim streetlamps, the lines of parked cars, and the occasional glimpse of white, as an intern or nurse hurried through the blowing snowfall.

"Dr. Haagstrom said he felt sure she won't get through the night," Caroline said. "When I think of how just a week ago she was sitting up and smiling and—"

"This turn came so quickly," Gail exclaimed.

Caroline nodded, her cheek pressed against the coolness of the window glass. "I was at the *Morning Journal,* meeting the editor-in-chief. The hospital called me there, just after we heard about the embassy takeover in Iran."

Gail shook her head slowly. "The world is full of maniacs," she murmured, as she leaned back against the wall in the softly lit white corridor and watched two nurses walk past them, giggling at something one of them had said. She had hurried from the Shubert as soon as the final curtain fell on *Princess of Delancey Street,* her newest musical, not even waiting to take her makeup off. When the two nurses looked over their shoulders and stared at her, she shifted around and slid in a half-sitting position onto the windowsill. "God, I'd love a cigarette. This is when I'd really love a cigarette."

"Stop it," Caroline said automatically.

"Well, I would!"

"After all of that agony, the hypnotists, the stop-smoking programs, the rationing, the stops and starts—?"

"That doesn't make me not crave one." They were murmuring, Gail's voice a hiss through the muffled quiet, the distant sound of call-bells chiming, the rustle of a starched uniform and rubber-soled feet as another nurse hurried by, the intermittent soft gurgle of a drinking fountain in the wall.

"You're impossible," Caroline said, but she smiled and reached out to touch Gail's cheek. "I remember when we were about nine and ten, how you sneaked a bar of candy out of the drugstore in Newport into your pocket, and I saw you do it. You'd bought it while Ellie was busy at the back getting a prescription filled. I wanted to tell Ellie because I knew it would make your face break out, but—"

Gail laughed softly. "But you didn't, because you were my friend. But you had such a terrible expression on your face, Mama turned and looked at us before we got into the car, and right there on the sidewalk, she said, 'Gail, I can tell from Caroline's face that you've just done something you shouldn't have.' I tried to hide the bulge in my pocket, but she saw me and pulled the candy bar out. I was so mad at you." She smiled at Caroline with affection. "You always *did* have a lousy poker face."

"You, too. How about the time I hid a turtle in a box under my bed? When Nanny Grace was looking for it, you kept staring at the bed and saying, 'I don't know where it is, Nanny Grace, honestly I don't.' But your eyes were glued to the dust ruffle on the bed like a telescope."

They laughed softly. "That was nothing!" Gail said. "How about the time Meacham told your mother he thought we'd taken one of the cars out? Remember? Jamie's little red Ford convertible? Remember how we drove it up and down Bellevue Avenue at five o'clock in the morning?" She was laughing again. "Damn! If it hadn't been for that old fool, the gardener at the Vanderbilt house, who saw us and squealed. And you said to your mother, 'Oh, but we didn't drive very far. Just a few blocks on Bellevue Avenue.' She wasn't really certain about it until you gave us away."

Caroline smiled. "And we couldn't go to the beach for a week."

They became silent again, recalling the sunny summer childhood days at Newport, the wintry weeks in the playroom on the top floor of the house on Fifth Avenue, the trips to the ski lodge in Vermont.

Gail was leaning her forehead against the cold pane of the window. "Remember that night your mother let us sit in that little room off of the ballroom so we could watch everyone come in?" She smiled, remembering. "The Vice President and his wife, and the Governor. Alfred Lunt and Lynn Fontanne—" She giggled softly. "Fat Mrs. Pierpont in that awful yellow dress. But your mother . . . Oh, I'll never forget." She moved her forehead dreamily against the glass. "More beautiful than anyone there. It was between Christmas and New Year's, wasn't it?" When Caroline nodded, she went on. "She had on a green velvet gown, cut very low, and her emeralds. That beautiful dark hair was swept up into a cluster of curls. She and your father stood near the door, greeting everyone, and your father—he couldn't take his eyes off her. What marvelous years those were . . ." Her voice drifted off.

Caroline nodded again. "I remember wishing I could somehow go back and be a child again, when everything was wonderful, when—"

"Caro, it may take a long time, but someday Steve will see how foolish he's—"

"No." It was such an abrupt but expressionless *no* that Gail was startled. "He'll never come back to me."

"You can't be sure."

"He'll never come back. It's over, Gail. He despises everything the Kendall name stands for."

"But he's wildly in love with you." She watched Caroline, where she leaned against the wall, a slender figure in the softly tailored blue suit, the exquisite face a haunted mask in the dusky light. "Jack said that one of these days, he'll wake up and—"

Caroline turned to her and grasped her hands. "Thank God, one of us made it work. It helps, Gail, just knowing how happy you are. I'm so pleased you finally married Jack, that you realize how much you really love him."

Gail gazed off into space, and then a curious expression came into her face. She turned slowly to Caroline. "Richard . . . is always in the back of my mind," she said softly.

"Of course he is, darling." Caroline put her arms around her, and for several moments they held each other. "As he should be. That was a very important part of your life." She drew back and gazed at the bleak and empty darkness in the street below. "Just as Steve was of mine. No matter what happens, I'll always have the memories."

With hands tightly clasped, they walked back slowly into the room where Elizabeth Kendall lay. They sat through the night, dozing from time to time in chairs pulled close to the bed, rousing when the private nurse bent over the prone figure to adjust a tube, or take her pulse, or change one of the plastic bottles on the intravenous.

Only once through the long hours did either of them speak. "When Daddy died six months ago," Caroline said softly, as she held Elizabeth's hand on hearing Elizabeth sigh, "she gave up, I think. Nothing in her life mattered after that."

"It was perfection, wasn't it?" Gail said, almost wistfully. "The perfect love affair, with nothing ever marring it."

"Is that really possible?" Caroline whispered. And they fell silent again.

When dawn fingered the sky with dreary gray streaks, the snow had changed to a drizzling sleet slashing against the windows. They struggled out of their chairs, cold and stiff, when the nurse suggested they go to the cafeteria for some breakfast while she changed the sheets on the bed.

They walked along the corridor arm in arm, not speaking, and waited for the elevator. As the elevator descended, they watched the lighted floor signals.

"Some of the family, those who are around, will be arriving in a few hours," Caroline said in a weary voice.

"Who, Caro?" Caroline's half-brothers, she thought, and Warren Leland, her step-uncle.

"Larry, I'm sure. Maybe Avery—" She frowned at both of their names. "That is, if he's in town." She smiled with a suddenness. "Jamie, I hope." She looked at Gail. "He loves her so, you know. He never really knew his own mother. She died when he was so young."

"Lovely, lovely Jamie," Gail said. "How did he ever manage to come out of that bunch? Strange. I never think of Larry and Avery as even your half-brothers. But Jamie . . ."

They left the elevator and brightened some at the bustle and chatter of voices in the corridor just outside the gleaming cafeteria, at the blaze of lights and aroma of coffee and food. They even laughed a little as three young interns stopped Gail and asked for her autograph, just as they were entering the cafeteria behind a stream of nurses and doctors. Inching their way past the cashier's counter, Gail picked up two trays and started toward the food counters, then stopped to look around for Caroline. She saw her by the stacks of morning newspapers next to the cashier, paying for one, her body hunched forward tensely as she read past one of the headlines. Walking back to her, she said, with foreboding, "What is it, Caro?"

"Three newsmen were kidnapped in Beirut." Caroline looked up at Gail, her face white, filled with shock. "Steve . . . is one of them."

Her hands trembled as she held the newspaper out to Gail. "Read it." She pointed to the story in the upper-right column of the *Morning Journal.* "Steve McCallum. Read it."

Gail led her to a table and made her sit down. "I'll get some coffee. Stay right there until I get back."

She hurried through the line, scooping up fruit juice, some danish, and coffee in two steaming mugs. When she got to the table, she saw that Caroline had turned to an inside page and was staring at a picture of Steve, between pictures of the other two newsmen, one from an Australian newspaper, the other an Italian, all pictures taken in earlier days when they could smile into cameras. While moving the food from the tray onto the table, Gail glanced at the picture of Steve, the rumpled brown hair smooth for once, but the same crooked smile and laughing eyes, the big shoulders crowding the picture, the mouth sensitive and sensual, even when caught in a smile.

She pushed the mug of coffee closer to Caroline. "Here, drink some of this. You need something warm in your stomach. And try to eat the danish." As Caroline took a sip, her eyes never wavering from the newspaper, Gail knew it was useless to try and persuade her not to read the story.

"What does it say?" For a moment there was silence.

"They were seized when Alec Harwood, the Australian, drove them over into Moslem West Beirut to cover a story. Gunfire had been erupting there all through the night." She began reading aloud. " 'A witness said the three men were pulled from the car after it had been ambushed in a dead-end street and were pushed into a tan-colored van, which was driven away, deeper into West Beirut. The two militia organizations, that of the Druse Progressive Socialist Party and the Shiite Moslem Amal, were notified immediately, with spokesmen from each promising to organize search operations.' "

She looked up at Gail with terrible dread in her eyes. "Oh, my God, Gail, these are madmen who do these things, fanatics who think nothing of killing—"

"Stop!" Gail put her hand on Caroline's wrist and clenched it hard.

"Don't even think about it that way. Keep your mind open, positive. Keep telling yourself he'll be released and safely." But as she said it, her heart sank. In all of the political kidnappings she had read about, she couldn't remember more than a few who had been released unharmed.

"They commit these terrible acts believing they're on some kind of religious mission, thinking they will go to Paradise when they kill and *are* killed—"

"Stop, Caroline," Gail said firmly. "There's no point in torturing yourself. That will accomplish nothing."

They sipped at their coffee in silence and went back to Elizabeth's room, hand in hand, not speaking. For several hours they kept their vigil, cold rain slashing against the glass panes.

In mid-morning, they were standing at one of the windows, both gazing up at the sky. The sun was trying to break through the leaden overcast. Caroline turned first, hearing something. When she saw that Elizabeth's eyes were half open, she rushed across to the bed, Gail following her.

". . . hoped you were here," Elizabeth was whispering, and Caroline, clasping her hand, put her cheek down against her mother's, each feeling the other's tears. Again Elizabeth whispered, seeing Gail, who was leaning toward her from the other side of the bed.

"Lovely little Gail . . ."

"Not so little anymore," Gail said roughly, trying to hide the anguish in her voice.

". . . like my own," Elizabeth was murmuring, and tears slid down Gail's cheeks. "Always felt you were like my own." She slowly looked from one to the other, as they both leaned close to her. ". . . loved you both so much . . . so much." As though exhausted from the few words she had spoken, she closed her eyes once more. They watched her for a long time, then slowly walked to the window again, realizing Elizabeth had slipped back into that twilight of consciousness. For more than an hour, they stood there, almost motionless, only stirring when they heard the soft sound of the door opening.

"Mama!" Gail exclaimed in a hushed tone, and flew across to the woman standing in the doorway, snow sprinkled on the wide lapels of her beaver coat, the still-blonde hair curling from beneath a gray felt hat. Her pretty face, almost unlined, was drawn from weariness but she clutched at Gail and Caroline when they rushed to her. Holding them closely for a moment, she finally let Gail take her coat and

26

hat, and walked toward the bed. When she reached it, she stood very still for several minutes, then put one hand out to touch Elizabeth's cheek.

"Don't leave us, Elizabeth," they heard her whisper, and Caroline put a hand up to her mouth to stifle the sound of a sob. "It's Ellie, Elizabeth. Ellie." And then she sat down beside the bed and began to talk in a low voice, as though she were certain Elizabeth was listening. "I know. I know how lonely it is since he's been gone. But don't . . . don't leave us, darling. Come back to us, and come to Switzerland with me. Georges wants you there, too. Remember the winters at Bellone? So beautiful and white. You loved it there."

With her hand still over her mouth, Caroline slowly shook her head. Didn't Ellie know how ill Elizabeth was? But then, as Elizabeth's eyes fluttered open again, she knew why Ellie had kept talking to her in that soft, prodding voice. She wanted to say goodbye, wanted Elizabeth to know she had come, wanted her to know how she was loved and how much she would be missed.

"Yes, darling, I'm here," Ellie said, as a slow smile crept over Elizabeth's lips. "We're all here. Caroline, Gail . . . three of the four of us who cared for you the most."

"I loved him so, Ellie . . ." Elizabeth whispered and Ellie nodded. Caroline suddenly realized that, in a way, Ellie had been the person closest to her mother all through the years, except for her father, sharing their most secret thoughts and wishes with each other, just as she and Gail always had.

"I know, darling, I know," Ellie was saying as Caroline and Gail stood on either side of her.

"Love all of you so . . ."

Caroline watched as something burned in the deep, violet depths of her mother's eyes. And then it was as if a light went out slowly. She cried out with a soft *no* and knelt beside the bed, holding her mother's hand, while Ellie's arm stole around her shoulders and Gail put her head in Ellie's lap and quietly wept.

"Of course, with Amy and Coley away at boarding school now, it means I can travel with Larry *wherever* and *whenever* he goes," Honey was saying to Enid Leland across the table from her, moving her head from side to side to see her past the flower arrangement. She finally reached out and moved the flowers an inch or two.

"Oh, I *do* envy you that," Enid said, the usual little whine to her voice and the usual little pat to the side of her silvery hair to make certain the heavy earrings she always wore weren't falling off. "When the children were young, I never seemed able to go with Warren."

Caroline carefully watched along both sides of the long table as she drank her demitasse. She had driven up the Hudson from Manhattan that afternoon, then asked everyone to come to Kendall Hills to tell them what the funeral plans were. Elizabeth had wanted the service to be held at the Kendall Chapel down in Rijksville.

"Well, when Katherine and Brenda were small, we didn't have as much help in the house as we have now," Warren said heartily, cutting off the end of his cigar with a silver clipper. He held the cigar up with one hand and his gold lighter with the other. "Do you mind, Caroline?"

"No, it's quite all right," she said, carefully masking her feelings. She wished she were back in the Manhattan apartment or upstairs with her shoes off, in a robe, sitting in front of her fireplace, with a tape of Rachmaninoff's Second Symphony playing, or soaking in the tub with moistened pads of cotton on her eyelids. Instead, here she was, listening to the idiotic small talk that her half-brothers' wives, Honey and Faye, were making with a step-aunt by marriage.

Enid Leland wasn't even that, she thought. But if she wasn't, what was she? Her father had explained it to her when she was very small. He had pulled her up into his lap and said, "Well, you see, sweetheart, before I married your mother—before I even met her—I was married to someone else." Caroline had nodded her head solemnly, and said, "To Larry and Avery and Jamie's mother? A lady named Anne." She thought for a moment. "She died."

"Yes, she died." He had held her a little closer then. "And she had a brother. That's your Uncle Warren."

"But he's not my uncle," she said, a stubbornness coming into her eyes, a look that Lawrence Kendall knew only too well.

"Well, let's not hurt his feelings," he had whispered to her as though in conspiracy. "He likes to think he's your uncle."

"All right," Caroline said, pretending he was right. But she knew *Uncle* Warren didn't really like her very much. She could tell by the way his voice always filled up with a kind of false heartiness when he talked to her. But then Larry didn't like her very much, either. Or Avery. Only Jamie liked her.

"So that makes Aunt Enid your aunt."

She had sighed and slipped down from her father's lap, turned and looked at him, and said, "If you want me to, I'll call her Aunt Enid. But I won't like it."

He had smiled back at her, trying not to laugh, and just nodded. Then he whispered, "That's my lovely girl."

"Don't you think so, Caroline?"

Her head snapped up. "I—I'm sorry, Faye, I didn't hear what you said."

All eyes were watching her, down both sides of the table with its massive silver candelabra and flowers, its crystal stemware and heavy silver that had the engraved K for Kendall on it. They look like poised penguins, she thought, Larry and Avery and Warren, in their starched shirts and tuxedos. Only Jamie with a soft shirt and black bow tie that was a bit crooked, a little off to one side, looked human. He was slouched in his chair, one hand on his highball glass. "Must you have a highball, James, when everyone else is having demitasse and liqueurs?" Barbara had asked peevishly. But he had acted as if he didn't even hear her. One eyebrow was raised quizzically at Caroline. She heard Faye repeat her question.

"I was wondering—well, if you were going to be able to chair the Rijksville Hospital benefit in—well, in view of what's happened?"

Caroline smiled. "No, I suggested they ask you to take over, Faye. I wrote them a note this morning."

"Oh, well, of course, darling, anything I can do to help." Faye smiled graciously, but with that condescending little twist to her mouth.

How like Honey she is, Caroline thought, the same Le Cirque hairstyle; she had even affected the same tinkling little laugh, had Honey's way of thrusting her chin forward when she talked to give it that finishing school kind of sound.

"Of course, I'd love to help," Honey was saying, "but with Larry going to Cairo on Sunday, I'm going to go as far as Cairo while he goes on to Kuwait and Bahrain. Women don't *go* to Kuwait or Bahrain, you know. I mean, you *can* go, if you really, really want to, but women are treated like cattle there, no, like *servants*. I mean, you rarely see them, except with those veils over their faces and those long—"

"I thought that was Saudi Arabia," Enid said, catching an earring as it slid off her right ear.

"Well, all of those strange places. I mean, the women are so second-rate—no, third- or fourth-rate, really. Of course, *Cairo!* Well, all of those dreadful black flies. I mean, you simply can't go some places, you know. You have to be terribly careful where you go or these dreadful flies just swarm around you, and—"

"How is the new steward on the *Lear,* Warren?" Larry asked, finally cutting the unending stream of words with a pat on Honey's hand. She dropped her voice several decibels, and simply turned to her other side and continued talking to Jamie about the delights of Cairo.

"Seemed very capable," Warren said, leaning back and expansively sending circles of smoke into the air. "But I had to tell him to make certain he keeps a stock of Chivas on board."

"And those wonderful little petit fours from Bonte Patisserie . . ." Faye began.

"Really, darling, with all of that dieting you do." Honey slid a cigarette into the gold holder and slowly flicked her lighter. "I would think—"

"I'm flying to Beirut right after the funeral," Caroline suddenly said.

She saw Larry's head turn. How many times a day does he shave? she wondered. He still had that bluish look about his jowls. Some people thought him handsome, the carefully brushed dark hair, the carefully maintained figure. She suspected he plucked his eyebrows in the middle. They looked as though they would grow straight across otherwise.

"Beirut?" He looked puzzled. "Why Beirut?"

"Did you read about the kidnappings there yesterday?"

"Some newsmen, weren't they? Oh, yes, someone from the *Inquirer.* I recall now."

"The someone"—she caught herself quickly. They had never known. Why tell them anything now?—"just happens to be a Pulitzer Prize-winning reporter and correspondent in our employ."

"Does that require the presence of the owner and publisher?" Avery asked. Avery's mouth was weak where Larry's was strong. The same dark hair. The same impeccable grooming. Several inches shorter. Fifty, two years younger than Larry, he somehow managed to look older. Maybe it was because of the way he carried himself, stooped shoulders, always looking at Larry for approval of whatever he said.

"What a terrible place to go. With all of that killing and those crazy people running around," Barbara said, her rings flashing as she fluttered her hands about, the diamonds catching the candlelight. She would be pretty if she weren't so discontented-looking, Caroline thought, that luscious red hair curling around her face, the fair skin, and wide green eyes. Jamie didn't deserve that, she told herself for the thousandth time. Once again she wondered if Jamie drank because of Barbara's disposition or had Barbara become sour because of his drinking? She had forgotten what they were like when they were younger than young. Such a stunning couple, everyone had said, Jamie with his marvelous gray eyes that were always amused and lazy-looking, his grace on the tennis court, his lopsided smile that always said, *Who really gives a damn about all this bull, the houses and stables and cars and thirty-room apartments on Fifth Avenue?* Jamie loved the lodge at Stowe, Vermont. It was the only place he had ever been really happy.

"It will . . . help, getting away right now," Caroline said, rising. She would tell them no more. They deserved nothing from her. Only Jamie, she thought.

They all stared at her again, the penguins and the sculptured heads. Enid's other earring fell off and rolled to the floor. Jamie grinned at Caroline, and his eyes said, *Good for you, old girl.*

She watched them for a moment, a slim, lovely figure, the black jersey clinging to every curve, the dark hair falling in soft waves on her shoulders. The men had all risen to their feet—Larry, the one who had stepped heavily into at least one of his father's shoes when Lawrence Kendall had died several months before. Avery, who jumped when Larry crooked a finger. Warren, a handsome, well-preserved man of sixty-six and a senior officer in Kendall, Inc. And Jamie—Jamie who was paid to stay home. She smiled at Jamie and started from the room, giving him her special signal with her eyes.

He followed her and they walked along the gallery, hand in hand, saying nothing, but feeling the warmth between them. When they reached the library, Caroline curled up in a corner of the couch before the fire and Jamie went to the bar to pour liqueurs for them. He flopped onto the floor with his back to the fire after handing her her glass.

"Isn't this the guy you once told me you were in love with?" he asked.

"Yes," she said, nodding.

He smiled. "Okay. I won't ask any more."

"Someday, when I can talk about it, I'll tell you."

"Fair enough."

There was a long silence, and then she looked down at him. "Jamie, before I leave . . ."

But he was slowly shaking his head. He smiled at her with that sardonic, lopsided smile. "It's too late, beautiful."

"No—"

"Much, much, much too late," he said softly.

"There's a good place for you in Boston. You're marvelous with people. They love you. You could sell anything. The advertising director there is in his sixties. One of these days he'll be retiring. He's a marvelous man who knows the business through and through, a perfect kind of person to train under. In time you could take over—"

"Caro, Caro." His voice was still soft. He took one of her hands in his. "I'm forty-eight, my liver's like a rock, and my stomach probably looks like a tennis net. I couldn't make it twenty, twenty-five years ago. So I certainly can't make it now."

"Why, Jamie, why . . . ?" she asked, a pleading in her voice.

He sat up, resting his arms on his knees, and looked into the fire. He had pulled the small black tie loose and opened the dress shirt at the neck, the effect giving him a boyish look in the firelight. Although he was still handsome, the formerly sharp lines of youth were puffed and blurred. He shrugged.

"Just say I had a mother complex. My mother deserted me. She died before I was four—" He laughed derisively.

"No, Jamie." Caroline was slowly shaking her head. "Not good enough. When our father married my mother, she adored you and you adored her."

He was quiet for a long moment as the crooked smile faded. "No . . . you're right. Not good enough." He spoke so softly, she leaned forward a little to hear him. When he spoke again, his voice was very far away, as though he had forgotten she was there.

"He said, 'You killed her. She had cancer of the uterus! You know what the uterus is, you dumb kid? That's what the baby grows in. And after Avery was born, the doctors said she shouldn't have any more children. But she had you and you killed her!'" He was shaking his head a little.

"Larry?" Caroline said sharply. She suddenly slid to the floor and put her arms around him. "Darling, no. Oh, no, Jamie. You had nothing to do with it. It was four years before—"

But he didn't seem to have heard her. "But that was just the beginning. When Elizabeth came, I loved her. And that made it worse. They didn't want her there. You and Elizabeth were all I had. He—our father—he was always busy—away from me and Larry and Avery—and I was always with them." He looked around at her, as though catching himself from drifting farther away. The self-mocking smile returned. "It was easier from then on to play the fool . . ."

"Oh, Jamie, it's not too late." She was clutching his hands.

He suddenly got to his feet, walked to the bar, and poured himself a scotch on the rocks, then stood there shaking the glass and listening to the ice tinkle.

"Bring me back some worry beads from Beirut," he said, the self-mocking tone growing as he smiled across the room at her. "I will sit quietly in the corner with my glass in one hand and the worry beads in the other, and no one"—he raised a finger and said a long Shhhhh—"will even know that I am there." He turned then and walked out of the room. "Least of all Barbara."

2

She fumbled for the light switch, turned the bedside lamp on, and sat up staring at the phone. It was several moments before she realized she had dreamed she heard it ringing . . . dreamed that there was a voice at the other end, a mocking voice, waiting to tell her that Steve's body had been found, thrown into a West Beirut street in the deep darkness of night while guns rumbled across the city, a voice that laughed and said, *First your mother and now your lover . . . first your mother and now your lover.*

She shuddered and, tossing the long dark hair back, she reached for her heavy satin robe, then pulled it on, struggling with one sleeve that was turned inside out, while looking about wildly, as though searching for someone. But the vast corners of the pale blue and white room were lost in shadows.

Caroline pushed her feet into satin mules and, tying her robe, crossed to the door. She slipped along the wide hallway and down the staircase to the lower floor of the triplex, footsteps silent in the deep pile of pale carpeting. It was a large apartment, twenty rooms on the three floors, and then there were the kitchen, butler's pantry, and servants' quarters. It was small actually, compared to the other houses. Only the apartment in London was smaller. Her father had loved London. Said it was his second home. After he married Elizabeth, she had made him give up the apartment in Paris. "Such silly baroque splendor," her mother had said, laughing. "I felt like someone's paramour there."

At the door of the music room, she stopped, then walked in, not knowing why; perhaps because her mother had loved it so. For support, she leaned on the grand piano, then slid down onto the cushioned bench. Four tall palladian windows reflected glimmers of light from Fifth Avenue far below and from clear, cold moonlight in the sky beyond.

She touched a finger to an ivory key, then several others, listening to the silvery sound, sad and lonely in the half darkness. With a discordant crash, she brought her hands and arms down on the keyboard, then rose and ran toward the center foyer, panic beating wildly in her throat, an unbearable ache deep inside.

But she stopped just inside the double doors. She pressed a button on the wall and watched the tiny museum lights above the row of paintings along the dark-paneled walls flick on. So many times she had come into the music room to find her mother standing in front of one or the other of the paintings, so lost in thought she was unaware anyone had entered. The last time, just a month or so before, she had been wearing a long mauve hostess gown. Smoke from a cigarette—the inevitable cigarette, much to Caroline's dismay—in a long jade holder drifted lazily upward as, with her head tipped to one side, she studied the Vermeer, a small smile on her lips. It was her favorite, Elizabeth often said. She loved its contrasts of light and shadow. Caroline's gaze wandered along the walls—the Frans Hals, the Seurat, the Signac, and the Mary Cassatt. There were Cézannes and Homers and Hoppers, a Renoir, a Dufy, several Picassos. "They're like friends," her mother had once said, her lovely face pensive, dark head arching back.

Caroline pressed the button again and the paintings disappeared into the darkness. She walked out to the foyer and stood for a moment as though listening for something. She could smell the delicate fragrance of the flower arrangement on the lacquered lowboy, another on the chinoiserie chest. The apartment had been her grandmother's. But Sybil Stuart had died several years before, and Elizabeth had kept it vacant until the death of Lawrence Kendall. It was then that she moved from the five-story townhouse to the Fifth Avenue apartment, a place that held all of the lovely feminine touches first of Caroline's grandmother and then of her mother. And now it was the place that Caroline had come home to, wearily . . . gratefully . . . painfully.

She walked down the wide gallery to the dining room, flicked on the soft sidelights with their small, rose-colored silk shades, and sat at her mother's place at the end of the long table. She could see herself in the mirrored wall—pale, drawn. It was like looking at a stranger.

There had been a time when she was perpetually tanned, always a golden glow that moved from season to season and from place to place, Palm Beach to the ski slopes at Kitzbühel or Verbier in the Valaise, or when they cruised on the Sapphire in the Cyclades. The month of July without fail in Newport at Kendall Hall. Aspen, Sardinia, St. Moritz, Mykonos . . . But that had been years ago. Before Boston. Before Steve.

Pale light was stealing through the transparent curtains. She heard a stirring behind the swinging doors to the butler's pantry and the kitchen beyond. Turning her head, she again looked at herself in the mirror, trying to see past the pale skin and dark smudge of eyes. When people first looked at her, they did so just as they would anyone else. But when they heard her name, the same expression came into all of their faces—surprise, then a fawning kind of smile. She learned when she was terribly young to pretend she hadn't seen this reaction. And though they always treated her like . . . yes, like some member of a royal family, she had been taught, from the time she could first walk, to be gracious and unaffected and well mannered. Sometimes she had wanted to stick her tongue out, jump up and down, shout something silly, but instead she had merely curtsied and murmured, "I'm very happy to meet you." Often, when she was alone, she stood in front of the mirror in her bedroom and stared at herself, trying to see down deep inside, feeling guilt and a strangely nagging unhappiness, wondering at the core of anxiety that never left her as a child. Did anyone at school like her for herself or was it the name *Kendall?* Even Evelyn Henredin, whose family was synonymous with Vanderbilts and Fords, with Du Ponts and Rockefellers, once asked her in an odd tone what it was like to be a Kendall. She had learned that aggressive activity was the smartest answer. She became the best field hockey player, the best swimmer.

"Why, Miss Caroline!" She heard the surprise in Morgan's voice as he pushed through the swinging door. He was hastily pulling on the black alpaca coat that he wore mornings, his wispy gray hair standing a little on end. He turned back, holding the door ajar. "I'll tell Katy you're here."

"Just ask her if I could have a cup of coffee, Morgan," she said.

In moments, Katy was hovering over her, pouring the coffee, gently touching her shoulder, her cheerfully lined face anxious. She felt tears flooding her eyes and turned to Katy, on whose ample bosom she sobbed for several moments.

"There, there, dearie," she heard Katy say, over and over.

When she straightened up, and wiped her eyes with a tissue Katy pushed into her hand, she said, "I'm all right." She tried to smile. "Don't feel sorry for me, or I'll crack into little pieces." But she was glad that Katy kept on gripping her shoulders. Morgan and Katy had been with the Kendall family even before Caroline was born, first in the townhouse and then in the apartment when Elizabeth moved there six months before. More than forty years, starting their employment with Lawrence Kendall when he had brought his new bride to the Manhattan townhouse.

In control once more, she smiled at Katy, then picked up her cup and saucer, and walked to the door at the far end of the dining room.

"I'm home to stay, Katy," she said, turning, and the old woman nodded, a smile on her face.

Ellie found her in the library an hour later when she came down, her pale blue velvet robe making a swishing sound on the carpet as she walked through the door. Caroline, who'd been seated before a crackling fire, went to the small wall telephone, phoned the kitchen, and asked Morgan to bring coffee and toast.

"I phoned Gail," Ellie said. "Jack got in late last night from San Francisco. They'll be here in an hour, in time to ride with us for the . . . the funeral." She held Caroline for a moment.

Caroline nodded, as they sat on the deep couch in front of the fireplace, Caroline's feet curled beneath her. For several moments they were both silent. Before Ellie had come down, Caroline had phoned the *Inquirer* in Boston. She had talked to Ed Pinckney, the political columnist. She had known he would have been there through the night, waiting for more reports on the kidnapping in Beirut. He and Steve had been close friends from the start.

"I . . . I'm sorry, Caro. But . . . well, nothing." She could almost see him—sleepy brown eyes and sardonic smile, thinning blond hair and near-skeletal frame—standing at his cluttered desk, tie askew, coffee mug in hand. There would be no smile this morning and the eyes would be wide with anger. "No one has taken any responsibility for it as yet. So they don't even know who or what to look for." He paused for a moment. "Caro, I'm sorry about your mother—"

"Thank you, Ed," she said quickly, cutting him off. There was just so much grief she could handle in one conversation. "I'll call you again tonight."

She had hung up and walked back to the fireplace, where she gazed into the sputtering flames. When Ellie had come through the door, she'd felt a flooding wave of relief at Ellie's having come from Switzerland. She knew it hadn't been easy. The small private school she and Georges had run there for so many years took all of their skills and close attention. She looked at her, saw the fine lines around her eyes and her mouth. But the china-blue eyes were as clear as ever. She was still delicate and apparently fragile, the pale blonde hair curling about her face.

"You know how I feel, Ellie, that you were able to come."

Ellie put her hand on Caroline's. "Elizabeth was my friend and you have always been as close to me as Gail."

Caroline nodded and whispered, "Thank you." She forced a smile. "But poor Georges."

Ellie laughed softly. "Georges is perfectly capable of taking care of things alone for a week or so. Why, he has as much energy and enthusiasm as he had the first day I ever met him. Evening, I should say, I guess, because he was teaching English to immigrants and the refugees and that evening class in French I took so many years ago down at Washington Square." She sighed. "So many years ago."

Caroline looked at her curiously. "When Gail and I were very small, you once told us how you and Mummy met, when you were both just in your teens."

Ellie looked up at her, startled; then, smiling, she gazed back into the fire. "Your mother was such an independent creature. Even then. When children were seen and not heard. You're very much like her."

"Tell me again," Caroline begged softly. "I've forgotten so much of it. And I want to . . . remember everything about her."

There was silence for a long moment.

"Well, it was during the Depression, you know. And I had to get a job. I'd finished high school . . ." She looked off, smiling, remembering. "That was quite an accomplishment in those days for people in our circumstances. We all worked in the textile mills, you know, fathers, mothers, aunts and uncles, the children in their later teens. But so many of the New England mills had closed down."

They both watched Morgan as he wheeled in the cart with its silver covered dishes and coffee service. Caroline smiled at him, murmured her thanks, and began pouring their coffee as he quietly left the room, his old face sad and gray-looking.

Ellie took a cup and saucer from Caroline. "A friend of mine from

Fall River had gotten a job at one of the big mansions in Newport as a kitchen helper. Scullery maid, they used to call it. She wrote me a letter and told me she'd heard of a job that was open with the Kendall family. So"—she smiled—"I set out for Newport one morning . . ."

3
1932

The black Pierce-Arrow churned up clouds of dust as it sped down from Providence past Portsmouth and Middletown, skirting the towns and taking the less-traveled road from the Bristol Ferry, blue ocean sparkling on one side, dune grass waving on the other.

Elizabeth, sitting on one of the jump seats in front of her mother and her Aunt Vivian, kept staring at the back of Jackson's neck through the glass partition that separated the open front of the long limousine from the gray upholstered rear. She was feeling queasy again. It was one of her bouts of car sickness coming on, the kind that had a way of appearing on a sunny, hot day such as this one. When she was about ten, she had discovered that if she stared at a stationary object, her stomach would flutter down to normal again. Seventeen years old, she thought disgustedly, and still carsick.

She glanced quickly toward the ocean, wishing fervently she were one of the two persons in the Flying Dutchman she saw sailing down-wind about a quarter-mile offshore. Oddly enough, she never felt seasick.

"Just let her get into an automobile!" her father always said with a teasing laugh. He and her brother, Dana, found it amusing.

"Dr. Downing says she will outgrow it," her mother always answered with a reprimanding look and a toss of her fashionably bobbed head. But so far his prediction had been unfulfilled.

She looked quickly back at Jackson's neck again, wondering why it was so red beneath his chauffeur's cap. *Your collar is too tight,* she wanted to tell him, but she knew he would just smile and shake his head at the way she always said exactly what she thought, blurting it out bluntly. That Elizabeth! they always said backstairs in the servants' quarters. *She's a caution, she is! Says what she thinks, does what she feels like.*

She wished she dared light a cigarette, but she knew if she did her mother would let out a little scream and say, "Just wait until tonight when I talk to your father!" Aunt Vivian would simply smile and try to wink at her. Aunt Vivian had been divorced twice and was what her father called a flapper. She rouged her knees, wore intriguing dark spitcurls over her ears, and bound her breasts tightly to make herself look boyish and flat-chested in her little print chiffon dresses with the short, pleated skirts. She smoked long, thin brown cigarettes that she called cigarillos. Her second husband, an Army colonel, had first had them imported from Havana for her, then complained about how she was clogging up his lungs "with that damned smoke of yours."

Elizabeth glanced back at the two women for a moment, only half-listening as they quarreled pleasantly about some unimportant matter, their voices high and musical, like two chirping birds on a branch. They were sisters, but so different, she thought. Her mother was handsome, almost regal, with a slender elegance that made her seem tall, although she was not. Her dark hair was cut short in the new fashion, but it was carefully waved back from her face, which had only the merest touches of makeup, some powder and a bit of pink lipstick. Her gray-and-white-print frock had flowing sleeves and was accented with a single strand of milky pearls.

Aunt Vivian, however, had an exotic look about her. Her brows and lashes were darkened and her lips were a glistening red. She had pasted a tiny beauty spot just below one corner of her mouth, and a lovely, haunting hint of her perfume filled the car.

When the Pierce-Arrow suddenly slowed, Elizabeth looked ahead. Another automobile was coming from the opposite direction, an open touring car with a white canvas top, the isinglass flaps on the sides removed to let the breeze blow in. It careened along the road toward them with five or six young men waving and shouting from the sides, leaning over the doors and pushing one another aside as they tried to look out. Dartmouth, Yale, and Amherst banners were fastened to the spare tires on both running boards and the rear.

"Oh, Mother, look!" Elizabeth said in an alarmed voice.

A young woman in a drab, brown cotton dress, heavy tan stockings, and black oxfords was walking along the side of the road, going in the same direction the Pierce-Arrow was traveling. She was carrying a small bag and a shabby pocketbook and she moved slowly, struggling, obviously weary and hot. She merely glanced at the auto filled with the shouting young men, even when they slowed almost to a stop. She plodded on, looking neither to right nor left, all her concentration on putting one weary leg in front of the other.

"They're going to try to make her get in their automobile," Elizabeth cried out as she started tapping on the glass partition to Jackson. They had almost passed the girl when he looked around and nodded at Elizabeth's gesture toward the young woman.

"Stop!" she shouted. "Stop, Jackson."

"Elizabeth," her mother said with soft reproval. "I don't think we should—"

"And let those dreadful boys taunt her, try to pick her up?" Elizabeth exploded. "Who knows *what* they might do to her?"

"Elizabeth is right, Sybil," Vivian said, leaning forward and looking out at the blonde young woman as the Pierce-Arrow came to a stop just ahead of her. "She looks exhausted, ready to faint."

Before Sybil could say anything more, Elizabeth had jumped from the car and was running back a short distance to where the young woman had stopped. She was staring, first at the Pierce-Arrow, then at the touring car that had pulled over about two hundred yards farther on. She looked back at Elizabeth, who was running toward her.

"Come on and get in," Elizabeth called out. "Are you going to Newport?" When the young woman nodded, her mouth open in a kind of numb surprise, they looked at each other for a long silent moment.

The young woman's face and neck slowly flushed with embarrassment as she studied the beautiful young girl with blue-violet eyes and dark curling hair standing before her. Elizabeth was wearing a fine voile dress of lavender and pink flowers on white, with a skirt that blew fetchingly in the wind. Long, tanned bare legs and feet in pretty white sandals were planted firmly on the dust along the side of the road.

"Come on," Elizabeth said, taking hold of her elbow and pulling her along with her. "It's much too hot for you to be out here on this road and dangerous too." She looked over her shoulder with a dark, angry glance at the young men who were still shouting and beckoning, three of them out on the road, jumping up and down in their white duck trousers at the sight of two pretty girls instead of just one. But when Jackson stepped out of the driver's seat and started toward them, threateningly, they jumped into the touring car and sped off, still calling out and hanging from the sides, one on the running board, holding on, but with a leg and arm outstretched as though to take off and fly.

"Fools! Utter fools!" Elizabeth said, looking over her shoulder once more, as she tugged at the young woman's arm and dragged her to the Pierce-Arrow. When Jackson hurried around and held open the door of the car, the young woman shrank back.

"Please, Miss, I—"

"Get in," Elizabeth insisted as she pushed her inside and climbed in after her, "there's plenty of room."

Vivian had edged Sybil to the far side of the car to make room for Elizabeth as the young woman hesitatingly sat on the jump seat, a terrified expression on her face, hands clutching her purse.

"Why, you poor thing," Sybil Stuart suddenly said, reaching out and putting a reassuring hand on the young woman's arm. One look at her heat-grimed face, the tendrils of blonde hair that clung damply to her brow, the trembling mouth and frightened blue eyes, and Sybil melted. "Of course there's plenty of room. And if you're going to Newport, we'll be glad to let you off there wherever it is you want."

Elizabeth stared at her. The young woman looked hardly a day older than herself, yet there was a mature, older set to her mouth and eyes. Her hair was pale blonde, like spun gold, and her eyes were a lovely intense blue. She had white skin that was tinged with red, burned from the glaring sun. There was a delicate, almost fragile look about her, and yet her hands were red and chafed, as though she had kept them in water too long.

"Where are you going in Newport?" Sybil asked gently.

"To"—fumbling, the young woman quickly opened the worn purse and searched around, finally pulling out a scrap of paper—"to Belle-vue Avenue—" When all three women looked at her in surprise, she hurriedly explained. "To Kendall Hall. I'm applying for a job there as one of the upstairs maids. Mrs. Kendall wrote me a note . . ." She fumbled again in her pocketbook and brought out a small embossed white envelope and extracted the note. "She told me to be there today at two o'clock for the interview."

"We go right past Kendall Hall," Sybil said, again touching the young woman reassuringly on the arm. There was the merest hint of scorn in her voice as she went on. "Although I don't know the Kendalls personally—they're fairly new to Newport—I *do* know where they live, and we'll drop you off right inside the gates, if they're open."

She picked up the speaking tube and spoke into it, softly giving Jackson directions as he put the Pierce-Arrow in gear to start it gliding on along the road.

"Where are you coming from?" Vivian asked curiously.

"Fall River," the young woman said nervously.

"Why would you go all the way from Fall River to Newport for a position?" Sybil asked, her voice curious.

"Well, ma'am, with jobs so hard to get, an' with so many of the mills closing down—"

"My dear Sybil, you *do* recall we're in the depths of a depression, don't you?" Vivian asked wryly as she lit one of her cigarillos and lazily blew the smoke toward the window, while the young woman watched her in frozen fascination.

Sybil merely cast Vivian a quick look of annoyance. "But surely there must be positions in Fall River or nearby?"

"Not hardly, ma'am," the young woman said, her clear blue eyes watching Sybil without faltering. "An' besides, ma'am, I thought that if I could get a position in one of the big houses at Newport, maybe I could go back to New York or Philadelphia or Boston with the family when the season ends here. To tell the truth, ma'am, there's more money there than in Fall River or thereabouts for an upstairs maid or a serving girl." She suddenly blushed. She had seen the New York license plates on the Pierce-Arrow. "I—I mean—"

"Good thinking," Vivian said with a smile. "You're probably right."

Elizabeth suddenly put her hand out and, grasping the young woman's, shook it, ignoring the glance of reproval on her mother's face. "My name is Elizabeth Stuart, and this is my mother, Mrs. Stuart, and my aunt, Mrs. Chase."

"I'm pleased to meet you," the young woman said, looking embarrassed again. "And I thank you for the ride."

"What's *your* name?" Elizabeth asked.

"Ellie Halloran, Miss."

They had reached the outskirts of Newport and were already traveling along Farewell and Thames streets. There was little traffic. On a lazy, sunny, mid-week afternoon, most Newporters were at Easton's or Bailey's Beach, or sailing on Narragansett Bay.

While stealing guarded glances at the Halloran girl, who was staring straight ahead as she sat on the small jump seat, Elizabeth was slowly struck by the difference in their lives. On this summer day, with her mother and her aunt, she was on the way to Seacliff, her grandparents' summer home, to stay for the month of August. By some quirk of fate, she had been born to Sybil and Howard Ellison Stuart, the department-store Stuarts, newspapers always added after their name. By that same quirk of fate, she lived in a tall townhouse on New York's East Sixty-second Street, she had gone all through Brearley and was now entering Vassar. She would make her debut in December, but not at the Ritz-Carlton at her own coming-out party as her mother had hoped and planned. Sybil had made a concession after hearing Howard's complaints about business and "these hard times," which were simply getting worse since the stock market crash in '29, just three years before. Elizabeth would be introduced to society at the Debutante Cotillion and Christmas Ball, and also the Junior Assembly, the one for *old* New York families. She made a face as she looked away and out the window. A phrase, something she remembered reading from her Sunday School days when she was little, leaped into her mind—*Ten virgins, who took their lamps, and went forth to meet the bridegroom*—and she smiled wryly.

Without seeming to stare, she saw the cheap fabric of the young woman's dress, the runover heels on her tightly laced black oxfords, the coarse and shapeless tan stockings, her imitation leather pocketbook, ugly and worn.

For the first time in her life, she began to wonder about people like Ellie Halloran. Who was she, really? Was she from a big family, how far had she gone in school, what was her home like? What did she and her family and friends talk about? Certainly not about what Doris Duke and Alice Belmont and Gladys Rockefeller wore to Barbara Hutton's dinner dance at the Central Park Casino. Or who won the polo matches at Meadow Brook this past weekend. Or the name of the strange young man who was Nadia Pierpont's escort at El Morocco Saturday night.

They were just passing the Travers block, and then the shingled Casino and the Audrain Building. She saw the young woman turn her head to look at the deep striped awnings, the summer frocks on the women shoppers as they strolled along the sidewalk. There was a curious expression on her face as she watched two boisterous young couples tumble out of a roadster and run toward the Casino, tennis rackets in hand, heads thrown back in laughter, skin tanned to a golden brown.

"Where will you stay tonight?" Elizabeth suddenly asked her, eyes wide with concern. "And how will you get back to Fall River?"

"A friend and her husband brought me in their truck as far as Portsmouth," she said, smiling at Elizabeth. "They are going back tomorrow and will take me with them. Mrs. Kendall said in her note that I could stay the night in the servants' quarters."

They were traveling along Bellevue Avenue, the tree-lined road cool in the sultry afternoon. Elizabeth watched Ellie as she gazed past the soaring wrought-iron gates that guarded the vast grounds and the mansions one could see resting like jewels on velvety green lawns. When the Pierce-Arrow turned and halted before closed iron gates, flanked on both sides by tall columns of white marble gleaming in the sun, she saw the young woman's face begin to pale again.

"It's going to be all right," she said, reaching over and warmly clasping her hand. "Mrs. Kendall will hire you in a minute."

Again, Ellie Halloran cast her a quick but nervous little smile, then looked back once more as the gate man swung the gates wide and the limousine rolled silently through, on along the curving driveway.

Kendall Hall was an enormous stone and marble mansion, like those that had been built in the late nineteenth and early twentieth centuries by immensely wealthy men as spectacular showplaces and luxurious villas for their families to live in through the summer months. Called *cottages* by both the owners and the townsfolk, the mansions and estates were comparable to almost anything to be found for royalty in Europe.

Even Elizabeth was a bit overwhelmed by Kendall Hall. Her grandparents' summer place, Seacliff, was huge and rambling, a weathered, shingle-clad house with gleaming white trim, airy rooms, and large windows facing the sea. Comfortably informal, it seemed to invite the sea and the air and sun inside.

But Kendall Hall shimmered majestically in the tree-dappled sunlight, its white marble and stone walls rising in intimidating splendor, neo-classical in detail with Ionic columns, palladian doors and windows, and wide terraced steps to the main entrance. The door of filigreed brass and gold and glass glittered in the afternoon sun.

"Wait," Elizabeth said, touching Ellie Halloran's arm, as they watched Jackson mount the steps just as a footman in livery came from the door. Through the open window they could hear fragments of conversation, then they saw the footman hurry in through the entrance and in a few moments return with a tall, imposing, half-balding man in a black tailcoat and trousers.

46

"Good heavens, the palace guard," Vivian tittered softly.

"Tell her to go around to the service entrance," they heard the tall man say as he pointed around past manicured green shrubbery toward the far side of the mansion.

At that moment, Elizabeth leaped from the Pierce-Arrow, pulling a startled Ellie Halloran with her. She hurried up the steps and swept past the butler and footman, who stared open-mouthed.

"I say there, wait a moment," the butler called out, but Elizabeth ignored him and continued on into the entrance hall of the house, her high heels tapping impudently on the marble floor.

"Here now, Miss," the butler said, his voice echoing across the cavernous hall as he hurried in after her.

"My name is Elizabeth Stuart, and my mother and aunt and I are on our way to Seacliff on Ocean Drive, where my grandparents, the Venables, live. We gave Miss Halloran a ride. She is here to see Mrs. Kendall." Elizabeth had planted her feet rather wide apart on the gleaming floor, a signal that she wasn't to be trifled with. She had a determined expression on her face and an imperious tone in her voice.

Not immediately recognizing the names, the butler stepped forward a little with a slight bow. "Of course, Miss Stuart. And I will give Mrs. Kendall your message, but the young lady must still go around to the service entrance—"

"No," Elizabeth said stubbornly. "She'll wait here and I'm going to wait with her."

"Miss Stuart," Ellie said timidly, "I'll—" She had started to turn back toward the entrance, but Elizabeth grasped her arm.

"We'll wait here."

"I'm afraid, Miss Stuart," the butler said with a slight curl of contempt on his thin mouth, "that she will have to—"

"The young lady is quite right." The man's voice was deep, echoing.

Elizabeth looked around in surprise. The massive entrance hall, three stories high, with balustraded galleries running around on three sides on the second and third floors, was dim and cool. She heard a fountain trickling and saw it from the corner of her eye off to the right, the water coming from the mouth of a carved marble lion's head. A wide, central, red-carpeted staircase separated on a landing halfway up, with two staircases continuing upward in opposite directions. The man was standing on the landing. He was tall and slim, well-built, with premature touches of silver in his dark hair, tanned skin stretched tautly over good bones, a thin mouth flaring at one corner in amusement. He was a graceful figure in white flannels and a white V-neck sweater, leaning casually against the railing of white marble.

"Sir?" the butler said in surprise, looking upward.

"Go along, Abbott. I'll take care of the young women."

"Yes, Mr. Kendall," Abbott said, backing away for several steps, then turning and hurrying off toward a door beyond and below the staircase.

Mr. Kendall. Elizabeth stared at him as he came slowly down the stairs. *Lawrence Robertson Kendall the Second. The* Lawrence Kendall. The name always mentioned in the same breath with John D. Rockefeller, J. P. Morgan, Andrew Mellon, with a Du Pont, Vanderbilt, Astor, McCormick—but younger. She recalled an article she had recently read about him in *The New York Times.* His grandfather, the first Lawrence Robertson Kendall, had started the Kendall fortune in a somewhat modest way. He had sold the family farm in western Pennsylvania during the financial panic of 1873 and with the money he received he had bought thousands of shares of almost worthless railroad stock that had sunk to a fraction of their original cost.

When the boom of the 1880s came, he went to New York, sold some of the railroad stock, which had rallied upward in price again, and with it bought a small freighter line. Then, with the help of his only son, Samuel, he had built it into a successful steamship company. Fulfilling his youthful dream of going to sea, as he frequently did in his later years on one or the other of his ships, he died a happy man in his sixties.

On his father's death, Samuel Kendall sold the steamship line at a large profit and purchased more railroad stock, until he had control of the line. That's when he began building the Kendall fortune, block by block, wisely diversifying and delivering daily preachments on the flexible rules, the clever intricacies and hidden loopholes of business to his only child. Lawrence Robertson Kendall II was born in 1893, and from the age of six he stood head and shoulders over his classmates.

One limpid night in May, young Lawrence was informed in the room of his fraternity house at Yale that the British steamship *Lusitania* had been sunk by a German submarine off the coast of Ireland, with more than a thousand lives lost, many of them Americans, his parents among them. One carefree moment, he had been a senior student about to graduate with the class of 1915. The next, he was heir not only to the sizable Kendall fortune, but also to his father's position as head of Kendall, Inc.

"My father and mother were on a pleasure trip," he insisted to newspaper reporters the following morning at a meeting in the office of the president of the university, denying that his father had been on his way to London to negotiate the sale of more munitions from his New Jersey factory to the British government for the war with Germany. "And they were returning in three weeks so that they could attend my commencement from the university. It was a pleasure trip, a hop over to the Continent for a week after a few days in London, and then home to the United States."

However convincing he was—and Lawrence *was* an engagingly convincing young man—the reporters didn't believe him.

"There are rumors, strong rumors," said one, "that there were munitions *on* the *Lusitania,* Mr. Kendall, munitions from your father's factories in New Jersey and Connecticut."

"Nothing but rumors," young Lawrence said, looking the reporter directly in the eye. "And now, if you would—"

"Yes, if you will excuse us, please?" said Pernell Beckwith, one of his father's lawyers, who had rushed up from New York to New Haven that morning. "Mr. Kendall has to return to New York immediately, gentlemen." He added in a low aside, his gray head nodding solemnly as Lawrence with an apologetic smile left the room, "The funeral arrangements, y'know. A memorial service, but nevertheless, a sad and burdensome business."

Young Lawrence, with characteristic abruptness, did not return to Yale. His diploma was hand-delivered to his father's—now his—New York City offices by an assistant dean. Within a matter of days, no one in the higher echelons of Kendall, Inc., had any doubt about who was running things. His father had schooled him well, and what he did not know about Kendall, Inc. and all of its diversified interests, he learned swiftly. He had a quick, facile mind and a feel for finance, while at the same time an inherited shrewdness and wily instinct carried him through board meetings and business conferences with his father's trusted lieutenants in the firm. These men, in those first few weeks, watched him and listened to him with open-mouthed admiration, almost in awe. His grasp of information and knowledge about both the munitions and railroad business was not only impressive, but caused them to pause and examine their own lesser gifts and wonder at the genetic imbalances in life.

And their awe grew. Just as Kendall, Inc.—soon referred to as the holding company or the Trust—grew. Samuel Kendall had ventured in a small way into the petroleum business. His son took it to new heights, purchasing refineries along the New Jersey shore. His son also took to other heights. While still in prep school at Andover, he had become fascinated with the first airplane flight that took mail from Garden City to Jamaica, New York. Within two years after becoming head of Kendall, Inc., he built a factory in Connecticut for the manufacture of airplanes, and by 1921 he had established a passenger airline that flew between Boston and New York, one that rapidly expanded to become Trans-Global Airlines, a major mail and passenger line.

During the next ten years, the holding company spread to include steel, banking, and mining interests. And in 1924, at the urging of his trusted business advisers and directors, he married Anne Leland, a woman seven years younger than he whose widowed mother had been his mother's closest friend and whose frail qualities had appealed to his protective nature. She was looking for a father figure in a husband, and he had begun to want some stability.

Elizabeth vaguely remembered much of this as she watched the tall, smiling man walking toward them. Again she noticed the way sun-bronzed skin was drawn tautly, attractively over his face. He walked with his hands in the pockets of his white flannels, and the smile on his thin, flaring mouth had spread to deeply set gray eyes, eyes that warmed as he watched her, but eyes that she sensed could be cold and remote.

"Ben?" he said, calling out to the young footman who stood stiffly near the entrance where sun spilled onto the marble floor in a filagree pattern through the glass and ornamental bronze door. "Take the young woman back to Mrs. Abbott and tell her to give her something cool to drink and something to eat if she wishes it, before she has her interview with Mrs. Kendall." For a fleeting moment, he saw his wife, Anne, in his mind's eye. She would be sitting on the loggia off her bedroom suite, gazing at the ocean, with a book in her hands, a light robe over her lap. Miss Lidstrom, the nurse-companion, would be bringing her the early-afternoon medicine just about now. Luminal— to make her sleep, the doctor had said, to relieve the anxiety. In about fifteen minutes, she would lead her into her bedroom for her afternoon nap . . . listless . . . frail . . . never quite recovering her strength after the radiation treatments. "Mrs. Kendall isn't well," he said, mildly rebuking himself for this sudden interest he felt as he watched Elizabeth's face with a steady intensity. "She'll be resting until after three o'clock."

When Ben moved toward them, Elizabeth grasped Ellie's hand for a moment, the young woman looking around her with awe, with an uneasy fear in her eyes, which nevertheless had a certain spark in them.

"Good luck, Miss Halloran," Elizabeth said warmly, shaking her hand up and down. "I'm certain everything is going to be fine." She looked quickly at Lawrence Kendall on the last few words, the emphasis one he couldn't avoid understanding, and he smiled, pleasantly surprised by her outspokenness. "I'm certain you'll get the position. They'll be lucky to have you here."

"I'll put in a good word for you," he said, smiling now at Ellie, while glancing with amused eyes at Elizabeth. He was clearly piqued by her daring and brashness.

"Thank you, sir," Ellie said, dropping slightly in a curtsy, then almost running as she followed the stiffly walking footman toward a high marble archway near the rear. "And thank *you,* Miss Stuart," she said, looking over her shoulder with a quick smile. Something in their eyes held for a moment and then she was gone.

When they had disappeared, Elizabeth walked toward the front entrance.

"Miss Stuart?" Suddenly, Lawrence didn't want her to leave. But as she turned, almost reluctantly, he felt a small measure of guilt. For several seconds they simply stared at each other. The smile had left his face and for an unguarded moment she saw an expression in the gray eyes that sent a shiver along her spine. He walked slowly toward her, while she tried to watch him with a dispassionate air. But she could feel the warm flush in her cheeks, the thrill of excitement as it tingled along the bare skin of her arms.

"That was extremely kind of you, giving the girl a ride," he said softly, feeling the undercurrent, but trying to make it sound as casual and inconsequential as the words.

"Miss Halloran," she said with a reprimand in her voice, glad to feel the sudden annoyance, finding a flaw, leaping upon it. "Her name is Ellie Halloran. I think people should be called by their names. And she's not a girl. She's a young woman."

"Of course," he said. "Ellie Halloran." He grinned. "Young woman." His smile flashed with gracious apology. His eyes had a recognition of something she couldn't ignore and so she looked away. She heard the commanding timbre of his voice, and when he took her hand and held it, she felt a little faint. She wanted to walk away, but something in his tone held her. "Did I hear you say you're visiting your grandparents here in Newport? For the rest of the summer, I hope."

"Yes," she said, feeling the warm blush flame up in her cheeks again as she tried to pull her hand away. She stepped back, but he held onto her hand. "I must go," she said. "My mother and my aunt are waiting."

He would let her leave, he thought, turn and walk back to his study.

"I'll walk you to your car," he said, still watching her with unwavering, unconcealed admiration, as he let her pull her hand away and walked along beside her. When he opened the door, she kept her eyes straight ahead of her. He was married . . . had children . . . sons, weren't they? How dare he? she thought in a fit of anger.

As they walked down the wide steps, cool in the heavy shade of tall elms and oaks, she noted with a smug kind of satisfaction that the ivy trailing up the marble and stone walls of the soaring mansion was sparse—too new to have acquired the thick, luxuriant appearance that gave houses an old and dignified look. Seacliff had stood on the small bluff overlooking the ocean for more than seventy-five years. Three generations of Venables had summered there.

Lawrence Kendall had *built* Kendall Hall. Just as, in a little more than fifteen years, he had built his massive fortune.

But then she felt shame burn in her face. What difference did it make if all of this was new? What difference did it make if all the wealth and power and influence were recently acquired? *Nouveau riche.* That was a term her mother used. But what an ugly term, what an ugly thought! She despised that kind of thing, had always hated it in school. Girls snickering behind their books in class when a new girl stood up to recite. *Position* and *money.* They talked about somebody's *new money,* as though it were something ugly and dirty.

In a stiff tone, she introduced Lawrence Kendall to her aunt and her mother, who reached out from the shadowy depths of the limousine with a cool white hand to his while Vivian smiled impishly at Elizabeth through a cloud of curling smoke.

"How nice to meet you," Sybil Stuart said in a tone that implied it wasn't nice at all. But Lawrence Kendall simply smiled, his eyes amused. He had met her kind before. Not a bad woman. Just a little too closely inbred was all. And too sheltered from the realities of life. He knew the Stuart department store empire. It was on shaky financial legs, the Depression slowly eroding its foundations. Three generations of conservative fiscal policy, and lack of growth and modernization, had taken their toll. If what he had heard was true, the underpinnings were about to collapse and the walls of Stuart's would at any moment come tumbling down. Howard Ellison Stuart was known as a gentleman in business. Too much so for his own, and Stuart's, good. Still believed in the closing of agreements and deals on a handshake. Too hesitant in decision-making. No vision, always talking of the past rather than looking to the future. Now the son, Dana, he showed promise, according to what Lawrence had heard about him.

Young Dana Stuart had already spent two summers during his years at Princeton working in the family business, and from the talk that Lawrence Kendall had heard, the young man, much to his father's dismay, had tried to introduce new merchandising methods and payment procedures.

"I understand from your daughter that you will be spending the rest of the summer in Newport, Mrs. Stuart?"

"But of course," she said, her smile distant, tone amused. "We spend *every* August in Newport, Mr. Kendall. We always have."

"And always will," Vivian said, her eyes rolling upward in boredom.

Lawrence smiled, unperturbed by Sybil Stuart's snub while chuckling inwardly at Vivian Chase's blunt honesty.

"Then you can understand the pleasure I feel looking forward to these next four weeks, even though it will by necessity be only long weekends that I will be spending here for the most part."

"Oh, I do sympathize. You'll have that atrocious drive," Sybil said, fanning herself with a limp, white glove that she picked up from her lap. "I dread it so awf'ly that we stopped overnight this time with some friends in Watch Hill. To think that you make it twice each week from New York."

"Well—I travel at night each Monday and Thursday," he said. "By train."

"Oh, yes." She spoke slowly, recalling something. "I seem to remember someone speaking about it." He then heard the mocking note in her voice. Such gauche extravagance, it was saying. "You have a private railroad car, I understand."

"It gives me a place to work while I'm traveling," he said, the bemused smile still in place. "And room for people to travel with me *while* we work."

"And for your wife and children as well, I'm sure." The implication was unmistakable. She had seen how he looked at Elizabeth as they came down the terraced steps.

"That too," he agreed. As he straightened up from the door, he stepped back a little. "Well, perhaps we will all see each other in the next few weeks." He stared unblinkingly at Elizabeth as she settled back into the cool shadows of the limousine.

"Oh, probably not," Sybil said with more sharpness than she had intended. "I doubt that we know the same people, Mr. Kendall."

"If that is the case, Mrs. Stuart," he said with a slight bow, his smile now boldly confident, "I will have to change that."

Elizabeth smiled in spite of herself as he closed the door. When Jackson drove off, she glanced back and saw him smile and raise his hand in farewell, one foot casually resting against the carved paw of one of the stone lions guarding the entrance. She felt an odd disappointment at leaving. There was a strange sort of excitement, a magnetism about Lawrence Kendall that filled her with a shimmering kind of light. He had a compelling power about him, a subtle sexuality that she had never come face to face with before. It's because he's so much older, she told herself. In his late thirties, she recalled reading in the *Times* article. She was accustomed to young men of seventeen and eighteen with damp, white cotton gloves and clumsy feet at Miss Damon's Dancing Classes on Central Park West, or sophomoric college boys who carried flasks and got sick at parties or tried to unbutton her blouse in somebody's rumble seat.

". . . and such an obvious show of money," her mother was saying disgustedly. She suddenly waved her glove in irritation. "Really, Vivian, that's the third one of those awful things you've lighted in the last hour."

But Vivian ignored her as she inhaled deeply on the cigarillo. "Oh, I don't know," she said lazily. "I thought he was charming and terribly well-mannered. Quite good-looking, didn't you think so?"

"I wish you'd wait until we get to Seacliff, then go out and sit on the rocks in front and smoke to your heart's content."

Vivian flicked her ashes into the small ashtray on the side. "Handsome really, in a terribly virile way." She smiled at Sybil wickedly, squinting through the smoke.

"If you dare to—" Sybil exploded, as Elizabeth felt a quick stab of jealousy.

54

"Of course I won't." Vivian laughed. "He's much too young for me. Even for idle flirting." She winked at Elizabeth. There was nothing Vivian liked better than teasing her proper sister. "Seven or eight years, I rather imagine."

"And married!" Sybil exploded. "A devoted family man, someone told me not long ago."

Much older and married. Elizabeth felt the disappointment twist inside her as the limousine turned and drove through the stone pillars on each side of the long road that led up to Seacliff. And then, whatever she had been thinking slowly drifted from her mind as she saw her grandmother and Nanny Grace, who had arrived two days earlier. They were coming down from the long, wide veranda that swept around three sides of the big old house, the two red setters running around them in circles on the green lawn that sloped to the rocks overlooking the sea. But the feeling of strength in his hand as he held hers and the expression in his gray eyes lingered.

"Well, here we go again," she heard her Aunt Vivian mutter. "And to think I could have sailed for Cherbourg on the Berengaria with the Wallaces and spent the rest of August in Antibes."

"*Really,* Vivian." Sybil sighed. "Must we go through this every summer? Need I repeat that it's the least you can do, spending four little short weeks with Mother and Father?" She was leaning forward eagerly and waving to her mother as the car slowed on the upgrade, the voice for Vivian and the smile for her mother and Nanny Grace not matching.

"Bridge, beach, and bores," Vivian muttered in an even lower voice. "Well, perhaps Mr. Kendall will have a handsome older friend hanging about somewhere."

"Really, Vivian." Sybil sighed again. "Your trashy little affairs."

4

Howard Stuart pulled at the damp neckband of his shirt while looking down into the deep canyon-like side street. A fan on the wall whirred behind him, but the air in the large dark-paneled office was heavy and humid, barely moving. A fastidious man, he disliked the feeling of dampness on his shirt, felt a severe sense of defeat that he had finally succumbed to taking his suit jacket off. Or was defeat simply coming from all directions, unchecked and without any specific plan of attack? Was he finally so vulnerable that even the merest problem seemed insurmountable?

The few dim street lamps in the short block below between Sixth and Seventh avenues seemed to quiver in the closeness and heat. Just a few hours earlier, the street had teemed with trucks backing into the loading docks, the shining maroon-colored trucks with the gold letters on the side saying STUART'S, and customers had streamed out of the revolving doors, the same maroon boxes and paper bags in their arms, headed for the subways or the suburbs or to apartments uptown.

He rested his hands on the wide windowsill and watched as a few cars drove past below, their headlights cutting a swath in the dim canyon as they turned the corner and headed toward a brighter thoroughfare at Thirty-fourth Street. With all the windows flung open to the top, he could hear the sounds of the city, horns and taxi brakes screeching, the clattering wheels of the Sixth Avenue El and the trolleys as they rattled past the corner, bound for Herald Square.

Lights in a bank of offices across the way winked off. He heard a window slam shut, then the distant voice of a newsboy hawking his papers as he ran toward the corner. Far off, a ship's whistle cried out eerily, then another one, as though in sorrowful answer. He leaned on the windowsill and looked down again, feeling the suffocating heat rise from the sidewalks and pavement. Just one car crawled along the narrow street, as though looking for an address, but then it sped on and turned the corner, disappearing.

For several hours he had known what he had come back to his offices to do. Now that he knew, he felt strangely calm. But he had left the store at five, telling Janet Worden, his secretary, that he was going uptown to his club. She had stared at him with worried eyes.

"Go home, Janet," he had said wearily and then, for the first time in fifteen years, wondered what home in Flushing was like. Sybil had been there once, carrying Christmas gifts one year when Janet had been ill and unable to come to the office. "It's one of those narrow little bungalows," she had told him that evening as they sat in the candlelit dining room at dinner. "Hundreds and hundreds of them, block after block, all in a row." She had shivered a little. "Dreadful, Howard. So—so monotonous and dreary."

"I daresay," he had answered, not really thinking about it.

But now he did think about it as he stared down into the darkened street ten floors below. All of Stuart's sprawled below him, nine floors of dresses and suits and furniture for homes, of notions and toys and layettes for infants, of hats in the millinery department, fur coats on fifth, shoes on second, and the tea rooms on seventh. Floor after floor of merchandise for all of those little bungalows in Flushing that Sybil had told him about.

Sybil. Sybil was in Newport.

What was she thinking right now? What was she doing at this moment? He glanced at his watch. Nine-fifteen. Was she at a dinner party? A game of Ping-Pong with Elizabeth? Or reading one of her endless popular novels? Sometimes she hid one of the trashier kind inside the dust jacket of a book by another author, one that had received some kind of literary acclaim or glorification. "What are you reading, Sybil?" someone might ask. She would flick her hand in a bored kind of way. "Oh, another of Scott Fitzgerald's. We met him with that wife of his at the Fraziers', you know."

Yes, she was probably reading, while Vivian and Laura and Wharton played three-handed bridge. She hated bridge. He could almost see her, stretched out gracefully on the chaise in her sitting room with the french doors open to the night sky and a breeze from the ocean.

Elizabeth would have flown through the hallway door about an hour ago, her tiny high heels tapping across the patches of bare floor between the colorful throw rugs, dark hair flowing down over her shoulders, her lovely face alight with excitement in anticipation of the evening ahead—a dance at the Casino or a moonlight party on the Bannister yacht, or maybe just a movie or a play at the straw-hat theatre up at Ocean Grove. "I'm off," she would say, leaning down to kiss her mother on the cheek, then, with a saucy little flip of the skirt on her bright summer dress, she would turn and dash out the door.

Sybil would be staring at the door where her daughter had disappeared, a fleeting little expression of wistful yearning—or was it envy? —on her face. She spent hours before her dressing table mirror each day putting on her makeup or creaming her skin, peering closely in search of fine lines, even the terrifying sight of a wrinkle. When he teased her once about the weekly facials and massages, the careful recordkeeping in a small white leather diary of her weight, the exercises, and spartan denial of sweets and fattening foods, she turned on him sharply and said, "Would you rather be married to an obese hag?"

She *was* beautiful. At forty-five, she looked far from her age and could still turn male heads when she entered a room. How she loved it, laughing softly, when someone exclaimed to her as Elizabeth stood by her side, "Oh, but you look just like sisters!"

He felt a terrible jolting tug inside and gripped the windowsill. *Why, he would never see her again.* Howard shook his head a little, as though to clear it. He had almost forgotten how much he loved her.

"Howard, you will have to be patient with me," she had whispered to him that first night so long ago, a small hint of fear in her eyes, her lips trembling as he looked down into her face. They were spending the first night of their honeymoon at the Plaza Hotel, before sailing for Europe the following day.

"Of course, darling," he had said, touching her cheek, then bending down to softly kiss her before putting the key into the door of their hotel suite. So long ago . . . so long ago . . .

A light in the office across the street suddenly blazed on and he saw a cleaning woman with bucket and mops come into the room. He turned and leaned against the windowsill for a moment, then slowly walked to a place in the room where he could look through the soft light and see her picture on his desk. It stood between the pictures of

Elizabeth and Dana. His marriage to Sybil, with ups and downs, had settled into something of a routine, but those first years . . .

"Lovely," he whispered. "So lovely." Yes, those first years had been worth it all.

He could almost feel her skin beneath his hands, the satin ripple of flesh over hipbone. A woman of New England reserve, she had surprised him behind closed doors with the amount of passion she felt. *Well, old girl,* he thought, *it was always good in that way.*

He pulled at his collar again, felt the dampness, then, with a complete departure from his usual custom of propriety, no matter what the circumstances were, he loosened his tie and unbuttoned the top button. Slowly turning, he looked across the big room toward his desk again. The single, dark-shaded lamp burned there, casting shadows up the walls. A bottle of scotch stood unopened where he had placed it just moments before, a tall glass beside it, next to the gold and onyx pen-stand.

He had left at five, but not for his club. As he came out onto the street, the summer sun had been low in the west, but burning with the intensity of high noon. Everyone had looked wilted. Two hours before, his lawyers, Ellis Babcock and Herbert Sheehan, had come to his offices with the bankruptcy papers in their briefcases for him to look over. When they left, Janet Worden had stood in the doorway, watching their receding black-suited backs, then she had turned and looked at him as he sat at his desk with his head in his hands.

He had finally glanced up at her. "It's all right," he had said, as he tried to smile.

She had watched him, dark eyes wide with sadness, her wispy brown hair escaping from the tight bun in back as though she had been running her fingers through it, her white face whiter than ever. She couldn't seem to speak, but simply swallowed several times as though her throat hurt. "I'm sorry," she finally managed, in a strangled half-whisper. She had loved him for so many years, but he had never known.

"It's all right," he said again. Then he had gotten to his feet, feeling the panic rise in his chest, and had left the offices, telling her he was going to his club, while her heart stumbled after him.

He had hurried across the street in the middle of the block. As he stepped up on the curb, he turned around and looked back. Howard almost felt surprise, seeing that it was still there, soaring ten stories into the air and stretching like some monstrous animal one entire block in length and width. The gray stone facade, with its set-in columns at each corner and wide entrance, was weathered and stately; there was a quiet kind of grandeur about it. Stone urns at each side of the wide entrances held clipped evergreens; dark maroon canvas awnings, each with the large gold initial S in its center, shielded the broad plate-glass show-windows from the shafts of afternoon sun that suddenly flooded into the narrow street on its way westward.

"More restrained-appearing than Macy's or Gimbel's," Howard's father had explained to him when he was a boy, "but we carry much the same kind of merchandise. And in our East Building, we will continue to carry those items that appeal to the wealthier customer."

The East and West buildings, both under the same roof, were separated in the interior by a kind of arcade walkway that had small-paned glass walls on either side

As he stood across the street, oblivious to the occasional bump of his shoulder or arm by a hurrying passerby, he stared at his empire and wondered where everything had begun to go wrong. With the stock market, of course, in '29, the rumbling chaotic crash, and then the Depression that set in, eroding the unseen foundations of his kingdom, the legacy of stone and steel and shining glass, of deep-pile carpets and glittering brass elevators and dark paneled walls, given into his care, bequeathed to him by his father, and his grandfather and great-grandfather before him.

He looked distractedly along the street, half-expecting to see the long, dark Pierce-Arrow limousine, with Jackson at the wheel, turning the corner and sliding silently up to the east entrance to pick him up. But then he remembered with dull relief that he had instructed Jackson to stay in Newport for the month of August.

Wrenching his glance away, he plunged toward Thirty-second Street, the chaos and panic inside unrevealed to those he passed. To them, if they looked his way, he was expressionless, simply an expensively dressed gentleman with dark, gleaming hair, a narrow, well-bred, handsome face, slightly rakish-looking with its well-groomed mustache and dark flaring eyebrows.

There was a speakeasy on Thirty-second Street that he had occasionally frequented when someone else insisted. It was not exactly his type of place. He rang the bell and was ushered inside, relieved to be unrecognized. He felt the cool dimness swallow him, clothing him in an anonymity that he welcomed with a closely guarded silence. And as he stood at the bar, he glanced only once in each direction, seeing a group of men with four loudly talking and laughing young women. There were other men, alone, in dark suits with pale oval faces in the half darkness, hunched over their drinks while silently staring at nothing.

He had stayed there for perhaps an hour, then, as darkness began to slip over the city, he started walking. He had no destination in mind, but simply walked, swiftly moving through one street after another, his mind seething with a different darkness from the one that surrounded him, great livid forks of agony leaping out of that darkness within and tearing at his insides, burning in his brain, sending dry sobs upward to heave in his throat.

You always knew, he thought with an anguish that suddenly rushed at him like a glaring white blizzard of light. *You always knew, Father.* He looked up to where the tall, dark buildings parted above to leave a strip of deep, dark blue sky, strangely empty of stars or moon. Yes, though they had never spoken it aloud, they both knew there was a flaw, he and his father. He had fulfilled all of the traditions that had been carried down through generations of Stuarts, first Groton, then Princeton and the Ivy Club, marriage to the right girl, a Venable of Boston in his case, membership in the New York Yacht Club and the country club in Greenwich, the month of August always spent in Newport, crewing twice when he was younger for the America's Cup contender, his apprenticeship at Stuart's, first in the Philadelphia branch and then Manhattan.

He had done everything that was expected of him as a Stuart, but . . . something had always been missing, and both he and his father, though never speaking of it, had known. He had heard his grandfather talk about how his father had "that factor of audacity," the ability to take risks, to move ahead with the Stuart boldness and daring to outwit his competitors.

Dana has it, he thought, as he stared through the lamplight of his office. If anything could be salvaged somehow out of the financial shambles that was now Stuart's, perhaps his son would be the one to do it. Once he had finished college . . .

He walked across the room to his desk, poured a long glass of scotch, and raised it to his lips. As he felt it burn its fiery way down his throat, he sat down at the desk, pulled out the heavy vellum stationery, and opened his fountain pen.

"My dearest Sybil . . ." he wrote.

* * *

Jackson received the phone call in his quarters over the old coach-house at Seacliff, where all the servants had their rooms. The call, from Ellis Babcock, came at midnight, asking him to inform Mrs. Stuart that Howard Stuart had taken his life by pointing a gun to his head and pulling the trigger.

"He said he thought it was better if you heard it in person from someone in the family or like me, Mrs. Stuart," Jackson explained in a voice choked with grief. They were in the large main living room with its wide windows that looked out to the ocean. Gently blowing white curtains, bright flowers arranged in large vases, white wicker chintz-cushioned furniture jarred with the scene. Sybil Stuart and her father, Wharton Venable, were sitting on a long settee, with Jackson standing nervously in front of them.

Sybil was wearing a gray silk robe, but Wharton Venable was still dressed in a hastily pulled-on golf sweater with his white flannels. He and his wife, Laura, had been playing three-handed bridge with their other daughter, Vivian, in the upstairs sitting room.

Jackson saw Mr. Venable's hand go out and grasp Sybil's hand, saw her face go white and her body become rigid.

"I'm sorry, ma'am, to be having to tell you this way," Jackson said, his voice breaking a little. He had liked Mr. Stuart, liked him best, perhaps, for the qualities that were missing in his character—the gentle manner, the stepping back in a crowd, the lack of aggressive heartiness that was so evident in his father.

"It's—it's all right, Jackson," Sybil said in a half-whisper. She was staring at him, seemed not to have quite understood what he had told her. "You had no choice. And I—I appreciate your courage in doing so."

Wharton Venable was nodding at him. "Thank you, Jackson," he said, the piercing blue eyes suddenly tired-looking. "You can go along now. And thank you." The briskness was gone from the Boston banker's voice.

As Jackson hurried from the room, he glanced over his shoulder to see Sybil Stuart turn and put her face against her father's shoulder and his arm go around to support her as she softly cried out, "Oh, Father, how am I going to tell Elizabeth and Dana?"

The Stuarts returned to New York and Elizabeth did not see Lawrence Kendall again. A large arrangement of flowers with his card on it was sent to the funeral home, but it was almost lost in the sea of flowers that arrived. Weeks later, when Sybil Stuart looked through the cards that had been sent, she frowned when she saw the bold scrawl of his name and quickly dropped the card into the wastebasket beside her small French desk.

But at the moment the small white card was fluttering into the wastebasket, Lawrence Kendall was looking across his broad shining desk at Dexter Venable, Sybil's brother, who was general manager of Stuart's in Manhattan. The forty-three-year-old Venable was as fair-haired as his sisters were dark, a capable, uncomplicated, pleasant man who seemed perfect for Kendall's plan.

"Howard Stuart held the controlling stock in Stuart's, I understand?" Lawrence said as he fingered a dark leather portfolio on his desk that Dexter knew held information about all of the Stuart stores. There were three smaller ones, in St. Louis, Cleveland, and Detroit, in addition to the big stores in New York and Philadelphia. He knew that Kendall had ordered a complete financial study for acquisition purposes.

"Yes, that's right," Dexter said, nodding with his lopsided, good-natured smile. "It's been that way for three generations, handed down from father to son to grandson."

He watched as the tall, handsome, cold-eyed man rose from his chair and walked to the window. He was wearing a suit of well-cut gray flannel, which seemed rather casual to Dexter, accustomed to the severe pin-stripes and dark blue worsted suits in the boardrooms and business offices of his acquaintances.

As the silence lengthened in the large, walnut-paneled office, Dexter watched Lawrence Kendall with curiosity. He had heard quite a few stories about him, many of them uncomplimentary. Kendall had a reputation for being calculating and cold, a shrewd driver of hard bargains, a genius with financial figures, a man with the uncanny cunning to be in the right place when opportunity presented itself. All of this combined with a bold, sometimes almost reckless courage and extraordinary vision seemed to place him head and shoulders above most other men. A myth had grown around him. Comparatively few men within the canyons of Wall Street and throughout the other business establishments that stretched from coast to coast had met him. But all knew his name, his reputation, talked about his rumored millions that were said to be sliding without any effort toward the billion mark—a young King Midas whose mere touch turned everything to gold.

Although the gray eyes had pierced coldly across the broad desk, Dexter had found him to be thoroughly approachable. His soft, deep voice had been faultlessly polite. He had rung for coffee that had been served in fine bone china cups and saucers. He had insisted that Dexter sit in a more comfortable chair and considerately adjusted a window blind so that the sun wouldn't shine in his eyes.

"We would like to see Stuart's survive and continue to operate," he said as he slowly turned around and sat behind his desk again, his voice soft but filled with confidence. Dexter had noticed that Lawrence Kendall always spoke in terms of *we* when referring to Kendall, Inc. "Whatever I say to you here, at this moment, must remain confidential."

Dexter nodded. "Of course."

"This is an acquisition that we prefer remain without notice. Stuart's is a department store operation with much tradition in its long background, a group of stores that has been owned by one family for several generations. And regardless of Mr. Stuart's recent death, and"—he continued in an even, unhurried tone—"the manner in which that death occurred, I am convinced the customers of Stuart's would be happiest served by an uninterrupted flow of business, undisturbed by the jarring knowledge that unknowns were taking over their favorite department store."

"I agree with that," Dexter said, lounging back a bit in the deep, comfortable leather chair and snipping off the end of the fine Havana cigar that Lawrence had given him. He took a moment to light it and to puff smoothly, then studied the curling stream of smoke as it rose to the ceiling. "But if you are taking over Stuart's, how do you propose to do it without all the newspapers printing it in the next morning's news?"

"One of our holding companies will take it on, with a dummy corporation as the operating division."

Dexter nodded his approval.

"The legal department is working out the details," Lawrence said. "The important thing is a smooth transition. You have been acting on the family's behalf in Howard Stuart's position as president, I've been told."

Again Dexter nodded. "It seemed the natural thing to do. I have been the vice-president and general manager for three years now."

"Excellent," Lawrence said, his hands coming together in a steeple effect in front of him. "I also understand that the tradition of succes-

64

sion in the Stuart family is a strong one, and that young Dana, when he is graduated from Princeton, would be expected to step into the presidency?"

Dexter leaned forward with a reassuring smile. "That would be clearly understood, and I would willingly step down when that time—"

"On the contrary, Mr. Venable," Lawrence said softly, a slow smile spreading over his face as he came around to the front of the desk and leaned back against it. "At that time you will step up to the position of chairman of the board."

Dexter stared at him. "But—"

"Smooth transitions, Mr. Venable?"

"Well—er, yes," Dexter said, looking down at his well-manicured hands and smoothing an unseen wrinkle on the knee of his trousers. "I understand what you mean. But there has never been a position above the presidency—"

"The Board of Directors will create one."

Dexter stared again, for a moment. The gray eyes before him were smiling, but the mouth was hard with decision. "Dana Stuart, in just his two summers of work at Stuart's, left a commendable record behind him. He tried to institute some really brilliant merchandising ideas. One or two of them might have exploded in his face—" Lawrence smiled. "But on the whole, he revealed a keen mind for the business and some truly innovative ideas that could drag Stuart's out of the nineteenth century and into the twentieth."

"Well, I suppose—"

"Come now. Admit that the store is run with antiquated practices, Dexter." Lawrence stood erect and bowed slightly. "If I may? Call you Dexter?"

"Oh, please do—er, Lawrence."

Kendall's hand suddenly reached out to grasp Dexter's.

"Then it's all settled."

Dexter slowly rose. "Why—yes. Of course. Dana has another two years at Princeton, you understand."

"The timing could not be better. By then everything will be in place."

He was walking Dexter to the door, holding his arm and smiling down at him. "And now, supposing we have that lunch I was talking about earlier?"

"Fine. There are some questions I would like to ask you, and—"

"How does Keen's suit you? It's close and—"

"I would very much like to take you uptown to my club, if you can take the time," Dexter insisted as they paused by the door.

"That's very kind of you," Lawrence said, again with that formal little half-bow that Dexter had come to associate with him. He had turned to get their hats from a brass rack in the corner, so that Dexter did not see the sudden small gleam of triumph in his gray eyes. "But some other time, perhaps. At this moment in our acquisition, it would perhaps be best if we were not seen together in a place where you are so well known."

"But Keen's?"

"There's a small private room there that my secretary already reserved for us."

Dexter nodded as they left the office. "Well, then Keen's it is, Lawrence."

5

When the financial shambles that was Howard Ellison Stuart's personal estate was finally settled, there was barely enough left for Dana to continue at Princeton, Elizabeth at Vassar, and for Sybil to keep the townhouse on East Sixty-second Street.

But one morning in October of 1932, readers of New York's many newspapers were surprised when they read that "in spite of the untimely recent death of Howard Ellison Stuart, the department store group long known as Stuart's will continue under Stuart family leadership, with the late Howard Stuart's brother-in-law, Dexter Venable of the Boston banking family, stepping into the presidency of the corporation."

A second announcement, later that month and in the society pages, said, "Miss Elizabeth Venable Stuart, daughter of Mrs. Howard E. Stuart of New York City and Newport, Rhode Island, and the late Mr. Howard Ellison Stuart, will be introduced to society in December at a ball at the Ritz-Carlton Hotel in New York."

Although Elizabeth had protested, her grandparents, Wharton and Laura Venable, insisted. They would bear the cost and head the receiving line with her mother.

"It's important," Wharton Venable said on one of Sybil and Elizabeth's weekend visits to the Beacon Hill house in Boston, "that you put on a calm and confident face, in view of everything that has happened, and particularly in view of the fact that this company, A. and W. Leland Ltd., has managed to operate as quietly as it has in the receivership of Stuart's."

"What does all of this mean, Father?" Sybil asked as they lingered over coffee and liqueurs in the dining room, the row of ancestors' gold-framed portraits gazing down at them, while candlelight flickered across her sad but handsome face.

"It means, quite generously, as Dexter has described it to me, that the Stuarts have lost individual proprietorship of the company but gained a partner through a merger. A. and W. Leland Ltd. has absorbed Stuart's, formed a corporation, and invested a strong capital base and expenditures in exchange for a majority of the stock." As a cloud crossed Sybil's face and she started forward as though in protest, he hurried on. "Quite frankly, my dear, in times like these, Stuart's is most fortunate that a benefactor such as this one came along when it did. It was about to go completely under, which is why Howard— well, my dear, need I say any more?"

"I suppose not, Father," Sybil said stiffly, her coffee cup clinking ominously against the china saucer. She was gowned all in black, and her face rose like a pale oval in the candlelight, the dark hair carefully outlining white brow and cheeks.

"Sybil, dear," Laura Venable said, her voice soft as she reached out and patted her daughter's hand. "Wharton has told me that it means you will be able to go on living in quite the same manner you have in the past, with only a somewhat reduced income—"

"It isn't that!" Sybil almost spat the words. "It's—it's just that"— she was fighting tears, hot tears of resentment—"that it's all so humiliating."

Elizabeth turned to her in shock. She had been quietly listening as she toyed with her silverware, her face, like her mother's, pale with grief but still exquisite in the flickering light. "But, Mother, no one will know." She added quietly, "And now people will stop saying the dreadful things about Father that they've been saying."

"*We* know. And *they* know—whoever *they* are—these people at A. and W. Leland, whatever that is."

Her father smiled as he folded his napkin and placed it on the table. His white hair and the white front of his dinner clothes gleamed in the candlelight, while he waited for Chin, the elderly houseman, to pad back through the swinging door into the butler's pantry.

"It's an investment company, Sybil," he said. "They saw a good thing in Stuart's and decided to invest in it, to keep it from slipping into oblivion. You should be very happy about it. Dexter will take over the general management of the group and the running of the New York store, and when Dana is through school and ready to step in, a place will be there waiting for him."

"Just think what this means for Dana, Sybil," Laura said, her silvery head tipped toward her daughter, as though to try to convince her.

"Mother, for heaven's sake, none of your friends are going to know a thing," Elizabeth said rather drily. She stood up quickly, the folds of her amethyst satin gown swirling about her as she turned and pushed the tall carved chair back to the table.

"And where are you off to?" her grandfather asked her cheerfully.

"Gavin Armstead asked me to go dancing."

"Oh, I don't think you should—" Sybil said, but her father cut her off with a quick smile.

"Gavin's a perfectly respectable and acceptable young man from my offices, Sybil."

"But it's so soon after her father—"

"Sybil, she's young," Laura said softly. "And two months have passed."

"Well," Sybil said grudgingly, nodding at Elizabeth. "As long as it's with someone your grandfather knows."

Elizabeth quickly kissed her mother on the cheek and ran to the door. "I'm not going to marry him, Mother," she said, a teasing look in her eyes. "I'm simply going dancing." And she disappeared.

For several moments there was silence in the long room with its portraits on one wall, murals of Boston Harbor before the Revolutionary War on another, and the long narrow windows that faced out on the street. When Sybil looked up, first at her father, then her mother, there were tears in her eyes. "It's just that it's so hard . . . with her away at college. For the first time in my life . . . I find that I'm lonely."

Elizabeth made her debut that winter. It was held in the Crystal Room of the Ritz-Carlton, with less than four hundred guests, small by comparison with some of the other elaborate and showy coming-out parties of recent years.

"I simply won't permit one of these *nouveau* extravaganzas," Sybil had said while they were in the planning stages.

"That's all right with me," Wharton said cheerfully. "I hear that Barbara Hutton's cost sixty thousand dollars two years ago, and the party favors were small gold jewelry cases filled with diamonds and other precious, unmounted gems."

"Well, the most dreadful party of all," said Laura Venable, her merry eyes twinkling a bright blue, "was back in 1906 when the parents of Mary Astor-Paul had thousands and thousands of butterflies brought from Brazil. They were hung in gossamer nets up at the ceiling of the ballroom. And when the butterflies were released at midnight, as planned, they were dead and fell all over the horrified guests down below." Her husband stared at her open-mouthed, then burst into laughter.

Gavin Armstead came from Boston to be Elizabeth's escort at her debut, a matter that had now become pleasing to Sybil. He was a nice young man with reddish blond hair and a ready smile. He came from an old and prominent Boston family, one with wealth, social standing. Sybil found him easily acceptable.

But Elizabeth had different ideas. Often, when she was still a student at Brearley riding her horse each day in Central Park, she would watch young couples lolling about on the grass or riding in roadsters with the top down, one couple in the front and sometimes another in the rumble seat, openly kissing. She would feel a sudden emptiness inside, a strange kind of loneliness—strange, because she was surrounded by love in her family. But this was different. As she grew older, the feeling became intense at times, whenever she saw couples together, whenever she saw a young man and young woman walking along the street holding hands, or in the shadows of a doorway in a close embrace. She knew that she hadn't yet met anyone who could fill that emptiness. Several times Gavin had tried to kiss her, but she had laughingly evaded him. It had been that way with most of the boys she had gone places with.

The evening of her debut, she and Gavin stepped from the Pierce-Arrow into a flood of light beneath the hotel marquee. Fresh snow had fallen in the afternoon and the streets of Manhattan were like a fairyland. They had ridden down Fifth Avenue to Forty-sixth Street so that Gavin could see the Christmas tree decorations and lights along the avenue. Dana and Gavin were sitting in the small jump seats, while Elizabeth and her friend Missy Wainwright spread the skirts of their gowns across the entire width of the rear seat.

"Later tonight we'll take you down to see the windows at Stuart's, Gavin," Dana was saying as the gleaming limousine sped down the snow-cleared street, and turned east toward Madison Avenue. "After the party, we'll all go down to the Village, where we can have some *real* fun." He was laughing.

"Oh, Dana," Missy said, patting at her hair, "that's not a nice thing to say. Elizabeth's party is going to be absolutely scrumptious." Her mother's diamond earrings winked in her ears.

"Don't you mean sumptuous?" he asked, still laughing as he looked over his shoulder, dark eyes suddenly softening at the sight of her, a vision in pink tulle and peau de soie. She was so pretty, so soft and cuddly, rather like a soft little kitten. But he wasn't in love with her and had tried to tell her so without actually saying it.

Dana Stuart had a dark, brooding handsomeness that was very appealing. Missy Wainwright was just one of many young New York women who had fallen in love with him. But that's one of the nice things about Dana, his sister thought as she looked at him in the half-darkness of the limousine. He doesn't know how attractive he is, how women fall all over themselves because of him.

She sat quietly in her corner of the Pierce-Arrow, wondering why they were going through all of this nonsense—yes, *nonsense,* she had told Missy the day before—for what was called her introduction to society. She had studied herself in the long mirror of her bedroom earlier. Everything was in place, everything was ready. Her dark hair was piled high on her head in the front and fell in shining waves down the back to drift across her bare, gleaming shoulders; her eyes were an intense dark blue with that heat of violet, widely set, burning with some fire that she didn't understand, wanting something she couldn't name.

She had looked at the gown, white with a sweeping wide skirt and tiny bodice, touched from breasts to toe with pearls and winking crystals. Her mouth and cheeks were the palest pink, and tiny pearls clung to her ears.

What is it I want? she asked silently, watching the words form on her lips. *I don't want this, hundreds of people staring at me.* She would have to smile until her cheeks ached, shake hands until she felt limp, say all the right words, feel others stepping on her toes as she danced, remember names, laugh at all the right places . . .

". . . When Morton threw that pass to McCall in the last game," Gavin was saying in heated but friendly argument with Dana. Gavin was a sophomore at Dartmouth and Bill Morton was his idol. "That gave us our winning touchdown."

"All right, all right, all right, I'll give you that much, but when Dartmouth plays Harvard next year, the jig's up, my friend . . ." Dana was saying. Elizabeth looked with impatience through the side window, her cheek brushing the soft, white ermine fur of her evening wrap. She wished she were somewhere else, anywhere else but on her way to her coming-out party at the Ritz-Carlton.

"Here we are," Dana called out, as he leaped to the sidewalk and held the door wide before Jackson could come around from the other side. The lights from the marquee blazed and Elizabeth hesitated, hanging back for a moment while Missy stood on the sidewalk peering in at her. She could see the crowds of people, all in evening dress, as they moved toward the revolving glass doors of the hotel. A long black limousine slid in ahead of them and she watched the driver go around to open the rear door as a tall couple hurried toward it.

"Why, Miss Stuart!"

She heard the voice just as she climbed out of the Pierce-Arrow, and her blood seemed to freeze in her veins, then it rushed on hotly to beat in her throat and flush her cheeks. He was walking toward her, leaving the handsome older couple standing near the limousine door. His white tie and tails were impeccable, and he was carrying a tall silk hat and a black chesterfield over his arm.

"Mr. Kendall," she said in a voice that sounded strange to her ears. She quickly introduced him to Missy and Dana and Gavin, catching a glimpse past him at the couple with him, the woman's face curious, but also annoyed. As she pulled her hand from his, she knew it was trembling and was angry with herself for it.

"Well, nice to have seen you," she said as she walked toward the revolving door, hoping it sounded as offhand and casual as she intended it. Halfway through the door, she glanced back and saw him still standing there, a knowing smile on his mouth, his eyes dark with some message. Angrily, she pushed her way on, but in moments, as they walked toward the Crystal Room, she felt the familiar emptiness she had known so often, now stronger than ever before.

"I can't wait to dance with you," Gavin was whispering in her ear.

She looked ahead and saw Missy clinging to Dana's arm. *Nothing is right,* she thought with despair. *Nothing is the way it's supposed to be.*

The Dartmouth Winter Carnival was something that Elizabeth had always heard about and for years she had longed to be there. She loved to ski and ice skate, so she settled in at the Hanover Inn with a feeling of jubilation. She had arrived at White River Junction, where Gavin did not meet the train, as she had expected, but a young man by the name of Glen Bassett, a neatly dressed young man with an insolent mouth and blond good looks. His shoulders seemed to almost bulge out of the somewhat shabby-looking ski jacket and he moved with the lithe grace of a panther. He led her to Gavin's car slinging her suitcases into the back seat. *Football scholarship,* she thought, as she stepped into the car.

"Gavin's on the judging committee for the ice-carving contest," the young man explained. "They're having a meeting. That's why he asked me to meet you." He slid behind the wheel, started the motor, and sent the car skidding out into the road toward Hanover. As he looked around at her, he grinned. "I work at his fraternity house. I'm one of the paid drudges."

She ignored that. "You play football?"

"Swimming," he said, grinning again as he glanced at her, then back at the snow-covered road.

She looked away and kept her head turned from him, away from those remarkable eyes, like sun glinting on blue steel, as insolent as his mouth, the smile flashing in a deeply tanned face. "I'm on a swimming scholarship." When she didn't respond to that but kept looking out the car window, he went on. "So you're Gavin's girl?"

"Gavin and I are good friends," she snapped.

"Mmm-hmmm. Interesting. He says you're his girl and you say you're good friends. Very interesting."

When she stole a quick glance at him, he was looking intently at the road. She turned her head away again and watched the forest fly by. The sun was blazing down on pristine stretches of white snow, glittering like millions of tiny diamonds, the whiteness banking up against the stately pines, making them so green that she blinked back tears at the sheer beauty of it all. They passed small white, green-shuttered houses nestled back against the soaring foothills, with smoke curling from the chimneys. A tall belfry and spire rose from a white clapboard church in the middle of a small commons. A deserted bandstand stood in the center and a cluster of white buildings around the edges.

"Pretty, isn't it?" Glen Bassett said, smiling down at her, and when she nodded, he chuckled. "But boring. I like cities, bright lights, lots of people, noise, confusion, theatre marquees, restaurants, the excitement on any day of the week when you step out of your front door."

"New York, I suppose you mean?" she said drily.

He looked at her for a long moment before returning his steady gaze to the road. She was wearing a gray squirrel coat and hat, the silky fur bringing out the deep blue-violet of her eyes, accentuating the dark sweep of eyebrows and tendrils of hair that peeked out from the cossack-type hat, etching the delicate face in loveliness. Her gray velvet ankle boots were edged in squirrel, and above them he could see long silken legs.

He glanced in the rear-view mirror. Her initialed gray leather luggage was expensive, as were her clothes. *She* was expensive. He whistled to himself silently. She was *marvelous*. Not only expensive, but beautiful. And wary. He had to be careful. But he had just a few days to work in. Goddammit, he thought, just his luck. Here was the girl he had been looking for all of his life, and he had only a matter of days to do something about it. Oh, he didn't worry about Armstead. Gavin Armstead was a chump—a nice chump, but a chump all the same. He went by the book. Nonathletic and not the best student, he tried to make up for it by volunteering for committees and councils. Like the ice-carving judges' committee. No, he only worried about Elizabeth Stuart herself. She was the kind who could see through almost any kind of deception.

Well-bred and well-tuned. No, finely tuned, to any kind of fakery. He saw it in her eyes the moment he first looked at her, heard it in her voice, soft and silvery, but with an edge to it when she said, *New York, I suppose you mean?*

"I grew up in a small town," he said, with an apologetic kind of grin, his voice with just the right amount of sheepishness in it. "I guess we small-towners always yearn for the bright lights. But maybe once we got there, we wouldn't like it so much."

"Oh, I think you would," she said with a cool smile, her voice softening a little, but still edged with a slight chill.

That's it, he thought, that's the right tack to take.

"But it's nice to be able to get away from it once in a while." She laughed softly, a row of small, perfectly formed white teeth like pearls against the soft pink of her lips. "Even for small-towners who quickly become city slickers."

"Oh, I'd never do that." He laughed along with her. "I'd be much too busy looking up at the tall buildings and stumbling over my own feet."

"Hardly," she said softly. "Hardly, Mr. Glen Bassett. You talk a good country-bumpkin line, but I suspect there's a certain charm and slickness underneath."

"Do you now?" he said, his voice matching hers in softness, as he looked at her with his remarkable eyes. "Well, maybe while Gavin is charging around from one ice-carving to another and taking notes, I can do him a favor and keep you from getting bored. Then we could find out if there's this certain *charm* and *slickness* underneath."

"Oh, you're one of those, are you?" She was still smiling, but with a wariness. "Taking over someone else's date?"

"When it comes to a beautiful girl like you?" he said, the voice still low and touched with insolence. "I'd be a fool if I weren't, wouldn't I?"

She looked at him for a long moment, her face unreadable, then glanced away. "After you've dropped me off at the Inn, will you find Gavin for me and tell him I'll be expecting him to pick me up for dinner at about seven?"

"Be glad to," he said, looking straight ahead at the road with a secret smile on his face. "But, you might as well know. He'll be busy with all the little ice-carvers and sculptors most of the day tomorrow."

She frowned and gazed off through the window as the town of Hanover came into view, the lovely colonial buildings rising up out of the snow. This Glen Bassett *did* have a way of making poor Gavin sound like a bumbling fool.

"You can go along with Tom Williston's girl. Her name is Debbie, I think. Yes, Debbie Hudson. And Marcia Freeling. She's here with Bud Mather. They'll all be going to the skating exhibitions." Gavin was pulling at his pocket for his wallet, while trying to signal the waiter. His pleasant face was flushed with concern over having to leave Elizabeth to his friends the next day.

"Gavin, I'd rather go with you," Elizabeth insisted.

"But I'll be with the other judges most of the day, Elizabeth," he said as he pulled a bill from his wallet after looking at the check. They were sitting in George's, a popular gathering place and restaurant in the middle of town. They had gone to the hockey game in late afternoon and a fraternity dance that evening after dinner, then stopped at George's for a late snack and were now ready to shuffle through the snow back to the Inn. "That wouldn't be any fun for you. You'll have a much better time with Debbie and Marcia."

Several times during the evening, she had caught a glimpse of Glen Bassett. He worked as a waiter at the fraternity house, except during parties and dances, when he did the bartending. Whenever she was dancing with Gavin or one of his fraternity brothers and looked over her shoulder toward the bar, she saw his eyes on her and quickly glanced away. They were in the big living room of the fraternity house with the rugs rolled back, the lights turned low, muic from a small student combo playing slow, pulsing music, and dancers jamming the floor in closely swaying couples.

Everything was so right, yet something was wrong. Missing. She felt as though she were floating on the music. The rush of voices and laughter from another room seemed far away and yet close enough to be part of the evening's magic. But . . . something was missing.

A young man with curly blond hair was crooning into a megaphone like Rudy Vallee, his voice soft and sweet and sad. Elizabeth watched him over Gavin's shoulder. His eyes were closed, and he tipped his head and almost whispered the words, as though he were crooning them into a girl's ear. The saxophone was wailing and the pianist's fingers rippled with sultry insinuation over the keys. She felt a small thrill shiver up her back and wished she were dancing with—yes, with Glen Bassett, she thought ashamedly, as her eyes met his and clung for too long a moment, long enough to see the ironic twist of his smile, the bold admiration in his eyes, as he shook a silver cocktail shaker, his white mess jacket gleaming in the distance.

When the song came to an end, she quickly excused herself and pushed through the packed couples as they stood waiting for the next song, some of them clapping their hands, the long dresses of the young women like bright slashes of color against the black tuxedos of the young men. She inched through the crowded room toward the staircase, smelling the heavy fragrance of gardenia corsages, the rippling laughter and voices assaulting her ears. Free of the close crush of dancers, she ran up the stairs toward the room and adjoining bath that had been turned into a powder room by the young men for their dates.

She took her time refreshing her lipstick and powdering her shiny nose, just sitting before the dressing table staring at herself. The low-cut bodice of her pale blue satin dress was scalloped and edged with tiny seed pearls and brilliants, and curved seductively over small firm breasts. Her dark hair rose high on the front and sides, where it was caught with gardenias, and fell in long shining waves over her shoulders, illuminating the high cheekbones and wide-set eyes, giving the pearls in her ears a shimmering luminescence. Her dress fell to her silver sandals in molded panels that clung to her figure.

What on earth are you thinking? she thought, aghast for a moment as she realized she had been imagining his arms around her, the thin flaring mouth closing over hers, a hand touching her throat and stealing down to the bodice of her dress, where it lingered. She didn't even like him—didn't even know him.

Rising quickly, she hurried toward the door and opened it, then stopped. He was leaning against the wall in the dim corridor just outside.

"Hello," he said softly, his mouth smiling but his eyes smoldering with an expression that made her step back nervously.

"What are you doing here?" she demanded, but realized she had said it barely above a whisper.

"Waiting for you," he said. "I've been watching you. You're really bored, aren't you?"

"Of course I'm not," she said hotly.

"No?" He tipped her chin up and gently put the tip of his finger on her nose. "My eyes told me something else."

"You know, you really have a nerve—"

"I know," he said, suddenly pulling her to him and kissing her. His mouth was hard, demanding. She tried to push away, but his arms held her against him in a vise-like embrace. When his lips moved against hers and parted, the tip of his tongue probing inward, she shuddered, again tried to push away, then surprisingly felt the rigidness go from her body, as it curved against his.

The music was pulsing on the floor below, slow, sensual music that seemed to crawl like silken fingers along her skin.

"Some friends of mine are having a party at a house where we all live over in Norwich just a few miles from here," he whispered. "We've rented a sleigh to go there."

"Don't be ridiculous—" she said, but he pulled her against him again.

"I'll pick you up in front of the Inn at one o'clock."

"You must be crazy—"

"Tell Gavin you're tired and want to turn in early."

She pushed away from him and ran along the corridor toward the staircase just as they heard voices and bursts of laughter coming from the stairwell.

"I'll be there at one," he called out softly.

At the top of the stairs, she glanced back quickly, but he had disappeared along the corridor, apparently toward a back stairway. How dare he! she thought, the anger rising in her in a flooding tide. But it was more than anger, she realized, as she started slowly down

77

the staircase, one finger touching her lips where he had kissed her. She smiled absently at the two young women coming up the stairs. They were laughing and chattering, passing her in a rush of drifting perfume and rustling taffeta and silk, their pert blonde heads nodding hard as they giddily laughed over some idle piece of gossip.

The rest of the evening swept past in waves of dizzying color and music and the rise and fall of voices and laughter. When the tempo of the music raced, the lights blazed up and couples swung onto the floor in a frenzy of fast-moving dance steps, but when it slowed to a sensuous flow of liquid silver, the lamps were turned low and just the vague sway of bodies in close embrace cast shadows up the walls. She felt removed from it all, even though she floated from one set of arms to another; as the saxophones moaned, she yearned for something, for someone. At midnight she asked Gavin to take her back to the Inn, pleading that she was tired.

He left her in the lobby, watching as she slowly walked away from him. But once she was out of sight, she ran toward her room, quickly changed her clothes to a dark ski outfit, and sat waiting with her eyes glancing frequently to her watch, until the small gold hands stood at five minutes to one.

She started toward the door, but turned and sat down again. She waited in rigid silence, not moving, but her mind racing. Part of her wanted to run from the room. She squeezed her eyes shut, remembering the feel of his mouth on hers, his hands touching her throat and drifting down to her breasts, the hardness of his body as he pulled her against him. A weakness flowed through her and she slowly shook her head as though trying to push the thoughts, the memory of his mouth, away from her, into the dark corners of the room.

She looked around her at the softly glowing lamps, the smooth green rug and flowered drapes, the comfortable deep chairs and pretty bedspreads on the twin beds. *I'm Gavin's guest here,* she kept telling herself, as she tried to recall what he looked like. Twice she started to rise, but forced herself to sit down again. She had no problem remembering what Glen Bassett looked like, the sun-bleached blond head and dark blue eyes beneath thick black lashes.

It was fifteen minutes past one when she heard the soft rap on the door. She didn't move. She hardly breathed, as she sat in one of the deep chairs, holding herself across the front of her heavy wool ski jacket. When the rapping came again, a second and then a third time, she slowly rose and walked to the door. She waited there for a long moment. When he knocked a fourth time, she put her mouth close to the door.

"Go away, Glen."

"Not until you come out."

"Then I'll have to call down to the desk."

There was a long pause. "You *would* do that, wouldn't you?"

"Yes. . . . I would."

Again there was a long pause. "You'll never know what you missed, Elizabeth." When she didn't answer, he finally spoke again. "Well, when you get married, that's the kind you'll marry. A boring chump, like Gavin Armstead, and you'll be bored the rest of your life."

Elizabeth waited until long after she knew he had left. Then she rose and undressed for bed, a strange emptiness, even more intense than she had known before, drifting through her like a cold damp mist. But oddly, as she drifted off to sleep, she wasn't thinking of Glen Bassett. She was thinking of a man named Kendall.

She left two days later, never seeing Glen again. And from the day she left, she saw Gavin only at occasional debutante parties and once across a restaurant in Boston when she was lunching with her grandparents. She waved but avoided his eyes after seeing the hurt and confusion.

"But he's such a nice young man," her grandmother said, her eyes puzzled.

"I know," Elizabeth said and turned the subject to something else.

6
1934

"Dana is delaying his homecoming again," Sybil said across the table in the breakfast room as she scanned a letter, the loose sleeves of her heavy, rose silk morning gown falling back to reveal pale, thin wrists and arms.

"Why?" Elizabeth asked, biting into a piece of toast as she glanced at the morning headlines. She was dressed for a day at the beach with friends and was anxious to be on her way. But since returning home for the summer months from Poughkeepsie, she had quickly learned that her mother was becoming more and more dependent upon her.

"Spend the summer with her," Aunt Vivian had begged. She was off to Tokyo with her third husband, a diplomat, who had just received a new assignment as a chargé d'affaires in the Far East. "Since your father—well, since he's been gone, she seems so lost."

Elizabeth had promised, but now with the summer half over, she felt smothered, hemmed in, without the wonderful freedom she had always had during summers at Seacliff. She adored her mother, but . . .

"I don't know," Sybil said slowly, as she read further. "He says he's having such a marvelous time that he decided to stay on for the month of August as well." She looked up, a puzzled expression on her face. "But he's still in Rome."

"Hasn't he been there for most of July?"

"Yes," Sybil said, looking back at the letter once more. "A week in Paris, then he went down to Rome."

"Well," Elizabeth said, starting to rise. She could see the two red setters through the long windows, cavorting over the lawn. "I told the gang I'd meet them at ten."

She started toward the door.

"Elizabeth?"

She turned, a bright ray of sunlight catching her in its path, her hair loosely flowing about her shoulders, the white linen slacks and blouse accentuating her golden tan.

"Yes?"

"I'm going to call Cunard and have them get us passage to Europe."

Elizabeth's face lighted up. She had crossed to Europe twice before, but not for several years. And then she laughed.

"Poor Dana."

"I'm curious," Sybil said.

"You're suspicious, that's what you are." Elizabeth laughed again.

"Well, he mentioned a girl in his last letter. A Lucia somebody-or-other."

"Mother, much as I'd love to go—and I'm dying to—isn't it rather unfair to go prying into Dana's affairs at this point? After all, he *has* graduated from college and he *is* starting work next month—"

"I need the trip," Sybil said stubbornly, as she folded the letter and slipped it back into the envelope.

"Mother, Dana is—"

"I'm restless, Elizabeth, and I need a change."

"Well, we could go to London. Visit the Marshalls. Take a week down at Torquay."

"I want to go to Italy." She was immovable.

Elizabeth looked at her mother. She had never looked fragile before. Always slim and graceful, there still had been a substantial quality about her figure, a wiriness that did well on the tennis courts and the back of a horse. But now she looked frail, had deep shadows beneath her eyes, a weary sound in her voice.

Elizabeth knew there was no point in arguing further. "All right." She smiled. "But I'm due back at school by September twentieth."

"I'll see if I can book staterooms for the end of this week. We can be back by September tenth. That will give us more than a month. We can stop off in Paris on our way home and get whatever you need for school there. And sail from Cherbourg."

Elizabeth was standing by the door. "I'll write the Timmermans and tell them I can't come to the Vineyard on the fifteenth."

Sybil sighed. "Well, you might have met someone new. But then again, you might meet someone on the crossing."

"Mother, you just never give up, do you?" Elizabeth said in a burst of laughter.

"Well, you're impossible to please," Sybil scolded.

"Yes, I am," Elizabeth said softly. "I wonder why." She turned and went out the door.

They sailed that weekend on the new *Roma,* after deciding to go directly to Genoa instead of Southampton. Sybil watched hopefully as Elizabeth spent much of her time with three young men, one in particular who was bound for Italy, where he—as Dana had done, but starting in Paris, and one month earlier—would begin his Grand Tour of Europe following graduation from college.

"It's sort of a ritual, isn't it, for—well, for people like us?" Elizabeth said as she sat in the small satin boudoir chair waiting while her mother dressed for dinner one night.

"A rather nice practice, I think," Sybil said, leaning toward the mirror and smoothing on the palest hint of rouge. She smiled. "Your father called it 'a young man's rite of passage.' Before he enters the world of finance or one of the professions." She was flicking a powder puff over her nose, her shoulders gleaming in the light from the dressing table. "Your father had the Grand Tour just a year before we were married"—she smiled softly—"then he took me to France on our honeymoon and showed me all of the places that he had been, Paris, the Normandy coast, then down to Mont St. Michel and on to Aix and Antibes. It was heaven." She sighed and lowered her head for a moment, then determinedly went on making up her face.

"A nice practice if you have the money," Elizabeth said softly.

"Well, of course," her mother said somewhat absently.

"Your friend, Scott Fitzgerald, wrote in *The Great Gatsby* about the vast carelessness of the rich." Her voice had a wry note in it.

Sybil turned sharply to look at her. "You never talked this way until recently. What is it?"

Elizabeth wandered to a porthole and looked out at the moonlit sea. She wore a long gown of pale green silk, the back plunging to deep folds that formed a cowl, the waist caught with a wide gold kid belt that matched her tiny high-heeled sandals.

"At college we talked about it quite a bit this year. I guess I never thought about it before." She turned and looked at her mother. "About being *rich,* I guess."

"That's an unattractive word."

Elizabeth ignored the remark. "There are some girls there that

82

come from families who are not very rich. And others who are much richer than we."

Sybil decided to change the subject as she looked into her beaded bag to make certain she had a hanky, a lipstick, and a compact. "This young man I've seen you with several times?"

"Emory Bennett. He's from San Francisco."

"The San Francisco Bennetts? Malcolm and Dorothy Bennett's son?"

Elizabeth laughed softly. "Yes, the San Francisco Bennetts, Mother. But he's just very nice."

"Really, Elizabeth," Sybil said, rising and walking toward the door, the folds of her red chiffon gown falling gracefully into place. "You could at least give it a chance, to find out what he's really like and how you really feel about him."

"I knew in about five minutes," Elizabeth said bluntly as she followed her mother.

"I've seen how he looks at you."

"*Please,* Mother." She heard Sybil sigh as they went out the door.

Elizabeth leaned over the rail and waved wildly when she saw Dana standing on the dock in a vast crowd of people. The ship had slipped into the half-moon port and eased up to a pier near the Stazione Marittima. She looked up to the hills that sloped right down to the water, then gazed beyond the golden haze of old buildings to the narrow medieval streets beyond that wound their way up the hillsides.

"There's a young woman with him," Sybil said sharply.

Elizabeth shielded her eyes from the sun with her hand, then waved again, leaning out over the rail dangerously as Sybil clung to her arm. "Dana, Dana," she shouted. "Over here!"

She could see him clearly now, the rumpled white suit and rakishly tilted panama hat over that broodingly handsome face. And then she saw the girl—small and dark-haired, wearing a large white hat that was all that Elizabeth could see from the distance. *How lovely and feminine she looks* was Elizabeth's first thought.

"What a theatrical-looking costume," Sybil said bitingly.

"I was just thinking how lovely she looks."

"Well, we shall see," Sybil said grudgingly.

Whatever stiffness Sybil revealed after kissing Dana and holding him to her for several long moments, Elizabeth made up for by greeting the young woman warmly.

"This is Lucia Daniello," Dana said, his eyes, as he looked down at the beautiful young woman, leaving no doubt as to his feelings. "My mother, Mrs. Stuart, and my sister, Elizabeth." He was hugging Elizabeth to his side and leaned down to kiss her cheek.

"I am so pleased," the young woman said in a low and silvery voice, her accent almost nonexistent as she spoke in English.

"It's very nice to meet you," Sybil said from beneath the wide black straw hat, her smile distant, her tone polite.

"I want you all to get to know each other, and well," Dana said pointedly, as he led them toward the Via Gramsci where he had left his car, a perspiring porter following them at a half run as he pushed his cart, piled high with their luggage. "We'll stop for lunch on the way. By leaving immediately, we can reach Rome by evening."

"But I had our agents make reservations for us here for tonight at the Colombia, as I cabled you, Dana—"

"I canceled them" he said as he walked briskly on a little ahead of them, still holding Lucia by the arm, while she looked over her shoulder with an apologetic little smile on her pretty face. Elizabeth smiled a quick wide smile in response, marveling at the large, luminous brown eyes that gazed at them with such warmth, at the rosily tinged olive skin and delicate features.

There was little discussion in Dana's car. Its canvas top was up to shield them from the sun, but the sides were wide open, and normal conversation was impossible.

They stopped in Siena, first driving slowly through the town, admiring the shell-shaped Piazza Del Campo while Dana described the Palio delle Contrade, where a horse race is held each summer with much pageantry in costumes of the fifteenth century, thousands gathering for the spectacle. They lunched at shaded tables outside, which overlooked the Palazzo Pubblico, and watched the groups of tourists that crowded into the thirteenth-century building, cameras in hand, their bright summer clothing a moving mosaic as they lined up near the entrance.

"Lucia is a student of opera," Dana said, after the waiter had taken their order and put green bottles of cool mineral water on the white-clothed table, along with a platter of slices of ripened dewy melon and clusters of green and purple grapes.

"Opera?" Sybil said in surprise, her eyebrows rising as she looked around at the young woman and gazed at her from within the shadow of her broad-brimmed hat. "How interesting."

"She has an amazingly beautiful voice," he said proudly as he openly held her hand on the edge of the tablecloth. "She gave a concert last week, a small private one at the Palazzo del Giorno, and the critic Beniamino Volpi was there. He compared her to Galli-Curci. He said she had a voice with a rare timbre, that as a coloratura she had *breathtaking brilliance,* and that she was ready for La Scala or Rome, and of course Naples and Venice."

"How wonderful!" Elizabeth was breathless with the wonder of it. "Oh, my gosh, I wish I had some kind of talent." She impatiently pushed her hair back as she ate some grapes.

"I heard Galli-Curci at the Metropolitan Opera House about ten or eleven years ago," Sybil said, her voice mellowing somewhat. "She was absolutely magnificent, in spite of what I heard was a goiter problem. She seemed to sag somewhat in pitch, but there was still that exceptional brilliance, that remarkable tonal beauty."

Lucia leaned forward eagerly, a dainty figure in her ruffled white dress. "But then you are a lover of opera, Mrs. Stuart," she said, pronouncing it Meesus and somehow managing to trill the "r" in Stuart. "Oh!" she said with a puff of relief. "I am so glad of that."

"We have a season box at the Metropolitan Opera House each year." Sybil smiled a bit less archly. "Perhaps someday we will hear you there."

"When you do," Dana said, "it will be when she comes to New York to be *Mrs. Dana Stuart.*" He quickly gulped half of his wine.

A deathly silence fell over the table. Suddenly Elizabeth could hear the rush of voices from the groups of tourists, the louder voices of the guides as they shouted at their groups to follow them, the ringing shouts of some children across the piazza who were rolling hoops. She looked at her mother, but Sybil seemed stunned.

"Well, I . . ." Lucia finally said, breaking the silence. "I don't know, Dana." She was speaking softly, and turned her hand to place it gently over his on the table. And then she looked from Sybil's face to Elizabeth's pleadingly. "You see, my family—they make great sacrifice for me to study singing. I must do nothing that would stand in its way." She then looked at Dana and her beautiful eyes filled with tears. "Even though I love Dana so very much, I cannot hurt my parents for all they have done for me."

"You can do both," Dana said stubbornly, grasping her hand. "Have a singing career and marry me."

"Of course you can," Elizabeth said eagerly, leaning toward them, her eyes filled with excitement. "Mother once said to me, when our father died, 'If you love someone, don't let anything stand in your way.'" She suddenly looked at Sybil. "Do you remember that, Mother?"

But Sybil was looking at Dana. She was seeing the expression of worship in his face as he watched Lucia. She slowly turned her head until her gaze met Lucia's. "Your family, you say, has made great sacrifices?"

"My parents, they come from a small village near Arezzo. My father, he has—he is owner of"—she searched for the words—"un' osteria."

"A small inn," Dana explained. "The kind that serves simple kinds of food and wine."

"They do not have much," Lucia went on after smiling at Dana for his help. "But they send me to Florence, and after Florence, to Rome, for study. It is in Rome I meet Dana." She put her hand in his again, as her eyes brimmed with love.

There was silence again for a moment, as the waiter brought a steaming platter of pasta and another of prawns in an herbed butter sauce. When he hurried back to the café at the side of the small terrace, Sybil let her gaze wander across the piazza. When she spoke, her voice was soft and trembled a little.

"I can see that you are both very much in love." She looked at Lucia and smiled. "And Dana is right. Yes, you *can* have both marriage and a career, Lucia. In America you can certainly have both. And we will all help you."

Tears ran down Lucia's face unashamedly, while Elizabeth leaned to her mother and kissed her cheek. After a moment, Dana reached across the table and clasped Sybil's hand while he looked at Lucia.

"You see, darling, I told you I had a wonderful family."

Dana and Lucia were married in the Church of St. Francis in the Piazza di S. Francesco, standing beneath the magnificent fresco cycle that had been painted in the fifteenth century by Piero della Francesco. Many of her relatives came from the surrounding countryside and villages to crowd into the cathedral and the fine old villa nearby that had become an albergo, for wine and a dozen kinds of pasta and chickens cooked on outside spits, while the young people danced the traditional peasant dances in the sunshine.

Sybil and Elizabeth watched with troubled expressions as Lucia tried to break away from her parents and brothers and sisters in a torrent of wailing cries. She had sung earlier while one of her brothers had played the violin with infinite sweetness; tears caught in their throats as they heard her voice soar. They watched tears run down her mother's face, and her father's face twist with anguish, both feeling certain they would never see her again, but unwilling to stand in her way.

"I am afraid that we must go now," Sybil said apologetically.

"Temo propio che sia ora di andarcene," the young priest said to Lucia's parents as he translated what Sybil had said, explaining that they must leave if they were to get to the ship in time.

Sybil was holding Lucia's mother's hand. She was almost as beautiful as Lucia, with just a soft sprinkling of silver in her carefully dressed hair. The black lace shawl she had worn on her head in the cathedral had fallen to her shoulders and she smiled at Sybil with tears in her eyes while telling the young priest to ask Sybil to watch over her child. When Sybil kissed her cheek, she kept exclaiming, *"Molto gentile!"* The priest translated, "You are so kind!"

They climbed into the chauffeur-driven automobile that Sybil had rented, for Dana had sold his in Rome. As they drove off, Lucia watched from the small rear window, frantically waving, until she could no longer even see the ancient walls of the town. Tightly clasping Dana's hand, she watched the road ahead in silence, tears clinging to her lashes. After a time, in exhaustion, she fell asleep, her head on Dana's shoulder.

He listened to the soft purr of her breath beside him and smiled into the darkness. Turning his head he could see the shadowy outline of her profile. He raised himself on one elbow until he was looking down at her, head resting on his hand, the heat of her body seeping across the small space between them. With one finger he slowly, softly traced down the line of her nose and across the delicately shaped upper lip. She stirred and murmured, the dark fan of her hair slipping across the pillow and falling like a cascade onto the sheet.

As he slid down onto his back again, he stared above him. A warm, drowsy kind of peace was stealing through him. He felt . . . what was it? . . . a wholeness. Yes. He felt whole, in utter, wonderful peace with himself. Something . . . something had gone from him. A kind of anxiety, an anxiety he had known all his life, ever since he was a little boy.

He had always dreaded certain things. The first day of school. Big family parties. Holidays. The opening day of ballroom dancing school when he was small. The afternoon he had first arrived at Princeton. There were always so many strange people . . . dozens of boys his age, laughing and shouting, tripping each other, pulling off someone's hat and throwing it across the room. And the girls at dancing school, giggling and whispering in their white flouncy dresses and hair ribbons, shrieking in delight when someone bolder than he pulled their curls from behind.

By the time he had arrived at Princeton four years before, he had learned how to disguise the dreaded shyness.

"I wish I could be like you," a studious-looking new student had said to him one day in his third year of prep school at Exeter as they stood by and watched a group of boisterous classmates demolish the peace and quiet of a local ice cream shop with good-natured but overloud shouting and pushing.

Dana had looked around at him in surprise and stopped sipping his malt. "Me?" he exclaimed, vigorously stirring his malt with the straw.

"You just watch it and smile, but keep slightly aloof from it all."

That was when Dana realized he appeared aloof rather than shy. Although the feelings of anxiety and unsureness never completely left him, he simply learned how to disguise them. He was a good student and a fair athlete, qualities that helped in his disguise. Even his few close friends never guessed. Only Elizabeth and his father knew.

"It's all right, son," his father had once said to him softly as they stood gazing across the ballroom in his Grandmother Stuart's house in Philadelphia, where a Christmas dance for all the grandchildren was being held. Dana was twelve, his new shoes pinching, the palms of his hands damp with fear. "You outgrow it. I felt the same way you did when I was your age." He had ruffled Dana's hair while they stood there watching nine-year-old Elizabeth laugh and chatter as she struggled with the clumsy feet of her partner, while managing to look graceful at the same time.

Dana turned his head again and watched the sleeping Lucia. It was the third night out of Genoa, where they had boarded the *Augustus* in late evening, in plenty of time for a midnight sailing. Ever since, his mother and Elizabeth had been most discreet, leaving the honeymooning couple to their own devices most of the time, seeing them only when they had their meals together.

"Dana," she whispered, rolling toward him until her body curved in to his, fitting like hand in glove, he thought.

He kissed her, gently at first, while stroking her hair back from her face. The first night, he had sensed her timidity and had ventured slowly. But tonight she came to him eagerly as she wakened. He felt the length of her body, stretched beneath him, moving almost imperceptibly at first, then rising to him and catching the rhythm of *his* body. Their passion rose quickly, as though they had hungered long for each other.

"Lucia, Lucia," he moaned, as his hands roved across her flesh.

She was kissing him with a new wildness, her hands tearing at his back, her body writhing under his. There was only her mouth, her hands, the motion of her body, and the darkness that held them.

When he slipped inside of her, her legs curled up and clasped around him. All drowsiness was gone. Everything else slid away, leaving them suspended in an exquisite kind of madness that plunged ahead and pulled them on.

Until this night he knew it had ended in pain and confusion for her. But at this moment he felt as though his heart would burst with joy. It was happening as it should, in long sensual waves, her excitement matching his and racing onward until it climaxed in a series of sensations that made them cling to each other in sudden stillness.

It was several moments before he became aware again of the ship's motion, the slight pulse of the motors, and the fresh, salty odor that came from the portholes. He pulled her close to him until he felt her head beneath his chin.

"For the first time in my life I feel whole," he whispered.

She burrowed deeper against his neck and he felt her lips roam across his skin. "I, too," she said in a soft voice. "I, too, Dana." When she slept again, he carefully rose from the bed, pulled on a light robe, and walked to the open porthole. He lit a cigarette, watching the path of moonlight ripple across the water, and smiled. It was just as though his life were now beginning.

The traffic on Broadway between Thirty-ninth and Fortieth streets was almost at a standstill. The normal evening crush of vehicles fought to get past the entrance of the Metropolitan Opera House, where taxicabs and limousines inched forward to discharge their passengers.

Lucia stood in the tangle of ermine and sable and black broadcloth, a sea of tall silk hats, even a tiara or two. Light flowed from the arched doorways as the crowd pushed through. Just that morning, Dana had taken her into the fur salon at Stuart's and told her to choose anything she wished. She walked about with wide eyes, touching the soft furs while smiling salesladies and Mr. Purdom, the fur buyer, stood by watching.

And now, as she stood in the waiting crowd before the opera house, she looked down for a moment and smiled. Her new gown of gold cloth flowed from beneath the slightly darker mink coat, its folds falling softly about her throat in a shawl effect. She turned suddenly and smiled up at Dana, who stood beside her, white tie and tails gleaming, tall hat at just the right angle, his white silk scarf blowing a little in the brisk November wind. She could see Elizabeth and Sybil up ahead, past the signs and pictures of Rosa Ponselle as Carmen, waiting at one of the doorways for them as they pushed through the glittering crowd. A very tall man in dinner clothes and black top hat was looking down at Elizabeth in her white velvet gown and cloak. A handsome, somewhat older man, he had a lean, casual grace and manner.

"Oh-oh," Dana said with a soft laugh as he guided Lucia through the jammed crowd with his hand on her arm. "Look at Mother's face. Stormy seas ahead."

"What is this you say, Dana?" Lucia looked up at him, then ahead at Sybil. She looked puzzled. "What is it you mean, *stormy seas?*"

"That's what we always said when we were little and Mother was angry about something. Her storm cloud face."

"But why?" Lucia's voice was softly inquiring.

"See the man talking to Elizabeth?" When Lucia nodded, he said, "That's Lawrence Kendall."

"Parli chiaro, Dana," she said. "Please explain to me."

"Mother dislikes him."

They were drawing closer. "But why?"

"He's extremely rich."

"That is a reason?"

"No—no, that's not the reason." He held her back for a moment and looked down at her. "Haven't you ever heard of Lawrence Robertson Kendall?"

Lucia thought for a moment. "Ye-es," she said slowly, her eyes widening. "But that is—?" She was startled.

He nodded. "Yes, *the* Lawrence Kendall."

"But he is so young for a man to have done so much."

"In his forties, early forties. His father started the fortune. But this is the man who made it grow to what it is today." Dana was openly admiring, as he said softly, "One of the richest men in the world, they say."

"And your mother? Why does she—?"

"It's the *way* the Kendalls made their money and—well . . ." How could he possibly explain? How could anyone explain to someone like Lucia about this kind of wealth and how it was made, the monopolistic controls, the timing of it, being in the right place at the exact time, the brilliance, the shrewdness, the painstaking decision-making, the ability to act boldly and sometimes ruthlessly. There was talk—there was always talk when it came to Lawrence Kendall—about covert purchases of stock to obtain ailing railroad lines, coal mines, and oil fields, about buying countless smaller competitors out of business— "not *driving* them out, as the muckrakers would have it," Kendall's associates always insisted—about the reinvestment of profits, the centralization of his wealth in his banking interests, the stock market manipulations and proxy fights. Much of it, or certainly some of it, Dana was certain, was not true. But because Kendall rarely, if ever, responded to his accusers—who frequently gained newspaper space with their castigations—the rumors persisted.

"It's much too difficult to explain," he said hastily as they pushed on toward Sybil and Elizabeth, caught up in the aura of perfume and flowers, in the babble of excited laughter and voices, until at last they stood next to them, Lucia breathless with the excitement and glitter.

"Here you are," Elizabeth said, a radiance in her face that Lucia had not seen before, as she looked back at Lawrence Kendall again. "I don't believe you've met my brother, Dana—"

"No, I haven't had the pleasure," Lawrence said with a warm smile as he shook Dana's hand, the slightly hooded gray eyes searching Dana's face with interest.

"And my sister-in-law, Lucia," Elizabeth said as she clasped Lucia's arm.

"Delighted," Lawrence said, holding Lucia's small white-gloved hand for a brief moment.

"*Molto piacere,*" she said. "It is with pleasure, Mr. Kendall, that I meet you."

"Ah, what a lovely accent," he said, smiling again.

"Lucia is from Italy," Sybil said stiffly, her face closed and unfriendly. She moved with a slight impatience toward the doorway, her black velvet gown and white ermine cape swirling as she turned.

"And this is her first night here at the opera," Elizabeth said, as they all slowly followed Sybil. Lawrence took Elizabeth's arm to guide her. "Lucia is a singer. She studied opera in Florence and Rome. She has *such* a beautiful voice." She trembled a little at his touch.

"Until I lured her away with marriage," Dana said laughingly.

"You have given it up?" Lawrence asked, looking past Elizabeth to Dana's wife, his grasp on Elizabeth's arm tightening slightly.

"Oh, no," she exclaimed. "I want to continue, and"—she impulsively threw her arms wide as they came into the glowing lobby—"someday sing here at the Metropolitan Opera House."

"She has tried to get an audition," Elizabeth said. "But it's very difficult. I'm hoping this evening to go backstage after Miss Ponselle's performance. I met her once at a party and thought she might perhaps introduce us to Signor Gatti-Casazza—"

"The general manager here?" Lawrence asked with a quick raise of his eyebrows.

"Yes," she said, slightly surprised. She had not expected Lawrence Kendall to be the kind who would know general managers of opera companies.

"Perhaps I will see you later," he said, as he gazed over heads toward the far side of the lobby, then made a gesture to someone. "I see my party waiting over there for me." He turned back to Elizabeth and Sybil for a moment. "I would be delighted if you would join us later at the Colony—"

"I'm sorry," Sybil said abruptly. "But we have other plans."

"Well . . ." He bowed slightly, his eyes amused while looking directly into Elizabeth's eyes. "Some other time perhaps."

She watched as he pushed across the crowded lobby, unaware that people were bumping past her. A woman with a pale face and light brown hair pulled back into a severe bun at the back of her head also watched Lawrence anxiously as he walked toward where she waited, surrounded by a group of people. He took her arm.

"Come along, Elizabeth," she heard her mother call out and, looking once more in his direction, she caught up with Sybil and Lucia and Dana as they climbed the staircase to their box.

As the lights came on during the intermission and the applause subsided, Lawrence stood up and gazed around from his box at the other boxes, eyes narrowed and hidden as they skimmed over faces. When he caught sight of her, he stood motionless for a moment, then, annoyed with himself, dropped his eyes and quickly turned to the frail woman wearing a dark fur cape at his side and clasped her hand. "If you're not feeling well, we can leave any time you want, Anne."

The following day, Lucia received a phone call from Signor Gatti-Casazza's office. An audition date was scheduled, one week away. Several days later, Elizabeth read in *The New York Times* that Lawrence Robertson Kendall would underwrite a new production of *La Bohème* at the Metropolitan Opera House.

7
1935

Elizabeth let her head fall back as the voices soared. Without really seeing it, she stared at the gold frieze and richly ornamented ceiling far above, her throat aching with unshed tears as the death of Mimi was played out on the great stage. At times through the performance she and Missy had clutched hands, so overwhelmed were they by Lucia's voice as it rose in brilliance and beauty. Several times during the first act, Dana had gone to the small salon at the entrance way to their box to smoke in nervousness, but now he sat enthralled, unashamed tears in his eyes as he looked down to the tiny figure on the stage. And then the curtain swept closed on the final act.

Suddenly, caught by the excitement and with a burst of exultation, Elizabeth leaped to her feet, tears running down her face. A deafening clamor had broken throughout the opera house. The entire audience was on its feet and shouts of "Brava, brava!" rose above the thundering applause. She grabbed Dana and kissed him, then kissed her mother and hugged Missy.

She was clapping again, her hands and arms aching as the principals came out from between the folds of the gold curtain time and time again to bow, catching the flowers that were flung to them and sweeping them up from the footlights where they had fallen. As she turned to see Dana run from their box, something drew her gaze. Standing in another box, not far from theirs, was Lawrence Kendall. For a brief second, her heart seemed to stop. He stood forward against the velvet-cushioned rail, applauding, his figure slim and tall in his impeccable tails and white tie, the handsome face smiling down toward the stage.

Then, as though she had called out, he turned and looked at her.

She smiled and bowed slightly, and he bowed back. There was no mistaking the expression in his eyes, nor what she knew was in hers. She quickly looked down to the stage again, but she knew that he was still watching her and a warm glow flooded through her.

She had just arrived at Vassar for her final year. It was an afternoon in autumn of 1935, a lovely afternoon with the sun slanting low, leaving a shimmer of golden triangles on the blue rug of her sitting room. She had unpacked her clothes and started to change from her yellow and brown tweed suit into slacks when she heard the thud of the newspaper against the door to the corridor.

Well, that's service! she thought as she padded in bare feet and her slip to the door.

She sat in the chintz-cushioned window seat to read the paper. Suddenly she leapt up, stiff with shock. While leafing past the obituary page, a headline had caught her eye: MRS. LAWRENCE R. KENDALL DEAD AFTER LONG ILLNESS. She read it through twice, feeling a quaver when learning that Anne Kendall was only thirty-four, that she had been ill with cancer, and had been hospitalized in late August. She had finally been brought home from St. Vincent's Hospital by her husband and had died one week later.

"In addition to her husband, she is survived by three sons," the obituary read, "Lawrence R. III, nine years old, Avery L., seven, and James R., five. She is also survived by a brother, Warren J. Leland of New York City and Rijksville, New York."

Elizabeth slowly raised her head and looked out the window, only vaguely aware of the ivy-covered buildings opposite, of the brightly dressed young women hurrying along the paths or sitting beneath the tall leafy trees. The grass was so green it almost seemed to shimmer in the sunlight and became like a carpet in the patches of vivid shade.

Leland. She spelled the name out silently, slowly. *Leland.* Wasn't that part of the name of the firm that brought a large capital investment to Stuart's, making it possible not only for the doors to stay open in the future but giving it a solvency that assured its future, regardless of what the stock market might do? Yes, A. and W. Leland Ltd. *W. Leland.* She closed her eyes for a moment. *Warren* Leland.

That meant . . . that Lawrence Kendall was behind it all.

She felt a strange weakness flow through her limbs. *Lawrence Kendall.* But . . . why?

She slowly rose and walked to the mirror hanging over the small marble fireplace. She had been unpacking in her slip, a thin wisp of silk and lace that just barely covered her small breasts and clung to her tiny waist and narrow hips. Dark gleaming hair with reddish lights tumbled over her shoulders. Her eyes stared back at her with that dark, intense violet shade and haunting expression that, at moments like this, revealed a passion, a raw kind of desire within. Is this what he saw when he looked at me? she wondered. Is this what I am feeling when I think of him?

Slowly she pulled the straps of her slip from her shoulders and let it fall to the floor. For several moments, as she stepped back until she could see herself full-length, she let her gaze roam down her body, seeing it as someone else might see it, the perfectly formed small breasts and curve at her waist, the softly molded hips and long tapering legs.

Is it he? Is he the one I want to be looking at me in this way? "Yes," she whispered aloud. "Yes, it has always been, from the first moment I met him."

Something fiery but sweet rose in her. It crawled along just inside her flesh, tingling and warm, making her hold her breath and cradle herself with her own arms as she rocked from side to side. *Oh, my darling,* she thought . . . *my darling.*

And then she remembered the newspaper and she felt the flood of shame. She quickly drew on slacks and a sweater and ran out into the corridor.

"Elizabeth!" Gwen Harrington shouted from the stairway as she labored upward under two armloads of coats and field hockey sticks and tennis rackets and a stuffed kangaroo, her bright red curls a tangle around her merry blue eyes.

The two girls embraced with cries of excitement, overjoyed at seeing each other again after the long hot summer.

"Well, here we go again," Gwen said in a burst of enthusiasm as they rushed along the corridor toward her rooms. "But this time it's the final year." She stopped and suddenly dropped everything on the floor as the enormity of it swept over her. "Oh, my God, Elizabeth, what will we do when it's all over?"

8
1936

She drove up the road toward Seacliff with her head thrown back and her hair blowing. The top of the roadster was down, the sun drying the bathing suit she wore. It was a white two-piece wool, much too daring, her mother had said, with its exposed midriff. Aunt Vivian, who was visiting for a month, had brought it from Hawaii, and had laughed when Sybil objected to the suit.

"Good Lord, Sybil, come into the twentieth century. You're still so Victorian."

They had been sitting on the lawn the afternoon before, the big striped umbrella tipped against the sun and white wicker chairs pulled up to the round table so that they could all sit in the shade. Henry had served drinks, carefully suppressing a smile on his long thin face as even Mrs. Venable scoffed at Mrs. Stuart for her objection to the bathing suit.

"She said, 'If you want to stay young-thinking, Sybil, you have to go along with the young people and the changes they're making,'" he repeated in the kitchen, as he returned to refill the cocktail shaker with another batch of Mr. Venable's Carstarters, the gin and rum drink he claimed to have invented in college. "Yes, indeed, that's exactly what Mrs. Venable said."

Elizabeth had been standing in the butler's pantry, with her hand on the swinging door ready to open it, when she paused for a moment to listen.

"Well, I never!" Mrs. MacIntosh, the Venables' housekeeper and Henry's wife, said. Elizabeth could just see her with her hands planted on her ample hips, standing in the middle of the huge kitchen with the copper pots and pans hanging on the walls.

"Hurry along, boy." Although Elizabeth couldn't see, Henry was obviously fussing at Chin about chipping the ice faster. Chin was at least twenty years older than Henry, and yet Henry called him *boy*.

"Well, I must admit Miss Elizabeth looks like something out of one of those magazines in that bathing suit, but I never thought I'd see the day when Mrs. Venable would think it was all right for her granddaughter." It was Mrs. MacIntosh's voice again.

Elizabeth had suppressed a giggle and returned through the main part of the house to go out onto the lawn. Now, as she drove up the long sloping hill toward the house, she saw people on the lawn again under the striped umbrella. And as she sped along the driveway that circled the house to the coach-house in back, her wheels crunching through the thick white gravel, she suddenly pushed on the brakes and came to a stop. A long black Rolls Royce was parked in front of the coach-house, a uniformed driver leaning against the fender.

When he saw her climb from her roadster, he straightened up and tipped his hat. She nodded and smiled, and ran into the back entrance of the house.

Once inside, she pulled on her white beach robe and ran through the house until she came to the enclosed part of the veranda where the wide windows looked out to the sea. Her mother and grandparents and Aunt Vivian were all sitting under the umbrella with a tall man who was leaning forward, one arm on a knee, and talking, while they listened intently. Somehow she knew that he was talking about her.

She walked slowly to the french doors that led out onto the open veranda, crossed to the steps, and smiled while moving toward them. Her grandfather and Lawrence Kendall had risen.

"We were just talking about you, darling," Aunt Vivian said with a signal in her eye. She was smiling impishly, the inevitable cigarette in a long jade holder, the heavy diamonds glittering on her fingers, her lips a deep crimson to match the splashing poppies on her thin summery dress.

"How nice to see you again," Elizabeth said, looking up at Lawrence, their eyes touching like the brush of a bird's wing.

"Could we walk for a little?" he asked.

What she had seen in his eyes made her spine tingle and her heart pound in her throat. He was wearing sports clothes and looked tanned and slim. His brown hair was ruffled a little, as though he had run his hands through it, and his jaw was set hard.

She glanced at her mother, ignoring the warning expression. "If you'll excuse us, please?" He nodded and half bowed to the others, then walked across the lawn with her toward the beach below.

When they reached the edge of the water, he stopped and turned her toward him. She knew that her mother would have left the others on the lawn and would now be watching from her upstairs sitting room, but it didn't matter.

"You . . . knew I would come here to you this summer, didn't you?"

"Yes. I knew."

"Then we've both known . . . for a long time, haven't we?"

She nodded and for a long moment they simply looked into each other's eyes. When he took her in his arms, it was as if she had always been there, but when he kissed her, she felt as though she were drowning, felt as though she were being pulled down through soft liquid waters, dark and dangerous, and thrilling beyond belief. She became lost in the kiss, giving herself to him completely. When he slowly pulled away, he said, "I think we had better be married soon."

"Yes," she whispered, "soon."

Their marriage that September was the most talked-about event of the season. It was held at St. Thomas's Episcopal Church, but with less pomp and ceremony than everyone had expected. Once Sybil had adjusted to the fact that nothing would stop Elizabeth from marrying *that man,* as she first called Lawrence Kendall, she began making elaborate plans.

"No," Elizabeth said one afternoon, as they sat in her mother's small sitting room on the second floor of the East Side townhouse, "I don't want one of those huge weddings." She was sitting on the carpet in front of her mother, legs crossed like an Indian's, the blue linen slacks and crisp blue shirt making her eyes turn a periwinkle color. "I want just Lucia and Missy, and Grandfather to give me away, and Lawrence wants Dana as his best man."

"That's all?" Sybil asked, aghast. She was sitting at her small cherry-wood desk, pen in hand, beginning to work on a guest list.

"And no more than—than—" Elizabeth fumbled for a number. "No more than one hundred guests."

"But Elizabeth!" Sybil was crushed.

Elizabeth was suddenly on her knees and clasping her mother's hands. "Oh, Mother, please, we don't want all of that fuss, dozens of bridesmaids and ushers and all those people and—"

"I should think it would be your decision."

"It is my decision. Lawrence said I must do whatever I wanted. But it's what he wants too, and it's important to me that he has as much to say in this as I."

"I'm surprised," Sybil said grudgingly. "I would have expected him to want the most elaborate kind of wedding possible."

"No, you're wrong, Mother," Elizabeth said softly, smiling up at Sybil. "When you know him better, you'll understand what a terribly private man he is."

As titillated and curious as everyone was about Lawrence Kendall's marriage to Elizabeth Stuart, the social world of New York that was Sybil and Elizabeth Stuart's was nonetheless shocked. *Social climber* was a phrase that was whispered over and over. More than ever gossip spread like wildfire about *how* Lawrence Kendall had built his massive fortune. When Dana Stuart proposed Lawrence Kendall's name for membership in the exclusive Union Club, other members were aghast. But at Dana's insistence and with the help of a number of close and loyal friends, he was accepted.

While the wedding plans were being made, Sybil Stuart learned just how private a man Lawrence Kendall was. When Elizabeth protested that she didn't want a reception in a hotel and Sybil with equally vehement protests said that the East Side townhouse was neither appropriate nor large enough for a reception, Lawrence suggested that perhaps *his* townhouse would serve. Sybil had been unaware that he even had a townhouse, one only a short distance from her own. And it had a large ballroom in a wing off to the side that would be more than adequate for a hundred guests. It would, in fact, hold several hundred people quite easily, she saw, when she and Elizabeth went there for an inspection.

"It's very beautiful," Sybil said as her high, silvery voice echoed through the cavernous room. "Ornate, of course, but beautiful." Elizabeth's footsteps were making a sharp tapping sound as she walked about pulling back heavy velvet draperies from the long palladian windows to let some light in. Morgan, the butler, stood at the wide doorway, rather formidable-looking in his black tailcoat. Then he smiled, suddenly seeming friendly.

100

"You can just ring for me, Madame, here by the door, when you're ready to leave." He pointed to a buzzer on the wall.

"Thank you," Sybil said, with a small nod. She was wearing a small, chic black hat with a tiny veil that pulled down over her nose, a black fitted suit, and was swathed in silver fox furs that fell about her shoulders. When Morgan had left, closing the double glass and bronze doors behind him, she walked the length of the massive room, her black high heels echoing sharply. She turned at the end and looked about her.

"This house was built by one of the Vanderbilts, I think. I've forgotten which one. He built it for a daughter or a son, I seem to recall someone telling me. I can't remember which."

"It's huge," Elizabeth said. She was standing in the middle of the room wearing a bright leopard coat and hat, dark hair tumbling over the collar. Her deep-lashed eyes were wide with amazement. "The room, the house, everything. I'm not sure I like it."

"Well, you had better make yourself like it, my darling, for this is where you will be living." Sybil looked up to the ceiling painting, one that reminded her of the Tintorettos she had seen in Venice. The marble walls were inset with gilt and mirrored panels and the mantel-piece over the great fireplace was of pink marble topped with sculptures of bronze. Each corner of the room had tall marble and bronze sculpture pieces with a branch of bronzework above that held candle-type lights. Three massive chandeliers in bronze hung from the ceiling. The gleaming floor was set in a parquetry design. All of it was meant to overwhelm, to impress, and to provide a setting of splendor for whatever took place within its walls.

"I had forgotten that there are still people who live like this," Sybil said softly.

"You heard Morgan," Elizabeth said. "He said the room has never been used since the Kendalls have lived here."

"Well, I'm not surprised. With his—with his wife so ill."

Elizabeth turned away so that her mother wouldn't see her face. How she has changed, she thought. Now that Lawrence and I are going to be married, she almost seems to like him. She sighed and walked over to a window again, where she stared out at the traffic on Fifth Avenue. It was all terribly overwhelming. Lawrence had taken her to Kendall Hills the Sunday before, for tea. In each of these massive houses she had felt swallowed, small. So terribly small.

"It's so big," she had protested to him after he had taken her through Belvedere. "I wouldn't even know which direction to start out in to find anything."

He had laughed softly and pulled her against his side as they walked down the grand staircase into the main hall. "It won't take long. And you'll be glad it's so big, once you hear the racket the boys can make and how much room they need to spread out in." He had led her into the library, a beautiful room with dark paneled wood, and walls and walls of books. A fire crackled in the fireplace and tea had been set, with the firelight flickering on the silver tea set.

"There's both tea and coffee there, ma'am," a pretty little maid said.

"Thank you," Elizabeth said, crossing to the fire, her cheeks flushed. Lawrence had trained his servants well. They were already treating her as though she were the lady of the house. She had sat down and begun to pour the tea, when she slowly looked up at the young woman in a gray uniform and white apron and cap. "Why—why, you're Ellie," she exclaimed in surprise, a sudden smile transforming her face. "Ellie Halloran." She jumped up.

"Oh, Miss, you remembered," Ellie said excitedly.

"I told her you would," Lawrence said, laughing softly. He was wearing flannels and a soft beige cashmere sweater over his sport shirt, looking very much the country squire, Elizabeth had thought earlier. "I told her you were the kind who didn't forget, or—let others forget."

In a rush of affection, Elizabeth clasped Ellie and hugged her, then stood back and looked at her. The pale blonde hair was pulled back into a bun under her frilly cap, but her eyes seemed bluer than ever, and her delicate beauty was unmarred by the fear and embarrassment she had been suffering on the day four years earlier when they had given her a ride to Newport.

"Ellie is going to be your personal maid," Lawrence said, as Elizabeth sat down again and resumed pouring the tea.

"I don't need a personal maid," she said with a pretty scowl.

"Ellie says you do." There was a twinkle in his eyes as he sat down next to her on the settee.

"Yes, Miss," Ellie said. "I certainly think you do."

Elizabeth looked from Lawrence to Ellie and then back to Lawrence again, her laughter soft. "What a conspiracy!"

"I was so excited, Miss, when Mr. Kendall told me you would be coming here, that you were getting married." She was deftly rearranging things on the teacart, putting several small finger sandwiches on a plate for Lawrence and handling it to him, then taking the cup and saucer Elizabeth held out, and with knowing fingers, measuring sugar and cream into his cup before giving it to him.

"Ellie has spoiled me badly." He grinned.

"I can see that," Elizabeth said with a sly expression.

"Well, sir," Ellie said, her eyes misting a little as she stepped back and started to turn. "It's the least I could do after all you've done for me." She looked at Elizabeth. "And you, Miss, being so nice to me that day and takin' me right in when Abbott told me to go around to the service entrance."

She had walked to the door, where she paused for a moment. "If there's anythin' else you want, Miss, Mr. Kendall will show you where to ring for me." She dipped in a tiny curtsy and disappeared.

"Now whatever will I do with Nanny Grace?" Elizabeth said, as she lifted her cup and sipped at it.

"And *who* is Nanny Grace?"

Elizabeth laughed and curled up in the corner of the couch with her legs tucked beneath her. "I'm almost ashamed to admit who she is. She was my nurse, brought over from England when I was born. When I grew up and didn't need a nurse any longer, well—by that time she had become a member of the family, so Mother kept her on as a seamstress and, oh, lots of other little things, mostly just bossing everybody about, including my father." Her laugh tinkled like bells of silver. "Now that I'm back home once more, she tries to take care of me again. But I am a bit old for that." She smiled a droll smile.

He touched her hair. "Well, I'll tell you what. If your mother will let her go, we'll bring her here. I'm not at all satisfied with the woman who looks after the boys. We've had a string of them and none have worked out. Your Nanny Grace sounds as though she could handle them. What do you say?"

"It sounds perfect, Lawrence. And of course I'll love having her with us."

He suddenly took her in his arms. "And I will love having you with me." He kissed her, a long, deep kiss. Slowly she pulled herself back. She looked up into his eyes, one finger tracing his lips.

"If it weren't for Ellie, we . . . never would have met," she said, then shivered. "How awful that would have been."

He looked at the way the firelight played over her face, how it caught and glittered in her eyes, how it turned the pale gold wool dress into a glowing thing of wonder. He leaned down, letting his face touch hers, breathing the perfume of her skin. "I can't imagine any part of my life without you now," he said.

"I would have been an old maid the rest of my life." She laughed softly.

"Never. Not you."

"Well, then I would have made someone a miserable, unhappy wife."

He lifted her hand and kissed the palm. "I worship you," he whispered, and for a long, long moment, they looked into each other's eyes.

When he rose and leaned back against the mantel of the fireplace, he was smiling, but there was a sadness in the smile.

"I want to tell you about Anne," he said.

She nodded and sipped at her tea.

"She was wonderful. Kind and thoughtful, the sort of woman who lived for her family, for her children. She spoiled them, of course."

"They must be devastated."

"It's getting better," he said, nodding. He lit a cigarette and blew the smoke out slowly, watching it curl above his head and disappear. "I—I wasn't in love with her."

Elizabeth caught her lower lip between her teeth.

"But I cared about her. Can you understand the difference?" he asked, his face almost pleading.

"Yes—I think I can."

"She died very young. But I think she was happy, most of her life, the part of it that had anything to do with our marriage—the children."

Elizabeth nodded. There was nothing she could say. She finally rose, and said, "Would you take me home now, Lawrence?"

He held her in his arms for several moments. When they walked out to the main hall hand in hand, she felt weightless, a singing inside, a shimmering glow that she had never known before.

The reception was almost as Elizabeth had imagined it would be. Even though the guest list had swelled to two hundred, the great ballroom did not seem crowded. Guests were dancing at the far end to the music of Meyer Davis's orchestra. Small round tables with pink tablecloths and tall candles in silver candleholders were placed on newly laid rose carpeting at the near end of the room and around the edges of the dance floor. Each table was centered with a vase of pink roses, and great pink flower arrangements cascaded from large urns that were placed around the massive room.

The dinner was over, but many of the guests still sat at the tables, drinking and chattering, voices and laughter bright chips rising above the music as though in counterpoint to it. Lucia had sung earlier and the crowd had risen, shouting for more. Now a pretty redhead in a blue satin gown was singing into a microphone, a slow love song. As Elizabeth floated in Lawrence's arms, her white satin gown flowing around her, she closed her eyes and let herself drift. There had been only one jarring note. At one point she had looked up, feeling someone's eyes on her. Lawrence's oldest son was standing near the door and staring at her. She had met his sons only once, and the meeting had been polite and civil, if not overwhelmingly friendly. They were so young, she thought, only nine, seven, and five. But in that brief glance across the ballroom she saw what seemed to be a deep hatred in his eyes. In a moment it was gone. He was gone. And she wondered if she had imagined it.

"Shall we go now?" Lawrence whispered to her. When she nodded, he pulled her along with him, out a side door of the ballroom to the broad center staircase in the entrance hall. At the top of the stairs, they parted.

"Half an hour," Lawrence said in a whisper, and she nodded again.

They boarded his private railroad car in Grand Central Station in a flurry of excitement, suitcases, rice, and good-natured teasing. Dana and several of Lawrence's associates had, unknown to Lawrence and Elizabeth, preceded them to the railroad station and were waiting with rice and confetti. There were toasts with champagne on the train, and when it finally began to move and pull out of the station, it was almost midnight. She had not known about the trip to the West Coast by train. He had simply told her their honeymoon would be a surprise.

Elizabeth was unprepared for the luxury of the private car. It was the last car on the train and had a small open platform on the rear. A lounge like a living room, with couches and chairs and softly shaded lamps, took up a third of the car. There were also a bar, a small dining room and galley, and two staterooms, one a full bedroom all done in a soft, silken peach, with heavy silk drapes at the windows. It seemed newly done—done for her, she suspected.

Elizabeth was thrilled to find Ellie in the bedroom. She had pulled down the spread on the large double bed, and was hanging her clothing in the closets.

"I just couldn't believe it when Mr. Kendall asked me if I wanted to make the trip with you," she said, one word tripping over the other in a small blizzard of excitement. She was placing lingerie in a narrow set of drawers to one side of one of the closets. "Five of us came. Edward, Mr. Kendall's valet, Mr. Wicksham, the chef, and Ben, both from Kendall Hall. He'll serve at meals and tend bar. And Mr. Kendall's secretary, Stephen Tilton."

"But where does everybody sleep?"

"We have compartments in the car ahead." She smiled as she turned around. She walked slowly over to Elizabeth and took hold of her hands. "You just don't know how many times I've thought about you and said a little prayer, a prayer of thanks for meeting you on that road that day. If it hadn't been for you—"

"It just would have taken you a little longer to get there, that's all."

"No." Ellie shook her head solemnly, her blue eyes round and far away, remembering. "No, those—those boys might have made me get into their car." She shivered a little. "I hate to think what might have happened then."

"Oh, I'm sure they were just being ridiculous. They think that's clever, shouting at girls as they pass them . . ." Elizabeth had thrown her fur coat and matching hat across the bed, and sat down to kick off her pumps. She suddenly frowned. "At least, I hope that's all it was."

She didn't see Ellie's expression as the young woman turned to put Caroline's hat and coat in the closet. Her mouth had a grim set to it. A cousin of hers had been pulled into a car filled with college boys who had been drinking, over near Providence. She shivered a little in the warm railroad car, remembering what had happened to Doris.

She opened another suitcase and started unpacking it.

"Let that go until morning, Ellie. It's late and you must be tired."

"Yes'm," Ellie said, turning back with a smile. "Can I help you with anything else now, Mrs. Kendall?"

"*Mrs. Kendall.*" Elizabeth seemed startled. Then her face broke into a smile. "You're the first one to call me that, Ellie."

Ellie was at the door. "He's a fine man." She gazed softly at Elizabeth. "He always treated me like I was *somebody.*" When she was gone, Elizabeth undressed, taking each garment off slowly, knowing Lawrence was at the far end of the lounge, dictating telegrams to Stephen

Tilton. She creamed her face and brushed her hair with long, firm strokes.

She slipped between the silken sheets and lay on her back, listening to the sound the train wheels were making beneath her, the *clickety-clickety-click* rhythmic and soothing. Just one small lamp burned in the room. It had turned everything to a soft glow. She heard voices in the outside corridor and her breath quickened.

When he opened the door, he stood there for a moment, then slowly closed it, the remarkable eyes never leaving her. She watched him as he undressed. There was no hesitation, and her eyes never wavered.

He stood beside the bed above her, straight and tall, his body gleaming golden in the soft light. A lock of dark hair had slipped down onto his forehead. Slowly she raised her arms and he came down to her. When he slid beneath the sheet next to her, she felt the stretching length of his body, hard against her, pulling her slowly until she curved her body to his.

His lovemaking was as she had known it would be, filled with infinite tenderness, his hands gentle but exploring as she arched and yielded, her body like a dancer's, twisting and turning beneath his touch.

The almost imperceptible sway of the train became a part of them, the click of the wheels and the haunting, eerie cry of the whistle far up ahead—all of it became part of their love, his hands, his mouth on hers, the sudden clanging of bells as they thundered past a railroad crossing, the methodic, soft clicking of the wheels again.

It is what I thought it would be, she thought, rejoicing. *It is beautiful, warm, flowing, relentless in its journey . . . exquisite in its pain . . . darkly sensual, filled with all the grief and joy of life . . .*

Her body rose and became part of his. She cried out in soft whimpers that told him to go on. He grasped her to him, hard, demanding, pulled her slimness upward, sank within her and held her as they soared on the edge of pain, only to find their way again, the pain becoming joy, musky, tangled, melting, wondrous *joy*. And then there was that moment . . . that moment when they became weightless, without bodies or souls, when they reeled from the earth and were caught in motionless space, somewhere, she whispered later, "between life and death."

When reality returned to her, their bodies were warm and damp and fragrant, her mouth was crushed against his shoulder, and his hand was caressing her, gently pulling her hair upward and away from her neck. When he slipped down and lay beside her, he murmured and laughed softly, but it was a laugh of wonder. He pulled her to him again and held her close.

"I want to give you everything," he whispered.

"I only want you," she said.

BOOK
II

9
1937

"Stupid little kid!" Larry said, looking down from his ten-year-old wisdom at his six-year-old brother.

"Yes, stupid little kid!" Avery repeated, looking to his brother, Larry, who was two years older, looking for a smile or even just a gleam in his eye to let Avery know that he wanted and appreciated his support. And Larry didn't disappoint him, but he took his time. He turned an arch smile at Avery.

They were bouncing around in the rear of the long Chrysler station wagon that was always used to take them to Tarrytown to the private school they attended. Jamie tried to ignore them. With steadfast stubbornness, he kept staring up front to the blue band on the nurse's hat and the back of the driver's neck, lip trembling a little, tears pushing at his eyelids and threatening to quiver on his eyelashes. He glanced at the nurse, Nanny Grace, but she was busy talking to the driver, Karl Wancek. He wondered what she was saying. Karl Wancek didn't know much English. He had come over to America a year before. Jamie remembered hearing his father tell Elizabeth that Karl had had a letter from a man in Berlin, a man named Gunther Blaumberg, who did some kind of business with the Kendall aircraft factory in Connecticut. The man had asked Warren Leland to please give Karl Wancek a job. Yes, that was what Jamie had heard his father tell Elizabeth, and Jamie was glad. He had grown to like Karl. Just as he liked Elizabeth. And Ellie and Nanny Grace.

"You've got to be the stupidest, dumbest kid in the world," Larry hissed, one eye on Nanny Grace and Karl before he leaned over and poked Jamie, who huddled against the door. Larry leaned closer.

"And if you tell anybody what I said, I just might kill you some night when you're alseep."

Jamie flinched. *Kill* in Larry's vocabulary meant some kind of minor torture, like scattered thumb tacks in Jamie's bed, or soaking the bottom sheet, or folding the bottom sheet in half so that he couldn't straighten his legs out—and then forcing him to sleep in the bed without a complaint to anyone.

"Leave me alone," he said softly, tears blurring his eyes.

"Well then, take it back, take back what you said," Larry said with another poke in the ribs.

"Yes, dummy, take back what you said," Avery repeated, kicking at his shins.

"I will not," Jamie said stubbornly. "I like her. She's nice to me."

"Oh, huggie, huggie, kissie, kissie!" Larry sneered, kicking sideways and giving Jamie a painful thrust in the leg.

"Leave me alone!" Jamie wailed softly.

" 'Ere now, what's going on back there?" Nanny Grace said, turning around and giving Larry the steel of her eye.

"Oh, he's nothing but a crybaby. I bumped into him accidentally," Larry said, looking out the window with a look of utter contempt, suddenly pretending interest in a group of public-school children who were standing on the corner near the Tudor-style plaster and timber building, waiting to cross the road. "Look at those dummies," he said. "Walking in the snow—"

"That's enough of that, laddie," Nanny Grace said, shaking her finger at him. When she turned her face forward again, Larry stuck his tongue out at her back, then quickly looked out the window again, as he saw Karl Wancek watching him with a grave expression in the rear-view mirror.

Such nice-looking boys, Karl was thinking, as he saw them reflected in his mirror. Jamie the most open, with a sweet expression on his narrow, sensitive face, the golden-brown curls spilling out from beneath his small school cap. Avery? There was something about his mouth. A weakness, Karl thought, an indecisiveness. And the way his blue eyes shifted about—he would never look at anyone directly. And Larry? Karl glanced at him again, his gaze lingering for a long moment as he watched him in the rear-view mirror. Odd. Strange that a man as kind, as fair as Mr. Kendall was could have a son with such a cruel streak in him. Even his mouth had a hard, cruel look to it. He was a handsome child, dark, stocky, unsmiling. Like his mother's family,

Ellie had told him slowly as he fought to understand the words in English. Yes, like his mother's family. More like his uncle, Mr. Leland. The same straight line of a mouth, the same dark hair and close-set eyes.

That one took some watching, he thought. Little Jamie was not much of a match for him. He would have to make his warning stronger, tell Ellie again to keep a watch over young Jamie. Until he was some years older he would need protection. Both Ellie and the nursemaid had to know how serious it was.

Ellie, he thought. He smiled. She made him feel warm, feel good all over when he thought of her. Such a fine young lady. Yes, he would have to tell Ellie.

He looked over at the nursemaid and grinned. She chattered on and on, like a magpie, just as though he understood every word she was saying. And yet, she didn't seem to expect him to answer. She simply talked on and on in her cheerful, friendly manner. Someday soon, he would be able to understand much more of what she said. Ellie had urged him to accompany her down to Rijksville to the high school for night classes. He was studying English and learning quickly. While Ellie went to her typing and shorthand class, he went to his English class, and afterward they went to the coffee shop across the street. Two nights each week they did this, and while they sat and drank their coffee, she asked him questions and he practiced his new English on her. The *Lady,* Mrs. Kendall—she had insisted they go to school.

"What a handsome-looking couple," said the old lady who owned the coffee shop. She always poked at her husband with her elbow as he stood behind the counter filling the metal containers with paper napkins or pouring sugar into the big glass shakers. She would say to him, "Look at them, Jim, don't they make a nice-looking couple? Handsome devil, isn't he?"

One night as he was standing at the counter waiting to pay for their coffee, Ellie beside him, he looked in the wavy mirror on the wall behind the counter and studied himself and Ellie. He was tall and blond. She was small and blonde. They both had bright blue eyes and wide smiles. He shrugged. Blond, yes. Nice-looking? Fine-looking? Handsome devil? He shrugged again. He didn't know. He was just Karl Wancek.

A sad expression came into his eyes. Only one other person had ever said that to him, that he was handsome. Mrs. Blaumberg. Miriam had smiled when her mother said that. "Such a handsome young man,

Miriam. Where did you find him?" *Miriam.* He sighed. Miriam.

"All right, you youngsters," Nanny Grace was saying as the three boys spilled out of the car and ran across the snow toward the ivy-covered gothic building. "We'll pick you up at three o'clock."

Elizabeth smiled and looked ahead. She could see Ellie's head bobbing as she nodded and talked to Karl, he turning from time to time, taking his eyes from the curving road to look down at her. The glass partition separating the front of the limousine from the back was closed, so she couldn't hear anything they were saying. But in the growing dusk she could see the happiness in Ellie's face.

"How much longer before we get there?" she heard a sleepy voice murmur, the question interrupting her thoughts about Ellie and Karl. She reached down and tousled Jamie's hair. His head lay in her lap.

"Soon, darling," she said softly, not wanting to waken Larry and Avery, who were still asleep, sprawled on the other part of the rear seat. "Another half hour, I think." As Jamie closed his eyes again, she smiled. Nanny Grace was facing front, upright on one of the jump seats where she had insisted on sitting, saying she could never sleep while in a moving automobile. But Elizabeth could see her head nodding.

She watched from the window as the Vermont countryside slipped by, smoke curling from chimneys, the soft lights from passing houses reflecting on the sparkling snow, twilight deepening.

The smile disappeared from her lips. Lawrence had been coming with them right until the last moment. They had planned the week at the ski lodge in Vermont at Elizabeth's insistence.

"The boys don't see half enough of you," she pleaded one evening, turning from her dressing table to watch him as he stood at a long mirror and tied his black bow tie, then slipped into his tuxedo jacket. "There's always some interruption when we're here or at the house in the city. Just a week in Vermont, darling, please."

He had walked to her then and stood behind her, his hands sliding around under her hair and down her neck. Then he had bent and kissed her. "How can I say no to anyone as beautiful as you are this evening?" As he stood straight again, a small smile lifting one corner of his mouth, he stared at her. In the lavender gown with its low neckline, she took his breath away, the swell of her breasts molding the gown's bodice and rising above it in an enticing glow of flesh. He bent again and let his lips whisper there, while she pulled his head

114

against her, then rose and wound her arms about him beneath his jacket.

"Then it's yes?" she whispered.

"It's yes," he said, and kissed her deeply.

But at the final moment, an explosion and fire at one of the refineries in New Jersey had called him away, and she had left with the children. He had promised to join them by the middle of the week.

When they arrived at the lodge, Karl carried the sleeping Jamie into the house while Elizabeth and Nanny Grace herded the other two boys ahead of them. They found fires blazing in all the fireplaces. The beaming caretaker and his wife, Ben and Cleo Martin, waited with Effie MacWorter, a woman from the town who worked as cook for the Kendalls when they were at the lodge.

For the next two days, even the doubting Nanny Grace admitted that Elizabeth's idea of a week in Vermont with the three boys had been a good one. Ellie and Karl, at Elizabeth's insistence, joined her and the children when they skated on the pond and took sleigh rides through the forests. Mornings, Larry and Avery skied with Karl at Stowe, while Elizabeth took Jamie for his skiing lessons. On the third afternoon, while Elizabeth and Ellie walked down to the village to browse through a new handicraft shop that had opened, Karl took the three boys skating.

"I don't like it," Karl muttered to Ellie in a low voice as he sat with her in the kitchen over a cup of coffee when they all returned in late afternoon.

"You don't like what, Karl?" Ellie asked. The big country kitchen glowed with a fire on the hearth, reflecting off the long rows of copper pots and pans on one wall. They could smell the aroma of a roasting leg of lamb and hear the cheerful Effie as she sang off-tune in the butler's pantry, where she was washing vegetables. It was cozy and warm, with snow drifting down past the wide windows, the rising wind just beginning to whine in the bending treetops. They sat in the corner breakfast nook, stirring their coffee.

"What the two older boys do to the little one."

Ellie looked around at him, sharply alert. "What happened?"

"Whenever I would turn my back or look the other way," he said slowly, searching for the correct words, "they were—were—"

"Taunting him?"

"That means saying words to frighten or make him feel badly?"

"Yes."

"Then—yes. Taunting him."

"It's Larry," Ellie said grimly, shaking her head. "Avery would probably be all right if it weren't for Larry. He's—well, weak, I think, easily led."

"Why is Larry this way?" Karl spread his hands, puzzled.

Ellie looked around, to make certain Effie couldn't hear her, then lowered her voice. "His mother. From the moment Jamie was born, she pushed the other two aside. Even as a baby, the other help have told me, Larry was not an affectionate child. But Jamie, from the moment he arrived, was warm and clinging. She seemed to need this. In the years of her illness, something began to be missing from her life. Everything seemed to be going on without her, she told Katy Morgan once. No one really needed her. Only Jamie, when learning how to walk and to talk. There was a succession of nursemaids, but she sent them all away."

Karl was nodding his head. "And now the older boys—they take this out on Jamie. For something a sick woman did."

"Yes," Ellie said, shaking her head sadly. "Mrs. Kendall tries so hard. From the moment she and Mr. Kendall were married, she's spent so much time with them, taking them to matinees and the museums, horseback riding and on shopping trips. Two and three times a week, she plans outings with them. But the more she does, the more Larry seems to resent her."

"Mr. Kendall? He knows this?"

"She keeps it from him, and he thinks everything is fine."

"He should know the truth," Karl said, almost angrily.

"No. She insists that someday Larry will begin to understand, begin to realize that she loves him, that she has no favorites among them—"

Karl glowered. "She does not know. There is a bad streak in the boy. He will never change."

"Oh, don't say that, Karl. He's only a child."

"You listen to what I say, Ellie. There is a streak in him that she will never change. I know about cruelty, I know about this kind of streak in men."

Ellie thought of those words as she sat by the window, shivering, the rebuilt blaze of the fire on the hearth not yet permeating the room. She looked over her shoulder at the two boys who huddled by the fire, their warm bathrobes drawn tightly about them, Larry staring stonily

116

into the fire's depth, Avery glancing at her with fear in his eyes. She looked back to the window and saw the moving lights, bobbing in the dark against the snowy mountainside, deeply forested and soaring to almost three thousand feet at the rear of the sprawling lodge. Elizabeth had fiercely insisted on accompanying the large group of men that Ben Martin and Karl had quickly recruited from the village and nearby farms. While she had gone to change into heavy ski clothing and boots, Karl had reassured Ellie that he would not let her out of his sight. When Elizabeth came down to the large living room again, Nanny Grace had said, "Should I get in touch with Mr. Kendall?"

Ellie had seen Larry's head turn, fear in his eyes, his face pale, and then the small quickly disappearing smile when Elizabeth said, "No. Not at the moment." And she knew then that Karl was right. If Jamie was safely found, Larry would be uncontrite. Ellie somehow knew, as did Karl, that Larry was in some way responsible for Jamie's disappearance. But if the child were not . . . safely found, then no one would ever know what happened—and Larry's secret would be safe.

In the middle of the night, Nanny Grace had gone to Jamie's room before she retired, to make certain the youngster was warmly covered and that Larry or Avery hadn't sneaked in and thrown all of the windows open wide to the below-zero air. She had found Jamie's bed empty and the child nowhere in the house. It was then that she roused Elizabeth and Ellie and the others.

Ellie looked at Nanny Grace, sitting by another window, the gray hair hanging in two plaits down her back over the gray flannel robe. "It's five below out there," she said in a grim voice, with a quick glance over her shoulder at Larry, who merely looked away and back at the fire again.

But an hour later, when Nanny Grace suddenly stood up, put her hand out, and said, "Come, Avery. Come with me to 'elp me make some 'ot chocolate," Larry grasped Avery's arm to hold him back. Nanny Grace walked to him, pulled Larry's hand from Avery's arm, and said, "I wasn't speaking to you, Larry. I was speaking to Avery." And grimly holding Avery's hand, she led him away and in the direction of the kitchen.

When she hurried back to the living room five or ten minutes later, she was shouting, "Avery's told me everything!" Larry was standing by a window looking upward. He didn't turn when Nanny Grace spoke. She was pointing to Larry, her voice hoarse with anger. But he was glaring at Avery with a murderous rage.

"That one!" she said to Ellie, who slowly rose from her chair. " 'E took 'im up to the Boy Scout cabin, 'alfway up the mountain, an' told 'im to find 'is way down by 'imself. Avery and 'im and some boys from the village, they 'ave a secret society, Larry told 'im, and if 'e wanted to join, be a member of this secret society, 'e had to prove 'e was strong and fearless by coming down from the cabin in the night by 'imself."

"Oh, no!" Ellie cried out. She ran to Larry with her hands out. "How could you, Larry? It's below zero, and there's a snowstorm coming up."

"I've done it lots of times," Larry said scornfully.

"Jamie is only six years old," she almost shouted as she took him by the shoulders and shook him. She suddenly turned and started from the room, calling out as she ran, "I'm going out to tell them."

When she came back a few minutes later, dressed in warm ski clothes, she paused by the door. "For your sake, Larry, as well as his, I hope that Jamie is all right." And for the first time, Nanny Grace saw fear in his eyes.

It was more than an hour before Nanny Grace and the two boys heard shouting voices and loud stamping of feet. She had watched the lights come down the mountainside and converge toward the back of the lodge. "Please, Lord, please, Lord," she kept muttering as she hurried to the door and threw it open. Elizabeth rushed in, followed by Karl, carrying the limp form of Jamie, bundled up in a blanket. Ben and Ellie were just behind them.

"Run a warm bath, Nanny Grace," Elizabeth called out as Nanny Grace and Ellie ran up the stairs after Karl. "I'll call the doctor."

She waited for a moment, looking across the room to where Larry and Avery stood. "Please sit down," she said, "while I phone Dr. Sherman." Her voice was soft, trembling.

Avery watched her with frightened eyes, while Larry picked a spot on the wall above her head and looked at it. His mouth was set hard and his eyes had a defiant look in them. When she had finished with the call, she turned around. She pulled off the woolly white stocking cap and shook her hair out until it flowed over the collar of her red ski suit. Slowly unzipping her jacket, she pulled it off and walked toward them. She stopped about six feet away; suddenly caving in, she slipped to her knees and began to weep, her face in her hands. The two boys stared at her, Avery bewildered, Larry with a wary expression on his face.

When she became quiet once more, she looked up at them. "If Jamie is all right . . . and I feel certain he will be . . . I am not going to tell your father." She saw the flicker of relief in Larry's eyes. "But —I want your promise that nothing like this will ever happen again." Her voice hardened. "I think you should know that if it does, I will tell your father."

10

"You more than like him, don't you, Ellie?" Elizabeth said softly as she folded a tweed skirt and put it into the box they were packing to give to the Ladies' Auxiliary at St. Matthew's Church down in Rijksville. Standing in Elizabeth's large walk-in closet, where two wide windows looked down over the south gardens, they had watched the station wagon with Karl and Nanny Grace inside as it drove around the curved driveway and toward the garages. A few minutes later they had seen Karl cross the snow-covered garden and go toward a long red sled that one of the boys had left on the hill beyond. He was lithe and graceful, even in the heavy dark jacket that covered his black chauffeur's uniform.

Karl was one of the three drivers who worked for the Kendall family. He had already become the favorite of both Lawrence and Elizabeth, but worked mostly for Elizabeth and the Kendall children.

"Well, ye-e-es, I guess I do, Mrs. Kendall." Her face was prettily flushed. They had filled the large cardboard carton, and between them carried it through the bedroom and out into the sitting room, where they placed it near the door, along with four others. When they returned to the closet, they saw Karl kneeling beside the sled, retying the rope that pulled it.

"Tell me about him, Ellie," Elizabeth said, as she took more clothing from the hangers.

"About Karl?" Ellie looked surprised and her face flushed again.

"Yes. All I know is that he came from Germany three months ago. With a letter of introduction to Warren Leland from a man in Berlin who had been doing business with one of the Kendall companies."

She tossed a dark blue coat into a box, then several skirts and jackets. Ellie knelt down and carefully folded them.

"He comes from Czechoslovakia, originally. Prague. And before that, some small village near Prague, I think he said. His brother was —is—a very talented musician. Karl told me that he composes music. They went to Prague and then Berlin so that his brother could get more training, while Karl worked in a factory."

Just then Elizabeth glanced out the window again and saw Karl pulling the sled and hurrying with long, easy strides back toward the garages. She pushed the casement window wide and leaned out a little.

"Karl," she called out, and he stopped, then looked up. She saw a strange expression on his face and paused a moment before calling out again. "Could you come upstairs and get some boxes?" Ellie had come up beside her and was smiling down at him.

"Clothing, Karl," Ellie shouted. "That we just packed to go down to St. Matthew's Church."

He nodded, and they turned away from the window to carry the last box into the sitting room.

Karl stared up at the window. When the voice had called out to him and he looked up and saw the two young women standing there, smiling down at him, he had suddenly been carried back to another time and place. For several moments he felt confused, trying to recall when and where it had been. He looked up at the window, eyes puzzled. And then . . . slowly he remembered. It had been 1934 . . . in Prague. He was hurrying along a street and a young woman's voice had called out to him. He stopped to look up and saw two pretty, laughing faces, hands waving at him from a schoolroom window. Waving back, he shouted something as they all laughed again, and he strode on once more along the cobblestones, swinging his metal lunchbox in his hand and whistling a cheerful tune.

Prague, he thought . . . how long ago it seemed. That day. It had started out like so many others. He had run across Wenceslas Square. It was summer. He had seen flowers, daffodils and crocus, near the factory where he worked. Pretty girls and flowers, he thought, almost shouting out with the simple joy of living. A lady passing by with her string bag of parcels from the Zeltergasse fruit market smiled when he laughed aloud. Oh yes, he felt good.

Herr Brodas, his foreman at the factory, had given him the letter he had promised. It was addressed to the foreman's cousin in Berlin, and Karl hoped it would get him work in a factory that made electrical parts like the one here in Prague. With the post-war unemployment still a problem in Berlin, the letter would be gold in Karl's pocket. Now Anton could study at the Conservatory in Berlin and Karl could enter the Technical University for study at night.

His eagerness grew as he turned into the Niklasstrasse, where he and Anton had taken rooms upon their arrival from Lidice. He could see the bridge and the blue of the Moldau, sparkling in the sun. "You must take your brother to Prague," his father had urged him. "Jan Mohryzek said he has taught him everything he knows."

"He is already more proficient than I on the violin," the music teacher had said. "And now, to learn composition, he must go to Prague."

So two years before, they had left Lidice and gone to Prague, where Anton had begun his studies with Professor Brokoff, and Karl had first found work in an ill-smelling butcher shop in the Fleischmarktgasse, a warren of narrow winding lanes where the *holátka,* the prostitutes, prowled day and night. But soon he was able to leave the squalid area for work in a factory that made electrical coils. Willing to work long hours, he was young and strong and eager, and Herr Brodas knew a good thing when he saw it. Before long, Karl was earning enough that he could begin his studies of electrical engineering at night.

"Well, if your brother would not need so many lessons and so many hours of work with the music professor, who lives on such an expensive street in the Hradcany district, you would be able to—" Herr Brodas once started to say.

"No," Karl said stubbornly. "Anton is the one with the *gift.* And it is a promise I made to my parents. I will keep that promise."

And Professor Brokoff was the best in Prague. Sometimes when Karl joined Anton and his teacher in the evening at the Café Arco, at the corner of Hybernergasse and Pflastergasse, he saw how the artists and writers and musicians gathered there listened to Professor Brokoff, how they revered him.

"Well, I guess you know what you're doing, Karl," Herr Brodas had said, scratching his head. He was fond of Karl and admired his appetite for hard work. "But you must also think of yourself. You must have a life of your own, meet a young woman, get married, have children."

"Time enough for that, Herr Brodas," Karl had said with his flash of a smile. Then he had winked and nudged the foreman. "And I know many young ladies. Sometimes I take them to the *pivnice* or the *vinárny,* for a little wine, beer, and we dance, then walk by the river, and if there's a moon—eh?" They'd laughed softly.

He found a note in their rooms from Anton saying he would be at the café. While Karl changed his clothes, he hummed softly, planning what they would do. First they would go to Lidice to say goodbye to their parents. Then they would take a train to Berlin. They would leave within a week. In the past two years he had saved enough to buy their train fare, to pay for rooms in Berlin, and to get Anton started at the Conservatory. A colleague of Professor Brokoff's from Berlin, who had studied with him when they were young, had heard Anton's composition, which had been performed just two months earlier by the Kleinseite Ensemble.

"If ever you come to Berlin, young man," Professor Annschbinder had said, "you must come to me at the Conservatory."

Karl and Anton had sat by a window of the café. The sun was slanting into the Hybernergasse, turning the gothic buildings opposite into stones of gold. Karl turned and smiled at his brother. *Berlin.* It had been their dream, but one that had never quite formed. They were like two sides of a coin, both with the same fine features, the sensitive mouth and bright-blue eyes. As children their hair had been flaxen. Now it was sun-streaked, but still fair. But where Karl was tall and broad across the shoulders, Anton was half a head shorter, with a slightly stooped figure that had a frailty about it.

They had walked from the café that early evening still smiling. Lights from the bridge shone down on the flowing water. They had walked to the center of it, running part of the way, shouting their joy and now beginning to plan. Soon they would go to Berlin. Berlin, the *mecca. Berlin.* A jewel in Europe's glittering crown.

"I cannot believe it," Anton said in a soft, trembling voice. They were coming back from the center of the bridge where they had run about and shouted into the night sky. Karl had slung an arm across his brother's shoulder. They were happily sated with wine and excitement and the lights of the city. "That a man so great as Professor Annschbinder was impressed with my work."

"A man so great!" Karl scoffed. "Someday you will be even greater. Someday you will not only go to Berlin. But to Paris, and London. Even New York, I think. They will hear your music all over the world and you will conduct for them all over the world."

They had thrown back their heads and laughed, running just to feel the wind on their faces. They had run until they came to their rooms on the Niklasstrasse, where they fell into their beds and slept through the night and rose the next morning knowing they would make their dreams come to be.

"But must you go so far?" Selma said. She was kneading dough for the bread she would soon slide into the brick oven, the fire underneath now settling to a nice glow. She looked at him while wiping her hands on a voluminous white apron.

"Quiet, woman," Stefan, her husband, said in a not unkindly way. "They will go where they must go. If it is Berlin, then Berlin is where they must go."

He and his two older sons, Karl and Anton, were sitting about the big, round wooden table with its blue and white cover, sipping the good Moravian wine that Karl had brought as a gift from Prague. It was pleasant, sitting there, Karl thought. There were times he had missed the sprawling cottage that sat halfway up the hillside at the edge of Lidice, missed the sound of the brook, the sight of the black and white cattle that dotted the hillside, the smoke winding upward from the three chimneys, the fields of yellow daffodils and sweeping tall trees that sheltered the cottage.

There were even times when he wondered if he would have been content to stay here, to follow in his father's footsteps. But it was foolish to even think it. It was all decided. He had a skill. He worked well with his hands. Anton had a gift. Magnificent music sprang from his head and hands. Perhaps . . . perhaps he, too, could study in Berlin.

"Professor Brokoff says he could be another Antonin Dvořák," he said, while watching their younger brother, Josef, bring in wood for the stove and pile it in the corner. Josef, at seventeen, was already taking over some of the duties and responsibilities of their father. Yes, Josef was the one who would stay in Lidice.

Stefan had risen and from an earthen jar on a shelf near the stove he took an envelope. He handed it to Karl and sat down again in his chair. "I have been saving this. I have always known that the time would come when you and Anton would go farther than Prague. This will carry you until you are settled in Berlin." He then reached out and put a hand on Karl's sleeve, his rough thatch of graying hair catching a ray of sunlight that fell through a window, his lined face heavy with thought. "You have worked hard, Karl, and given up a lot. I know how much this schooling means to you. There is enough there to help pay for the schooling—"

Karl felt tears come to his eyes. He looked at the envelope, turned it over in his hands, keeping his face lowered so that they wouldn't see the tears. He brushed at them quickly with his sleeve.

"Thank you, Father," he said, unable to say any more.

"Such long faces," Selma said with a smile from the big black iron stove where she stirred onions into a broth with a large wooden spoon. Her face was still round and merry looking, even with her blonde hair pulled back tightly into a bun.

Stefan looked up at her and shook his head. "It's . . . Berlin. I don't like the sound of what is happening there. That madman would destroy us all—"

"Oh, Stefan, what Hitler does in Germany—" Selma began.

"No, it is far more than Germany!" he thundered, his first pounding on the table. "Germany now, yes. Soon it will be all of Europe. Those who so foolishly believe that this— this military madness is only something that Frederick the Great or the Kaiser believed was Germany's right—oh, how foolish they are. It is something *in* the Germans. And this man with his tanks and his soldiers and yes, it is believed, his airplanes—the Versailles Treaty, it is nothing to him. Look at what happened to Dollfuss in Austria. Even the Chancellor of Austria was assassinated, cut down by thugs—local Nazis masquerading in uniforms of the Austrian army."

"But, Father," Karl tried to argue, "there can't be another war—"

"And there are other things," his father said with dark trembling anger. He was trying to fill his pipe, but his hands were shaking. "Who knows what he is planning to do? This is the kind of fanaticism that can bring down nations, destroy everything in its path, while the rest of the world sleeps on."

There was a long, long silence. He then looked up at both Karl and Anton. "Don't ever forget who you are." He paused and watched them, the blue eyes hardening like the ice on the brook when it froze in the winter. *"Don't ever forget who you are."*

Within a week of arriving in Berlin, Karl had found work in a factory that manufactured motors. Herr Brodas's note had done that for him. He and Anton settled in rooms near the Conservatory, which meant that Karl had to ride some distance by trolley to reach his place of work. But he was insistent that they live near where Anton would be studying.

The night they arrived, as they were unpacking their clothing and some of the personal belongings they had brought along—Anton's small radio, Karl's ice skates, some books and phonograph records, other odds and ends—Karl carefully broke open a box that he had placed on a table in the center of their small sitting room.

"What is it?" Anton said curiously, walking around to the other side of the table and gazing down into the box, his blue eyes wide.

"It's something I've been working on," Karl said, carefully lifting it from the box and putting it down on the table. "Herr Brodas let me keep it in a small storeroom off his office, where I would stay late occasionally and tinker with it."

"Yes," Anton said, smiling. "But what is it?"

"Well, it's something I—well, I guess you could say it's an invention." He grinned sheepishly.

"What does it do?"

"It helps to carry current more efficiently into a generator," Karl said. He bent down, and with a long pencil began to trace the different components and what they were used for, how they performed, and exactly what he could expect them to do.

"Wait a minute," Anton said, laughing. "That is all very wonderful, but I don't understand a word you have said." He was becoming excited. "But what I *do* understand is that you have invented something that is not only very valuable and necessary, but something that has been missing until now. Is that right?"

"Well, I guess you could say that."

"Karl, that is wonderful," Anton said, sounding out of breath. "What are you going to do with it?"

Karl scratched his head. "I don't know."

"Well, one thing even I know is that you must not show it to just anybody. It must only be shown to people you trust."

Karl laughed. "Well, Brother Anton, considering that we don't know anyone in Berlin, that will not be too difficult."

"That's true," Anton said, joining his brother in laughter. "But sometime you will meet someone you can show it to, someone you can trust, and then you will become a very important man because you will be a recognized inventor."

"Yes, that would be fine, wouldn't it?" He put it back into the box, and slid the box into a closet near the door. Until I meet someone I can trust, I shall not discuss it." He looked up and smiled at Anton. "And now I suggest that we see what this city of Berlin is all about."

That evening they had dinner in the Bavarian dining room of a vast restaurant called Haus Vaterland, and enjoyed the sounds of a brass orchestra and yodelers. They ate ravenously, both agreeing that the roast goose and potato dumplings were not as good as their mother's. The following morning they set out to see the city. They rode on the Untergrundbahn, their first experience on an underground railway, and then they climbed the steps to the Hochbahnhof Bulowstrasse, this time to board an elevated train and look down on the city.

They visited the sprawling Lustgarten, standing in the center of the Leipziger Platz, and looked with admiration at the baroque buildings that formed an octagon all around them. They had lunch in a café in the Unter den Linden and visited the famed Berlin Zoo. That evening they attended a performance in the Komödie Theatre; then, weary from their hours and hours of walking, they returned to their rooms, strangely disturbed by the city, but not knowing really why.

"Perhaps—well, perhaps we are not accustomed to seeing so many military uniforms," Anton said as they prepared for bed, calling out from his room to Karl's in a tired voice.

"They look as though they are wearing costumes on the Komödie Theatre stage," Karl said in a disgusted voice. "I counted five monocles and lost count of the jackboots."

Anton was standing in the door, slowly unbuttoning his shirt. "You aren't sorry, are you, Karl? Would you rather go back to Prague?"

"Of course I'm not sorry, Anton," Karl said, bending to pull off his boots, his voice rather more blustery than Anton had ever heard it. He looked up and smiled. "Tomorrow I am going to start looking for that person I can trust."

It was only a matter of months before that occurred. Karl turned one morning at a shout in his ear, one he could hear over the roar of the motors that were being tested in the shop of Teltow Fabrik, the factory on the Teltow Canal in the Steglitz district where he had found employment.

"Come with me, Wancek," Joachim Schering, the foreman, shouted at him.

Karl put down the tools he was working with and followed the older man through a narrow path of workers and machinery, the roaring din following them until they were in Schering's small office with the door closed.

"What you told me, about your invention, that you have tested it completely and it performs as you said with the generator? It's all true?"

Karl nodded. "Of course, Herr Schering. I would not tell you anything but the truth about it. That wouldn't be to my advantage."

"All right," Schering said, motioning at Karl to sit opposite him while he sat down behind the desk. "I told the factory manager about it, the little bit you told me. And he told Herr Blaumberg."

"Herr Blaumberg?"

"Herr Blaumberg owns Teltow Fabrik!"

"I see," Karl said, nodding.

"Something . . . something wrong?" Schering peered at him with hard suspicion in his eyes.

"Wrong?" Karl appeared surprised at the sudden change of tone.

Schering spoke carefully. He even lowered his voice and looked at the door as though to make certain it was completely closed. "You —you have certain—well, er—*politics*?"

"Politics, Herr Schering?" Karl looked at him with a puzzled expression. Slowly he began to understand, and shook his head. "No. I have no politics. I just came here from Prague, as you know. Before that I lived in a very small village twenty miles from Prague. Mining and farming are what the people are concerned with in Lidice. Not politics."

But as he said it, he remembered his last conversation with his father, the angry talk about Herr Hitler and his father's warning, *Don't ever forget who you are.*

"Herr Blaumberg is a Jew!"

Karl stared at the foreman for fully a minute, and then spoke slowly and softly. "I'm not certain I know what you are trying to say."

"There is a feeling in Germany about Jews." Schering's voice was almost expressionless.

Karl rose and walked to the small window. He looked out at the canal flowing by and at a small boat chugging past below, faintly hearing the *chup chup chup* sound it was making. He looked up at the gray sky and felt its dreariness invade him. "I am not a German, Herr Schering. I am a Czech," he said without looking around.

"And I am not *that* kind of German, Karl." Schering's voice was low, but it had a fierce ring in it.

128

Karl turned and looked at him. "I am glad of that."

They solemnly shook hands. "Come now," Schering said. "Herr Blaumberg would like to speak to you."

"To me?" Karl was shocked. He poked his own finger at himself.

"About the invention." Schering laughed and took his arm. "Come along." They started from the office.

"But the owner of such a big factory—"

"Herr Blaumberg is a very good man. Treats his employees well, pays good wages, and comes into the factory now and then to talk to the workers." He looked around and laughed again. "He won't bite you."

"This new coil and armature structure? You have tested it?" Herr Blaumberg was standing by the window of his large office, looking down at the road as though searching for something. Apparently not seeing what he was looking for, he turned back to Karl, who stood on the other side of the massive, ornately carved desk. Karl had never seen an office like this one before, with thick carpeting, heavy dark red velvet drapes, paneled walls, and little shaded lamps on the walls. There were several silver-framed photographs on the desk, which he couldn't see from where he was standing.

"Sit. Sit, Herr Wancek," the factory owner said. Karl sat in a deep, cushioned leather chair and studied the man before him, careful not to seem to be staring. Blaumberg was as tall as he, with carefully brushed steel-gray hair and searching gray-green eyes. He seemed stern, almost forbidding, but when he smiled his face lit up and the eyes grew warm and humorous. He was a handsome man with straight shoulders and proudly arching eyebrows that contrasted darkly with his silvery hair. "Tell me how this invention of yours works."

For half an hour, Karl sat there explaining the coil and armature structure, his hands and arms forming arcs and circles and other quick gestures. ". . . and it would have many windings, sir, which would sit in narrow cuts, longitudinal cuts in the core of the armature. And then these would be connected, you see, to the correct elements of this cylindrical arrangement of insulated metal bars . . ."

He saw that Blaumberg was sketching quickly with a pencil on a piece of paper. He looked up.

"You say you have built a model?"

Karl nodded.

"Will you bring it to me?"

Karl hesitated, then said, "Yes, sir."

Blaumberg watched him from beneath lowered eyebrows. "You are very trusting. Perhaps it is not so wise to be so trusting."

"You have the face and the sound of a man that I feel I can trust," Karl said with a simplicity but also with a confidence that made Blaumberg straighten up, lean back in his chair, and smile.

"I appreciate your trust," Blaumberg said quietly. "And I will honor it."

He stood up and walked to the window again, once more studying the street as though watching for something. He looked over his shoulder at Karl. "Could I see it soon?"

"Yes, Herr Blaumberg."

"This is an imposition, I'm afraid, but I am most anxious to have a look at it. Could you bring it to my house this evening?"

"Yes, Herr Blaumberg."

The factory owner crossed to his desk and quickly wrote something on a slip of paper, which he handed across the desk to Karl. "My address. You will take a taxicab, please, for which I will give you the cost in return."

"That is not necessary—"

"I insist. We live in the Spandau. You will need a taxi to get there. Eight o'clock?"

Karl nodded, and as he stood up to shake Herr Blaumberg's hand, he could see two of the photographs. One was of a slender, handsome woman, her dark hair parted in the middle and drawn softly over her ears to a coil in the back. Frau Blaumberg, he imagined, from her appearance and the place of importance the photograph took on the desk. The other was a group, with the same woman seated at a grand piano, two teenage children on the bench on either side of her, and Herr Blaumberg standing and leaning on the piano. The boy and girl were looking up at him and smiling, while the woman watched the music in front of her as she played.

"At eight then," Herr Blaumberg said, walking to the door with Karl.

The taxi turned between two stone pillars at the road and followed a winding drive past thick pine trees. In the distance through the trees Karl could see carriage lights on either side of a massive carved door. When the house came into view it towered, three stories of stone—like a fortress, he thought. He paid the driver and climbed the stone steps to a terrace that ran across the front of the house and on around to the side.

It was several moments before the door was opened. Herr Blaumberg stood there, an open book dangling in one hand. "Come in, come in," he said with a hearty voice.

Karl followed him through a dimly lit hall that had a broad staircase curving up the three stories. It was all paneled in dark gleaming wood; Oriental rugs covered the floors. He was led into a library, with three walls of books from floor to ceiling, and one wall a long stretch of french doors that seemed to open out on a garden. The embers of an earlier fire glowed on the hearth. Just one reading lamp was turned on by a deep, comfortable chair with high wings, a cushioned footstool before it.

Blaumberg went about turning on lamps, while motioning Karl to put the box on a long heavily carved table in the center of the room. "Put it there and let us have a look at it."

"Yes, Herr Blaumberg," Karl said, placing the box on the table, then gently lifting the mechanism out and placing it on the table.

He watched for the next fifteen minutes as Herr Blaumberg bent, peered, and lovingly ran a finger over the various segments and connections. "Yes . . . yes . . . yes . . ." he was murmuring. At one point he looked up and smiled. "My father started out as a machinist. One day when I was about fourteen, he said to me, 'If you are going to take over this factory someday, when you are grown and I am old, you are going to know everything you can possibly know about what you are running. Today you will start learning about machinery.' " He laughed softly. "And from then on my life was miserable. That is, until I began to understand. That part fits here. This part goes here —this coil fits into this. . . . It was then that I started to like it more and more. One day I told my father that I didn't want to run the factory, that I simply wanted to be one of the men who made the machines work." He laughed again and for another few moments was silent as he studied the model once more.

A large gold-framed portrait with a small museum light at the top hung over the fireplace, a portrait of the same handsome woman Karl had seen in the photograph. She was beautiful in the portrait, wearing a flowing blue dress, a cutting basket in her lap filled with long-stemmed flowers. As he watched and waited, he slowly shifted his head a little. In the distance he heard a ripple of music, a phonograph record of some American jazz tune, and then a spill of laughter, silvery and high. A door slammed and the music stopped, but he heard running footsteps, muffled as someone ran down the staircase, and then the sharp tapping of high heels as they hit the bare floor between the Oriental rugs in the hall.

Blaumberg suddenly hurried to the library door, opened it, and called out, "Drive slowly, Miriam. Max tells me you drive too fast."

He heard a voice answering, melodious and filled with high tones, with something edging laughter, and then it was gone as a door closed. Moments later there was the sound of a motor outside, driving away and fading in the farther distance.

Herr Blaumberg had returned to the model. With one hand placed on the top, he said to Karl, "If it can be patented, I will arrange for it in your name."

"Herr Blaumberg—"

"No," he said, raising his hand to stop Karl. "This is the way we do business. As the proprietor you will receive the royalties and we will receive the benefits of your invention, if—" He paused, one finger in the air. "If it works as you say it does."

"It works as I said," Karl answered with a simplicity that made Blaumberg nod with a smile. Then he added softly, "And you, young man, are not to be wasted in the division you are now working. Herr Schering has told me of your talents, your intelligence. We are going to make better use of you in a position where you will be overseeing—"

"If I may interrupt, Herr Blaumberg," Karl said, then smiled a bit sheepishly. "I would prefer to stay where I am, sir, for a while at least. You see, I am attending the Technical University, in the evenings."

"You don't say?" Blaumberg said with a small measure of surprise.

"Yes, Herr Blaumberg. I am studying to be an electrical engineer."

"Why, that's splendid. Splendid. But why do you wish to stay where you are?"

"There's much I must learn, sir, before I take a job of more importance, and—"

"Nonsense. You already know more, from what I can see here—" he touched the model—"than most machine workers could ever learn in five lifetimes. Schering wants you as an assistant."

"But—"

"He says you are the man he wants for the job."

Karl smiled and nodded his head finally. "I cannot believe all of our good luck."

"All? Our?" Blaumberg peered at him. "Schering tells me you are single."

"My brother. We came to Berlin together. He is studying at the Conservatory with Professor Annschbinder—"

"Ah, I am acquainted with the professor."

"And just today Anton learned he has been accepted at the Hochschule für Musik to study composition."

"Well, that is fine news." He walked Karl from the room, then stopped in the hall. "My son, Max, will drive you back." He went to the staircase and started up.

"A taxi, sir, if you will just telephone for a—"

"Max is meeting friends in the Kurfürstendamm. He will be happy to take you."

Karl watched him disappear up the stairs and waited by the door, twisting his black leather cap in his hands.

"Have a cigarette, Wancek."

"Thank you, but I don't smoke," Karl said quietly. He had been listening to the purring sound of the motor on the big Mercedes-Benz.

"My father tells me you came here from Prague," young Max said, glancing occasionally away from the road at Karl. When he had come down the staircase with his father, Karl had admired his well-tailored clothing and suave manner. He could not be more than twenty-one or -two, he thought, yet he had the poise of a much older man. His dark good looks and serious smile made Karl warm to him.

"Yes. My brother and I have been here only a short time."

"You don't speak German too badly."

"Well, we studied it in school, you see." He laughed apologetically. "It is getting better as I speak it more."

"I've seen you at the factory several times," Max said, smiling at him in a quick side glance, then turning his eyes back to the road again.

"Yes, well, I have seen you as well, but I would not have expected you to have noticed me."

"How could I miss you?" Max asked in a burst of laughter. "You're head and shoulders over everybody else there."

Karl smiled. "Oh, I am not so tall. I am told I had a great-grandfather who stood almost seven feet. I am only three inches more than six feet."

"Seven feet! He must have been a giant!" Max exclaimed. He

rolled down the window and tossed his cigarette away. "What is it like where you come from, Karl?" He made a gesture with his hand. "Is it all right if I call you Karl?"

"Yes, please do." Karl looked from the window, the beauty of the area called the Spandau Forest, even in the darkness, bringing on a wave of homesickness. It reminded him, in a way, of the thick dark forests of spruce and fir that rose up from the hillside above his home in Czechoslovakia.

"I come from Lidice, a small village north of Prague. Not far. Only a small distance to travel, but very far in the difference of life. Prague is a little like here, like Berlin, with cafés and many people, the beautiful buildings and the rivers. At Lidice you can hear the wolves at night. Sometimes a wild boar or a bear comes close." He laughed softly. "But we are snug and safe in our house, with the wind and rain beating at the windows. Nothing can come inside to do harm."

"Snug . . . and safe," Max said slowly. *"Nothing can come inside to . . . to do harm."* He lit another cigarette and it was then that Karl began to notice how brooding, how tense and apprehensive this young man was. "I once thought that, too. When I was a child growing up, when night would come and the wind would blow the tops of the trees so that they moaned, I would run to my mother's music room or to my father's study. I felt safe there, where it was light and warm and the sounds of the wind and the darkness were outside, far away."

Karl heard the thread of uneasiness in his voice.

"Now . . . one doesn't know. Everything is changing," Max said. For a long moment he was quiet. "Did you know that Chancellor Dollfuss, when he was shot in his cabinet rooms that day in Vienna, bled to death? They threw him on a sofa, where he pleaded for a doctor and a priest. But they ignored him and he slowly bled . . . until he died."

"Yes," Karl said, almost in a whisper. "My father told us. He said"—he spoke carefully—"he said that this kind of fanaticism will destroy everything in its path."

They were both silent as the car traveled several miles. They had come to the Altstadt, the old town where the Havel and Spree rivers met.

"Come with me this evening, Karl. I am meeting friends at the Café Kranzler. They are people you will like—"

"Oh, I am afraid I—" He looked down at his clothes.

"No, no, these are people who will like you as well."

They were already past Charlottenburg and were driving around the Siegessäule victory column in the Tiergarten.

"Well, perhaps just for a short while," Karl said. It would be pleasant, he thought, if Max Blaumberg's friends were as warm and friendly and interesting as he was.

They parked the automobile near the corner where Unter den Linden and the Friedrichstrasse came together, and hurried inside the café. In a smoky corner near the glassed-in front Karl saw a large group of young people sitting around a table. He paused for a moment in the clatter and clamor while following Max and drew in his breath. The most beautiful girl he had ever seen had turned her head and looked at him. She had been laughing up into the face of the young man seated next to her. For a brief second their eyes had held, and in that second or two he fell in love.

She was the first to break the spell. Pretending to pout, she had called out to the others at the table, saying, "Now that my brother is here, I shall have to behave myself."

Her brother? Of course, Karl thought, she was Miriam, Max's sister, the one who drives an automobile too fast. He saw that she looked like Max, and then realized they must be twins, not just brother and sister. She was wearing a vivid green dress of some soft and shining material—the color heightened the dark beauty, the arched brows and flashing eyes, the full mouth and hair that fell in soft waves about her face.

It seemed a miracle to Karl, but she made a place for him beside her. He had hardly heard the introductions, and went through the motions of shaking hands as though in a trance. He found it almost impossible to take his eyes from her, and wondered what stroke of luck had brought him to this place at this very moment.

"If Max brought you here to the café to meet his friends, then he must like you," she suddenly said to him with a directness that enchanted him.

"Well, I like Max." There was that locking of eyes again.

"And if Max likes you," she said softly so that only he could hear, "then I will like you as well."

"I am very glad for that." He knew a stein of beer had been placed in front of him, but he couldn't seem to turn his head or tear his eyes from hers. It was only when she looked down at the wineglass in front of her, lifted it, and slowly sipped from it, the rim of the glass barely touching her lips, that he grasped the handle on the stein and drank deeply. When he put it down, he said, without looking at her, "I work for your father, you know."

"You work at Teltow Fabrik," she said with a slow smile. "There *is* a difference, you understand. A man works for himself."

Remarkable, he thought, stealing another glance at her and finding his gaze hopelessly caught in the amused gray-green depths of her eyes.

"You are like a dream I have had," he whispered, no longer able to keep his thoughts from her.

She put her hand softly over his. "Karl? Is that right? Karl?" When he nodded, she said, her voice very low, "Would you meet me here on Sunday afternoon? At three o'clock?"

"Yes," he said, his voice husky, eyes shining.

"Three o'clock," she whispered. And he nodded.

They kept it a secret for months. Only Anton and Max and a few close friends knew. But by summer of 1935, they decided to wait no longer to tell her parents that they were in love and wished to marry. The motors being manufactured at Teltow Fabrik now had the revolutionary new improvements Karl had brought to Herr Blaumberg. He had been given a generous sum for the model and technical drawings, and would in future receive the royalties from its manufacture. As one of Herr Schering's four assistants, he was earning a good weekly wage, and he was attending the Technical Universität to become an electrical engineer.

They walked and walked one whole Sunday afternoon, discussing how they would approach her parents. It was sunny, not too hot, and the skies were a powdery blue with great puffy white clouds floating on the horizon. The broad streets and boulevards gleamed spotlessly, the facades of apartment buildings and handsome homes exploding in a riot of pink and purple petunias that bloomed in window boxes and on balconies. They strolled through the Hansaviertel and on into the Tiergarten, where they stopped for coffee at an outdoor café, dappled pools of sunlight falling through the leafy mass of green overhead. Ambling nannies and dog-walkers and romping children filled the pathways. Not even the frequent sight of jackbooted soldiers in twos and threes could dampen their happiness. They paused to watch two men engrossed in a chess game, the carved wooden chess figures as large as the men themselves. They rode in a small boat across the

Neuersee to the Zoologischer Garten, where they walked slowly past the Bahnhof Zoo.

"What are you so nervous about?" Karl finally asked as they sat at one of the white tables in front of the Café Kranzler. She sipped at the glass of wine, cradling it in both hands.

"They will give us every argument against it," she said at last. "But it will only be one argument that will matter, and that one is one they will hang onto."

"And what argument is that?"

She watched the traffic on the street, the passersby, and then let her gaze wander to a young couple at the next table.

"I am a Jew, Karl, and you are Christian," Miriam said in a low voice, her lovely face set, the gray-green eyes following the course of a double-decker bus as it careened around the corner.

"But that is nothing," he said, clasping her hand. "We are two people who will respect—"

"Don't say that is nothing!" she said, almost spitting it out, her face drawn hard, voice dropped to a pitch that was loud enough for only he, and no one else, to hear. "That is everything in Germany today."

Karl's face became flushed with anger. "I don't care about all of that."

"You have to care." She leaned toward him, grasping his hand hard. "These are the things my parents will say. This is the argument they will give. Oh, don't you see? Don't you realize what is happening here?"

"This—what is going on here"—he waved his hand in a wide circle —"it can't last. Talk to almost anyone here in Berlin and they laugh, they find him ridiculous."

"This is Berlin. Hitler hates Berlin. He finds the Berlin resident arrogant, too sure of himself, and the Berliner thinks like you, that it will go away." Her face grew dark with foreboding. "It will never go away. Never . . ."

A waiter passed close by, pausing to clear a table next to them. They sat in silence for several minutes. When the waiter left with a loaded tray, Karl looked at her.

"Does—does your father ever talk of leaving?"

She slowly shook her head. "Most German Jews are German first and Jewish second." She looked off into the distance, her head turning slowly from one side to the other as she gazed at the buildings, the people, the moving traffic. It all seemed so normal, just as it always

137

had been. "Try to understand. We are Germans. My grandfather and great-grandfather and his father before him. No one knows how far back."

She was silent again. "We have cousins who left more than a year ago. They came from Karlsruhe. It's very different in the smaller cities and towns. You see signs there. Signs like JEWS ARE NOT WANTED HERE. My father's cousin owned a bank in Karlsruhe. The bank was *purchased* from him." He heard the deep thread of sarcasm. "Who knows if any money changed hands? My father's cousin wouldn't say. For months he stayed as the manager of the bank, and then he took his family and left, went to Switzerland. But their passports will soon expire, my father said, and the German government won't renew them. This means they are now refugees, with no identity papers, no visas, nothing. My father sends them money. Without it, they would starve."

He watched her as she fought back tears, his hand clutching hers. She looked so beautiful. Her summery white dress had yellow flowers on it with tiny stems of green. She wore a band of yellow in her hair, and her bare arms were burned to a golden tan.

He suddenly pulled her to her feet. "We're going to be married," he said stubbornly. "And we will go to talk to your parents about it now."

She stopped him for a moment, holding onto his arms and looking up into his face.

"They will make it difficult for you."

"It doesn't matter," he said.

They were sitting in the garden, white wicker chairs pulled up to the round table set with a cloth and tea things. At the bottom of the hill, the small lake rippled blue in the sunlight and a slim red canoe bobbed at the end of a dock where Max had carelessly left it. No one was eating the small watercress sandwiches or tiny round iced cakes. Each was staring into his or her teacup or down at the canoe swinging about in lazy circles on the end of its short rope. Only Karl kept looking from one face to another, his jaw set stubbornly, his eyes blazing in determination. Gunther Blaumberg finally raised his head.

"I would not be so foolish as to say, 'No, you must not marry because you are a Jew and you are a Christian, because you do not have the same religion.' I can see by looking at you that this would not matter to you, this would be something you would try very hard to resolve. But this other matter . . ." He was gravely shaking his head.

He stood and walked to the top of the roughly hewn stones that formed steps down to the lake. He and his wife, Mala, had just been playing a game of tennis, and in his summer flannels and white casual shirt he looked very different to Karl. He walked back to the table and sat down again.

"For several years now, we Germans have been shaking our heads and telling ourselves that this was simply some ugly kind of mirage. That it would disappear. Some of us read *Mein Kampf*. Most of us bought it, took it home, and put it on the bookshelf, unread. Perhaps if most Germans had read *Mein Kampf* before 1933, when Adolf Hitler was made Chancellor, we might have been saved from what is coming. He left no doubt, between the covers of that book, of what he intends for Germany *and* for Europe."

"Gunther," Mala said softly when he paused for a moment. "I am going to speak out, say what I feel."

He smiled, and reached over to pat her hand. "Always, my dear. Even when I know it may not be what I want to hear."

She wore a white tennis dress and her hair was tied back with a white ribbon. She was an older Miriam, but with hazel eyes and hair several shades lighter than both of her children.

"With everything so uncertain, with none of us knowing what will happen—perhaps tomorrow, next month, next year—it may be that nothing is really important except grasping whatever happiness we can while it is there in front of us."

He patted her hand again. "I guess I would have been disappointed in you, Mala, if you had not said that."

When Miriam and Karl leaned forward hopefully, Gunther put his hand up in warning. He looked at Miriam.

"Your mother speaks from her heart. I am trying to say it from my head." He tapped his temple.

"Father, I would like to speak for Karl," Max said, jumping up from his chair and leaning on the back of Karl's chair.

"There is no need for that, Max," Gunther Blaumberg said. He looked with fondness at Karl. "He is a young man with talent, a young man who is going to do good things with his life, perhaps great things. These things have nothing to do with this matter." He gazed long, with sadness, first at Karl, then Miriam.

"If I were to say yes to you, then it means I am speaking from hope. Hope that Germany will get better, that this ugliness will disappear.

If I say no, it is because I see little or no hope. I must be honest with you. I can think of it in no other terms."

He rose and walked to the top of the stone steps again. The sun was slanting on the lake, turning it to crimson. A small sailboat scudded away from the far shore, and somewhere in the distance they heard children's voices, raised in laughter.

Miriam had stood up and walked halfway to her father. "We have to have hope, Father," she said softly.

"Yes," he said, nodding as he turned. Karl was standing next to Miriam, holding her hand. "We have to have hope." And as Miriam threw herself into his arms, sobbing happily, he looked at Karl, who watched them, a broad smile on his face.

The first days of September were merely an extension of August, hot and clear, the sky the clearest, most beautiful blue that Miriam had ever seen. It's for me, she thought when she rose each morning. It means good things, wonderful things, she mused as she carried her coffee onto the terrace above the lake, or rode her bicycle through the woodsy lanes of Spandau, or drove her little car into the narrow streets of the Old Town to shop or to the Kurfürstendamm at dusk to meet Karl for dinner.

"Not before the tenth of October," her mother had said firmly, ending the argument. "I can't possible get ready for a wedding before then."

"Mama says not before the tenth of October," Miriam said one evening, cheerfully, as she and Karl sat in the Eden Hotel Bar waiting for Anton and Max. "I had thought she was going to insist on November or December, but I had to pretend, of course, that the tenth is much too long to wait, so that she wouldn't suddenly say, 'Not possibly before January, you willful child.' "

"You *are* a willful child," he said softly, leaning over the small table and kissing her. Something soft and sweet was being played by the pianist, and the lights were low. How my life has changed, he thought, even since Prague, when I began to learn about things other than a small village and simple people who milked cows and worked in the mines and celebrated feast days.

"Sometimes you miss it, don't you?" she said softly, putting two fingers against his lips and then his cheek.

"It?" He thought, carefully. "I sometimes miss my parents and my brother Josef," he said.

140

"Your parents? What are their names?"

"Stefan and Selma."

"We'll go to visit them, Karl."

"Yes," he said eagerly, his eyes shining. "When spring comes, we will go to visit them." He thought about it for a moment, and his face quickly sobered. "It's very different, Miriam, from here—from anything you have known."

"Silly," she said, touching his lips again. "I'm not completely citified and spoiled."

"No," he said softly, the blue eyes darkening with desire. "You're everything I've ever wanted—" He looked up abruptly as someone roughly bumped Miriam's chair.

"Would you move your chair a bit, so that I can get through?"

Both Karl and Miriam looked up into the face of an officer wearing the wings of the new German Air Force. Karl slowly rose, his mouth tight, hands clenched. There was no question of the amount of space by Miriam's chair. There was more than enough room for anyone to pass. The German officer was with another one. Both were young and hard-faced, with piercing blue eyes and smooth shining hair beneath their caps, hair as blond as his, their eyes on a level with his.

Miriam quickly rose, picking up her drink and Karl's as she did. "Come, Karl, let's sit at the bar to wait for Anton and Max. The air is getting too warm on this side of the room."

Karl hesitated for a moment, his eyes never relenting, continuing to bore into the Nazi officer's. Only when the other's eyes dropped after a long, long moment did he turn and follow Miriam, anger and frustration seething and churning inside.

"Don't," she whispered as they sat at the bar and he cast one long enraged look over his shoulder. "It's useless to make anything of it. The insult is so slight that it doesn't even exist."

He looked around him. "I don't like coming to places like this."

"No, Karl," she said. "That's when they win. Don't you see that that's when they win?"

The Blaumbergs' house seemed the very soul of warmth and normalcy on that soft September evening when Karl and Anton arrived for the pre-nuptial party that Mala laughingly insisted upon, saying that there had not been an engagement party and that as a mother of the bride she felt deprived.

The servants had strung Japanese lanterns down in the garden, and three musicians walked about playing violins. The terrace overlooking the garden was filled with small tables; candles flickered in the soft breeze. The guests' dark shining cars had started rolling into the driveway shortly after seven o'clock. It was not a large party. Less than fifty relatives and friends had gathered for the evening, including Herr Schering, Professor Annschbinder, and their wives.

Gunther Blaumberg, Max, and Karl were standing near the doors leading into the house from the terrace when Anton, who had just arrived, came toward them. His face was white and strained as he slowly pulled a folded piece of white paper from his inner pocket. Without saying a word, he handed it to Gunther, who unfolded it. Later it seemed to Karl that it had all happened as if in a dream, the motions of everyone slow and hazy.

Gunther stared at the paper. It was a pamphlet-type paper, large, with heavy black printing on it, the kind that was found on tables in cafés and *weinhäusern,* the kind hungry-looking young men passed out on street corners to passersby.

"Nuremberg Laws," Gunther read slowly. Everyone standing within ten or twelve feet turned to listen. "It is dated fifteen September, 1935."

"It was handed to me as I came out of the Conservatory," Anton said, his blue eyes filled with pain.

Karl, hearing the dread in Gunther's voice and seeing the shock on Anton's face, looked about for Miriam, but he remembered she had said she was running upstairs to help her mother finish dressing.

"Fifteen September, 1935," Gunther read. "This is a law for the protection of German blood and German honor. . . ."

As he read on, Karl felt the blood rush to his head, felt his heart pounding in his chest, and stood there helplessly, clenching and unclenching his hands, recalling the cold but triumphant smile on the face of the Nazi officers at the Eden Hotel Bar.

The paper said that the law deprived all Jews of their German citizenship, that they were now confined to the status of "subjects." It also said that they were forbidden to enter into marriage with an Aryan, nor could they have extramarital relations with them.

Gunther stood, thunderstruck. His hands began to tremble violently. "Too late," he whispered. "Too late." He looked at Karl and staggered a little, and both Karl and Max caught him and held him up. "Good God, Karl, how are we going to tell Miriam?"

Karl kept shaking his head, unable to speak for a moment.

Just then, Miriam came running through the door, the short pink chiffon dress whirling about her slim figure, the tiny pearls in her ears and at her throat gleaming with milky opalescence. Mala, in a long, gray silk dinner gown with an emerald necklace and earrings, was just behind her. Miriam stopped outside the door, the smile freezing on her face. As she stopped, Mala caught hold of her shoulders from behind.

"What is it?" Miriam whispered.

Gunther could only shake his head. Max slowly took the paper from his hand as his father half fell into a chair by one of the tables. "Why?" Gunther was muttering. "Why is there so much hatred? Why?"

Karl had gone to Miriam's side and was holding her against him. When Max began to read aloud, she simply stared at him, unable to believe what she was hearing.

"Why?" she whispered, echoing her father. "Why?" She turned to Karl and put her arms about his neck, tears coursing down her face. "What did we do that was wrong? What have we done?" The words came out in broken sobs, like those of a small child who is lost in the dark.

"Dear God!" Mala gasped, as she leaned against the stone wall of the house and slowly beat her fist against it.

"All I wanted was to love you," Miriam said to Karl. He buried his face in her hair. "That was all I wanted. Such a tiny, little piece of life."

Gunther, tears running down his cheeks, watched his daughter as she clung to Karl.

The guests seemed frozen into immobility, as they watched the small group up on the terrace. The three musicians were playing Grieg's *Ich Liebe Dich* in the garden, the violins singing out in sweet lament.

"I love you, Miriam," Karl kept saying, over and over. Still holding her, he turned to her father. "We'll go to Czechoslovakia. Tomorrow. We'll leave tomorrow."

But Gunther slowly shook his head. "You have forgotten already. She is no longer a citizen. She has no rights. They will not permit her to be given a visa. She would be stopped at the border."

"I will go to the Czechoslovakian consulate tomorrow and get her a visa—"

"Karl, Karl," Gunther said softly, sorrowfully. "It is no use."

"I'll find a way," Karl said grimly. He looked down at Miriam.

"You'll see. I'll find a way." He held her closely, while the guests began to drift toward their cars, so he only half heard what Anton was saying to anyone who would listen.

"What are they afraid of? There are less than half a million Jews in Germany. What do they think? That less than half a million Jews could influence or dominate in any way almost seventy million Gentiles? Almost one-fifth of them Nazi Party members? How can they fear something that is an impossibility?"

And as Karl and Miriam, their arms about each other, slowly walked down into the garden, Anton watched them, helpless, angry tears in his eyes, while Gunther Blaumberg led his wife into the house.

Karl watched her coming toward him through the crowded tables of the Café Kranzler. Her face was tense, white, but she looked even more beautiful to him than ever. She was wearing a deep violet suit with a short peplum at the waist, one that softly revealed her figure and caused men to turn and smile. The weather had shifted during the night, bringing a chill and tangy fragrance of autumn to the air. In diffidence she wore a tiny lavender hat with a nose veil and a dark fur scarf over her shoulders. She approached the table nervously, and when Karl leaned to kiss her she clung to him a little longer than she would have before. But then she drew back, slowly, seeing the answer in his face even before he spoke.

Karl grasped her hands and held them, tersely giving the waiter their order. Suddenly the din in the café seemed louder than usual. The bursts of laughter from a table near the wall where a group of boisterous young men sat seemed macabre and strange to them, when on another night they would have smiled. The bright lights hurt her eyes, and the clamor of china and silverware and voices assaulted her ears. "At the consulate . . . ? There's nothing, is there?" Her voice was filled with despair.

"I talked to a man there," Karl said quickly, in a low voice. "He said there are ways of getting across the border. I know someone who might be able to help us—"

"Oh, Karl," she breathed softly, a glimmer of hope in her voice. And then she whispered to him. "Please, darling, let's leave here."

They quickly drank their coffee and hurried out of the café into the noisy street, with its flashing lights and crushing traffic. They found her little car, climbed in, and sat very still for several moments. The canvas top was up and the isinglass side curtains were snugly snapped

144

shut. For a long while they watched the passing vehicles in silence, and then she turned to him and slipped into his arms.

"I want to go with you, Karl," she whispered.

"Go with me?" he repeated, knowing what she meant, but almost afraid to believe it was so. It had startled him, yet he knew that somewhere deep in his subconscious he had been wanting it, hoping for it, willing it even.

In silence they drove to the house overlooking the Landwehrkanal, where he and Anton had their rooms. Still in silence, they parked the automobile and walked up the steps, holding hands. In the sitting room, they found Anton, huddled beneath a gooseneck lamp studying a score. He looked up at them as they stood in the half darkness of the large high-ceilinged room, and when he saw their faces, he knew.

Without saying a word, he rose, put his jacket on, wound his wool scarf about his neck, and went to the door.

"I have to go to see a friend of mine. Hansi Mueller. We want to work on some music together. I will probably be very late." He opened the door, hesitated, looked back at them. "About three o'clock, I would imagine."

Long after he had left and the echo of his footsteps had disappeared, they stood in the middle of the room looking at each other. With a cry, she suddenly threw herself into his arms. Karl slowly picked her up and carried her into his room. He sat her down on the bed and carefully took off her coat and hat. Kneeling in front of her, he kissed away the tears on her cheeks, then slowly undressed her, his hands gentle, his lips whispering that he loved her and would take care of her. "Somehow," he whispered, "somehow I will make something happen so that we can be together, be married. I will, Miriam. I promise you I will do everything I can . . ."

She leaned toward him and touched his lips with hers. Then, twining her arms around his neck, she clung to him as he lifted her into the bed, pulling him down to her. For a long while he kissed her, warmed her with his body hovering over hers. She had been shivering when they came into the flat, but now she felt drowsy and warm. He slipped from the bed, quickly stripped his clothes off, and slid beneath the thick eiderdown next to her.

Just one lamp in the far corner of the room sent shadows across the ceiling. He could hear the traffic beyond the windows, and wondered how life could be going on normally out there on the streets and boulevards, behind the walls and windows of houses and apartment buildings. How could people be laughing and eating and drinking, sitting in theaters and cafés, listening to radios, climbing into taxis, walking on the boulevards? But then the softness of her body curling against his pushed the cruel reality away.

He touched her throat and then her breasts, kissed her mouth, breathing the loveliness of her skin, a faintly musky odor floating through the perfumed surface. He felt her hand slipping down the hard curve of his thigh, instinctively sliding inward. For long, long minutes they explored, learning each other's bodies together, kissing softly, their mouths demanding more and more.

In the dim light, he looked down at her for a moment. Her eyes were closed and her lips were parted as her head arched back. The bareness of her shoulders made him lower his head and softly kiss the pulse at her throat. But her impatience grew. Her lips searched for his, her hands crept over his flesh. She felt the rush of his passion and she cried aloud as he swept her along with him. Her body, filled with sensations she had never experienced before, arched toward his. All barriers had slid away, had disappeared in the wildness of their love-making. When it ended, she cried out again, and he moaned—moaned with the exquisite pleasure she had brought him and with the love he felt for her.

They slept a little, enmeshed, their bodies tangled and warm and wearily content. Then, always touching, reaching out to each other every few moments, they dressed and left the flat. At the corner of the street he found a taxi and instructed the driver to follow the little car. It was almost three o'clock in the morning when they reached the road that led to her house in Spandau. While the taxi waited, he held her in his arms, and kissed her, whispering, "We'll get out, Miriam. Somehow we'll get out. Just let me think how to do it." She was clutching his hand.

"Yes, darling," she said through the darkness, and he heard the trust and belief in her voice.

"Meet me at the café tomorrow night, and we'll talk of what we will do." Their fingers were just touching. He looked up and saw lights on the second floor. Her mother would be frightened, wondering where her daughter was. Another light on the first floor told him that Gunther Blaumberg was pacing the floor of his library.

"Tomorrow night," she whispered.

Nodding, he stepped back and closed the door on her automobile. For a moment there was just the soft purr of the motor, and then she drove on, around the curving drive where it disappeared beyond the far side of the house. He looked into the darkness for several seconds before running toward the taxi in the road.

Karl arrived even earlier than usual at the factory. He went directly to Joachim Schering's small office and knocked several times.

"Yes?" the foreman's voice said on the other side of the door.

Karl pushed the door open and Schering waved him in, his big round face breaking into a smile, the heavy head of gray hair nodding affably. "Come in, come in, Karl." He had been sitting in his dark work clothes at his desk looking at several large sheets of paper spread out before him, sheets that indicated where everyone was working, and when, on the three new shifts that had gone into effect.

"Sit down," he said, at first busy pouring coffee from a large Thermos on his desk and pushing the cup across to Karl, then slowly looking up at Karl and leaning closer to stare into the younger man's face. "You are here very early." He became alarmed on seeing the haggard, weary expression, the wildness in his eyes.

"The . . . new decree. You were with us when we heard." Karl spoke with heavy dread. "The Nuremberg Laws. About the"—he almost whispered it—"Jews."

Schering was nodding his head. His eyes flashed angrily, and he peered hard at Karl. "Calm yourself, Karl. Drink some coffee."

Karl had rushed to the factory, eager and anxious to talk to the man who had questioned him so suspiciously on how he felt about Jews months earlier, angrily denouncing the Nazi thugs, as he called them, telling in a low voice what he had heard about concentration camps and the Gestapo. But suddenly, Karl pulled back a little, unsure. Other Germans that he knew and called friends, that he admired and trusted, simply threw up their hands when deploring the direction that Germany was heading, saying, Yes, we know, but what can we do?

"All right, you have something you want to say to me, Karl, so say it."

"This changes nothing in my feelings for her," Karl said haltingly. "More than ever . . . I care more than ever."

"Yes, I can see that you do," Schering said with a slight smile. "A nice girl." He waggled his head. "A bit high-spirited. But a nice girl. And it is obvious she cares for you." He suddenly stopped, and his eyes became grave. "Yes. The Nuremberg Laws. The Jews are now *subjects,* no longer citizens, and intermarriage is *verboten.* But this is only the beginning. When I heard . . ." He was shaking his head worriedly. "All I could think was 'What will happen to Teltow Fabrik? What will happen to Gunther Blaumberg and the factory?' Poor Blaumberg, I was thinking, it will probably mean he will lose the factory." He looked around him as though seeing beyond the walls of the cramped office and small sooty window. He looked back at Karl. "I hadn't thought about you and Fräulein Blaumberg. I wasn't sure how—"

"I still want to marry her, Joachim," Karl said, leaning across the desk, hands clenched around the coffee cup. "And I want to take her away."

"Away?"

"To Lidice. To Czechoslovakia."

Schering stared at him. "To Czechoslovakia," he repeated, as though weighing the possibility and finding it dismal.

"Do you understand what I am saying?" Karl's voice was low and urgent and filled with wariness.

"Yes, I understand." Schering slowly nodded his head. His eyes were darting about as though he might see something that would give him a clue as to a solution. "It would be . . . difficult."

"But possible?"

"Perhaps." Schering stood up and walked to the small window, where he stooped a little in order to look out. Without turning around, he said, "For you, it would be nothing. You would simply get onto a train, show your papers at the border, and travel on. For the fräulein, it would not be possible. They would take her from the train and—"

"Yes, I know, I know," Karl said impatiently. "But there has to be some way I can get her out. I thought you could help me, would know someone who would know what to do."

For a long moment, they were both silent, while Schering kept on looking out the window and Karl leaned toward him eagerly. When the older man slowly turned around and sat down again, Karl leaned even closer, arms resting on the desk.

"You know Straubing?" When Karl shook his head, he continued softly. "A small town in Bavaria. Near the Czech border, beyond Regensburg on the right bank of the Danube, at the edge of the Bohemian Forest." A grim smile touched the corners of his mouth. "Where it is, at this moment, easiest to cross the border. I have a brother there. He and his friends . . . they sometimes help others to cross—"

148

"I've saved enough money to pay people."

"He will take no money!" Schering's eyes flashed. And then he nodded. "But—well, there are others he must pay. At the border itself." He rose once more, walked to the small window, and peered out. "I am driving to see my brother come Saturday, leaving very early that morning, because it is a long trip, more than four hundred kilometers. It will take the full day."

Karl was smiling. He knew Joachim had made the decision that very moment.

"If you could have Fräulein Blaumberg here at the factory before dawn that morning—"

"We will be here." Karl was standing, eager.

"I will telephone my brother, to tell him we are coming."

Karl crossed to him and grasped his hand. "There aren't any words to say what I want to—"

"Then say nothing." Schering smiled. He patted Karl's shoulder. "There are some of us—not many, I am afraid—but some of us who care what happens." He sighed deeply. "This will go, you understand." He gestured around him. "Into other hands. Herr Blaumberg will be removed."

Karl nodded, anger narrowing his eyes. "When is it going to stop?"

"I am not so optimistic as those few who think it will stop here and go no further. And, of course, there are the others, the large numbers who think he is a great man because he is solving our social problems. They look over at England and see that they still have many unemployed, and they point here and say, 'See? See what he has done?' Because it is convenient, they choose to forget the Jews." He led Karl to the door, just as the factory whistle blew. "After I have talked with my brother, I will speak with you again."

Karl nodded, clasped his friend's hand again, and hurried out. Schering watched him, slowly shaking his head, then turned back into the office and picked up the telephone.

It had been dark for fully an hour when they began to see the lights of Straubing. Miriam stirred on Karl's shoulder as he gently shook her. Joachim Schering had borrowed a small truck for the trip from the factory pool of vehicles. "Less suspicious-looking," he had explained to Karl, "than my own automobile, in case we meet any road blocks or are stopped for any reason." As a precautionary measure, he had sent a truckload of machinery to Straubing two days before, the driver instructed to take two different routes on going and returning, then to report to Schering on whether he had encountered any difficulty. At one point, the driver said, near Bayreuth at the small town of Bindlach, he had seen a disturbance on the main road. Two carloads of SS in their black uniforms had been herding some people from a house and were stopping automobiles as they passed.

"Rasse-und Siedlungsamt," Schering muttered to Karl just as they started out before dawn the morning after the driver gave him his report.

"What does that mean?" Karl asked.

"It means," Miriam said slowly, "the SS Race and Settlement Service." She was sitting between them in the half darkness of the small truck, the faint aroma of her perfume reminding Schering of why they were there. He looked down at her profile in the dim light and for a moment he thought of his own daughter, the long dark hair and sharp, pretty features.

"It has gone that far already?" Karl expressed shock.

"Oh, yes," Schering said, his voice deeply sarcastic, as he turned sharply onto a dark road leading southeast from the city.

"Herr Himmler's SS Order of Teutonic Knights has come far in just two years. He has managed to take command of the political police in most of the states and now has his secret group, the Gestapo, as well as separate branches for different tasks, security, protection, race, and settlement—and one called Totenkopf Verbände, which we suspect guards the concentration camps."

"You know this for a fact?" Miriam exclaimed, and Karl knew that thoughts of her parents and Max were in her mind.

"There is a place called Dachau that Himmler established at least two years ago. For *political prisoners.*" They could see Schering's grim smile in the faint light from the dashboard.

As Miriam shivered, she felt Karl's hand clasp her shoulder, his arm around her. They had left her parents, standing in their warm robes in the library of the house in front of a crackling fire that Gunther had lit to take a chill off the room. Miriam had gone first to her father and then her mother.

"Just knowing you will be safe . . . and happy . . . is enough for me," Mala said in a broken voice, her fingers deep in Miriam's hair as they held each other closely, then touching her face as they pulled apart. Without looking back, Miriam had run from the room, while Karl solemnly shook hands with them both. He watched as Gunther pulled a white envelope from the pocket of his robe and handed it to him.

"Go to America, Karl. Take Miriam to America. There is where she will be safe." He glanced nervously toward the door where she had disappeared. "I did not want her to hear this. But I fear for what will happen here, for all of Europe." He tapped the white envelope that Karl was now holding. "Keep this safe. It is a letter to a man in America. An aircraft factory there that he controls. I have asked him to give you a position. We have done business with this company—"

Karl slipped it into his pocket, nodding, and turned to Miriam's mother. Tears came to his eyes when Mala Blaumberg pulled him to her and kissed both of his cheeks. Then he, too, had hurried from the room out to the graveled driveway where Max waited with his car to drive them to the factory. "I love her very much" was the last thing he had said to them.

"They will be all right, Miriam," Karl reassured her softly, while feeling just the opposite. "The Reich needs your father, it needs Teltow Fabrik." Although his voice sounded convincing, he knew differently. But when he felt her head resting on his shoulder once more, he felt certain he had alleviated her fears, at least for the time being.

Joachim Schering's brother, Horst, had a house on the outskirts of Straubing. It was a small farm of just a few acres, where he and his wife, Irma, kept some chickens and a cow, and grew vegetables. The house was small, quaint, of stucco and timber. It nestled in a grove of trees by a brook that ran down from heavily forested hills to the east. Horst was almost an exact copy of his brother, but a little younger, his big square face leathery from the outdoors, kindly gray eyes peering from beneath bushy eyebrows. His wife was apple-cheeked and plain-looking but smiled with a constancy that made Miriam and Karl feel welcome and at ease. First she fed them large quantities of sauerbraten and dumplings, and then, while Horst led Karl and Joachim to the loft over the barn where they would sleep, she tucked Miriam into bed in a tiny room off the kitchen.

"Horst will waken your young man before dawn," she said with her dazzling smile. "I will come for you, and soon after Horst will start you on your journey."

As the door closed, Miriam shivered a little in the darkness. *Start you on your journey.* It had such an ominous sound. Horst had explained that he would take them through the foothills and forests in his small truck, as far as the rutted narrow roads would permit, and then they would all proceed by foot into the mountains, where they would be met by two guides who would continue with Karl and Miriam. But soon her eyes grew heavy. It had been a long day. She snuggled into the eiderdown quilt and soon was fast asleep.

They said goodbye to Joachim in the warm kitchen where the hearth blazed. The aroma of strong coffee and home-cooked food had made Miriam hungrier than usual.

"Good! Eat all you can," Horst said. "You will need hot food in you." Karl stood in the doorway and watched Joachim's truck pull away, then walked back to the table, a sad expression on his face. Joachim had been a good friend and he would never see him again. But then, his farewell to Anton two days before had been even sadder. They had stood in the high-ceilinged living room of their flat in Berlin, hugging each other.

"Take her far away, Karl," Anton had said. "Who knows what will happen. The Nazis will swallow all of Europe, if they can." And Karl had then felt the knot of fear. Perhaps he would never see Anton again, either.

"Come!" Horst Schering said, as he rose from the table. "We want to be on our way before it gets light."

They said goodbye to the smiling Irma and walked to the truck, carrying their heavy outer clothing. It was still the warm days of autumn, but they knew it would get cold in the mountains.

The sun was just rising as they drove into the foothills. The forests closed around them as they climbed, the small truck chugging faithfully upward. Shards of sunlight burst through the thick canopy of trees overhead. At times they drove out from the trees onto high grassy plains where young boys and girls herded sheep and cows ahead of them, waving as they passed, their shepherd dogs racing around the herd, frantically barking.

They stopped by a stream to eat the bread and cheese that Irma had packed for them, and were on their way again, plunging into deep forests, then riding high on the green plateaus where tiny villages or farmhouses dozed in the sunlight.

When the afternoon began to fade, they stopped by an abandoned sawmill, where a narrow stream leaped down from the range of mountain peaks that loomed above them. Horst drove the truck to the far side where it would not be seen from the road, and they got out and stretched.

"This is where I will be leaving you," he said, and they both looked at him with apprehension. He smiled. "Oh, but not until Willi arrives." He looked at his watch. "He should be here soon."

Karl dug into his pocket and pulled out an envelope. He handed it to Horst. With curiosity, he asked, "Why will Willi take this money, but not you?"

Horst glanced at him sharply. "Willi doesn't keep it for himself. It is for bribes. He knows who will take money and who will not. There are those he pays to stay away from a certain place at a certain time."

"I see," Karl said softly. "I didn't understand."

Horst grinned. "There are two kinds of riches. We prefer this kind, knowing someone has beat them at their game." He suddenly raised his hand in a wave and they saw a young man striding toward them across the back meadow. He was tow-headed and square, and had a pack on his back, with a rifle slung across it. The introductions were hurried, and in moments they were waving goodbye to Horst and were following Willi back across the meadow toward the thick woods on the other side.

They had trudged upward for perhaps an hour before Willi stopped and told them to take a short rest. Karl had put all of their belongings into one large pack that he had strapped on his back. This meant Miriam had had to leave behind several pretty dresses and pairs of shoes at Irma and Horst's small house, but now, as she sat on a fragrant mound of pine needles, she was glad. Both she and Karl were breathing heavily from the climb.

"I've gotten too used to city ways," Karl said with soft laughter as he caught his breath.

For the first time Willi smiled. "Well, this is only the beginning. We have a long way to go before we settle down for the night." He grinned when Miriam groaned and rubbed her feet. She had taken off her sturdy walking shoes to pull up the sagging wool stockings Karl had insisted she wear. "Don't worry," he said with reassurance. "You are both doing much better than most I take this way. They are almost always older and always tell me they can go no farther."

"And do they?" Karl asked.

"Yes," Willi said, smiling. "They always do."

In moments they went on. By nightfall, after stumbling upward for the last half hour, Miriam collapsed onto the ground when Willi halted.

"You did well," Willi said softly as he stood over her. "We got much farther than usual." He turned then and trudged on beyond a short distance, up to a crest where he looked around. Karl watched him. He could see in the dim light that they were in a pass. After a few moments, when Willi waved his arm, they joined him.

"We will stay here for the night," he said. "This way I can see along the trail in both directions." He pointed off to the side, toward a thicket of trees. "Up in there, not more than one hundred steps, you will find a small hut. You can sleep there." As they straggled off in the direction he had pointed, he said, "I'll waken you while it is still dark."

In the hut, by a small flashlight, they ate more of the bread and cheese and drank some wine, then, holding each other close on a narrow shelf that was covered with hay, they fell into an exhausted sleep. Sometime during the long night, she wakened. Karl was kissing her, his hands softly caressing her. They had just fallen asleep again when they woke with a start upon hearing Willi's voice calling them from the door. They washed their faces in a small nearby stream, munched on some biscuits and drank cold coffee, and started on their way again, pushing through the silence and darkness on stiff legs.

After about an hour, Willi paused ahead of them, and pointed upward to a line where they could see daylight edging a formation of rock against the sky. It was at the top of the long mountain pass they had been climbing. "I won't be going past that point," he said. "Beyond there, it is Czechoslovakia. Another guide will take you on from there. Wait here." They watched him walk up the long sloping narrow pass. At the top he stood for several moments looking down on the other side. And then he waved to them to follow him. They hurried upward, eagerly, half running. "Czechoslovakia . . ." Karl heard Miriam say. "Oh, Karl, I can't believe it."

He heard the shots and looked up to the right side on the steep walls of the pass. Painted vividly on his mind's eye, for then and all time to come in his lifetime, were the silhouettes of two men against the dawn-gray sky, submachine guns pointed down and firing. And then in a split second he saw Miriam lunge ahead, upward, arms outstretched as though she would reach for freedom. In the narrow pants and wool jacket she looked like a slim boy running up a hillside after a kite, her long dark hair pushed inside a knitted cap. When shots rang out again, he was running toward her, but he saw her fall, just as more shots exploded. These came from below, fired at the men standing up above. He saw Willi, with his back shoved hard against the side of the rock formation and his rifle cocked upward, and he heard the sounds of gunfire repeating over and over.

Karl had fallen—thrown himself—over Miriam's body, while still looking up. The silhouettes had disappeared, but one body tumbled down the side of the steep wall and rolled to stillness not more than twenty feet away from him, the dark gray uniform and shining boots sprawled across the narrow path, face downward.

Willi ran to Karl in a low silent lope and saw that Karl had turned Miriam gently onto her back. He was holding her in his arms, murmuring her name over and over.

Willi pushed him back a little and first put his ear to her breast, then held her pulse for several moments. He looked up at Karl and sadly shook his head. "She's dead," he said. "Come. You must go."

Not waiting for an answer, Willi quickly climbed up the side of the canyon-like pass, holding onto the scrubby bushes, pulling himself upward until he reached the top. He stood there for several moments, looking down at something, then slid back down to the bottom again, where he pulled the body of the other soldier into a thicket nearby.

He turned to Karl again, as dawn lightened the sky, and stared at him. Karl had lifted her body and was walking across the crest of the pass and had started down the other side.

"You've got to leave her," Willi called out. But Karl stumbled on. He watched him for a moment, then slowly followed. He would take him at least to the bottom of the pass.

11
1938

"You can pick me up at Saks at four, Karl," Elizabeth said. She watched the stream of traffic ahead on Fifth Avenue, glanced at her wristwatch, and squashed her Camel out in the ashtray. "I think you'd better let me out at this corner. I'll get to my appointment more quickly if I walk."

"I'm sorry, Mrs. Kendall," he said, looking over his shoulder. The glass partition was down between the front and the rear of the limousine, the way she always wanted it. She liked to talk to him while they were driving anywhere.

"Don't apologize, Karl. It's not your fault." She laughed. "But the next time I see Mayor LaGuardia at a dinner, I'm going to tell him what I think of his traffic jams."

When the long car slid up to the corner, she opened the door herself.

"Don't get out, Karl. See you at four."

He watched her for a moment as she whirled away from the Rolls, her fur coat swinging loose. When he passed the intersection, he raised his hand and smiled at her. All the way down from Kendall Hills she had been asking probing questions.

"I don't want to pry, Karl. Just tell me to mind my own business if I ask too many questions, but Ellie tells me you were studying electrical engineering in Germany. Why don't you continue it here?"

"Well, learning to speak and read in English has taken much of my time," he said, without looking back at her, but he glanced in the rear-view mirror to see if she was watching. How could he tell her it had taken this long to try and pull his life together again? There was

156

no way he could speak of these things except to Ellie and he had sworn her to secrecy after she finally got him to unburden himself to her. Only Ellie in this new country knew about Miriam. He couldn't bear to talk to anyone else about what had happened.

"I've said this before, of course, Karl, but I'm going to keep saying it. Mr. Kendall said there's a job for you anytime you want it in the aircraft factory that Kendall, Inc., owns up in Connecticut."

He turned quickly with a smile, then looked at the road again. They were traveling down the Bronx River Parkway. The sun was welcome in this middle part of February after a long, dreary winter.

"Well, I think I may be almost ready, Mrs. Kendall. I feel my English is almost good enough to—"

"Your English is fine," she said quickly. "I told Ellie this morning that you have no more excuses."

Ellie. How patient she had been with him, he thought, and how wise. For a long time, it had simply been a warm friendship. She had encouraged him to go to night school, and they had gone together down to the high school in Rijksville. Even when the family was living in the city, he and Ellie would drive out to Rijksville. Mr. Kendall had told them they could use one of the cars. After their class, they usually would stop in at the coffee-shop across the street. Several times, they even went into a little bar and restaurant, like the bistros in Europe. They had talked for hours one night, the story of what had happened to Miriam spilling out in a torrent of words after a few glasses of wine. Ellie had tried to comfort him, but she had known, too, that it was something that would take time. Much time. Then one evening, when they walked out of the little bar and climbed into the car, he had turned and taken her in his arms and kissed her. After a few moments, he had pulled away from her and stared through the windshield into the darkness. His hands were clenched on the steering wheel.

"I—I'm sorry, Ellie."

"No, Karl, don't say that."

"But I—I don't know how I feel about you."

"It's all right," she had said softly. "It doesn't matter if you know or not. What matters is that you are feeling *something* again." He had started the car, and all during the long ride back into Manhattan neither of them spoke. And yet it wasn't a stiff, uncomfortable silence. It was warm, filled with the flood of understanding that he had heard in her voice. That night as he lay in his bed, looking up at the play of light and shadow on his ceiling, he realized that he needed her, and yes, loved her. But *in* love with her? It was different from the way he had loved Miriam. That had been young love, filled with anguish and frantic touching, drowned in unbearable excitement and the torment of separation. This was quiet and comforting, like the flow of a river. Slowly he realized that the terrible emptiness was gone, the tortured memories were fading. Two evenings later, as they drove back to New York, he told her that he wanted to marry her.

She wanted to reach out through the half darkness and touch him, but she hesitated. He had glanced at her and smiled when he saw the answer on her face, in the tremulous smile, the eyes swimming with happiness.

"You are very beautiful, Ellie," he had said softly, holding her chin with one hand. For a brief instant she had seen a small smile.

They were married that June, in 1937. Begging Elizabeth to keep their secret until they returned from a brief honeymoon, they had been married at City Hall with only Elizabeth and Nanny Grace there, driving on to the Kendall ski lodge in Vermont, where Elizabeth had insisted they stay. They arrived late that night and went to the small guest house behind the sprawling lodge, which sat halfway up the mountain. It was a chilly night. In minutes Karl had a fire crackling in the fireplace and Ellie had made coffee to go with the chicken sandwiches they had stopped to buy in the village below. They sat on cushions before the fire, while Karl opened the champagne Elizabeth had put in a wicker hamper in the car.

"To you," he said softly, raising his glass to her. "For giving my life meaning again."

"To us," she whispered, her eyes shining. And then because she couldn't bear not to say it, she said, "I love you, Karl."

She saw the flicker of pain cross his face. It was gone, almost as quickly as she saw it, and he turned to her and smiled, again raising his glass. "Let's drink to—to a long life."

"Yes," she said, raising her glass as well, smiling to hide the hurt. "To a long life."

An hour later, she went up the stairs to the small bedroom beneath the eaves, undressed slowly, and climbed into the big, high bed. He had put on a jacket and had gone outside. "To get some air," he had said.

She had left a small light on in the corner of the room and now she stared up to the dark beams across the white plaster ceiling that sloped down into the eaves of the roof. It was all so perfect, she thought, remembering how the firelight had reflected in the wide glass wall that looked down over the valley, how it had played against the pine walls and low chintz-covered couches and chairs. She had felt tingling and warm from the champagne, and had listened closely as Karl talked about Lidice and how they always gathered around the fireplace to talk and laugh and sing. She had wanted to reach out and touch him, wanted to say "I love you" again. But an emptiness had formed a barrier between them.

She turned her head, suddenly hearing soft footsteps on the stairs and then coming along the hallway. They paused outside, and her heart stopped. He came into the room and she saw him stand in the doorway for a moment, filling it with his broad shoulders. She lay perfectly still as he slowly undressed, and when he slid beneath the sheet and quilt, she held her breath. He had turned off the light, and in the darkness she could hear his soft breathing.

"Karl," she whispered, putting out her hand to touch him. He turned to her, slowly pulled her into his arms, and began to kiss her, his mouth gentle . . . but something held him back. When she felt him start to pull away a little, she crept up against him and wound her arms about his neck.

"It doesn't matter," she said softly. "I—I know how you feel, how hard it is for you. But, I love you, Karl . . ." She was curving in against him and was kissing his eyelids, her lips soft but seeking. Suddenly, when her mouth reached his, he pulled her hard against him and, with a groan that was like a sob, kissed her almost savagely. It was as though dikes had opened and the flood had burst through. With an unleashed wildness, his hands were roaming her body and he was kissing her with a hunger that almost frightened her.

"Karl," she cried, gasping and struggling beneath him.

"Oh, my God," he said. "Oh, my God, Ellie." It was a cry, and he was holding her close. She felt his tears on her cheek and on her bare shoulder. She touched his face, pushed the blond hair back from his forehead, and let her lips run across his eyes.

"It's all right," she whispered. "It's all right, my darling."

When he kissed her again, it was with a gentleness that grew slowly in intensity, that pulled her with him as though he were leading her by the hand. His touch was reverent at first, then explored her flesh with his careful but growing need. And she answered him, her fingers flicking over his body, her mouth yielding against his, his hand moving down the soft bare skin of her back.

"Ellie, Ellie . . ." he murmured, and she felt the solid, smooth flesh and muscle of his body as he slid onto her, felt the heat of his mouth, the soaring excitement as he thrust within her. Their hunger swept them on and on as though caught in a tide. Only their bodies were real, only their mouths and hands and flesh had meaning. Lost in a reeling passion, she drifted as it slowly ebbed in a series of sensations, leaving her with tears on her lashes and his lips whispering against her throat.

"I love you, Ellie." And she smiled into the darkness. "I didn't know . . . didn't believe it could happen again . . . but I love you, Ellie."

He smiled as he waited for another traffic light at the corner of Forty-sixth Street. It was strange . . . almost as though he had lived two completely different and separate lives. He would never forget Miriam, and yet . . . he couldn't imagine his life without Ellie. Even if he had only been away from her for a day, or an hour . . . a half hour . . . when he saw her again, something glowed inside. It was like the lifting of a bird's wings. When their eyes met, everything else fell away.

He parked the car on Forty-third Street and walked up the wide steps of the public library. His footsteps echoed through the huge cavernous hall. He picked up the book he had requested at the counter, one on electrical control panel design, and took it into a reading room. Just as he slipped into a chair, he looked up sharply. A young woman was passing who reminded him of Miriam. He watched her until she disappeared, her high heels tapping softly on the floor.

He opened the book, but his mind wandered. In a small village at the foot of the mountain, just inside the Czechoslovakian border, he had found people who helped him. He had brought her body there in a farmer's wagon, and from there he had taken her to Lidice in a truck. He had tried to hire it, but the owner, who drove him, had refused the money. With his parents and brother Josef standing beside him, he buried her there.

For a week he stayed in Lidice, watching the autumn leaves flutter down in a swirl of red and gold. And then when the blue faded from the sky and a canopy of gray spread from horizon to horizon, he left.

"I have to go, Mama," he had whispered as she stood next to him where he looked out the window. "Somewhere far far away, where I can try to forget."

And she had nodded. She understood.

* * *

Elizabeth closed the door of the doctor's waiting room. She walked along the corridor toward the elevators. So far, all of the tests she had taken over the past year had revealed no problem. There was no reason to believe she couldn't become pregnant.

"Darling," Lawrence had teased her. "Give it time." Just the night before he had held her close, ruffled her hair in the shadowy light of their bedroom, and laughed softly. "You want everything at once." He was above her, holding her face between his hands. "It doesn't matter," he was whispering between soft, searching kisses. "We have each other. We don't need anything else."

"But I want a child," she cried out softly, fiercely. "I want *your* child."

"All right . . ." Again that sensuously whispering voice, the hard, muscular body pressing down on hers. His mouth was teasing the skin on her throat, while his fingers traced circles—smaller and smaller—on her breast. And then he was lying next to her. He had slid her gown over her head and pulled her against him, against the hard, flat contours of his body. The fires that he had kindled were spreading and she threw back her head with a soft husky moan.

"Tonight," she had whispered. "Maybe tonight . . ."

She pushed the elevator button and waited. She had smiled at Dr. Fitzgerald and said, "You and Lawrence. He says the same thing. 'Give it time, Elizabeth.'" She picked up her pocketbook and then looked up at him. "We're leaving for Europe tomorrow. Lawrence will be involved with business there for about a month." Dr. Fitzgerald was holding out the sable coat for her to slip into. "Maybe when I get back—"

Dr. Fitzgerald nodded with a smile. "A great love match," his wife had told him just a week or so earlier. She read all the gossip columns and told him that Winchell had written that they were the great love match of the decade, second only to King Edward and Wally Simpson. "When Lawrence Robertson Kendall, one of the richest men in the world, married the beautiful 21-year-old New York debutante, Elizabeth Stuart," Winchell wrote, "it was front-page news on almost every newspaper throughout the world, the kind of coverage that is usually only accorded kings and princes, sons of Presidents, and Clark Gable."

The smile had slowly faded from her face. "Lawrence, as you know, has other children by his first marriage. But—it's not the same. I want one of my own."

"I understand," Dr. Fitzgerald said, taking his glasses off to polish them. He stood behind his desk in his white coat, watching her leave. She was his last patient for the afternoon, before he made his final rounds at the hospital.

Elizabeth walked to Madison Avenue, where she remembered having seen a small tearoom. It was getting colder. The sun had slid behind the buildings and lights were beginning to come on. She had three-quarters of an hour before Karl would pick her up at the Fifth Avenue entrance of Saks, time enough for a cup of tea.

She sat by a window and watched the traffic, slowly stirring her tea. She had never realized until this moment how desperately she wanted a baby. She recalled how she had scorned Dr. Fitzgerald's suggestion that he fit her for a diaphragm when she went to him for her blood tests and examination before she was married.

"Why?" she had asked him, looking up at him from the examination table, her feet still in the stirrups and the nurse rearranging the white sheet over her.

"So that you won't immediately become pregnant," he said with surprise, wondering that she would even ask such a silly question. He was a tall, scholarly-looking, stoop-shouldered man with a kindly, grandfatherly face and white hair.

"But I would *love* to get pregnant right away," she said, peering at him over the expanse of white sheeting.

"Yes, well, I suppose . . ." He let it drift off and bent to continue his examination. When you're married to someone who is rumored to be worth billions, it wouldn't make much difference about sleepless nights and bottles and diapers and teething rings and all that sort of thing, he was thinking. Even though his practice was fairly well limited to the Park Avenue and Fifth Avenue crowd, many of his mothers still had a nursery right next door to their bedroom, and the nursemaid was given one or two nights off a week. Elizabeth Kendall's nurse-maid would probably have an assistant who would have her *own* assistant.

"In fact, we *both* would love it," she had said. "Lawrence said he would adore having a little girl. He has all boys, you know, from his first marriage."

He had looked at her, marveling. Was this the same young girl who had first been brought to the office eight or nine years earlier, when he had prescribed a hot-water bottle and aspirin for her menstrual cramps?

"Elizabeth, Elizabeth," he had said softly.

"Dear Dr. Fitzgerald," she had said, sitting up and touching his cheek.

She smiled, while sitting in the tearoom window, thinking about how Dr. Fitzgerald occasionally talked to her as though she were still fourteen years old.

Well, she thought with a sigh, picking up her check and shrugging into her coat, she would stop talking about it. She was driving every-one crazy with her endless babble of wanting a baby. Even the doctor looked bored. She paid her bill, hurried outside to flag down a taxi, and arrived at the side door of Saks with just enough time to select some ties for Lawrence and a purse for Ellie's birthday, and get to the front entrance where Karl was waiting with the car.

"Drive over to Broadway, Karl," she said. She loosened the collar on her coat, pulled off her gloves, and lit a cigarette. "We're picking up my sister-in-law. She's at the opera house signing her contracts for next season."

"And then will we be picking Mr. Kendall up?"

"No. You will have to drive back for him later, I'm afraid. With our leaving tomorrow, he'll be tied up until well after nine o'clock tonight. That's why we'll be staying in town until we leave."

"Mrs. Kendall," Karl said hesitantly, glancing into the rear-view mirror. "Ellie made me promise not to ask you this. But it's no use. I must."

"What is it, Karl?" She looked at him curiously.

"Ellie—well, she's pregnant." He blurted it out.

"Ellie's pregnant?" Elizabeth pushed down one of the small jump seats in front of her and slid forward onto it so that she could lean on the partition. "Oh, Karl, how wonderful."

"She didn't want you to know yet because she said she didn't want to disappoint you about going with you tomorrow, and she felt if you knew you wouldn't let her go."

"Of course she can't go!" Elizabeth was ecstatic. "Oh, Karl, I'm so happy for you. When is the baby due?"

"In the summer," he said. "August."

"I never guessed." She slapped her hand on the partition. "Damn, why didn't I guess?"

He laughed. "She said she tried to avoid you in the mornings. She gets morning sickness."

She leaned across the partition a little way. "You go home to her tonight, Karl, and keep her there at Kendall Hills. You can send Meacham back to pick Mr. Kendall up."

When she slid back onto the rear seat again, she laughed. "And if she argues with you about it, you can tell her I can do without her morning sickness."

He smiled at her through the mirror. "I knew you would understand."

But through her happiness for Ellie and Karl, she felt a quick pang of envy. Knowing Ellie, she knew that was a large part of the reason she had delayed in telling her. Oh, Ellie, she thought with a hint of tears pressing at her eyelids, you crazy girl. After myself, I couldn't want it for anyone else more.

12

Elizabeth stood at one of the long windows gazing out to the Place de la Concorde, sipping her coffee. She was dressed for travel, the cocoa brown suit gracefully hugging her slenderness, the tiny brown hat and veil perched over her nose, gloves and purse and sable coat on a chair near the door. Her cocoa suede suitcases with the gold initials stood beside the door, ready to be taken downstairs.

When he came up behind her and encircled her with his arms, she leaned her head back and nestled it against him, loving the feel of him close to her, the fresh fragrance of his shaving lotion, the soft whispering in her ear. They had been in Paris for only a few days, after a week in London. When they first walked into the lobby of the Hotel de Crillon three days before, Lawrence had raised his hand for a newspaper. All through the day and into the evening, ever since first docking at Southampton, he called for newspapers, scanning the headlines, carefully reading the stories.

"Schuschnigg has resigned?" Lawrence said to the concierge, with a worried lift of his eyebrow.

"If one can call it *resignation,* Mr. Kendall," the concierge said. "German troops are at the Austrian border."

"Lebensraum," Lawrence murmured as he scanned the lead story of the *International Herald Tribune.* "Hitler says that Germany deserves this living space more than any other people."

He had slapped the newspaper down onto the concierge's desk and turned to sign the register. Ever since, it seemed that he talked of nothing else. The night before, he decided she would have to return to New York. When she protested, his mouth simply tightened and he took her arm. They were walking across the lobby of the opera house and, as he led her through the crowd, his grasp on her arm tightened. Their limousine had pulled up in front in the Place de l'Opéra, and he helped her into it. During the intermission, he had told an acquaintance he had spotted that they might join him and his party later at the nearby Café de la Paix. But when he tersely instructed the driver to take them to the Hotel de Crillon, she knew he had dismissed the idea.

As they turned onto the Rue Royale, he said, "I caught a glimpse of a newspaper earlier. The Reich army is marching into Austria at this moment."

"Oh, no," Elizabeth exclaimed. She gazed unseeingly at the passing shop windows.

Lawrence kept shaking his head. He had taken off the tall opera hat and was holding it in his hands, turning it round and round by the brim. "Without even so much as a shot." He turned to her and put his arm about her. "I want you to leave immediately for the States."

"But you?"

"I'll follow you just as soon as I can."

She boarded the *President Roosevelt* at Le Havre, hoping against hope right up until the last moment that she would receive word to return to Paris or to meet Lawrence in London. Or even that he would clear up his business and be on his way to Le Havre.

But, in her heart, she knew that none of these things was a probability. Once Lawrence made up his mind about something like this, nothing was liable to change it.

It was a midnight sailing. For a very short while, Elizabeth stood at the rail on deck, her fur coat clutched about her against the cold March wind, watching the lights of the port city float away. Her departure had been so abrupt that she felt part of her was still back in Paris. A call had come for Lawrence just as they were sitting down in their suite for breakfast, a call from the Paris offices of Kendall, Inc. A cable had arrived from New York informing him of an all-night roll call in the House of Representatives on a bill dealing with readjusted rates and schedules for corporation taxes. He had held her closely for a brief moment.

"The car will take you to Le Havre," he said briskly, while shrugging into the coat the valet was holding out for him. He crossed to her again, holding his hat, and kissed her. "I'm sorry about this, darling, but the trouble in Austria and now this House bill—it's all going to have an effect on the stock market. I'll follow you in a few days."

He was almost to the door when she called out, "Please, darling, let me wait for you—"

"No," he said. "Britain and France have made a public protest of Germany's march into Austria. There's no way of knowing what will happen. I want you back in New York."

"Please come with me," she begged, running across the drawing room of the suite toward him.

He quickly took hold of her hands and held her a little away from him. "Elizabeth," he said softly. "This isn't like you."

"I don't know why," she said, "but I feel afraid."

"You're leaving in plenty of time," he reassured her.

"It isn't that . . ."

Glancing quickly at his watch, he pulled her to him. "I have to go."

Although he still held her and she felt his arms around her, his lips against her hair, she knew he had already left her. She could almost see him striding through the marble-columned lobby, rushing past the Gobelin tapestries and priceless paintings, out onto the glittering Place de la Concorde where the limousine waited.

"Please come to Le Havre tonight." Her voice had a frantic note in it. He put both hands on either side of her face, kissed her, then gently pulled away from her.

"I'll only be a few days longer," he said, the door opening. "I'm stopping over in London for a day or two. I promised Charles McAlpin I would give him an interview when I was here next time."

And then he was gone.

She remembered this as she stood at the rail of the *President Roosevelt,* holding the broad collar of her coat up against her face. She had never felt this alone before. The wind was cold on her forehead and pulled at her hair. She looked up, but there were no stars, no moon. Nothing but a great black void stretching across the horizon. A bit startled, she realized with a suddenness that she had never been alone before. This was the first time. As a child, at camp, at school, there were always friends. And as she grew older, there was always someone, her mother, Aunt Vivian, her grandparents, Missy, her best friend from childhood.

She shivered, the loneliness settling on her like a mantle. She didn't even have Ellie. Ellie, who was more friend than maid.

With one last look at the fading lights of Le Havre, she turned and hurried inside, to soft lights and warmth, away from the lonely specter of a moonless black sky and the plunging sea.

She was standing on the boat deck in what seemed a bravely shining sun, pale and high and tempered by a brisk wind, when she heard a man's voice behind her. She had been watching the chop of whitecaps and looked back across her shoulder while leaning on the rail in her heavy gray and white tweed coat.

"It *is* Elizabeth Stuart, isn't it?"

She turned slowly until she was leaning back against the rail, trying to recognize the face beneath the billed uniform cap. Suddenly she remembered. "Why, I don't believe it! Glen Bassett." Her face broke into a wide smile and she put out her hand.

When he took her hand in his and held it, she felt a warm, hard clasp. "I saw the name on the passenger list this morning when I was going over it," he said, his smile matching hers. "Mrs. Lawrence Kendall. When I saw that, I thought, 'Good Lord, Elizabeth Stuart.'"

"But . . ."

"I read about your wedding in the newspapers." He took her arm and they started to slowly stroll along the deck.

"And you, Glen?" She pointed to his cap and the uniform. "You work for the United States Lines?"

"Purser," he said with a grin. "I guess I'd always wanted to go to sea. But what are you doing on the *President Roosevelt?* It isn't exactly—"

"It was the first ship that Lawrence could get me on after this dreadful thing in Austria." She smiled wryly. "And he insisted."

"I see by the passenger list that he is not with you?"

"He still had business in Paris." She turned to look at him, curious, and saw that he was as attractive as she remembered him. When he smiled down at her, she laughed softly, still disbelieving.

"Well, I knew you were probably headed for a better marriage than good old Gavin Armstead. But *Lawrence Kendall!* That's really starting at the top."

She looked up at him, trying to look annoyed, but laughing again. "You never were one to mince words, were you, Glen?"

They had dinner together, then sat in one of the smaller salons where a small trio played popular ballads. They danced, the low lights and soft music lulling them into a slowly swaying motion. They moved around the small floor as if in a dream. When she said it was time to leave, he walked her to her stateroom, held her hand briefly, and with great enthusiasm insisted they had to do it again the following night.

"I didn't realize how much I'd been missing," he said. "This run can get deadly boring." He grinned. "I should have looked for a pretty girl on each crossing. Of course, I'd never get this lucky again."

He stood there, straight and tall in his navy-blue uniform, gold buttons gleaming, his face wind-burned to an even tan beneath the dark-billed white hat, and she smiled as she pulled her hand from his. "It *was* fun, Glen. And thank you."

She closed the door and stood in the darkness for a moment, feeling the steady pulse of the ship, the fragrant warmth of the cabin enfolding her. When she moved toward a light, her taffeta dress rustled. She flicked on the switch and the lamp glowed toward the corners. Turning slowly, she looked in the full-length mirror for several moments, studying herself. She had worn the long red taffeta on purpose. It was bright and had a message. It looked *married.*

She smiled at her reflection, sleepily, and began to undress, warmth and drowsiness filling the emptiness she had felt the day before on the long ride from Paris to Le Havre, a desolate emptiness that had persisted through the first endless night.

At times through the next day, she caught a glimpse of Glen here and there. He joined her for a quick cup of coffee at breakfast, and while looking for a book in the sundries shop, she giggled as he put his head in the door and whistled in soft appreciation. Lunching with a couple she had just met from San Francisco, she waved back when he walked by and called out hello. And, after a late-afternoon game of shuffleboard, she saw him pass the purser's office, and nodded when he formed the words, "Will you have dinner with me?" He was interesting. Fun, she told herself. That was all.

They dined in the large salon on the top deck, near the wide expanses of plate glass that looked straight across the prow of the ship, toward the rolling sea that lay ahead of them. The sun was just setting and it seemed to hover on the far horizon, a fiery ball that flamed magnificently against the sky, then slowly sank into the water and disappeared, leaving fingers of red and gold reaching upward.

The martinis were perfectly chilled and biting, the beef bourguignon like nectar, the brandy warm and mellowing. They danced again in the small salon, almost reluctantly smiling their assent when an older couple from Boston, who had boarded the ship at Southampton, asked if they could join them at their table. Elizabeth left the table for several moments to "powder my nose," she said with a smile as she walked away. When she returned, they didn't see her skirting the small, crowded dance floor, and when she reached the table, she heard a scrap of conversation. The carefully marceled blue-gray head of Mrs. Lathrop of Boston was leaning toward her husband.

"But, Robert, didn't you say that was Mr. and Mrs. Lawrence Kendall you pointed out to me in the bar at the Savoy night before last, when we heard him say to that reporter from *Collier's* that they had just flown in an airplane across the Channel? Why, even the *London Times* said . . ."

Elizabeth was standing behind the woman and felt her arms and legs stiffen, her mouth caught in a grimace that had started out as a smile. In a reeling kind of daze, she heard Glen say, "I have to look in at the purser's office." He had jumped to his feet and taken her arm. She saw the woman's mouth go slack and her husband fumble to his feet, half knocking his chair over and catching it, all the while avoiding her eyes. She felt Glen lead her away and out of the salon.

They walked along the deserted corridor, the thick carpeting muffling their footsteps. He was holding her hand tightly and had tucked her arm inside of his, where he held it against him to try and still her trembling.

"Do you want to walk a while on deck?" he asked.

When she nodded yes, he led her to her stateroom and waited at the door while she got her coat. For perhaps an hour they circled the deck, never speaking for the first half hour, not touching. She walked beside him, matching her steps to his, her face straight ahead, the sable coat clutched around her, shielding her face as she held the collar up high. When they passed paths of light that fell from inside across the deck, he glanced at her and saw tears quivering on her lashes. He thought she had never looked so beautiful, the blue-violet eyes dark and tragic-looking in the milky moonlight, the high cheekbones sculpting her face in the dark frame of hair. *So one woman, even one as beautiful as Elizabeth, wasn't enough for Lawrence Kendall,* he thought with a wry kind of grimace that could have been a smile as he looked out toward the dark sea.

After a while, he carefully reached out and took her hand. At first it lay limp and lifeless in his. But as they walked on, he felt a timid pressure and he clasped it more closely. He held her arm close to his body and she didn't resist. They walked on for perhaps another fifteen minutes; then finally he spoke.

"The bar is still open. How about a nightcap?"

At first she didn't answer, but then she nodded. "Yes, I—I think I could use a drink."

The lights were dim and only two other couples—neither the one from Boston—were in the bar. He ordered them each a brandy, and she pulled a cigarette from her small satin bag. For a while she sat with her coat still wrapped closely about her, but as she sipped at the brandy, she finally loosened it and let it fall onto the back of her chair. He stared at her for a moment, while simply raising a hand to order another brandy for them. She was watching him, her eyes still filled with hurt, but a resolute kind of firmness in her mouth. Her pale violet silk gown fell away from creamy shoulders and the long graceful neck. Small diamond clips glittered in her ears.

"I'm sorry," he said in a low voice, actually meaning it. "I'm sorry you had to hear that."

She simply shook her head, as though unable to speak. Then she said, "Please, I don't want to talk about it, Glen."

He nodded, and carefully took her hand in his, as though to reassure and comfort her.

"But I want another brandy and then another. I don't want to feel what I am feeling."

He walked over to the bar, said something to the bartender, and came back with a bottle of brandy, and poured her glass full, then his own. She began to talk. She was reaching far back into her memory and Glen understood why. It hurt less to talk of things that had happened in her life before she met Lawrence Kendall.

Finally, she started to rise, pulling her coat about her shoulders. She had a drowsy look about her; the brandy had softened the blow, he thought.

"Everyone has left but us," she said.

He followed her, carrying the half-empty bottle at his side. In the corridor he took hold of her arm and steadied her, then held her close against him as they walked through the corridors to her stateroom. At the door, he slowly took the key from her hand and unlocked the door. When it swung wide, she walked in, flicked one low lamp on, and threw her coat across a couch. When she turned and looked at him, he closed the door behind him, and walked toward her. For several moments after he reached her, they didn't touch, but simply stood close, looking at each other. He leaned down and kissed her, gently, without even touching her with his hands. He kissed her again, this time a long, lingering kiss that made her sway toward him.

When she turned and walked from the small sitting room into the bedroom beyond, he followed her, leaning back against the doorjamb while she slowly undressed, dropping first her gown to the floor, then her underthings, until she stood naked in the light that fell from the sitting room.

For a long moment, he stared at her. Then he walked quickly across to her, swept her up into his arms, and carried her to the bed. In moments, he had stripped his clothing off and was beside her. For an instant, she thought of struggling upward, but the hurt and shock and the brandy had done their work. She floated for a while in a drowsy warmth, drifting in his tender but increasingly bold lovemaking. His hands barely touched her and yet she knew they were there, on her throat, her breasts, teasingly roaming across her body, his lips following.

When he cradled her in his arms and slipped on top of her, he whispered close to her ear, "If you belonged to me, I could never look at another woman."

A small sob heaved in her throat and she grasped him hard, pulling him closer. When he eased inside her, she moaned and moved against him, *with* him, wanting him to thrust harder and harder. She threw her head back, trying not to think, but something went dead inside of her. She grasped him closer, wanting to feel, wanting waves of desire to drown the hurt. *Don't think, just feel,* she cried silently, giving her body to a lost and hollow passion that vanished like mist and drifted away.

Later when he lay beside her, he smiled into the darkness. She had turned on her side and seemed to be sleeping. He waited a few minutes and carefully slipped from the bed, not wanting to waken her. He quietly dressed and left, never knowing her eyes were wide and staring into the darkness.

When Elizabeth awoke the following morning, she didn't move. She stared overhead, trying not to feel, trying not to think, a terrible pall settling through her like a thickly drifting fog. She heard the door buzzer from the sitting room, but didn't move. When finally she dressed, she walked the decks as though pursued, the gray of the skies matching her mood. Once, in the distance, when she saw an officer that she thought was Glen, she turned back and retraced her steps.

For the remainder of the crossing, she took all her meals in her suite. When he had notes delivered to her, she returned them unopened. During the following nights, she paced the dark salon of her suite, the confusion and hurt blurred with guilt. Each morning and afternoon, she took long walks along the deck at times she knew he was on duty, and only answered the buzzer or soft knocking on her door when she knew it was the maid or a waiter.

On the final morning, within hours of docking, she felt certain there would be a confrontation.

He found her, as the ship entered the Narrows, surrounded by the maid, two porters, and her packed suitcases. She stood by a porthole, looking out and smoking a cigarette. At first he couldn't see her face. The brim of her beige felt hat swept down on one side. She wore a closely tailored beige suit, and her brown gloves, purse, and fur coat were carefully placed on the end of the couch. As he approached her, she turned. Coolly, she put her hand out.

"We'll say goodbye here, Glen." The tone in her voice was low and final. She smiled, but it was one that put a distance between them.

With one hand, he took hers, and handed her a small slip of paper with the other. "My address in Manhattan." His jaw was clenched hard, but there was affection in his eyes. "I'll be here for two weeks before going out again."

"Goodbye, Glen," she said softly, while handing the still-folded piece of paper back to him.

He watched her for a moment, turned, and walked out the door.

A cable from Lawrence was waiting for Elizabeth when she reached Kendall Hills. Ellie met her with the cable in her hand as Elizabeth came through the entrance to the main hall and stopped to hug her. Karl, with Ben's help, was bringing the luggage in, as Elizabeth's two black spaniels, Robbie and Angus, raced around the suitcases, barking wildly and slipping and sliding on the marble floor. Two of the new little maids, their eyes wide, stood at the side, watching and waiting for orders from Ellie, who walked along beside Elizabeth rattling off messages and bits of household information.

"Oh, Ellie, I'm so thrilled about the baby," Elizabeth said, stopping to hug her again. "I missed having you on the trip with me, but I'm thrilled for you."

"Well, I'm sorry Karl told you so quickly," Ellie said, looking over her shoulder at Karl, who was following, leading Ben, with the luggage, the two little maids coming along behind them, each carrying a suitcase. "I was perfectly able to go along with you—"

"Absolutely not. And I want you to take it very easy for the next months . . ." She had pulled the cable from the envelope and was reading it when she stopped for a moment on the staircase at the wide landing halfway up. She read it slowly while everyone waited behind her. When she had finished, she looked at Ellie and in a low voice said, "He won't be home for another week."

Ellie saw the flash of distress in her eyes. But Elizabeth recovered quickly and continued up the stairs, speaking to Ellie over her shoulder. "I'll just change, Ellie, and go on back to Manhattan."

They were walking along the wide corridor and had come to her door. While Ellie waited for them all to put the eight pieces of luggage down in the sitting room, Elizabeth hurried into her bedroom and closed the door.

"All right, just leave everything there," Ellie said, "and I'll take care of it. Jessie—Edna," she called out to the two maids. "Come back in half an hour to help me unpack." When the others had left, she spoke to Karl in a low voice. "That cable upset her terribly. He won't be back for another week."

"Well, it's just that she expected him in a day or two," he said. "That's what she told me in the car." He started from the room, but slowly returned, put both hands on either side of her face, leaned down, and kissed her. "You worry too much about her, Ellie."

She had cut her blonde hair short and it waved and curled about her face, making her eyes seem rounder and bluer than ever. She gently touched his face. "Karl . . ."

"I know," he said softly. "She's more like a friend than the lady you work for." He held her close to him for a moment, then looked down at her again. "Do you know what else she told me in the car coming from the pier?" Ellie shook her head. "After the baby is born, when you're ready to work again, she's going to make you put that business course you've been taking to some use."

Ellie clasped her hands excitedly together. "Oh, Karl."

"She wants you to be her personal secretary." When she grasped hold of him and danced him around in a circle, he laughed, but made her slow down. "And she kept insisting that Mr. Kendall wants me to take that job in the aircraft plant over near Bridgeport."

She saw the familiar shadow cross his face and pulled away from him. "Karl . . . please think about it."

He walked to the door and opened it. For a moment, he stood there with his back to her. Slowly he looked around at her. "I . . . I keep feeling that there is something I must do."

Ellie's face became worried, but she said nothing.

"Somehow I feel I must go back . . ."

"No, Karl," she pleaded softly.

"War is coming there, Ellie." His eyes were far away, and a curl had twisted his mouth. "He has now made himself Supreme Commander of the Armed Forces of Germany. Austria is gone. Next will be the Sudetenland. And once the Sudetenland is gone, it will be all of Czechoslovakia—"

"Karl." She ran to him, but he caught her by the shoulders and looked deeply into her eyes.

"Help me by understanding, Ellie," he pleaded. "If I decide I must go, I want to go knowing you feel I am doing the right thing."

For several moments, she looked up at him, tears in her eyes. At last she nodded, and wordlessly he pulled her to him and held her close. "Thank you, my darling," he whispered. He watched her walk slowly to the door to the bedroom, tap softly, then open it, and disappear inside without looking back.

13

It was ten days before Elizabeth received a message from the Kendall offices that Lawrence would be arriving on the *Ile de France.* She rode that late afternoon with Karl to the French Line pier, her face a careful mask behind the small black and white hat that tipped over one eye. They waited in the passenger terminal and saw him as he was escorted by a French Line official past the customs lines. John Hendricks, one of Lawrence's several top lieutenants at Kendall, Inc., had joined them. A thin, serious-faced man who always carried a bulging brief-case and seemed to wear black, he paced back and forth in his black chesterfield and bowler hat until he caught a glimpse of Lawrence, then stood beside Elizabeth and kept repeating over and over, "Well, good, good, there he is. And not a day too soon."

Even at a distance, Lawrence looked tired, but his face broke into a smile when he saw her. He took her in his arms and held her, but over her head it was to Hendricks he was speaking.

"Sorry about the delay, but I had to rush over to London. I cabled you about the consortium that was pulled together. Well, it all worked out. We floated a loan of twenty million for the Argentine govern-ment . . ." He looked down at Elizabeth in his arms. "Darling, I'm sorry. John brought some contracts I must sign. We'll drop him off, then go right home." He shook Karl's hand. "Karl, you're looking well." Turning to the French Line official who was standing by pa-tiently, he said, "Thank you for shouldering me through. Damned nice of you."

Still holding her against him, he led the way from the terminal, with Karl hurrying ahead and two porters following with his luggage. In the tumult and hubbub all around them, and with John Hendricks walking beside them, she was saved the agony of having to face him alone the moment of his arrival. By the time they had been escorted out of the noisy crowded terminal, she had regained control of herself. But the terrible hurt remained, as did the eventual reckoning, the remorse over what she had done.

". . . and they came to our London headquarters. Rothschild was there, Needham of the Bank of England, people from the London house that has been carrying the blocks of unsalable Argentine bonds . . ." Lawrence was speaking rapidly to Hendricks.

In the Rolls, Elizabeth sat on the far side and Lawrence in the middle. Hendricks, on Lawrence's other side, immediately drew a sheaf of papers to be signed from his briefcase.

The limousine plunged eastward into midtown traffic, then turned south on Broadway, heading for the Kendall Building on Wall Street. From the corner of her eye she saw Lawrence signing the papers on top of Hendricks's briefcase and she half heard their rapid conversation. *He had left immediately for London,* he had told Hendricks earlier, *right after she left for Le Havre, called there for an emergency meeting.*

". . . and nice to see you again, Mrs. Kendall," John Hendricks was saying, while stepping from the car. She nodded and smiled, as the limousine pulled into traffic again.

". . . and this, darling, is something you'll be interested in," Lawrence was saying as he reached into an inner pocket and took out a folded newspaper clipping. When he handed it to her, she saw in the waning afternoon light that it was cut from the *London Times.* It was a picture of three people: Lawrence, Charles McAlpin, the writer from *Collier's* whom Lawrence had known since college days, and . . . and Missy Wainwright Devoe. She heard Lawrence chuckling as he talked on.

Elizabeth felt her hands begin to tremble.

". . . and I bumped into her in the lobby of Claridge's, as Chuck and I were going in to dinner. She and Ty were in London visiting his sister. Missy had just come from St. George's Hospital, where she'd left poor old Ty following an appendicitis attack and emergency surgery. She looked pretty done up, tired and needing a friend, so I asked her to join us for dinner. But damned if that young whippersnapper of a photographer from the *Times* didn't walk up and grab a picture. Of course, the concierge sent a battery of men across the lobby to throw the fellow out, so he just assumed the pretty young lady on my arm was Mrs. Lawrence Kendall."

Elizabeth felt as if all of the blood had drained from her.

She tried to laugh, to join Lawrence as he put his head back and softly chuckled. "Of course, the *Times* ran a correction of the caption the following day, after I had Berridge from our offices there call up and demand it, but Missy and I knew you'd be amused when you saw it."

Amused? She felt ill . . . dizzy . . . sickened at what she had done. "What damnable luck! Poor Ty," she said, surprised at the normalcy in her voice.

"We ran her back to the hospital after we'd eaten. She was determined to sit by Ty's bed until she knew he was completely out of the woods. And Chuck and I went on about our business. The interview I'd promised him, you know . . ."

When he suddenly put his arms about her again in the limousine's darkness, she put her face against his neck and held herself to him fiercely. "Don't ever send me away from you again," she said, pressing her face against the soft tweed of his coat.

"What's this?" he asked softly, putting his hand under her chin and lifting her face to him. "What is this all about?"

"Just—just that I love you so terribly. And I can't bear it when you send me away from you."

He kissed her, gently at first, then the kiss deepened, became more demanding. "I missed you, too," he whispered. "More than you'll ever know, Elizabeth. More than I ever thought possible."

He had planned to go to his offices after they finished their dinner. Hendricks and Dave Fisher would both be there, hammering out the terms of the Boland-Wymouth Mining Company contracts. And there would be the transatlantic calls on the Argentine matter, more calls from and to London and Brussels on which way the wind was blowing on the Czech situation. Hitler had summoned Czech President Emil Hácha to Berlin. God knows what the outcome of that will be, he thought, and how it will affect our banking interests there. If Czechoslovakia becomes a German Protectorate, we'll have to move fast, London and Brussels will have to move fast . . .

"I have to make one phone call," he said apologetically, as they rose from the table. He looked across the flickering candlelight at her, the burnished dark hair falling to her shoulders, the slim sheath of black and white silk that fell in a soft cowl at her throat and clung to her narrow hips, the eyes dark, almost mysterious in the fluttering light. He held out his hand and she walked to him, putting her hand in his.

They had their coffee and brandy in the library while he phoned

Hendricks. And with Brahms playing on the record player, they sat in front of the fire, all the lights turned off, Lawrence in a deep chair, Elizabeth on the floor, her head against his knee. When the concerto ended, they rose and went to the elevator in the main reception hall. Only the faintest light illuminated the massive tapestries. As the elevator hummed upward, she stood against him, feeling the familiar surge of longing. She saw their reflection in a section of mirror between the mahogany paneling and wished she could take a knife and cut out the memory of one night in her life.

"What are you thinking?" Lawrence asked, still holding her with one arm and tipping her chin up.

"About you," she said, closing her eyes, feeling his mouth brush hers while something inside cried, *Don't ever let him know.*

When he sat up in the darkness, flicked the bedside lamp on, and crossed to his dressing room, she still could feel his warmth next to her, the long, hard body as it curved her against him. She watched him in the low light, remembering his hands and mouth on her, and how she had responded in almost frantic hunger, then the exquisite flow of sensations that followed . . . that always followed.

"You sent me away from you," she had whispered, and he heard the pleading, the hurt in her voice, when later he cradled and held her.

"Never again," he said, his hands soothing her. "I promise."

She lingered around the edges of sleep, waiting for him to come back. But when he leaned down and kissed her, she saw that he was dressed. She sat up suddenly. "Where are you going?"

"The Bank of England opens in London in just a few moments." He was looking at his wristwatch.

She laughed softly, pushed pillows up behind her, and pulled a cigarette from the silver box on the table next to her.

"Well, at least I had you for a short while, first," she said as she drew her knees up beneath the silken coverlet. "Before the Bank of England."

"I'll be back by three." He was chuckling as he quietly closed the door behind him.

Never will I be free of the feeling of having betrayed him, she thought, and her smile disappeared. She smoked the cigarette until it almost burned her fingers, then turned off the light and stared up to the ceiling. Forgive me, she whispered, forgive me . . .

* * *

Gail Halloran Wancek was born on a bright, sunny August day in 1938, and, to the wonderment of her father, seemed like a delicate pink and white miniature of Ellie. A soft down of pale gold curls ringed her head and long dark lashes swept her cheeks.

"She's beautiful," Karl whispered when he returned to Ellie's room in the small hospital down in Rijksville after standing at the window of the nursery and staring at his new child.

When he bent down and kissed Ellie, she smiled and held onto him for a long moment. She had seen the look in his eyes and felt certain he would no longer talk of leaving, of going back to Czechoslovakia, even though just a week earlier, as they lay in bed in their cottage at Kendall Hills, he had said, "It would not be for long, Ellie. Just to see what is really happening there and if there is anything I can do, for my parents, for Josef, and to see Anton, if possible. Remember my father's letter said Anton was leaving Berlin for Prague. The newspapers say German troops are standing on the Czech border and the Czech army is mobilizing."

In the following weeks, she found continued reassurance that he wouldn't leave. He adored the new baby and spent every possible spare moment with her and Ellie, smiling and laughing as he had never done before.

"Ellie," he said, running into their cottage, close by the long twelve-car garage. He had been polishing one of the limousines on the tarmac. "Mrs. Kendall is coming down the hill. She called out, asking if you were here."

Ellie looked out the window and smoothed her dress and hair as she watched Elizabeth come through the white gate, her white tennis dress making the golden tan of her arms and legs glow. She ran to the door and said, "The baby is just about to wake up."

"Oh, I was hoping so," Elizabeth answered with the flood of a smile as she walked in. For the first time, when she saw Elizabeth's smile, Ellie thought the slight flicker of envy was gone, that fleeting expression in her eyes that Elizabeth always tried to hide whenever she looked down at Gail or held her in her arms. "Karl claims she actually smiled at him this morning," Elizabeth said, and they both laughed. They were walking toward the stairway of the narrow, sunny hall, Karl right behind them.

"Well, more likely a gas pain, the doctor always says," Ellie teased, looking at Karl over her shoulder.

180

"It was a smile," Karl said stubbornly. But he laughed as he turned around and went outside again, the screen door clicking shut behind him.

Upstairs in the yellow and white nursery, they stood looking down at the stirring child. Ellie glanced at Elizabeth's face curiously, seeing something she hadn't seen for a long time, a kind of serenity.

Finally she whispered, "Tea?" When Elizabeth nodded, they tiptoed from the room and went down the staircase.

It wasn't until Ellie had brought a tray of tea and cookies out to the small side terrace and put them down on the table that she said, "You look terribly pleased about something, Mrs. Kendall."

"Ellie, Nanny Grace says she doesn't have half enough to do with the boys in school most of the time, and she wants to take care of the baby during those hours you will be busy doing your new job. And if you are starting as my secretary next month, it's about time you call me by my first name." When Ellie started to protest, she reached out and touched her hand. "You're closer to me than almost anyone I've ever known," she said softly, "including Missy, I think. Friends call each other by their first names."

"All right," Ellie said excitedly. "But please tell me—!"

Elizabeth laughed. "When I was telling Aunt Vivian my news on the phone this morning, I said for the past twenty-four hours I had simply been walking around with a silly smile on my face. And she said, 'You sound like you're describing a cow!'"

"Oh, I don't believe it. You're going to have a baby," Ellie said with a little shriek, and they fell into each other's arms. "When?"

For a fleeting moment, Elizabeth remembered dark nights of anger, of humiliation, plunging blindly into a shipboard affair that filled her with self-loathing and despair. Don't think about it. It never happened, she thought, as relief flooded through her.

"February. Yes, in February." An expression so fleeting that Ellie almost thought she imagined it crossed Elizabeth's face. The relief flooding anew, Elizabeth hugged Ellie again. "Lawrence is thrilled, he's almost beside himself. He's certain it will be a girl."

"That means nothing." Ellie laughed delightedly, looking off in the distance where Karl was working on the engine of the long limousine. "Karl was so sure Gail was going to be a boy." Suddenly her face clouded.

"What is it, Ellie?" Elizabeth followed her eyes. "Is he talking about Czechoslovakia again?"

Ellie nodded, while measuring sugar into her cup and stirring it.

"One of the gardeners here comes from a town near Lidice, Karl's hometown. He told him that it's only a matter of time. That giving the Sudetenland to Germany will seal Czechoslovakia's fate. The Germans are appeasing Britain and France. Before it became so difficult to cross the borders, his nephew got out to England and joined the Royal Air Force." She gazed across the shining green lawns to where Karl stood, talking now to Meacham, who was looking down at the motor of the limousine, his red hair like a bright beacon in the September sunlight.

They were silent for several moments and then Ellie spoke again, her voice grave. "I just discovered that Karl has been taking flying lessons at a small airfield about twenty miles from here."

"I see," Elizabeth said. "The Royal Air Force . . ."

"But he has two more years at Polytechnic Institute and then he will have his electrical engineering degree. That was what he wanted, you know." When Elizabeth saw the desperation in Ellie's eyes, she took hold of her hand and squeezed it. "He wanted so much to be able to go to Mr. Kendall and say, 'I now have my degree and can work in the aircraft plant.' He always told me, 'In America, you must have a degree. That is important.' But now—"

"I'll see if Lawrence will talk to him."

Ellie slowly shook her head. "If the dismemberment of Czechoslovakia begins, nothing will stop him. Nothing."

On September the thirtieth, Prime Minister Neville Chamberlain of Great Britain flew back to London from Munich. He, Daladier of France, and Hitler had signed a paper and agreed that the Sudetenland, on Germany's eastern frontier, would be ceded to the Germans. Chamberlain told the world that Hitler had promised him faithfully that he had made "the last territorial demand that I have to make in Europe."

"Fools," Karl had said, his voice hoarse, his hands running wildly through the thick blond hair. "Fools! They listen to him and believe him because they want to believe him. This is just one big step toward the taking of all of Czechoslovakia. Bohemia, Moravia, all of it." He sat down with his head in his hands. "All of it will go."

Ellie had tried to console him, but he could not be comforted. It was the end of Czechoslovakia, the end of freedom in Europe. And Ellie knew it was only a matter of time before he would go.

He left in October. On the drive to New York City, he sat in the rear of the Rolls Royce, Meacham at the wheel in front, Ellie beside him on the other small jump seat, and Elizabeth and Lawrence Kendall sitting behind them. Lawrence had insisted that he was going to pay Karl's traveling expenses as far as London and until he was settled at the RAF training field where he would be stationed. Lawrence had also insisted on paying for a first-class cabin on the new *Queen Mary.*

They stood on the Cunard Line pier and watched him waving from one of the lower of the ten decks, where he had run with his long, loping gait after boarding the ship.

Elizabeth clutched Ellie's hand, knowing how devastated she was. She saw the tears in her eyes and felt her pain, as the young woman gazed upward to the distant figure of her husband, tall and bronzed, his hair blowing in the brisk wind.

And as he watched from above, it suddenly struck Karl, with the impact of a hard blow, how much he loved Ellie. I have never really let her know how much, he thought sadly, and in that moment he vowed that he would somehow survive what lay ahead and return to her and the baby. She looked so small standing down on the open pier between Elizabeth and Lawrence Kendall. She had begun working as Elizabeth's personal secretary the week before, and was wearing a bright blue suit and hat, and small navy-blue high-heeled pumps. He caught his breath for a moment, realizing he had never before been so aware of how lovely she was.

"Goodbye," he shouted, knowing the wind was carrying his voice upward and away, but shouting at her nevertheless. "I will be back, Ellie. I promise you, I will come back." Whistles were blowing and the crowds were shouting, but she nodded, as though she had under-stood what he said, just as the ship slowly began to slide away from the pier into the channel of the river. He waved and waved until he could no longer see her, and only then did he turn and walk away, toward the bow of the ship. For several hours he stood where the wind blew hardest. It stung his face and dried the tears he had tried to blink back, but finally let slide down his cheeks. Ever since that night in Berlin, when Anton had tried to comfort him, he had not shed a tear. He had closed a door inside, a door that shielded him against feeling, against the danger of being hurt.

But now the hurt was there again, the hurt of leaving Ellie and the beautiful new little child that had come into their lives. From that pain rose a simple, incontrovertible belief. He would come back to them.

* * *

Caroline Stuart Kendall was one month old when Hitler rode through the streets of Prague, standing in his big, open, black Mercedes, proclaiming to the people of Czechoslovakia and the world that he was the "Protector of Bohemia and Moravia." On that sixteenth day of March in 1939, he arrived in the beautiful gothic city, not as a savior, but as a conqueror. The American Ambassador was summoned home from Berlin. The French premier, Edouard Daladier, speeded up rearmament. British Prime Minister Neville Chamberlain remarked to the press that Hitler's word wasn't worth much. And Hitler began making demands of Poland. He wanted the strip of land, known as the Polish Corridor, that separated East Prussia from Germany proper. It had been given to Poland in the Versailles Treaty after World War I.

On March 31, Chamberlain announced that if Poland were attacked, Britain and France would honor their agreement to protect that country. It was reported that Hitler reacted with raging, screaming fury and ordered his general staff to plan the destruction of Poland.

But on that snowy day in February when Caroline was born at the hospital down in Rijksville, the newspaper headlines and radio bulletins faded away for Lawrence Kendall. Refusing all phone calls and messages, many of which were important ones from his offices in lower Manhattan, he paced the hospital corridor and maternity waiting room, right alongside an automobile mechanic from Rijksville and a gardener from the Roosevelt estate a short distance up the Hudson River. Elizabeth had refused to have the baby at the Margaret Reid Kendall Memorial Hospital in Manhattan, which Lawrence had built in memory of his mother.

"Kendall Hills feels more like home to me, Lawrence, than anyplace else. I want the baby to be born here—close to home," she had said several months earlier. The following day the Rijksville Hospital administrator received word from a David Fisher of Kendall, Inc., that the Kendall family was donating funds for a new maternity wing.

Elizabeth's suite at the hospital was already filled with flowers by the time Lucia rushed in with a huge bouquet of roses in her arms, Dana following with a broad smile on his face. Sybil, who had arrived at the hospital just before the baby was born, rose to take the flowers from Lucia and handed them to a nurse who stood at the door, smiling.

"Elizabeth!" Lucia exclaimed excitedly as she hugged her, then stood back a little to let Dana bend over to kiss his sister. "Oh, you look so beautiful, so happy, so . . . so . . . what is the word . . . what is it you say?"

"So pleased with herself," Dana supplied with a grin, as he took Lucia's fur coat, which she had let slide to the floor.

"Well, I should be," Elizabeth said, laughing. "Lawrence wanted a girl, and that's what she is."

"Well, doesn't he always get what he wants?" Sybil said, but with a smile. She liked Lawrence very much.

They stayed for only half an hour, then left when they were told the baby was coming in for her nursing.

"And Grandfather and Nana are on their way down from Boston to see you," Dana said as he planted a kiss on Elizabeth's cheek. "That will be enough visitors for one afternoon."

The day Caroline was brought home to Kendall Hills was the day that Lawrence finally returned to his offices and the servants heaved sighs of relief.

"I'll just be in New York for an hour or so and then I'll be back," Lawrence said, leaning down over the bed and kissing a laughing Elizabeth for the tenth or eleventh time, while Warren Leland paced up and down in the sitting room just beyond the door. "It's just that Warren said that merger with the Nickerson Newspapers in New England is about to go through . . ."

"Would you please go," Elizabeth exclaimed as he started back from the door again, but this time he sat on the bed beside her, took her face between his hands, and said softly, "You've given me another Elizabeth—"

"No, darling," she said, gently touching his face and kissing him. "She's very much herself, our Caroline Kendall is." A pucker of worry clouded her forehead. "They all are—the three boys. They miss you, Lawrence"

"The boys are fine," he said, his tone changing abruptly, becoming clipped. He stood up and walked to the door. For a moment his expression was hard. "Boys can't be coddled, Elizabeth, much as you would like to accomplish that with Larry and Avery and Jamie." She smiled a small triumphant smile. She had given the youngest boy his nickname of Jamie. A sweet-faced youngster, he followed her about adoringly whenever she was at Kendall Hills and on the rare occasions when the children were brought to the Manhattan townhouse. Lawrence had just called him Jamie. "They have to grow up understanding their responsibilities as men."

"Darling, they're only children—"

"They are boys." He smiled. "Little girls are for coddling, for spoiling. We'll do a good job of that with our little girl." For a long while she watched the door that had closed behind him.

Before lunch, the door opened and Jamie bounded excitedly across the room. She held out her arms and caught him, pulling him up onto the bed beside her. When she finished reading him a story from a book he had brought with him, he looked at her and, with solemn eyes, said, "I love you, 'Lisbeth."

She hugged him and said, "Why don't you call me Mummy, darling? I'd like it very much if you would."

They have to grow up understanding their responsibilities as men, Lawrence had said. She had tried hard to make the other boys begin to think of her as their mother, too. But Larry and Avery had stiffly resisted all overtures.

"I don't see them enough," she complained to Missy, who arrived at about three o'clock the next day in a flurry of furs and floating perfume.

"Well, the way that Lawrence insists on their attending Country Day School up here in Rijksville, I'm not surprised," Missy said as she lit a cigarette and puffed for a few moments pensively, one silken leg crossed over the other. She had thrown her fur scarf onto the chaise and was sitting on the end of it. "Good God, driving up here today, I felt like I was on my way to Alaska or Hudson Bay or some such place. It's so *remote,* Elizabeth, and there's so much *snow.*"

"It's wonderful and I love it," Elizabeth said, laughing. She was untying the pink ribbon on a tissue-wrapped gift, and exclaimed with pleasure as she took a small silver engraved cup out of the box. "How beautiful, Missy."

"For orange juice," Missy said absently while tapping her ashes into an ashtray beside her. "But you're not here that much."

"Lawrence prefers not having to commute during the week," Elizabeth said simply as she folded the tissue and ribbon and tossed them to the end of the bed. "In the cold months, that is. He insists on it in August, even though he only spends long weekends at Kendall Hall."

"Well, *Newport.* That's very different from—from *this.*" She waved her hand toward the window as though to indicate all of Kendall Hills. "Good heavens, there's nothing but trees and grass and ponds in the summer and snow and ice and miles of it in the winter out there."

Elizabeth laughed harder. "Missy, dear, you really are one of those provincial New Yorkers who think that civilization stops at the Hudson and Harlem rivers."

"Well," Missy admitted grudgingly, "I guess when you live in a place where you have your own fire department—"

"Oh, for heaven's sake, Missy, the fire department belongs to Rijksville."

"And who provides more than eighty percent of the tax base for Rijksville? Lawrence Kendall, I seem to recall reading in the newspapers one day about a month ago." There was no envy in her voice. She was, in fact, laughing. "Your own hospital, police department—"

"Oh, stop, Missy." Elizabeth laughed, but then her expression grew somber. "No, I'm really worried. About Larry and Avery. Jamie is only eight. He's accepted me. And he—well, he's different from the other two. He's so lovable and sweet and—"

"And young," Missy said bluntly, squashing her cigarette out. "After all, Elizabeth, Larry is what? Twelve? You're a bit young at twenty-four to have a twelve-year-old son."

"Yes," Elizabeth said softly. "There's that, I admit. But he won't even try to be friends." She slowly shook her head. "When Lawrence brought them in to see the baby last night, he just stared at her and finally turned around and started to walk out, with Avery following him. When Lawrence called out to him, 'Well, aren't you going to say anything about your sister?' Larry said, '*Half* sister.' And he ran out the door, Avery running right after him."

Missy sighed. "Oh, he'll probably come around, Elizabeth—"

"No." She shook her head again. "That is the way it's going to be. He's civil and that's about all. I think . . ." She was trying to find the right words. "I think—well, Lawrence is so hard on them. And he sees them so little. Perhaps if there was more . . . more . . ."

"More love?" Missy asked carefully.

Elizabeth nodded. "Oh, I know he loves them. It's just that he feels boys should be raised with—"

"With a straight spine and stiff upper lip." Missy smiled a bit sadly. "The dregs of Victorianism. I know. My father was like that with my brother, too." She laughed bitterly. "As a result, Jeff chases floozies, plays the horses, and cheats on his wife." She picked up her fur scarf and started pulling on her gloves. "When I asked Tyler if he didn't think he kissed and hugged our twins too much, he said, 'Time enough to teach them the harsh realities of growing up male when they don't make the varsity team or smash up their first roadster.' "

Elizabeth grinned as her friend walked toward her. "Tyler always was a softie."

Missy grinned back. "He meant what he said about the varsity team. That's when I fell in love, watching him run sixty yards for a touch-down at the Yale Bowl." She leaned down to hug Elizabeth. "Your Caroline is beautiful. Maybe she'll grow up and marry Dougy or Bruce."

"She might at that," Elizabeth said, laughing.

Missy was almost at the door when Nanny Grace appeared, filling the doorway with her friendly bulk. "Nanny Grace!" Missy hugged her, then stood back to look at her in her white uniform. "It's been ages since I last saw you."

"Well, we're country folk now." The nursemaid beamed. "I bin up 'ere watchin' over Ellie's baby an' the boys." When Missy made a face, she plowed right on. "That Larry's an 'andful, 'e is. Wouldn't even come to the nursery to see the new baby. Avery, too. But Jamie's sweet an' dear an' I love 'im like the child's me own. An' now we 'ave the new baby."

"And a beautiful one." Missy looked around at Caroline. "Worth waiting for?"

"Worth waiting for." Elizabeth smiled. "Oh, *so* worth it!"

"An' speakin' of 'er," Nanny Grace said, looking at Elizabeth. "She's awake an' shoutin' t' be fed."

"Bring her in, Nanny Grace," Elizabeth said, sitting up higher on the pillows, as the nursemaid hurried out.

From the door, Missy gave Elizabeth an uneasy glance. "Larry sounds like more of a horror than ever."

"I'm working on it." Elizabeth's mouth was set grimly.

"That's a situation you're never going to win," Missy said, waggling a gloved finger in warning. She added softly, "You might as well face it, Elizabeth. You came into his life and upset his little applecart. As far as Larry and Avery are concerned, you married their father and gave them a sister they didn't want, a little sister that will probably be their father's favorite child." She was speaking quietly and Elizabeth listened closely, with a sad look on her face. "I'm sorry if I sound blunt. But I think the sooner you understand it and accept it all, the better off you—and Caroline—will be." She left with a small wave.

* * *

188

During the first week in April, Benito Mussolini made a move. His troops boarded naval ships and crossed the Adriatic Sea to invade the tiny country of Albania. A somewhat small but highly vocal group of Albanian-Americans took to the streets of Manhattan and demonstrated loudly in front of Italian establishments that they thought to be sympathetic to Il Duce. Some even went beyond that and stormed the stage entrance of the Metropolitan Opera House, just below Fortieth Street on Broadway, during a performance of Norma with Lucia Daniello in the leading role.

It was Lucia's most taxing role, calling for a range that spanned the most exquisitely soft singing to rock-hard fury and rage, in full voice. She was always exhausted at the end of each performance, and Dana, if he was not able to sit in their box, made it a point to be there at the final curtain call to take her home.

He and Sybil had both attended that Saturday evening's production, but it wasn't until the final curtain had come down and the orchestra left the pit that they heard the chanting out in the street.

"What on earth—?" Sybil said, looking at her son. She was gathering up her beaded purse and velvet cape, and stopped to listen, as did numerous people below her in the orchestra and in the surrounding boxes.

"It . . . sounds strange," Dana said, pausing near the door of their box. He pushed the door open and caught an usher who was just rushing past. "What is it?"

The usher stopped, and began to stammer a little when he saw who Dana was. "Oh . . . er, Mr. Stuart." He was an older man with graying hair, and an old-timer at the House. "A big mob of people out there with signs, and marching up and down."

"Signs?"

"It's because of what happened with Italy. Marching into Albania."

"Oh, dear God!" Sybil said, understanding immediately what the man meant.

"Do the signs mention my wife?" Dana asked tersely. He had grasped the man's arm.

"Yes . . . er, yes they do, Mr. Stuart. And they're shoutin' that . . . well, that she shouldn't be allowed to sing here no more."

"Good Lord!"

Dana turned and took hold of Sybil's arm. Without another word, they rushed backstage and along the corridor to Lucia's dressing room. They expected to find her in tears, but instead found her nodding calmly, as the Metropolitan Opera's manager, Edward Johnson, stood in front of her explaining the situation.

"I must go out there and speak to them," she said to Dana as he and Sybil entered the flower-filled room.

"Go out there—?" Sybil exploded as she clutched one hand against her cheek in shock. "Why, Lucia, of course you can't go—"

"But I must." She was still wearing her costume and stood in front of all of them with her head thrown back. "Why, I can't run away from this. If I did, I would have to run every day of my life from this moment on, as long as all these terrible things are happening in Europe."

"Darling," Dana started to say.

"No, Dana," she said, turning to him and holding onto his hands. "You know that I am speaking the truth when I say there will be no end to it if I do not go out there and face them."

There was an odd kind of silence in the room, each of them realizing that she was probably right.

"It won't take me long to change," she said as she walked toward the door leading to her inner dressing room. When she closed the door, Johnson simply looked at Dana and Sybil and spread his hands as though to say, She's made up her mind.

They left the opera house through the lobby and main entrance and came out onto the sidewalk, where they were least expected. The main core of the crowd had gathered near the walkway leading to the stage door. But stragglers near the main entrance began to shout, and the crowd turned rapidly and moved like a shifting wave of water toward them. Police had been called, and many of them, both on foot and on horseback, rallied quickly. Three or four of the mounted police clattered up onto the sidewalk and stopped the sudden rush of the mob at the edge where they stood, shouting her name and loudly chorusing, "Go back to Italy, go back to Italy," over and over.

Police on foot closely circled Lucia, while Dana and Sybil hugged her arms to them as they stood at her side. For perhaps three or four minutes they listened to the chanting, and then suddenly Lucia stepped forward, Dana moving quickly with her. The crowd was surprised. There was a momentary lull in the shouting, and when she raised her voice and began to speak, there was a muttering, a low hum of voices, and then it became quiet.

"No," she said, her clear, silvery voice carrying out over the heads of the crowd, above the sound of trolleys and automobiles in the street, above the noise of a bus clattering by. "I will not go home to Italy. Italy is no longer my home. I, like many of you, am now an American citizen . . ." She paused and the hush that had fallen over the crowd made Dana slowly turn his head, his eyes carefully sweeping around to try to assess what had happened. ". . . and I, like all of you, love this country. What happened this week in Albania is too terrible to imagine. I am ashamed of what happened in Albania. I am filled with shame with what has happened to the country of my birth—"

Dana saw a camera flash explode, and then another, and held Lucia's hand tighter, but she never flinched.

"Please . . . do not ask me to go back to Italy. The Italy of my childhood no longer exists. Please understand how I want to stay here in this wonderful country, in this beautiful city, how I want to go on working in this magnificent opera house, singing for you—"

As more flashbulbs exploded, there was a sudden shout from the rear, and then the crowd began to applaud, a sprinkling of clapping at first, and then it grew to a groundswell, and they could hear whistling and cheering.

Dana saw their car pull slowly through the crowd to the curb in front of them. And as they walked toward it, Lucia reached out and touched hands that were outstretched to her. Dana and his driver, Quinlan, stood by the open rear door of the limousine, both grinning as Lucia slowly came across the wide sidewalk, Sybil just behind her, their long gowns sweeping about their ankles. The crowd was still cheering and applauding as they stepped into the car. As it pulled out into the center of Broadway, Lucia waved from the rear window, while hundreds broke from the crowd and raced along the street after her, calling out her name, the cheers and shouting echoing up into the canyon of walls on either side.

Elizabeth had asked Meacham to bring the car around at nine one sunny Saturday morning in April. When she came out of the elevator and crossed the reception hall, Jamie ran to her and grasped her hand, but Larry and Avery waited on the long, red upholstered bench by the vestibule door, fidgeting and looking at everything but her. They were all dressed in dark blue coats and small visored blue caps.

"Well, let's get going," she said in a cheerful voice, the words echoing across the marble-walled hall.

"Will they have leopards, too, Mummy?" Jamie asked excitedly as he skipped along beside her. "Leopards and tigers?"

"Mummy, Mummy . . ." she heard Larry mutter in mimicry under his breath as he and Avery followed along behind her. *"Stupid little kid."*

"Oh, lots of leopards and tigers, darling," she said, as they climbed into the car, Meacham holding the door and frowning at Larry, who was making signals behind her back to Avery.

"Jamie, you and Avery sit on the jump seats. Larry, you sit here next to me," Elizabeth said. The limousine was pulling around the circular driveway. She had taken a small notebook from her purse and opened it. "I want to read this wonderful story out loud, one that Larry wrote in school. The teacher sent it home to your father to read and he showed it to me. It's about that trip you all took to the Grand Canyon last summer." She saw that Larry was scowling but chose to ignore it. When she had finished reading, Jamie and Avery and she clapped their hands. She pretended to ignore the fact that Larry grasped the notebook from her hand and pushed it down on the seat beside him, then sat and stared out the window all the way down to Manhattan.

She and Meacham walked all through the Central Park Zoo with the boys for almost two hours. Then she took them to the Palm Court at the Plaza for lunch and to a matinee of *The Prince and the Pauper.* As they climbed into the limousine at the curb in front of the theater, she smiled to herself. The boys had seemed to enjoy themselves. Even Larry, somewhat grudgingly, had clapped when the final curtain had come down. This was what they wanted, she thought. Lawrence didn't have the time to spend with them, but she had plenty of it and would make a point of doing interesting things with them whenever she could. Saturdays. That was it. She would take them places on Saturdays. She had convinced Lawrence they should stay at Kendall Hills most of the time while the boys were still in school in Rijksville. She smiled again into the growing darkness as the Rolls drew near Kendall Hills. The lights of houses and shops flickered on in the twilight as they drove through the small village and finally turned through the big black iron gates.

"Well, darlings," she said gaily, as Jamie roused himself from sleep on her lap, and raised his tousled head of blond curls. "I've decided. Today was so much fun, we'll do something like this every Saturday." The limousine was rolling up the winding hill toward Belvedere, lights blazing from the tall windows on all four floors and glittering through the trees as they climbed higher. "Next Saturday we could go to the circus. Ringling Brothers and Barnum and Bailey opens—"

"I'm going to a ball game with Uncle Warren," Larry said. He was sitting on one of the jump seats, his face close to the side window.

"Well, then we'll go to the circus on the following Saturday, and next week Jamie and Avery and I will go to—"

Larry suddenly wrenched himself around to face her, a furious expression on his handsome face. "I'm not going with you any-where!" he snarled. Jamie stared at him with a frightened expression on his face, while Avery smiled hesitantly, almost timidly, not certain how he should react. But as he edged closer to Larry, his smile grew bolder. "I don't like you and I'm not going with you."

"Larry," she said softly. "Please. Let's try to be friends. I know that you don't want to think of me as your mother and I can understand that. But at least we can be friends—"

"We can't be anything! I don't want to be anything to you."

Elizabeth glanced at the glass partition behind Meacham and was glad to see it was raised. She could see the carriage lamps on each side of the entrance to Belvedere coming closer. They were almost there. "Larry, please."

"You shut up," he shouted. "You got what you wanted. A baby by my father—and now she's his favorite. So you got what you wanted!" He grabbed Avery's hand as the car pulled up before the entrance, quickly opened the door, and, dragging Avery with him, jumped out and ran up the steps. "Just leave Avery and me alone!"

She sat for a moment as an angry-faced Meacham, holding the limousine door for her, stared after the two boys, who disappeared into the vestibule. Jamie's arms were wound about her neck, his face frightened, tears glistening in his blue eyes.

"It's all right, darling," she whispered. Meacham reached in, took him, and put him on the steps, then climbed out.

"What that kid needs . . . !" Meacham was glowering.

"It's all right, Meacham," she said with a sad smile. "I guess it's just very hard, at his age, to accept the fact that someone else has taken his mother's place."

But Meacham was slowly shaking his head. "No, ma'am," he said. "He's just like that. I've seen him with other kids at the playground sometimes when I go to get them after school. He picks on the little kids, the ones who can't fight back." He was still shaking his head.

"Real mean, he is. I caught him one time just as he was about to put a stick into a little kid's ear. Had him down on the ground with his knee on the youngster's chest."

Elizabeth stared at him. Then she said softly, "I didn't dream—didn't dream it could possibly be as bad as that." She took Jamie's hand in hers and walked into the house.

BOOK
III

14
1939

On the morning of September 1, German troops crossed the border into Poland, and the world saw its first full-scale blitzkrieg, a bloody but lightning war, as newspapers described it in their headlines. Britain and France, joined by Australia and New Zealand, declared war on Germany three days later. Russia had signed its non-aggression pact with Germany the previous August, but even the Soviets had been caught off guard by Germany's sudden attack. And when invited by Hitler to *earn his half of Poland,* Stalin delayed until mid-September. Only then did Russian troops cross Poland's eastern border, while Polish government officials fled south to Rumania to escape the German and Russian squeeze.

On September 27, Warsaw surrendered, and by early October the last Polish resistance flickered out and died, leaving the country divided between the two victors. An attack on German naval bases in the North Sea in early September by the British Royal Air Force had proved courageous but ineffectual. And toward the end of September, when British land forces took positions along the Belgian border, it was too late.

Lawrence Kendall had watched the events unfold in Europe. With a certain amount of secrecy, he began making numerous trips to Washington. Because of his frequent absences, he moved Elizabeth, the baby, and Jamie to the New York townhouse, along with most of the household staff, and enrolled Larry and Avery at Phillips Exeter Academy in New Hampshire, "where coats and ties are required at all times," he explained to Elizabeth, "and learning is a challenge. It has the seminar system of exchange of ideas in the Socratic manner, rather than the brainless method of stuffing information into the head, which teaches nothing.''

In early 1939, at President Roosevelt's urging, Congress had approved a nine-billion-dollar budget for national defense. A large portion of this was allotted to military aviation. Having learned that the Kendall Aircraft factory had one of the most aggressive, boldest, and most far-seeing management policies in the country, the President had called Lawrence to the White House at that time to confer. It was then that Lawrence's almost weekly trips to Washington began and the Connecticut factory started its rapid expansion program.

"Our Neutrality Act, with its amendments and revisions that put an embargo on shipments to countries involved in war, has been repealed and we have a new act, *cash and carry,*" Lawrence explained to Elizabeth as the limousine rolled down the darkened Manhattan streets toward Pennsylvania Station. "Thanks to Secretary of State Hull."

"With some of that thanks also to you, Lawrence," she said softly with a smile, as she clasped his hand tighter on the seat between them.

"Ah, yes," he said, looking down at her with a grin. "You were Cordell's dinner partner last Saturday night at the Barkers'." He tucked her arm beside his and looked ahead at the traffic. "I merely filled him in on new developments in aircraft, what the needs of Britain and France will undoubtedly be, how we can ship aircraft without involving vessels of the United States."

"And how long will you be with the President and Mr. Hull this time?" she asked in a conspiratorial but teasing tone.

He chuckled in the darkness. "Do I talk in my sleep?" he asked, kissing the tip of her nose.

"It hasn't been difficult to guess."

"Nor will it be difficult for you to keep this just between us," he said in a matter-of-fact way but with his voice considerably lowered, even though the glass partition separating them from Meacham was closed.

"Would you believe it if I told you there are secrets Missy told me when we were seven years old that I haven't divulged yet?" she asked laughingly.

He grinned. "You can be trusted."

Ellie's office was a small room just beyond the library in the Manhattan townhouse. She worked not only as Elizabeth's secretary, keeping all records and handling the correspondence for the numerous charities Elizabeth had become involved in, but also for Lawrence, often taking dictation while he sat at breakfast or in the evening when he brought home a briefcase full of work.

"I'm going to steal her, she's that good," he often teased Elizabeth.

"If you do, I'll divorce you," was always her answer.

"I'd take her on myself," Warren Leland said one Saturday as the four of them sat in the small dining room at a late lunch. Warren had just returned from the West Coast, where he had begun the acquisition of a group of seven newspapers they were bringing into the Kendall chain, and he and Lawrence, with Ellie checking figures, were going to go over the contracts after they had eaten.

"Any news of Karl?" Lawrence suddenly asked her, noticing how silent she had been all during lunch.

She shook her head while still picking at her eggs benedict. "Not for almost a month," she said, looking up with a quick but strained smile at Elizabeth, who had put a hand over hers. "I had hoped he would be staying at Essex, where he was teaching flying to the Volunteer Reservists. Then in September, when Poland was invaded, he was moved, sent on somewhere. I couldn't tell from the postmarks where it was and his letters were heavily censored. But I got the feeling"— she toyed with her cup and saucer as she talked, twisting the cup on the saucer nervously—"the feeling that it was a base where they were in a constant readiness state. Somehow, I think it's France."

She looked pale and drawn in her dark blue dress.

"Well, in the best of times, mail from Europe is slow," Warren said, trying to ease her worry as he leaned back and lit a cigar. Even though he was only in his late twenties, Warren had dark hair streaked with a lock of gray. He was stocky and substantial-looking, smiled a great deal, had a joke for every occasion, and was, according to Lawrence, a genius at acquisition of other companies and firms. "If he is in France, as you seem to think, his mail will take even longer."

It was the summer of 1940 before Ellie finally got word. In May Karl had flown with an RAF squadron that attacked steel mills in the German Ruhr area, and had been wounded in the shoulder and arm. A number of planes had been shot down and others had limped back to base. Though worried about his injuries, Ellie was overwhelmed with relief on hearing that he was safe.

When he arrived back in the United States in late July, she vowed never to let him leave her again.

Elizabeth, Dana, and Lucia went with her to meet his boat on a soft summer evening. They pushed through the crowds at the President Line pier. Although America was not at war, there was a kind of wartime gaiety and near-hysteria where the *President Madison* was docking. Prowling U-boats made travel on the Atlantic hazardous, to say the least, and when Ellie and hundreds of others in the waiting crowd on the pier saw the ship starting to ease into the slip, the small tugboats hooting and howling, they sent up a din of greeting and exultation that shattered the air.

"There he is! I see him, Ellie," Dana shouted in her ear, while pointing up to the second deck.

"Karl!" Elizabeth and Lucia chorused.

"He looks all right," Ellie said, half crying and half laughing while standing on her toes and waving frantically. He was leaning over the rail, smiling and waving back. "He looks all right!" She grasped Elizabeth's arm.

But when she saw him fighting his way through the crowd to get to her after the ship had docked, she realized his arm was in a cast and ran to him, tears streaming down her face.

"It's nothing," he kept saying over and over, as he held her hard against him. He wore a dark small-billed Breton seaman's cap and jacket, and was thin but tanned.

"Let's get to the car," Dana said. He led them toward the car, his arms protectively around Elizabeth and Lucia, while Karl and Ellie followed. Ellie stopped every few steps to take Karl's face between her hands, reassuring herself that he was finally with her again.

"I'm all right," he whispered to her, his mouth against her ear. "Just a problem with some bone fragments. I was lucky, Ellie, very, very lucky. Some of my friends"—she heard the tremble in his voice—"I never saw them again."

Ellie and Karl both enrolled in school once more, for night classes, Ellie deciding she wanted to take some courses perhaps leading some-day to a degree in liberal arts. She signed up at New York University, while Karl reenrolled at Brooklyn Polytechnic Institute for his engineering courses. It was there they met many others like Karl, refugees from war-torn European countries, learning English, studying subjects that would lead them to productive jobs in their new country. They had made friends, among them a jolly, round-faced Hungarian, Miklós Rakósy, who was at the university to study English, and a handsome, dark-haired Frenchman, Georges Poncet, who taught classes in French.

Georges walked with a slight limp, the only outward reminder of a beach just east of Dunkirk when the Germans suddenly broke through in May at Abbeville. He, along with thousands of Frenchmen and other Allied troops, had waited for two days and nights beneath an unceasing barrage of air- and shore-based gunfire before they were rescued and taken to England.

"I was flown to the United States," he told them one evening as they sat in the Budapest at a late supper after classes. He smiled appreciatively, the dark eyes warm, the handsome face with its narrow mustache pale in the brightly lighted restaurant. "The kneecap was shattered, and there was a surgeon who had a new procedure." He laughed softly. "I was his guinea pig."

Although he and Karl rarely talked of what had happened to them in Europe, Ellie knew that it was always there, even in lighter moments such as this, when they were eating chicken paprikash and listening to Hungarian love songs. Ellie often took turns dancing with the men. Sometimes Miklós joined them. When he brought his pretty fiancée, Eva Horvath, along, she would get up and sing with the musicians.

There was a bright, frantic kind of gaiety about the Budapest. Ellie knew it was because of the war in Europe. Most who went there were New Americans, as Miklós proudly called himself at every possible opportunity. They had tasted bitterly of the war, and many would undoubtedly go back. Georges had tried, Karl had told Ellie. But the injuries to his leg, even though helped by a number of surgical procedures, had prevented his reenlistment. Instead he spent countless hours of his free time at the French Consulate translating documents that would be sent by special pouch to Washington for the U.S. State Department.

"In that way, he feels he is contributing *something*," Karl told Ellie, whereupon she quickly changed the subject. She *always* changed the subject when she felt Karl was getting too close to talk of something she knew he had buried deep inside—the feeling that again he must return to Europe.

In the next year, Karl and Lawrence spent hour upon hour behind closed doors at the townhouse in Manhattan and the aircraft plant in Connecticut, with plans for a new plane that Kendall Aircraft was developing spread out before them.

". . . fifty to one hundred bombers to a formation," Ellie heard Karl say one wintry Sunday afternoon as she brought a tray of sandwiches and coffee into the library, where blueprints covered the large carved walnut table. A fire crackled in the fireplace, sending ribbons of light up the paneled walls and rows of books, and music from the Philharmonic drifted softly from the speaker of the tall radio cabinet in the corner of the room. "Junker 88s, Dornier 17s, and with single-engine Messerschmitt 109s and twin-engine 110s as escorts."

Ellie sat down to pour the coffee for them at the low table before the fire. She heard the excitement in Karl's voice and it filled her with dread. But then she heard the answering excitement in Lawrence's, and she thought, It's just that they both love planes. I'm only imagining that he wants to go back.

"What we need here," Karl said, rapping at a drawing on one of the blueprints, "is the capability of a better ceiling than either the Spitfire or the Hurricane now has. That is what the Messerschmitt 109E has—and the best in guns, 20 mm. cannon, two of them, mounted in the wings, and two machine guns."

"In other words, the 110 is slower than the Hurricane, but the 109s, they were the ones that gave you trouble—" Lawrence was saying, when they both looked up sharply, something on the radio catching their attention. Ellie held the silver coffee pot in midair. All three turned their faces toward the radio as a man's deep voice cut through the music: "Here is a special bulletin!"

They heard a rustling of papers, then a man clear his throat.

"The United States was suddenly and unexpectedly attacked this morning at Pearl Harbor, our Pacific naval base in the Hawaiian Islands, by waves of Japanese bombers that struck without warning . . ."

"No," Ellie whispered with disbelief, while Karl and Lawrence strode across the room to the radio and stood there listening. She put the pot down, spilling some coffee on the silver tray.

"At this time," the voice continued, shaking with what sounded like uncontrolled rage, "we can only say that other United States possessions in the Pacific were also attacked by Japanese air force and naval units. The attack in Hawaii, carried out by torpedo-carrying bombers and submarines, has caused untold damage and death, with fires raging in the city of Honolulu and in the harbor, and also at Hickam Field, the Army Air Corps base. There are reports that the battleship *Oklahoma* is afire . . ."

When the double doors to the library were flung open, they all turned around. Elizabeth, in a soft gold wool sweater and tweed skirt, stood there.

"Have you heard?" she cried out and then saw the two men at the radio. She slowly crossed the room to Lawrence, who put his arm about her and held her as they listened.

"Karl?" Ellie said, fear and doubt in her voice, for she had seen his face.

He left the radio and walked to her, a sheepish kind of expression on his face. As he sat down beside her and took her face between his hands, he said slowly, "It means the United States is at war, Ellie."

"No!" she cried, hearing the real meaning in his words, knowing the inside battle that was beginning again in him.

"I have to try—"

"Your arm, Karl," she said frantically.

"There are other ways I can fight."

"Yes, with what you're doing at the aircraft factory."

"Somehow, some way, Ellie, I *must,*" Karl said, his voice low but pleading for understanding.

"No, Karl, now that we have the baby, now that we have Gail—"

"It is *because* of you and the baby, because of those I love, my mother and father, my brothers, Anton and Josef, those who may be lost to me, that I must find some way that I can help. I am a Czech, Ellie," he said with such utter simplicity that she let her head fall against his chest and became silent.

". . . but the news of these surprise attacks has fallen on Washington like a bombshell," the announcer was intoning. "The President has ordered the country and the Navy and Army onto a wartime footing, and has called a meeting of his Cabinet for this evening at the White House. We repeat now this bulletin for those who may have tuned in late. The United States was suddenly and unexpectedly attacked this morning in the Hawaiian Islands, at Pearl Harbor, our great Pacific naval base, by waves of Japanese bombers that struck without warning. . . ." Lawrence slowly reached down and lowered the volume.

"Well," he said heavily. "I guess this means we're at war."

He walked to the telephone and dialed a number. "Mr. Hendricks, please." He paused, and Elizabeth watched him, tall and gravely handsome in his smoking jacket. "Tell him Lawrence Kendall is calling." When Hendricks came to the phone, Lawrence spoke quickly. "John? Yes, we just heard. I want an emergency meeting of all available Kendall directors and officers this evening at eight in the boardroom." He nodded. "Yes, and all others should be in New York by

Wednesday at the latest." He nodded again. "Yes. I'll see you at eight."

When he hung up, Elizabeth was at his side. He put one arm around her, but looked at Karl. "I'll phone the plant manager, Karl, and tell him you're on your way. I want the production schedule changed to three shifts, starting by the end of this week, even if it means that some of the men will be working double shifts for a while. We'll start hiring in the morning."

Karl started for the door. "Tell him I've left."

"Sorry, darling," Lawrence said to Elizabeth as Karl walked out of the room with a wave of his hand. Lawrence picked up the phone and was dialing again. "I'm going to be on this phone for the rest of this afternoon, I'm afraid."

"Of course," she said quietly, smiling wanly at Ellie. "Let's go and work on those letters for the Red Cross, Ellie. They'll be needing these donations more than ever now."

"Please, Georges," Ellie was pleading in a low voice. "You talk to him. He just won't listen to anyone, least of all me. But you've been through it all, the war. You know what it is . . ."

"Ellie," Georges said gently, taking her hand and holding it in his, the giddy laughter and music of the Budapest swirling around them. "Karl has been through it as fully as I. He *knows* what he is getting into. I cannot tell him more than he already knows." They both looked around at Karl, who was stirring his coffee, a grim expression on his face. Georges leaned toward him. "There *is* no need, Karl, for you to go. You have done more than your share—"

"It is what I must do," Karl insisted stubbornly, his jaw set, eyes staring down into his coffee cup. He suddenly looked at Georges. "For you it is different, Georges. Your brother, he went to England with those who followed de Gaulle. And your parents, they are in Algeria. But my mother and father, and my two brothers, Anton and Josef, they are in Czechoslovakia still." He tapped his chest hard. "I have this feeling inside of me that I must do something for them, something that will help them." Still looking at Georges, he had clutched Ellie's hand and was holding it tightly.

Georges nodded slowly, his narrow face with the thin, dark mustache and warm brown eyes filled with understanding. He and Karl both smiled. In the short time they had known each other, they had become close friends, each always seeming to know what the other

204

was thinking. Georges, Karl knew, was a quiet stoic. He was rarely without pain. His leg had healed, but he would live with pain the rest of his life. And yet he never revealed it. Only Karl and Ellie were aware of the burden he bore.

"I am alive," he would always say, his eyes shining, the brilliant smile flashing. And then he would add in a soft voice, "And there are so many others, far worse . . . so many others who are dead. I am very, very lucky."

The two violinists had come to their table then, and launched into a fast and furious gypsy melody that had everyone in the restaurant clapping to the rhythm of the music. A waiter, with a big grin and a huge white apron almost touching the floor, was pouring šljivovica domaćá, a plum brandy, into small glasses for each of them.

"Drink! Drink!" he was shouting, his bright eyes dancing. "America is in the war!" He was reeling a little with excitement and slivovitz, and his heavy Hungarian accent was heavier than ever. "Now we will show that scum." And then he danced away, the bottle held aloft. "Drink! Drink!"

Karl and Georges raised their glasses, while Ellie hesitantly put one hand around hers. Her eyes were still pleading with Karl.

"Take care of her for me, Georges," Karl said softly.

"Of course."

"Karl!" Ellie begged, her eyes, beneath the blue hat, filling with tears.

But Karl merely squeezed her hand. "She is very . . . precious to me."

"And you, Karl—you take care of yourself," Georges said.

Karl laughed. "I am a most careful fella."

"Don't joke about it," Ellie cried.

"Dance with me, Ellie?" Karl suddenly said, pulling her to her feet as the music grew faster and couples whirled around the floor. Georges watched them admiringly while they floated off. He loved them both. They had become his closest friends in America.

Elizabeth had just asked Ellie to go upstairs. They had finally, after two days of work, finished the Red Cross donations mailing and had just returned from the post office. "Nanny Grace will be back from the park with the children, Ellie," she said as they handed their coats to Morgan. "Why don't you tell her to give them their supper in the playroom. I'll be along in a few minutes." As Ellie ran up the staircase,

Elizabeth heard a commotion and looked around at the entrance. Lucia was flying through the door, Dana just behind her.

"You tell him, Elizabeth!" Lucia was crying. "He won't listen to me."

She had thrown her arms around Elizabeth, engulfing her in a cloud of perfumed mink and chiffon, the scarf draped over her head and trailing over her shoulders, flakes of snow still clinging to it.

"Tell him what?" Elizabeth said, leading them along the gallery to the small drawing room, where a fire burned on the hearth. Morgan, following behind them, took Dana's and Lucia's coats. "Morgan, would you bring highballs, please."

"Yes, Madam," he said.

"What does she want you to tell me, Dana?" Elizabeth asked, standing by the fireplace, one arm leaning on the mantel.

"He wants to enlist in the Marine Corps," Lucia said in a sudden burst. "We have just come from your mother's. Sybil is distraught."

Elizabeth watched Dana, who stood quietly by a window looking out into the bitter cold twilight that had fallen over Fifth Avenue. *Dear Dana,* she thought, studying the handsome, brooding face in profile, *he would rush into it.* "Why not wait a little, darling?" Elizabeth said softly as she walked to him.

"Please, my love!" Lucia begged. She ran across the room to them, the dozen gold bangle bracelets on her arm jingling with the motion of her small frenzied body. "Listen to Elizabeth."

Dana turned slowly to Elizabeth and took one of her outstretched hands in his as he put an arm about Lucia. How beautiful she looks, he thought, even in a simple skirt and sweater, and then he looked down at Lucia, the dazzling little creature that was his wife, and he almost said, All right . . . I'll wait. He loved her so, all ninety-eight pounds of fragile energy and conflicting emotions, the dark dancing eyes flecked with gold, but now flooded with tears.

"I *have* to go," he said to Elizabeth, his eyes pleading with her to understand, the agony of decision in the grip of his hand and the low hard timbre of his voice. "They're going to call all men up to the age of thirty-five without children. I don't want to wait to be called."

"But it could be months, perhaps even years," Lucia pleaded with him. He put his arms around her, looking at Elizabeth over her head. "Please, Dana," she sobbed.

"Lucia," Elizabeth said, gently trying to turn her around in Dana's arms so that she could look into her face. "You musn't do this to yourself. You have a performance tonight, and—"

"No," Lucia wailed. "I can't do it, I can't go on."

Dana suddenly stood her away a little from him, grasping her by the arms. In a low voice, he said, "Don't say that, Lucia. Don't ever say that. Of course you'll go on. You'll walk on the stage at the Met, and you'll be wonderful, more than wonderful."

"I can't, I can't—"

"You can," he said, with a harshness that Elizabeth had never heard before. He was almost shaking Lucia, his hands gripping her arms, his face white and tense with stubborn determination. "The world doesn't stand still for us, Lucia. And because it doesn't, we do what we must do, no matter what happens. I have something that I have to do and you have what you must do." The sobs were slowly subsiding. He pulled her against him again and held her. Tears staining her cheeks, she looked up into his face.

"Yes," she whispered. "Yes, of course. We both will do what we must." She turned in his arms after a moment and looked at Elizabeth with a trembling smile. "Please come tonight to hear me. I will sing especially for you and Dana."

15
1942

Karl sat on a thick coil of rope and peered through the mist, marveling silently at the navigational skill of the man at the wheel of the long fishing boat. Just moments earlier he had been called up on deck from the dank, smelly hold below by the captain, a Pole named Wincenty Roclaw, who told him to get some air and a cup of coffee to warm his chilled bones. He sat in silence, feeling the roll of the sea, tasting the salt in the fine spray, and listened to the soft chug of the engine.

"In this fog, it will be safe for a time," the captain told Karl. "Until we start to approach the coast. Then I will ask you to go below again." Roclaw's sturdy shape was blurred in the heavy fog.

They were crossing the Baltic Sea at its narrowest point, below Ystad, the port on the lower tip of Sweden, where he had boarded a Swedish fishing boat. It had taken him to the midpoint of his journey, to Bornholm, on the isle of Rönne, where he had transferred to this Polish fishing boat. There were two others, Czechs like himself, Václav Bozema and Ludvic Halek, both members of the Underground who had fled to England when there was no longer any doubt that the Germans would march across the border into Czechoslovakia.

Karl smiled into the mist. They had met in London and gone into training with other members of the Czech Underground, learning the art of making and setting bombs. They were also drilled in survival tactics, given maps and photographs to memorize, and clothing and false identification papers that would let them blend in among the populace.

"Thinking of home, Karl?" Ludvic asked, sitting down next to him. He held his coffee cup so that it would warm both of his hands.

"Yes," Karl said softly, his eyes warm with memories, "thinking of home." He hadn't told Ellie until the night before he was to leave. He had been negotiating for months with the Underground in London, through the Czech Consulate, which still continued to operate in New York. When at last his orders had come, he first told Lawrence Kendall. That evening he had listened to Ellie read a story to Gail, played a game of hide-and-seek with their blonde, bouncing four-year-old, and helped to tuck her in bed, smiling sadly into the half darkness while Ellie sang her to sleep. Then they tiptoed from the nursery in their suite of rooms on the fourth floor of the Kendall townhouse.

She curled against him in their dark bedroom, feeling his warmth, the firm flesh and hardness against her as they listened to the lulling sound of rain tapping at the windows, of traffic far below them on the avenue. Finally, whispering, he told her. For a long moment, there was silence. Then he felt her body stiffen. She turned slowly and faced him.

"I hoped you had changed your mind," she said, all of the agony and loneliness and fear she had held at bay for so long crying out in the few whispered words.

"I *must* go, Ellie. Please try to understand."

She asked him no more. He gathered her to him and made love to her. All through the night she clung to him, sleeping fitfully. In the morning, when Meacham drove him to Pennsylvania Station, where he caught a train to Washington, he kept remembering how they had looked, Gail on Ellie's lap in her long white nightgown, her blue eyes round and sad, Ellie's filled with tears. He had left them in the small sitting room of their suite, in a shaft of early-morning light that fell through the window.

"I want to remember you both here," he had said softly, looking at them for a long moment. Then he had closed the door and hurried away, down through the corridors and staircases of the townhouse, still silent in the early-winter morning light.

"It . . . it was harder leaving this time," he said, without looking at Ludvic. The fog swirled around them, as Ludvic nodded. He had learned much about Karl Wancek in the almost four months they had been together, while training in England—about the young woman, Miriam, in Berlin, and then how finally he had married Ellie Halloran and they had had a child. He, Ludvic, had no ties back in England, where he had gone just before the Czech borders had closed. It was easier for a man who had no ties, easier to face the work that lay ahead of them.

Looking up, he sniffed the air. "We must be close," he whispered.

"I can smell land." He could smell the touches of spring.

Karl sniffed softly and nodded. "Poland," he said, his voice low. "It's . . . almost like being there already."

Karl, Ludvic, and Václav traveled short distances at a stretch. They arrived at the Polish coastal town of Kamien Pomorski at the busiest hour of sunset, when the hundreds of fishing boats were returning with the day's catch. They were immediately taken to a small house near the docks by two men who seemed to appear from nowhere out of the swarm of fishermen busy unloading. The men left them some food and a single candle.

They had been sitting on the dirt floor of the cellar for several hours, each occupied with his own thoughts, when Karl heard a soft chuckle and turned his head. In the flickering candlelight, Václav seemed to be sleeping, his face down on his knees, but Ludvic was whittling at a piece of wood.

"Who would have thought ten years ago that I would be sitting here in a cellar in a seacoast town of Poland, waiting to be smuggled back into my own country?" he said, smiling at the irony of it. "When I left my home village of Lidice—"

"Lidice? But you said you came from Pisek."

Ludvic grinned. "I came from many places, wherever there was work. I left Lidice when I was fifteen. I was born there."

"Lidice is where I, too, was born," Karl said excitedly.

Ludvic looked surprised. "But you said Prague—"

"My brother and I went to Prague, where he studied music."

Ludvic leaned over and clapped him on the shoulder. He suddenly snapped his fingers. "Wait! Your name is Wancek, you say?"

"Yes. Karl Wancek."

"Of course," Ludvic said, clapping his shoulder again. "I knew your father. Stefan Wancek." He laughed, remembering, and put his hand out as though measuring a child's height. "You must have been about this high, when I left Lidice. Always laughing. I remember, always laughing."

They talked warmly of home for another hour or two and then slept, their weariness catching up with them.

At about midnight, the two men who had brought them there— both middle-aged and with the eyes and wariness of animals that stalk in the night—returned and led them through narrow winding roads back to the dock area, where they hid them in a big truck that was loaded with fish.

"I hope this is not an omen," Václav said, laughing softly as he wrinkled his nose. "I hate fish." He was a handsome young man with dark hair and the sensitive features of a city-born youth of Hungarian origins, while Ludvic had the sturdier body and thicker features of a Slav and was older. He had been a miner, but had disliked working beneath the ground, so had gone to Brno, he told them.

"Well, I like fish," Ludvic said, pulling his knees up beneath his chin and a rough brown blanket about him to ward off the chill. "But to eat, in a restaurant, not to sleep next to."

They were huddled up near the front of the truck, the barrels of fish sloshing behind them as the truck rolled through the night. Before putting his head on his knees to try to get some sleep, Karl patted his jacket, feeling the slight bulge where he had put his forged papers. He was now Ladislaw Lehocki, a student at the university in Prague. The forgery was flawless, from all that Karl could detect, and the background closely matched his own. The fact that he spoke English as well as he did was supposedly attributed to three years of study of that language at the university. The scars on his shoulder and arm were from early service in the Polish Air Force, during the futile defense of Warsaw. He had since learned the error of his ways, his papers said, and was working at the university for a Professor Anders in the translating of English-language newspapers.

"Is there a Professor Anders?" he had asked one of the two men who had handed him his forged papers.

"Yes, and he will swear, if need be, that you work for him."

He awoke when the truck arrived, two hundred and fifty kilometers south, at the town of Zielona. Here they were met again, hurried into the cellar of a building that was dank with dripping water and wet earth. They were certain the scurrying sounds they heard in the dark came from rats. Once more, they were put into a truck in the dead of night, this one filled with hay, and were driven close to the Czech border near Walbrzych, where they were hidden until after darkness fell. It was then that they set out on foot, following two guides who were simply moving shadows in the dark, low-voiced shadows who spoke as little as possible. They pushed through rugged, mountainous terrain, through passes and ravines of the Sudetens, walking for hours, the thick bushes and scrub scratching their faces, the steep inclines and almost impenetrable underbrush exhausting them. But they pushed on, finally stopping for perhaps an hour while their guides left them and scouted up ahead.

"The border," Karl whispered to the others, and in the darkness he saw them nod their heads from where they crouched behind wide-trunked trees. When the guides returned, one kneeled down next to them and said, "From here, do not speak. Simply follow us and watch for arm signals. There is no barbed wire. But there are soldiers at intervals, with dogs. We are upwind of the closest guard-post. Follow me quickly, but when I signal you with one long sweep of my arm downward, that means you are across the border and must go on alone. You will be met about three hundred meters beyond where we leave you. Stop for nothing. Only for the word *Polonaise.* That is your password from those who will meet you. Come now."

They followed him, Karl at the head, the others in single file behind him. They ran swiftly, crouching low, each crackle of underbrush underfoot causing Karl to wonder if at any second shots would ring out.

When the guide suddenly stopped, Karl froze and held his breath. Sounds rose up out of the night, a stream nearby, a dog howling in the distance, a sharp snapping noise, as though an animal or man, walking stealthily, might have broken a twig. Just when he thought his lungs would burst out of his chest, the man began to run again.

They had leaped across a narrow brook when the guide stopped once more. He threw his arm up, held it there for a moment, then brought it with one long sweep downward. That was the signal to go on alone. Without hesitating, Karl and his companions ran on without looking back. They hurried across a broad open expanse, just as the moon came out from behind a deep bank of clouds. Karl's heart seemed to be lodged in his throat, pounding hard as he ran. He heard the running footsteps and strangled breath behind him of Ludvic and Václav, then the sound of a dog suddenly barking, two others taking up the call, a baying sound that sent chills of terror into him. The ground had turned steeply upward and he pushed on, the baying of the dogs coming closer. In the light of the moon, he could see a line of trees at the top of the hill up ahead, and somehow he knew that someone waited there for them, someone who would whisper the word *Polonaise.*

He looked over his shoulder. Ludvic was falling somewhat behind. "Hurry!" he said in a low voice, pausing to half turn and urge them on. Václav surged on past him, ragged bursts of breath tearing at the air. Karl suddenly grasped Ludvic's arm and pulled him up the incline with him, looking down just once, his gaze sweeping the valley below as the baying of the dogs drew even closer. Something was moving

in the distance. Or was it just a trick of the imagination? He pulled
Ludvic faster as Václav heaved past them. He heard the terrible rasp
of his own breath in his throat, felt the pain in his chest, the knife-like
stabbing in his side.

"Can't! Can't . . . !" Ludvic was sobbing as he staggered.

"You can!" Karl hissed as he pulled him onward. "We're almost
there."

Just a few more feet, he thought, his head throbbing as he stumbled
on, never loosening his grip on the man's arm. Suddenly strong hands
gripped them from each side. He tried to twist away, heaving upward,
then with a last superhuman ounce of strength he swerved and
wrenched his arm free, while reaching with the other toward the knife
at his belt.

"Polonaise!" a voice whispered harshly through the darkness.

Karl paused only for a moment, his hand clutching the scabbard at
his belt. He blinked hard, saw a white oval of a face, the eyes glittering. "Thank God!" he muttered.

"Come quickly," the other voice said as the man turned and pushed
into the forest, Karl following. He still supported Ludvic, who gasped,
"I can make it now, Karl."

Each day, Karl would go to the university, where it was believed
he and Professor Anders were poring over English-language newspapers. In reality he, Ludvic, Václav, and their instructors were closed
behind locked doors in a cellar room rehearsing over and over every
step of the action that had been planned for them by the Czech
Underground. And each day in late afternoon he would go to the
Hybernergasse, to the Café Arco in the long row of gray stone Gothic
buildings, looking for Anton.

Since arriving in Prague in early May he had found no one who
knew of Anton's whereabouts. All Karl knew was that Anton had
probably returned to Prague from Berlin. One day he fell into conversation at the café with an older man who wore a large, soft-brimmed
black hat over somewhat longish hair and carried a violin case. He was
sitting at a table by himself sipping a glass of wine, a long flowing black
cape about his shoulders.

"I wonder if I might join you?" Karl asked hesitantly, with a small
apologetic bow.

The man looked at him and smiled. "Of course. Please sit down."
The café was crowded and smoky, conversation and laughter ringing

up to the ceiling. Karl felt safe there. It was popular with the university students as well as with writers and musicians. Even if someone should recognize him, they would be careful, greet him with caution. Everyone in Prague was cautious these days, he thought, as he looked about and saw the sprinkling of Nazi uniforms.

"I see that you are a musician," Karl said.

"Yes," the man said, still smiling. "I am with the Philharmonic. A violinist. My name is Sebastian Feder."

"You would perhaps then know of a composer I once knew. Yes, he was a friend of mine some years ago. I was away for quite some time, and when I returned, I found he no longer lived at the same place he had before, and no one there knew where he had gone."

"A composer?" the musician said. "What is his name?"

"Wancek. Anton Wancek."

The man was staring at Karl with a curious expression. Suddenly he looked away and for a moment watched a group of Nazi officers who were laughing loudly at a table in the center of the room. The slight curl of disdain at the corner of his mouth told Karl everything he wanted to know. He leaned forward.

"Have you ever heard of him?"

The musician looked slowly around at him. "Ye-es," he said. "Anton Wancek is the assistant conductor of the Philharmonic."

Karl quickly hid the relief and surprise that he felt all at once. He took a quick drink of the schnapps in front of him, to play for time, wondering how to proceed. But he needn't have worried.

"Why don't I suggest to Anton that he stop here tomorrow afternoon at about this time?" The musician's eyes were guarded, but were also sending Karl a message. When Karl nodded gratefully, the man said, "Who shall I say would like to see him?"

"Why—why, just tell him that it's a friend of his brother Karl's." He rose then. "And thank you. You have been most kind."

"Not at all. It's—the very least I could do."

Karl had been waiting for fully an hour in the Café Arco when a waiter came to the table and in a low voice said, "Excuse me, sir. If you would follow me, there is someone waiting to see you in one of the private rooms."

Rising, Karl followed him at a distance, looking about him casually, as though he had had enough of the café for one day and was simply wandering out. But once he was beyond where most eyes from the main room could see him, he hurried after the waiter into a narrow corridor and through a door into a small room.

For several moments they stared at each other, while the waiter bowed out, closing the door behind him. Anton had risen from the table and slowly came around it. They suddenly began hugging each other, laughing softly, excitedly.

"I had begun to think I would never see you again," Anton said, as he finally stood back to look at Karl, then waved him into the seat opposite him at the table.

"I, too," Karl said, smiling broadly as he leaned on the table in eagerness.

For several moments, in low voices, they caught up on the years that had passed, Anton reassuring Karl that their parents and Josef were all right, Karl quickly telling Anton about Ellie and Gail, and their life at the Kendall homes.

Suddenly Anton's eyes narrowed and he leaned forward. "What are you doing here, Karl?"

"Why, my name is Ladislaw Lehocki and I am an English-language student at the university, where I help Professor Anders translate English-language newspapers. I served in the Czech Air Force and"—he stretched his arm out to the side and stiffly flexed it—"and was wounded in the defense of Warsaw." He smiled winningly. "Since then, of course, I have seen that that was wrong, have admitted the error of my ways, and am now helping the 'government' with this work I am doing with Professor Anders."

Anton nodded worriedly. "It would not be wise for us to be seen together. Sebastian Feder, the musician you met yesterday here—he said that he began to realize we must be brothers when you asked about me. Over the years, he has heard me speak of you and recognized you yesterday simply because we bear a strong resemblance."

Karl nodded, sober once more.

"I am watched, of course," Anton said casually. He pulled a silver-stemmed pipe from his pocket and tamped tobacco into it, then slowly lit it. "Most of us are. We are known to—er, to have liberal viewpoints, we artists." He laughed bitterly. "Oh, some of us have been taken away. But, for the most part, they leave us alone, while keeping a careful watch on us. After all, they need us. We provide the cultural cover for the city, the country. We are proof to the world that life in Czechoslovakia goes on as usual. My first concerto will be performed by the Philharmonic next autumn—"

"Anton!" Karl said excitedly, clasping Anton's hand across the table.

But Anton was shaking his head. "The audience will be filled with Nazi officers and their women—and those in the new Czech 'government' who, for reasons of greed or simply survival, have chosen to ally themselves with the Germans."

"Still," Karl said softly, "your first concerto."

Anton leaned slowly forward again. "Why are you really here, Karl?"

Karl shook his head and smiled, a sardonic kind of twist at one corner of his mouth. "I'm sorry, Anton. I can't tell you that."

Anton nodded. "Will you meet me here in this room each day? We can have supper and talk."

"I'd like that. But . . ." He looked through the gauzy curtains out the long casement window to the Hybernergasse. Windows in the three-story building opposite were open wide to the soft early evening. If he leaned close to the window frame and looked to his right, he could see the Powder Tower, rising with rococo majesty toward the lavender sky, wagons and vehicles rattling beneath its Byzantine arch. "When the day comes that I am not here, you will know my work is finished in Prague and I have left."

Anton stared at him. There was a strange mixture of fear and admiration in his eyes. He slowly rose and put his hands out to clasp Karl's. "I must go now. I have a rehearsal for Sunday's concert."

Karl also stood up and walked around the table to hold Anton to him for a moment. They clasped each other's arms, their eyes misty.

"Will you . . . somehow see Mama and Papa?" Anton asked.

"Yes," Karl said simply. "I couldn't leave Czechoslovakia without seeing them."

Anton nodded and slowly walked to the door. "Tomorrow then?"

Karl nodded with a smile. "Tomorrow."

Just as Anton had started to raise his baton, he heard the whisper of voices behind him. He paused and waited. It was his first public appearance as a conductor, a special performance at the State Opera House—of the Brahms Piano Concerto in B flat—for visiting Nazi officials from Berlin. Egon Karlovy, the regular conductor, had pleaded illness rather than perform "for the butchers from Berlin," as he called them. Anton, as assistant conductor, had not been able to refuse, much as he wanted to.

216

He turned slightly and looked over his shoulder to the center box that was reserved for the head of state. Just sitting down in one of the small red velvet and gilt chairs was Reinhard Heydrich, recently appointed Acting Protector of Bohemia and Moravia by Adolf Hitler. An icy-eyed young man of thirty-eight, known for his blond Aryan good looks, he was said to be one of Hitler's favorites. As his party settled in the box, Anton raised his baton, but with sinking heart. He nodded at Hector Czernek at the piano, who lowered his eyelids indicating that he was ready.

As Anton made his way through the crush of musicians backstage, most crowding in close to congratulate him and Czernek, he smiled and thanked them. As he had hoped would happen, once the glorious music of the Brahms concerto began to soar he became lost in it, until there was no one in the universe but himself, the composer, the pianist, and the orchestra. He still felt the elation as he floated through the excited crowd, nodding and smiling. For several moments he didn't notice that the hubbub of voices had sunk to a mere whisper. Suddenly he was the only one moving. He stopped.

Standing directly in front of him was Reinhard Heydrich. He stared at the man, noting the ice-cold eyes and long narrow nose. His uniform was impeccable and a row of colorful medals adorned his jacket. Two beautiful women stood to either side of him, with several smiling officers just behind them. Heydrich himself was smiling as he held his hand out.

"Maestro," he said, then looked quickly over his shoulder at one of the officers. "Would you translate for me, Zellner?"

"I understand German," Anton said curtly, but in perfect German.

"Good. Good," Heydrich said. "I simply wanted to offer my congratulations. I understand you are a composer and that your first works will be performed this autumn. I hope that I shall be here, Maestro, for I am an admirer of yours already." Anton tried to smile, but his face felt like hardened plaster. Heydrich went on. "I play the violin, quite well, I am told." The two women and the officers behind him were all nodding vehemently and murmuring. "My father was a composer and head of the Halle Conservatory. And my mother teaches voice and piano." He laughed. "I was headed for a musical career, but . . ." He spread his hands as though to say that fate had intervened. "But the Führer decided differently, as you can see."

Anton expressed his thanks, stiffly, while feeling a stir of nausea, and with a slight bow excused himself. Half-running, he reached his dressing room, slammed the door, and, tears running down his face, softly pounded his fist against the wall.

The man known only as Ziv asked for silence, then carefully searched the face of each of the six men before him. He would be the only one to stay in Prague. The others—all members of the Czech Underground, trained for this mission in London—would, by some means or other, get out of Czechoslovakia and return to England.

"I told you that I would decide now, and only now, which two of you would be the ones selected to carry out the actual mission. The other four will be in reserve. You will be in place several kilometers beyond the point we have chosen for the action, and you will remain there until you know it has been carried out. If something should happen"—he turned to a map on the wall in the low-ceilinged cellar room and pointed to a place along a winding road that led from the villa in the countryside outside of Prague into the city—"if the car approaches the point where you are hidden, you will know that the action, for some reason, was not carried out, and you must act and act quickly. Do you understand?"

They all nodded.

Ziv watched them from beneath half-lowered lids. "The two we have selected are Josef Gabeik and Jan Kubis."

The other four turned their heads to look at the two men, both short and stocky, with sandy hair, almost interchangeable, Karl thought. They had been parachuted in from England a week before and were known to have asked for the mission.

"You, Lehocki . . ." For a moment Karl didn't answer or turn his head. And then he jumped to his feet.

"Yes?"

"You will go with Gabeik and Kubis, to help carry the equipment."

He nodded, feeling a shiver run up his spine. It was an hour before dawn and they were to be in place before the sky grew light. He turned with Gabeik and Kubis, and headed for the door.

They had been in position for several hours, well hidden by heavy shrubbery along the side of the road. Heydrich's car, an open Mercedes sports model, would travel from his country villa along this road to his headquarters at Hradschin Castle in Prague, the castle that had been the ancient seat of Bohemian kings.

Karl sat hunched over the machine gun, fully aware, according to his instructions, that it was only to be used if the bomb did not go off or for self-protection. It was to be left behind when they ran for the small black car parked a hundred yards away in a well hidden spot.

They sat in silence and listened to insects buzzing softly in a clump of wildflowers near them. Karl looked at the yellow buttercups and thought of Ellie. She was like soft yellow and white flowers, eyes blue as the sky. What was she thinking? he wondered. Of him, he knew. She would just be going to bed, and would be lying there, looking up at the ceiling, perhaps reaching out to the other pillow as though to touch him, to . . .

"There it is!" Josef's deep voice was terse, tense.

Karl hunched lower, his hands tightening on the machine gun. He felt a ribbon of excitement charge from deep inside and spiral like lightning all through him. He hardly seemed to breathe and yet he felt a cold calm. He could see the vehicle containing Heydrich and his driver. The open Mercedes sports car was still in the distance, but the figures of two men were clearly discernible. He tightened his grip even more as the car drew closer. Then closer. And closer, until finally it was almost opposite them, a gleam of shining black metal and chrome against the intense, sun-washed green of shrubbery and trees.

With a sudden roaring shout, Josef rose to his feet and jumped high in the air, his arm curving in a wide arc. A split second later, Jan repeated the motion, following the first bomb with a smoke bomb, the two lethal objects soaring into the air.

Still crouched over the machine gun, Karl saw the first bomb strike and explode with the deafening sound of a close clap of thunder. With awe, he watched as, seconds later, large pieces of the automobile began to fly through the air. The car had splintered and shattered like a coconut, metal flying in all directions. He saw a wheel spiral upward against the sky, and then the smoke bomb cut off his vision and turned the sky to night.

"Run!" Josef shouted.

They leaped and ran through the underbrush down the embankment to a lower road, where they scrambled into a small car, Karl behind the wheel. In seconds, the car had screeched away, clouds of smoke still drifting overhead. None of them spoke, not until they were again back in the city, the little black car now traveling at a normal speed as it poked its way through the winding narrow back streets.

"Good show!" Josef said, letting his breath out in little spurts.

Jan laughed shakily and lightly punched Karl on the shoulder. "Six months in London and he talks like an Englishman."

For almost a week, Karl and the others remained hidden in the deep cellars of the Karl Borromaeus Church, along with other members of the Underground who had participated in acts of violence against the Nazis and were on the Wanted lists. News trickled down to them that Heydrich's spine had been shattered and that he was in a coma. Then on June fourth, they were told by one of the priests that Heydrich had died and that the newspapers were reporting the Nazis promised terrible revenge. It was then that Karl decided he must make his move. He wanted to see his parents and his brother Josef before leaving Czechoslovakia. When he told his companions that he was going to make his way to Lidice, they warned him against it, but he was determined.

"I want to get back to my wife and my child," he said. "More than anything I want that. But first, I must see my parents." He turned to Ludvic. "Come with me to Lidice."

But Ludvic shook his head. "I have more work I must do here before going to Lidice."

Karl clasped his hand and said he would go to his family and tell them that he was safe. He then shook hands all around and with one glance back at them pushed his way through the large cellar toward the winding stone staircase. When he reached the stairs, he looked across the sea of closely packed bodies for a moment. The room was big and dimly lit, candles flickering in the far corners where light from the two feeble hanging light bulbs didn't reach. More than one hundred men and women wandered about or were stretched out close together on pallets on the floor. Some sat with knees hunched up, staring into space. He shook his head a little, as though to clear the depressing sight from his eyes. Then he looked to the corner where his friends stood watching him, raised his hand in a brief salute, and quickly bounded up the staircase.

Karl had been in Lidice for three days and was preparing to leave and make his way back to the Polish seacoast town of Kamien Pomorski when Josef raced from the village into the house, shouting, "The radio. Turn on the radio."

Stefan quickly walked to the small radio and turned it on to a station broadcasting from Prague, then slowly returned to the table where he had been drinking tea with Selma and Karl. Karl's rucksack was ready and standing by the door. He had visited Ludvic's family and reassured them that Ludvic was safe and would soon come to see them. Within the hour he planned to be gone, back to Prague, where again he would be hidden in a truck driving north toward the border of Poland.

". . . where members of the SS, the *Schutzstaffel,* found one hundred and twenty members of the Czech Underground, among them five or six believed to be the actual murderers of Reinhard Heydrich, Reich Protector of Bohemia and Moravia, those who assassinated him in cold blood on a country road one week ago. All one hundred and twenty criminals were executed at—"

"No!" Karl shouted. He had leaped to his feet and was gripping the edge of the table.

"—were found in the large cellar rooms of the Karl Borromaeus Church in Prague, where priests of the church had hidden them . . ."

"No!" Karl shouted again as both his mother and his father grasped his arms and held onto him.

"There's nothing you can do, Karl," Stefan said as Karl lunged toward the door.

"I have to go there," he cried out.

"Why?" Selma asked, her face stricken. "There is nothing you can do now."

Stefan had walked to Karl and was holding him by the shoulders. "In fact, you must go nowhere at this moment. This is only the beginning, I feel certain." From the little Karl had said, Stefan had guessed his son had been involved with the assassination of Heydrich. They had been shocked when he arrived in the night at the house in Lidice, shocked but happy. The next three nights, after she and Stefan had gone to their room, Selma had wept in the darkness, knowing her son would leave again. Stefan had tried to comfort her, all the while feeling his own impending sense of loss. Now she became terribly frightened.

"Your father is right, Karl. You must wait. Wait until you know it is safer."

"They'll be watching all the roads," Josef said, "wondering if any slipped through and escaped, like you."

Karl looked at his younger brother, now as tall as he. "Yes," he said. "Yes, I will have to wait. A week perhaps."

"You will be safe here. No one ever comes to Lidice," Josef said, laughing hollowly, trying to make a joke of it.

Josef had picked up Karl's rucksack and was walking to the narrow staircase with it. "I'll take this back to your room," he said with a shy smile. This meant his brother would be with them longer.

"But I must leave at the end of the week." Karl looked at each of them, his mouth tight with determination. And then it softened a little. "I miss them, you see. I didn't realize how much I miss them —how much I love them, until this moment."

"Of course, son," Selma said softly, her eyes filling with tears. "And soon you will go home to them."

Anton Wancek could almost believe there was no occupation of his country, could almost believe there were no Germans, as he walked along the Hybernergasse toward the Café Arco. It was a balmy late-spring night. Lovers still strolled in the streets, the moon hung low over the rooftops, and if he breathed deeply he could smell the river. He paused for a moment before entering the café, then walked in and stood just inside the door to look around. It was then that he saw Sebastian Feder, the first violinist of the orchestra. He was sitting at a small table sipping coffee and looking around him nervously. The café was crowded, heavy with drifting smoke and outbursts of laughter, while the uneven drone of voices rose and fell. Feder didn't see him for a moment, but when he did, he raised his hand to Anton and waved him toward his table almost frantically.

"Ahhh, you are here," Feder said with relief. "I was afraid you would not stop here before going to the concert hall this evening."

As he sat down, Anton looked at the older man sharply. Something in his voice was warning him.

"You must not go to the theatre, Anton. No. It is better that you hear it here from me—" His voice was low, urgent, and he kept looking toward the café's door.

"What is it, Sebastian?" Anton had grasped his wrist and was holding it hard.

Feder leaned closer. "There is no way I can break this to you easily. It's Lidice—"

"Lidice?"

"The Germans. They have burned it to the ground."

"My God!" Anton gasped.

"As a lesson. For the killing of Heydrich." His grip tightened on Anton's arm as he saw the younger man's face turn ashen.

"My brother Karl. He said he would go there before—"

"Anton!" Feder's face was gray. He looked ill. "That is not all of it." For a long moment there was silence between them, as Anton began to understand. "The men. They killed all of the men, and took the women and children away in trucks. To a concentration camp. And then they burned and dynamited the town to rubble."

He held onto his friend's arm, then quickly picked up a bottle of brandy that was on the table and poured a glassful, pushing it into Anton's other hand. He watched as Anton swallowed it.

"Gone," Anton finally said. "All of them gone . . ."

He staggered to his feet and walked toward the door, Feder following him, the babble of voices and clatter of dishes rising around him and shattering against his ears while *Gone . . . All gone . . .* sang inside his head.

16

The August sunshine poured like molten gold from a cloudless blue sky, with only a puffing little breeze to relieve the suffocating heat. Ellie looked down from beneath her wide-brimmed straw hat and smiled. Caroline and Gail in starched white dresses were hopping about like bright little birds, trying to see everything at once, while Ellie held their hands. She watched for Georges, who had gone some distance to where a short, fat man was selling ice cream from a cart.

Even with the intense heat, the zoo was crowded with screaming children, weary parents, and perspiring nannies.

"No, Caroline," Gail was saying as she shook a tiny scolding finger at her smaller companion. "We can't go look at the monkeys until Georges brings us our ice cream cones."

"But I want to see the monkeys!" Caroline insisted stubbornly, her lower lip stuck out as she hopped on one foot.

"In just another few moments, sweetheart," Ellie said, only half-listening to the two little girls as their happy, chirping voices drifted up to her. "Georges is hurrying as fast as he can."

She sank down onto a nearby green bench as two nannies suddenly stood up and pushed their prams toward the lion house. "Now, sit here beside me, both of you," she said, watching them climb up onto the bench and sit at its edge on either side of her. She looked from one to the other, almost as though seeing them for the first time, Gail with her halo of golden curls and saucy blue eyes, Caroline, clapping her plump little hands, as a smiling organ grinder and his monkey came slowly toward them, the hand organ grinding out a merry tune. Long, shining dark curls tumbled down her back, and her eyes, a deep and lovely violet color, were filled with laughter as she watched the monkey, in his tiny cap and uniform with brass buttons, leap from the organ grinder's shoulder to the organ and back again.

Ellie pulled two coins from her purse and handed them to the two little girls, who held them out toward the monkey. When he grasped the coins and dropped them into a cup attached to the organ, they shrieked with joy. They were so much alike in some ways and yet so different in others. Gail was carefree and full of laughter, while Caroline was more thoughtful, more circumspect, often watching Gail with a quizzical smile on her face as though wondering how anyone could always be so full of high spirits and mischief.

"There's Georges, there's Georges!" Gail screeched. Ellie looked up and watched him coming toward them, balancing two ice cream cones in his hands, holding them out so that they wouldn't drip on his impeccable summer suit. He was dressed all in white, in a linen suit and panama hat, which sat jauntily over one eye. As dark as Karl was blond, he had eyes that, Ellie knew, made most women sigh. "He's so gorgeous!" Jessie said one day when he came to take Ellie out to lunch. She was whispering to Edna, while they peeked out at him from behind the half-closed drawing room door, as Morgan led him back toward Ellie's office. "I know," Edna mourned, "an' Miss Ellie, she don't even see him, she's so upset over her husband."

Ellie knew, in a far corner of her mind, that Georges was in love with her. But she pretended it wasn't so, pretended that they were just friends, that Georges was there as often as he was because he was Karl's friend as well and simply wanted to comfort her.

"Are you certain you do not have a sister who looks exactly like you?" Georges often asked in his precise but French-accented English, his voice mockingly mournful.

"I have two," Ellie would say, laughing delightedly, "but they are older, married, and each has four children."

He had become a fixture in their lives. Since Karl had left, Ellie found herself leaning on him for comfort and strength.

She watched him as he came toward them, laughingly holding out the dripping cones. Today was the first time she had seen him in several weeks. For some reason, he had stopped calling on the phone, and after a week or ten days had passed, she realized that she missed him.

They were strolling toward the lion house, the two little girls running ahead hand in hand, licking their ice cream cones.

"It's good to see you again, Georges," she said.

He turned to look at her, leaning forward a little to see her face beneath the floppy pink brim. She was wearing a pink-and-white flowered dress in some light material that blew prettily in the soft breeze, the pink suffusing her cheeks, golden hair framing her face. He suddenly stopped and turned her toward him.

"Is it really good to see me again, Ellie?" he asked her heatedly, the *is* sounding like *ees*. "Or do you just say this to make me feel better?"

"Of course not," she said, surprised at the agitation in his voice, the sudden grip of his hands. "I wouldn't say it if I didn't mean it." She gently eased her wrists from his grip.

"But you mean these words only as a friend, isn't that so?"

"We *are* friends, Georges. Good friends."

"We are more than friends, Ellie. I am more than a friend to you. I stayed away because it causes me pain to see you . . ."

She turned and started to walk on again, her face worried. But he stopped her again. "Georges, please—"

"No. I must say what I have to say. I have watched you all these months. You have heard nothing. There has been no word from Karl—"

"Please." She was trying to break from his clasp on her wrists again, but he held on tightly.

"No, you must listen. Then, when I am through, if you wish to walk away from me, I will not stop you." When she stopped struggling, he took her hand and they walked on.

"Please just let me say what I must say to you." He looked at her till she slowly nodded, then he looked away again. They had caught up to Gail and Caroline, and stood a small distance away while the little girls teetered on their toes to see up into the lion cages. "You must begin to face the fact that Karl will not be coming back, Ellie—"

"Don't say that!" she cried, watching a tree bough bend in the breeze, hearing the leaves as they rustled softly.

"You promised to listen," he said sternly, gripping her hands. "He has been gone for more than eight months and you have heard nothing since the early months."

"He—something could have happened. He is someplace where he can't let us know . . ."

He was slowly shaking his head. "Eight months, Ellie." He watched

226

her carefully as he saw her beginning to accept it. When he spoke again, it was with such simple honesty that she could only shake her head and force back the tears. "I love you, Ellie. I have loved you for a very long time. I only wanted you to know. Because I think you are very lonely and hurt right now, and perhaps it helps to know that someone cares as much as I do about you. I won't say any more. Not now. Not for a while. Not until you wish me to."

She nodded gratefully, and in a high voice that had a false note of gaiety in it, she called out to the children. "Come along, children. We want to see the monkeys before we have to go home."

They had strolled back up Fifth Avenue through the late-afternoon sunshine, Ellie's arm through his, the little girls skipping ahead, each of them clutching a stuffed teddy bear that Georges had bought at a booth in the zoo. When they reached the townhouse, they were almost reluctant to leave the sunny avenue with its procession of traffic and Sunday-afternoon strollers. As they followed Caroline and Gail up under the wide porte cochere, the door suddenly swung open. Morgan stood there, his young face filled with alarm.

"Miss Ellie, please go to the library," he said. Ellie saw Nanny Grace hurry up behind him, her lips in a grim line as she took the two youngsters by the hands and started to lead them away, calling over her shoulder.

"Miss Elizabeth's in there, Ellie," she said. "With Mrs. Stuart, and the young Mrs. Stuart."

Ellie turned to Georges, an expression of foreboding in her face. "Something must have happened, Georges, from the way Morgan and Nanny Grace—"

"I'll telephone you later," he said, holding her small white-gloved hand in his. Reluctantly, he let it go and half-backed down the wide stone steps beneath the porte cochere, leaving the invisible circle of her soft fragrance, the shaded prettiness of her face beneath the wide-brimmed hat.

"Thank you for a lovely afternoon," she said, as he raised his hand in a wave and smiled. When he had disappeared, she carried the image of him with her into the shadowy cool marble of the reception hall.

Pulling her gloves off, she hurried along the gallery to the library and walked through the open door. Elizabeth was sitting on one of the low couches, her arms about a sobbing Lucia. Sybil Stuart, in a severe black linen dress and broad-brimmed black straw hat, stood by a window looking out into the side street, her handsome features drawn in a sorrowful mask. When Elizabeth saw Ellie, she signaled to her to come on into the room. Lucia looked up and sobbed. "It's Dana, Ellie!" Ellie felt a sudden tug of warning. "Dana has been killed at Guadalcanal." The scene froze in Ellie's mind—the three women, the way the sun spilled diagonally down the shelves of books.

"No!" Ellie cried. From the corner of her eye, she saw Sybil Stuart's body shudder. Slowly the older woman turned toward her. "He had just been made a captain. I received that letter yesterday, and now . . ." She spread her hands helplessly, her eyes wide with shock. "Now he's gone." She seemed numb, still uncomprehending. Ellie moved toward her slowly and took her hands in hers.

"I'm so sorry," she said, barely above a whisper.

Dana Stuart had joined the Marine Corps, and after months of training had become a pilot in one of its aircraft wings. He had been shot down while flying a dive bomber attacking Japanese forces at the Ilu River, she learned later.

Ellie looked up just as Elizabeth, holding Lucia, started toward the door. "I'm going to take Lucia upstairs to lie down," she said, as Lucia quietly sobbed. "I've sent for Dr. Bernard. I think she needs a sedative. Please warn Morgan, Ellie. There will probably be reporters later."

Ellie nodded, watching them as they left the library. Then she pulled Sybil gently down onto a nearby settee, wondering how in the face of all the tragedy on this day, the sun could be falling through the long windows so brightly.

"It—it doesn't seem real," Sybil said, slowly shaking her head back and forth. "Happening so far away, it has no reality to it."

"I know," Ellie said softly, a small catch in her voice. She was nodding, as if trying to see something in the distance.

They were silent for several moments, Sybil studying Ellie's face. Then she nodded. "Of course you do," Sybil said. "You haven't heard from Karl since those first few months, have you?"

Ellie shook her head, unable to speak.

The first tears came to Sybil's eyes. She smiled a sad smile. "I remember that first day we saw you, Ellie, trudging along the road toward Newport. So much has happened to all of us since that day." She clasped Ellie's hands tightly. "And you've come to mean so much to us in that time."

"Thank you," Ellie whispered. "That means everything to me. I—I feel as though you are my family." They sat in warm silence again for several moments and then Sybil rose.

"I would like to see my granddaughter, Ellie." She tried to smile. "For some reason, it seems terribly important that I see Caroline right now."

Ellie nodded and, linking her arm through the older woman's, she led her out of the library toward the elevator in the main reception hall.

Elizabeth and Ellie had plunged heavily into war work by the time 1943 arrived. As the following year passed, Elizabeth headed Red Cross drives, War Bond campaigns, and supervised a local agency that placed British children in American homes—the children were sent from British towns and villages to be safe from German bombings. Ellie worked closely with Elizabeth, keeping all of the records for the drives and campaigns and even, on occasion, making speeches in Elizabeth's place when Elizabeth was obligated elsewhere. By the autumn of 1944 they were both veteran speakers at rallies and bonds sales meetings.

"I'm so thankful for Georges Poncet," Elizabeth said to Lawrence one evening as their limousine rolled down Fifth Avenue, a soft rain peppering the windows with quivering diamonds that glistened in the light from the streetlamps.

They were dressed for the theatre, Lawrence's white dress shirt and scarf gleaming in the dusk. He turned to look at her, catching his breath, as always, at her beauty, the cloud of dark hair framing softly chiseled features, the creamy swell of small firm breasts. She had pushed back the ermine cape and was taking a cigarette from the silver case in her purse. He leaned toward her, flicking his lighter. "One hell of a man, Georges," Lawrence said softly. "Thank God for him." He looked at the surging traffic. "But I worry about Lucia."

"Yes . . . Lucia." Elizabeth sighed deeply. "At least with Ellie—well, if it weren't for Georges, she would be in complete despair. As it is—"

"As it is, two years—more than two years—have passed," Lawrence said, putting one of her cigarettes between his lips and lighting it. He smoked rather grimly for a moment. "I'm afraid it means that Karl won't ever come back, Elizabeth."

She was shaking her head as she watched the Plaza slide past, the lines of taxis and limousines crushing around its entrance. "It's so hard to believe that he could be gone."

"Thousands are gone. Thousands," he said softly.

"But, most are . . ." She turned to him. "The wives and relatives receive telegrams. It's horrible, I know, but at least they're told, at least they know."

"Some of those telegrams say *missing in action.*"

"Ellie has nothing. It's as though he never existed. He just—just disappeared into nowhere. One day he was here, saying goodbye, and then there were letters from the government APO number, from England, and suddenly—nothing!"

Lawrence sighed as he crushed his cigarette out. "Well, we will simply have to wait until the war ends. Perhaps then we'll hear, or" —he turned to her with a smile and took her hand in his—"he will just appear one day, out of that nowhere."

"Oh, darling, I hope so." She spoke slowly, her voice low. "Dana . . . killed. Karl missing . . ."

"I know," he said softly, holding her hand tighter. "I know."

Sybil paced the long living room slowly, stopping every so often to peer down onto Fifth Avenue, her eyes worried, her heart giving a tiny leap each time she saw a small figure walking along in the dusk on the opposite side of the street.

She had given up the townhouse, turning it over to Dana and Lucia shortly after they were married, and had moved into this large triplex in one of the buildings Lawrence Kendall owned. Now, with Dana gone, Lucia had come to live with her, and they had sold the townhouse, both preferring to remember the happier years each had spent there.

"She goes out and walks for hours and hours, constantly," Sybil told Elizabeth on the phone earlier that day. "When her manager or anyone from the opera tries to reach her, she refuses to talk to them. Edward Johnson called her just this morning. She simply says she will never sing again and nothing I say or do will change her mind."

Elizabeth had arrived an hour or so later, catching Lucia just as she was about to leave, one of Dana's raincoats wrapped about her, almost hanging to the ground, a wide-brimmed hat drooping about her face, cheeks hollowed and eyes dark with grief.

"Lucia darling, you've got to pick up your life and start living again," Elizabeth said, taking her by the arms and holding her so that she couldn't break away and hurry out the door.

"I have no life to pick up," Lucia said dully, struggling a little.

"You have a brilliant career—"

"I have nothing. Nothing. Without Dana, there is nothing in my life."

"That's not true! And Dana would—"

She broke away from Elizabeth and ran to the door. "Don't say to me that Dana would want me to go on singing," she said, beginning to weep hysterically. "It doesn't matter, because I can no longer sing. Don't you understand, Elizabeth? I can no longer sing!"

She ran out the door, slamming it behind her. Sybil and Elizabeth stood in silence, staring first at the door, then at each other.

"It's just no use," Sybil had said. "She really believes she can no longer sing." Elizabeth sank into a chair, hopelessly shaking her head.

Sybil remembered that conversation as she paced the living room, waiting for Lucia, who had been gone for hours. When she suddenly heard the soft sound of a key going into the door in the foyer beyond, she sat down in a chair and picked up a book. When Lucia crossed the foyer, going toward the staircase, Sybil called out, "We'll have dinner, Lucia, as soon as you take off those wet things and come down again."

"I'm not hungry" was all that Lucia said as she disappeared into the shadowy well of the staircase.

V-E Day had passed and the family was at Kendall Hall in Newport when V-J Day arrived in mid-August, a little more than one week after the atomic bomb had been dropped on Hiroshima and Nagasaki. They were sitting on the side dining terrace where they could look to the west and see the fading sunset and to the ocean in the southeast where glints of gold danced on the whitecaps. Candles in tall hurricane lamps flickered over cascades of flowers and the glitter of wineglasses, over the gleaming cutlery, tiny gold-rimmed demitasse cups, and small iced cakes.

"Well, until this moment, I haven't known whether I'd suddenly find myself in the army or not," Larry was saying, as he lit a cigarette and tossed the match out onto the lawn, while his father frowned. Larry was sitting on the low parapet surrounding the terrace, the handsomeness of his face marred by an arrogant, almost insolent look about the mouth. He had bluish jowls that even at age eighteen showed up mere hours after he had shaved. His glance flicked over Elizabeth as she went around the table and gathered up the four little girls, Caroline, Gail, and Brenda and Katherine Leland, pushing them toward the wide doorway where Nanny Grace waited.

"Go along now," she was saying, her pale blue chiffon dinner gown floating like a morning mist all about her while, Larry noted, Lawrence's eyes never left her. "Ben is waiting in the theatre to show you the film of *A Midsummer Night's Dream.* Hurry, Jamie," she called out to the fourteen-year-old, who was scooping up his last drop of ice cream. She watched the children leave in a noisy wash of laughter and teasing, Katherine hanging back somewhat disdainfully from the others, her long dark curls swinging slowly from side to side.

"Well, if you'd worked harder and gotten better marks, Larry, you wouldn't have had to spend the past two years worrying about whether you were going to be drafted or not," Lawrence said with a sardonic kind of smile, taking Elizabeth's hand as she sat next to him.

"Oh, come now," Warren Leland said jovially, clipping the tip of the inevitable cigar and lighting it with a long series of puffs and then studying the faint glow. "That's being a bit hard on the lad, Lawrence. After all"—he laughed heartily—"we can't all be damned geniuses like you."

"How did you do in the tournament today, Larry?" Elizabeth asked quickly, wanting that course of conversation to go no further.

"We won the match and go back tomorrow," he said, a slight annoyance tinging his voice. Damn her, he thought, I don't need her pulling me out of these tugs-of-war with my father.

"Oh, wonderful," Enid Leland said, gushing as she turned to Elizabeth. "You simply can't imagine how far along he's brought Katherine with her tennis. She's developing quite a nice little backhand for a girl just ten." She turned to Larry. "You are a dear, giving her so much of your time this summer." She then looked around at Avery, who was eating his fourth cake, his eyes sliding back and forth at his father to make sure Lawrence wasn't watching. At seventeen, Avery's promise of good looks was lost in a plump face and a round body that had seen too many iced cakes, ice cream sodas, and candy bars. "And you, Avery, you can't imagine how thrilled she is at the times you've taken her sailing." She waggled her curly brown head from side to side and fluttered her eyelashes as she smiled at Lawrence. "It's been absolutely the most delicious August, Lawrence. I simply hate to see it end." She was rising, and extending her hand to Warren, who rose with her. "But now we must fly. I promised the Carringtons we'd fill in for bridge tonight."

Ellie had begun to rise from the table, as Larry and Avery drifted toward the doorway with them. She was painfully thin, but still pretty, in a pale rose dinner gown that swirled about her feet as she moved.

"Don't go, Ellie," Lawrence said, half rising, as he waved a good-bye at the Lelands. He waited until she had returned to her place at the table and the others had left, then slowly lit a cigarette and sipped at his demitasse before speaking. The sun sank below the horizon and a lavender twilight settled all around them.

Abbott was giving silent directions to Jessie and Edna, who were carrying plates from the table and placing a new silver pot of coffee before Elizabeth on the table. As Elizabeth poured Lawrence another demitasse, he leaned toward Ellie and put one hand over hers on the table, the candlelight sharpening the handsome lines of his face.

"I've been having inquiries made," he said. Startled, she looked up at him quickly. "Since V-E Day, I've had two men from the London office looking for information about Karl."

Ellie covered the lower part of her face with her hands, and her eyes darted excitedly from Elizabeth to Lawrence and back to Elizabeth again. "Elizabeth—oh, Elizabeth!"

"Wait!" Lawrence said, alarmed at her sudden excitement. "You mustn't get your hopes up. What we've learned so far still doesn't tell us anything about where Karl might be, even whether or not he might still be alive."

"All right," she said, trying hard to control what she was feeling. "But please—oh, please, tell me what you've been told."

He took a long sip of his liqueur, and slowly put the glass down. "He was one of a group who went from England to Czechoslovakia. Somehow he was smuggled into the country. Parachuted—some way. God knows how! That was after several months of training in England." He paused for a moment. "Karl apparently was part of the team who assassinated Reinhard Heydrich in June of 1942 in Prague."

"No!" Ellie gasped.

"Heydrich was the man they called The Hangman. We are just beginning to learn the worst about these monsters of the Third Reich, Hitler and his henchmen. Heydrich, most notably, was in charge of what they called the *Einsatzgruppen,* the action groups that were responsible for the mass murder of Jews and political officials, mainly in Poland and those in the wake of the Nazi advance into Russia. He also organized what the Allies are discovering were extermination camps for Jews, how many we don't yet know, and how many were killed there we also do not yet know." He was shaking his head at the horror of what he had learned. "We haven't been able to get any more information about Karl than just that. Not yet, but—"

"I want to go to Prague!" Ellie lunged forward, both hands on the table in front of her.

"Ellie, you—" Elizabeth began to argue.

"No, don't you see, Elizabeth, I must go," she pleaded.

"But travel in Europe is still almost an impossibility," Lawrence said.

"I have to try," she said with a determination that made him sit forward. "Where do I start? How do I find out—?"

"There's nothing you can do," he said. "But perhaps I can make some kind of arrangements."

"Oh, if you could!" she cried as she clasped one of his hands.

"I can't promise anything, Ellie," he said. "But I'll do the best I can."

It was more than a year before arrangements could be made. On a particularly cold February day in 1947 Ellie sailed on the *America* for Southampton. When they returned from the United States Line pier, Elizabeth urged Caroline and Gail to come into the library with her, saying they would all have some hot chocolate together. But when she looked around from the library door, Gail had disappeared. Caroline ran to one of the windows and stood there, quietly looking out across the expanse of snow that slipped down the hill from the terraces. Elizabeth came up behind her and, lightly resting her hands on Caroline's shoulders, thought how beautiful Kendall Hills was at very different times of the year. Even in dreary February. But then she started forward a little, seeing what Caroline was watching.

Gail, in her bright green snowsuit with the brilliant red stocking cap and mittens, was slowly trudging through the snow, aimlessly seeming to head nowhere. Just walking, slowly, sometimes stopping to trail one toe around on the snow to make a circle or square.

Elizabeth spoke quietly as her hands tightened a little on Caroline's shoulders. "Go out to her, darling. She's upset about Ellie leaving."

"She said she wanted to be by herself," Caroline said, looking up at her mother over her shoulder, the long dark braids giving her face a delicately sculptured look. She sounded almost hurt.

"But she doesn't. Not really. I'm sure she only said that because she's lonely . . . and a little confused."

234

"Why?" Caroline asked in her childish treble.

Elizabeth knelt down to hold her to her.

"Because she . . . well, she doesn't quite understand what has happened. About her father. She was a little angry, perhaps, because he went away and left them. And now her mother has left her and she feels the anger all over again."

Caroline thought about it for a moment, looked out the window again at Gail, and suddenly turned and raced across the room while calling out, "We'll be back in a little while."

Elizabeth stood at the window, watching. It was several minutes before she saw Caroline running toward Gail, her blue snowsuit and blue-and-white-striped stocking cap and gloves stark slashes of color against the snow.

Gail was sitting on one of the white stone benches, idly pushing the snow off the seat beside her, her legs dangling and swinging slowly just above the ground.

"Hi," Caroline said, coming to a sudden stop in front of the bench. When Gail didn't answer her or look up, Caroline sat down beside her. She didn't say anything for a long while, and finally Gail looked around at her.

"You'll get cold, just sitting here."

"So will you."

"I don't get cold as fast as you do."

"I'm not cold yet. My toes are just a little tiny bit cold. But the rest of me isn't."

"Well, in a minute, the rest of you will be cold, and then you'll go inside."

"No, I won't."

"Yes, you will."

"No, I won't."

"Yes, you will."

"Won't!"

"Will!"

"Won't, won't, won't!"

"Oh, Caroline," Gail said in her little-mother voice. "You're so stubborn." She took Caroline's gloved hand, and slipping down off of the bench, she pulled her along with her. They walked slowly toward the house, hand in hand, but then stopped near the bottom of the marble steps leading up to the side terrace.

"I don't want to go in yet," Gail said, pulling back a little.

Again they were silent, while Gail ran her glove along the railing, pushing the snow off it.

Caroline watched her. Pale golden curls peeked out from under Gail's hat. Her eyes were lowered and hidden by the long dark lashes that swept against her cheeks, but when she raised them for a moment, Caroline saw tears in her eyes. She walked to her and put her arms around her, and for several moments the two little girls clung to each other, while the tears slipped down Gail's face.

"She'll come home soon, Gail," Caroline said in a half-whisper, close to tears herself. "Honestly she will."

"She didn't have to go away!" The words wrenched out of her in a flow of anguish, as she pulled away.

"She wants to try to find your father and bring him back."

"He's never coming back."

Caroline stared at her. Gail sounded almost angry.

"He's never coming back . . . never!" She suddenly turned to Caroline and they put their arms about each other again. "Oh, Caroline, maybe she'll never come back either." She was crying hard.

"No, Gail. I promise you. Ellie's coming back. She said in just a few weeks; she said maybe even sooner." But Gail wasn't listening.

"And then I'd have no one." The anguish had deepened, and she sat down on the snowy steps, Caroline right beside her and holding onto her.

"Ellie's coming back," Caroline said staunchly. "She promised. And until she does, you have me, Gail. You always have me."

They were both weeping and rocking back and forth, clumsily falling over in their thick snowsuits, until finally the sobs subsided and they became quiet again, still huddling together on the steps.

"I don't remember him very well," Gail said in a soft voice. "I just remember a little bit how he looked." She smiled through her tears. "He used to put me up on his shoulders and ride me around, like he was the horse and I was the rider. He was very tall and he told me stories. About when he was a little boy, back in—back in Czechoslovakia . . ." She pronounced it slowly, enunciating each syllable.

"Is that the name of the town?"

"That's a country, silly!" Gail said scathingly as she pushed away the last of the tears with her glove. "Don't you know anything?"

Caroline beamed. Gail was her old self again. "Is it near Bermuda? Where we went last summer?"

"It's in *Europe,* Caroline." Gail looked at her, pulling back in amazement. "Honestly, you don't know anything."

"Will you show me on the globe in the library?"

"Sure," Gail said, taking her hand and pulling her up. "Come on." Then she stopped and softly touched Caroline's cheek. "I love you, Caroline," she said solemnly. "You're my best friend."

"And you're my best friend, Gail," Caroline said. "You always will be, forever and ever and ever and ever." They gazed at each other for a long moment. Then, holding hands, they turned and ran along the terrace around to the front entrance and hurried inside.

Travel through Europe in 1947 was even more depressing and disturbing than Ellie had expected it to be. With the proper visas and other papers, she made her way to Prague by train—crossing the English Channel by boat train, then winding across France and into Germany in damp, cold, unheated coaches. She watched the endless miles of devastation and endured countless delays because of equipment that kept breaking down, because of detours, and work crews who were still repairing bombed stretches of rail. When she arrived in Munich, she had several hours' wait for another train and decided to walk about a little. She left the railway station, which was under heavy repair, and went out into the Bahnhofplatz and stared about her in disbelief. They were just beginning to rebuild Munich. It had been badly bombed, so badly that she could see nothing as she looked across the Schutzenstrasse and Karlsplatz that wasn't a mountain of rubble.

She walked on, stunned by what she saw, even more stunned as she looked into the faces of the people of Munich who passed by, hurrying in one direction or another, their clothing shabby and drab, coat collars and scarves pulled closely about their faces in the damp cold, faces that were almost expressionless. One or another occasionally glanced at her and at what seemed obviously new to them, her brown fur coat and hat.

She stood before the gray stone Palace of Justice, its walls crumbling, even nonexistent in some places, a jaggedly soaring corner reaching toward the sky as though in a plea for pity or forgiveness. Two scraggly brown dogs with skeletal ribs pawed at something in the rubble, and she turned away and walked on.

The few vehicles on the streets were mostly small trucks, ramshackle buses, and a small number of cars. There were people everywhere, carrying string bags that contained meager packages, brown-paper-wrapped parcels of food, for the most part. But there was something about the people, something strange that at first she couldn't put her finger on. And then suddenly she knew. The people were mostly women. Women and children. Realization slowly grew. Perhaps half a generation of men had been wounded or killed in the war. She turned back toward the railway station after an hour of wandering, went through the partially destroyed building with half-closed eyes, and boarded the train that would take her to Prague.

She dozed for a while, waking when she heard the hissing of steam. The train began to move, continuing her journey into Czechoslovakia. As the train crawled through the barren countryside, she saw almost nothing but miles and miles of snow, frozen rivers, lonely forests, and white mountain peaks. But occasionally across the horizon she would see what was left of a town or village, the walls of its houses rising in jagged edges and spikes above a snowy wasteland—no curls of smoke spiraling from chimneys, no barking dogs, no children waving as the train wound its way past. Where had all the people gone? she wondered sadly, as she aimlessly traced circles on the frost that had formed on the inside of the window. She was the only person in the compartment and had wrapped herself in a ragged brown blanket the conductor had given her. At times she dozed, but for most of the daylight hours, she watched with sinking heart as the terrible havoc wreaked by the war swept past, a desolation and destruction that seemed to have no end.

There was a long delay at the border, while border guards went through the train, carefully checking all papers. The two young men who came into her compartment, both wearing shabby coats and pieces of various military uniforms, stared at her unrelentingly. She tried to smile at them, but their eyes were cold and hard like marbles, their faces expressionless, closed. And when they left, she realized she was trembling. A terrible, desperate loneliness swept through her, touched with fear and foreboding. Pulling the pretty brown fur hat closer over her ears and the beaver collar up around her neck, she burrowed down into the corner of the seat and leaned her head back. It was night—she glanced at her wristwatch—past midnight and the train was moving again. The light overhead flickered dimly, threatening to go out at any moment. She had never felt so alone, so fearful of what lay ahead. Sleep, she told herself, as she shut her eyes. Sleep, Ellie. In the daylight it would all seem more hopeful again.

She wakened just as it was beginning to get light, and huddled for a moment in her blanket, unmoving, dazed, wondering where she was, the steady clicking of the wheels on the rails below confusing her. Then she remembered and she stirred, feeling the chill and stiffness in her bones. She stared at the blankness of the landscape, bleak under a leaden sky, the unending white stretch of snow, punctuated with dark green pines.

"*Guten tag, gnädige Frau.*"

Ellie turned her head sharply to see a young woman on the seat opposite her. She was pretty, with delicate features, dark eyes and hair beneath a warm wool cap, her loden coat expensive but worn, patched at the sleeves. Ellie shook her head.

"I'm sorry. I don't speak German," she said.

The girl smiled. "I speak little English," she said, her rather peaked face and brown eyes lighting up with friendliness. "You go to Prague?" When Ellie nodded and murmured, "Yes," wondering at how this young woman could be so forward and friendly with someone whose country had just defeated her country in war, the young woman nodded eagerly.

"I speak German, but I am Czech."

"Oh, I see," Ellie said, with some relief. She had found it difficult, the few hours she had waited in Munich for her train, just being in the country that had caused so much tragedy and horror in the years past.

"My parents, they were taken to Germany in 1939, to work in the factories. I was just ten. We were taken to Regensburg, where they made the ball bearings. But before this, my father, he was *Herausgeber* —how you say?—*Redakteur* of newspaper—"

"The editor?" Ellie offered, leaning forward.

"Yes. The editor. But he try to warn people, he write the truth in Prague about the *Sudetendeutsche Partei,* about Konrad Henlein." When she saw that Ellie didn't understand, she tried to explain. "He was head of a minor party of Germans in Czechoslovakia who stir up revolt."

"Yes," Ellie said, "I remember Karl talking about it."

"Karl?"

"My husband. He is a Czech." She then began to speak in a low voice, telling this strange young woman with the warm and sympathetic eyes about how Karl had gone to America and then had returned to Europe again when America went to war. While she talked, she pulled a Thermos and some bread from a small leather bag she was carrying, poured the Thermos cap full of steaming coffee for the girl, and drank from the mouth of the Thermos herself. "Do you still live in Germany?" she asked the young woman, who was gratefully sipping at the coffee.

"No. My mother and I go back to Prague. But my father . . . he is buried at Regensburg. My mother say he was never strong. He died of the lungs . . ." She was tapping her chest.

"Pneumonia."

"Yes. Pneumonia. In the bad winter, just three years ago. My mother, she is ill, so I go to his grave. 'You must go, Franceska,' my mother say. So on day he die, three years later, I put flowers on his grave and talk to him, tell him we are safe, tell him we are now back in Prague."

"I—I'm sorry, Franceska," Ellie said softly.

They talked for hours as the train crawled on toward Prague, Franceska telling her how hopeful the Czechs had been when the war ended, but how repression had come again. Her eyes constantly darting to the door of the compartment, in hushed tones she told of how, in the wake of the German defeat, a new government of Communists had gained control of the police and threatened Russian intervention if the Democrats did not fall into line. "I work in the Prague University Library," she said. "And there I see and talk to the *dissident,* the *scribe* . . ."

"Writers?" Ellie asked.

Franceska nodded. "Yes, the writers. Some of them were friends and workers with my father. And there are artists who come there also, sometimes musicians—"

"Musicians?" Ellie leaned toward her a little. "Perhaps you have heard of a man named Anton Wancek, a musician and composer—"

"But of course," Franceska said. "He is conductor for the Philharmonic."

"In Prague?" Ellie asked excitedly. "He is my husband's brother."

"I have met him," the young woman said. "I have cousin who plays viola with Philharmonic. I could take you to him."

"Oh, would you, Franceska?"

"Of course," she said warmly. "And you will stay with us. We have big flat that was my grandfather's. It is near Náměstí Krasnoarmejců. Such a beautiful square. That is where Philharmonic is. At the House of Artists. Not far from the Charles Bridge." She suddenly enthused, "Ah, Prague is beautiful city. I will show it to you."

*   *   *

Karl had told Ellie of Prague, but she had not been prepared for the grace and beauty of the city, the great baroque buildings and shadowed streets, the steel gray of the sky reflecting down into the massive stones and cobbled roads, the arches and gabled windows, the massive squares with their gothic vaultings and splendid carvings, the narrow alleys and ancient courtyards. She felt its pull and understood why Karl had loved it so.

They rode in a battered taxi with a driver who muttered and complained, while Franceska sat forward to scold him because he had made a wrong turn to extend his fare. Ellie watched from the window, feeling somehow a subdued, muted quality about the city. There were not many vehicles about, and those that were moving in the streets appeared old and battered. In some places the streets seemed almost empty, but in others, shabby-looking people stood in long lines, queued in front of stores, string shopping bags in their hands, impatience and unhappiness embedded in their eyes.

The flat where Franceska lived was in a large apartment house that loomed heavily over the narrow street, some of its upper windows hanging in deep bays that seemed held up by the baroque carvings of gargoyles and lions and evilly grinning cherubs.

They entered through a small side door that was part of a larger one opening onto a small dark courtyard. A steep spiral stairway led to the big fourth-floor flat where soaring ceilings dwarfed everything beneath and sent deep shadows into corners. Mme. Corescu, Franceska's mother, was a frail, tiny woman who spent most of her time in bed, hanging onto life by a thread, but she greeted Ellie warmly. It had been a luxurious flat once, with fine paintings and furniture, and Oriental rugs that were now almost threadbare.

"We will go to the Philharmonic tomorrow morning," Franceska said as they sat at supper over a thick lentil soup. "That is when they are there, rehearsing."

They set out the next day, first stopping at the Alcron hotel, where Ellie had told the border guards and customs man she would be staying. Leaving Franceska's address with the concierge, they walked on to Náměstí Krasnoarmejců. When they entered the empty theatre, great swells of magnificent music made them stop at the top of the aisle to listen. For several moments, Ellie could think of nothing but the music, but when the conductor suddenly rapped sharply with a baton on his music stand, she studied him from the back. And when he turned his head, she leaned forward a little, struck by his resemblance to Karl.

As she stared at him, she saw that he was shorter than Karl, somewhat narrower about the shoulders. The orchestra repeated a passage of the Dvořák symphony, then went on with the music until its end. Franceska had quietly pulled her down into a seat at the rear of the darkened and empty hall. The stage was a blaze of light.

She watched as members of the orchestra rose and walked about, stretching their legs, walking into the wings with cigarettes in their mouths, a murmur of voices rising as they talked and laughed. When Franceska tapped her arm, she stood up and walked slowly down the dark aisle until she stood below the stage, where the conductor was talking to the first violinist. In a moment, they felt her standing there and turned.

"Yes?" Anton said, a strange expression coming across his face. "You"—he stared at her—"you . . . are Ellie," he said, speaking English. When she nodded, he hurried to the side of the stage and came down the curving steps, then walked to where she stood. He took her hands in his and held them for several moments. "Come," he said, starting to lead her up the aisle, but paused for a moment and spoke several words to a man who was watching them from the stage. The man nodded and ran offstage for a moment, returning with a coat he threw to him. Anton led her toward the rear of the theatre, not saying anything. When they reached the back, she saw that Franceska had disappeared. Silently he took her out to the street in front and they climbed into a taxi, as he pulled his coat on.

"Café Arco," he said to the driver, then shook his head at her, as though to say they musn't talk in the taxi. In something of a daze she watched the streets and buildings pass, saw him pay the driver, and walked with him into the café. It wasn't until they were seated in a corner that he spoke. He ordered coffee for them, and when the waiter left, he sat forward, arms on the table, and said, "I recognized you from your pictures that Karl carried with him." And added softly, "I never knew where to find you, to write and let you know—"

"Know what?" she asked sharply.

He watched her for several moments until he saw some kind of acceptance in her eyes. She was sitting rigidly, one hand a fist on the edge of the table. Slowly she put her other hand out to him while her head shook back and forth.

"That Karl . . . is gone," he said. He quickly slid around the table

242

until he was sitting next to her, clutching her hand hard. When the waiter put their coffee in front of them and murmured *Maestro* in a deferential way, Anton hardly nodded.

She kept slowly swinging her head from side to side, as though refusing to accept it. But as the silence continued between them, she grew still.

"Tell me," Ellie said, her voice low and trembling, her eyes far away on some unfixed point, as though she couldn't bear to look at him and his strong resemblance to Karl. "We had heard he may have been with the men who assassinated Heydrich."

"He was a national hero, Ellie." He looked away. "When we still had heroes."

"Hero?" She looked around quickly, her gaze clinging pitifully to his. Her face was thin and white, but still lovely, and Anton could see how Karl had fallen in love with her. The skin, almost translucent, was finely stretched over delicate bone structure. Her eyes were large and of an intense blue—like bluebells in the fields of Lidice, he thought sadly. "Then he *is* dead." It was a sharp low cry.

"He left the cellar beneath the church where they were all hiding, before the SS suddenly swarmed in and killed everyone hiding there, more than one hundred of the Underground. The last time I saw him, before the assassination, he told me that all he wanted now was to go back to America, to you and your child, but that first he would go to Lidice to see our parents and brother Josef."

"Then . . . ?" A light of hope had flickered in her eyes. But he was slowly shaking his head, and the light faded away.

"He went there and then soldiers came. The Nazis. One of the men who had thrown the bombs at Heydrich's automobile had come from Lidice, had lived there many years before. In revenge, the Nazis killed all of the men and burned the village to the ground." He spoke so low that Ellie strained to hear him. She heard the dark river of despair in his voice, the currents of hatred and horror swirling in fury. "The women and their small children—some of them—were sent to the Ravensbruck concentration camp, where many of them died. Our . . . mother was one of them. All of them are gone. I am the only one who is left." He put his head in his hands and slowly shook it from side to side, while Ellie sat watching across the crowded café, seeing nothing but a blur of faces through the endless tears.

"I'm sorry, Anton," she whispered. "I'm sorry."

* * *

She left Prague the following day, unable to bear it any longer, saying goodbye to Franceska and her mother. Anton took her to the railway station, where they stood on the wind-swept platform of the glass- and iron-covered shed, hissing steam from the train enveloping them in floating white clouds, until she felt they were caught and held in a dream. He was holding her hands and looking down at her as their breath puffed on the bitter cold air. She looked pale and drawn, but beautiful, the soft brown fur of her hat and collar framing her face, the dark lashes sweeping her cheeks when she blinked to try to keep the tears back.

"He told me how much he loved you," Anton said. "It was all he could think and talk of when we met each afternoon at the café. You and the child. It gave me hope that there was something so much better, beyond"—he waved an arm—"beyond all this."

A whistle blew shrilly from the distant engine on the train.

"You have your music, Anton," she said softly. "You still have that. And it's such beautiful music."

He nodded and tried to smile as she climbed the steps of the train. She waved at him from the platform as the train began to move. He waved back and walked slowly beside it, then faster and faster, until he could keep alongside no longer. The last glimpse he had of her was the blur of her face and her gloved hand raised in a wave, and then the train curved on the distant track and her fluttering hand disappeared. He stood there until the train was gone, two red lanterns on the last coach tiny specks of light far down the track curving away and out of sight.

17
1949

The *Sapphire,* when cruising, stayed at sea much of the time. More than three hundred feet long, it dominated any harbor it entered with its sheer size and splendor, the long, dazzling white hull and gleaming brass catching the sun's rays in southern or Mediterranean ports, and drawing crowds to quayside like children to a circus parade. A crew of more than thirty manned the floating mansion at all times, while a staff of ten to fifteen servants who moved with the Kendall family from estate to estate came on board when members of the entire family were cruising. When Larry or Avery Kendall brought their own parties aboard, in the absence of other members of the family, they took their personal staffs with them.

Designed and built for Lawrence Kendall to his own specifications, the *Sapphire* had been done with the utmost taste, but with a luxury and opulence, however understated, that had astonished Elizabeth and her mother the first time they saw it. Eight guest rooms and three guest suites were each furnished and decorated in a different pastel color; the three suites had marble bathrooms and small private decks. The four-room suite for Lawrence and Elizabeth was like a penthouse, with a long secluded deck, a glass-covered solarium, a paneled study, a living room and bedroom, and two marble bathrooms with gold fixtures in each. Next to their suite was a three-room suite for Caroline and Nanny Grace, the two bedrooms off a large playroom that was filled with dolls and toys.

The glass-enclosed dining salon, just below the captain's quarters and wheelhouse, seated thirty at one long table—that is, until Lawrence's marriage to Elizabeth. After her first cruise aboard the *Sap-*

phire, she had the long table removed and replaced with eight small tables that would seat four each in a graceful and informal arrangement.

"Ugh!" she had said to Lawrence, when she first saw the stiff formality of the dining salon, so incongruously planned with the openness of sea and air and sky all around it on three sides. "I love you very much, darling, and this wonderful hotel that you have put out to sea. But I absolutely refuse to sit in the dining salon on another trip if it has to stay the way it is."

"Do anything you want with it," he said, catching her in his arms and whirling her about. "Do anything with the whole damn thing from stem to stern that you wish. It's yours and I am going to rename it the *Elizabeth.*"

"You will do nothing of the kind," she said. "If you do, I'll never set foot aboard again."

There were several salons on the three-deck yacht, one with a fireplace, paneled mahogany walls, deep leather couches and chairs, and two full walls of books; another for movies; a third with a piano and bar, a small dance floor, and café tables and chairs that drifted through sliding glass walls out onto a deck; and still another with chintz-cushioned window seats, permanently set-up card tables, and white wicker furniture, all in a garden setting and light pastels, with greenery and real flower beds that were bright with blooms.

A telephone system connected each room. There was a small infirmary with a registered nurse aboard at all times; and near the large outdoor swimming pool on the top rear deck, with striped awnings at each end, were deck chairs and luncheon tables for informal dining.

Behind the captain's quarters was a three-room office suite with the most sophisticated communications system available, serving as the Kendall, Inc., executive quarters whenever Lawrence and his most trusted assistants were on board. Ship-to-shore telephones and wireless equipment kept him in touch with all corners of the world at all times. Elizabeth grew to expect his absence throughout most of each day while they traveled on the *Sapphire,* but she always knew he could be found in the office suite at almost any time between early morning and late afternoon, keeping two secretaries busy at their typewriters, with Ellie, more often than not, coordinating all of the work.

In March of 1949, after Caroline had turned ten, Lawrence and Elizabeth took her and other members of the family, as well as Ellie and Gail, on a long cruise, starting at Nice on the French Riviera and sailing down through the Mediterranean. Lucia and Sybil Stuart came aboard the *Sapphire* at Monte Carlo, where they had been spending the winter months. Enid Leland, with her two daughters, Katherine, now thirteen, and Brenda, just a year older than Caroline, could not have been more charming and cloyingly friendly.

"She is such a snake!" Sybil complained to Elizabeth, as they sunned along the edge of the pool one morning, while steaming past the northern port of Bastia on the island of Corsica, the sea stretching like a carpet of white-flecked blue beneath the dazzling golden sun and banks of fleecy clouds. Elizabeth stirred only minimally as she lay in the long deck chair, her one-piece blue bathing suit molding to her like a second skin, her long, glossy dark hair flung like a cascade over the edge of the canvas chair. She smiled but didn't open her eyes. "Such a nasty little phony, gushing when Lawrence is around—"

"Lawrence finds it amusing."

"Well, I find it revolting."

With one eye still closed against the sun, Elizabeth looked at her mother and grinned. "She's a mass of insecurities. She comes from Brookline, while Honey comes from Beacon Hill."

"*Honey!*" Sybil exploded. She was knitting and the needles clicked ominously. "What kind of a ridiculous name is that?"

"The kind of a name that a doting father gives you," Elizabeth said with another grin. "Unfortunately it stuck."

"I must love you very much to have agreed to come on this cruise with those two along." Sybil smiled, then made a face as she dropped a stitch.

"Caroline will never get that sweater if you don't watch what you're doing."

Sybil was knitting furiously now. "When do Larry and Honey come aboard?"

"In Mykonos, I think. That's where Larry bought a villa as a gift to her."

"Well, why don't they just stay there?"

"Really, Mother," Elizabeth said, laughing, as she stood up and pulled a thin white robe around her shoulders. "You hide your feelings so well." She started away with a wave of her hand. "See you at lunch."

At Naples, an entourage of men, bowing and smiling and led by the *direttore* of the San Carlo Opera, came aboard to see Lucia, who insisted that Elizabeth be with her when she received them in the garden salon. For several moments, there was a flurry of greetings, while the men kissed the hands of the two women. Elizabeth smiled as she listened to the volley of Italian flying all about her, and then Lawrence came in and asked the four men to join them for lunch. Later, Lucia and the *direttore* spent an hour behind the closed doors of the library, and when they came out, his face was crestfallen, while Lucia's mouth was tight, her face white.

"I am sorry, Madame," the *direttore* kept saying as he bent over Lucia's hand and kissed it three or four times, his three companions standing behind him, all looking as though someone's death had taken place. "We had so hoped we could add you to our coming season, Signora. The glorious voice of Lucia Daniello should be heard once more in Italy and at La Scala. But we in Naples had looked forward to her being at the San Carlo—"

"There is nothing more I can say, Signore," Lucia kept repeating over and over, her voice cracking. Elizabeth could see that she was upset, near the breaking point, and stepped in.

"I'm sorry," she said, signaling Lawrence with her eyes. "But we're sailing soon and . . ."

Lawrence had taken the arm of the *direttore* and was leading him toward the gangplank, while the other men followed. They look like a funeral procession, Elizabeth thought, in their black suits and Homburg hats in this heat.

"I think I would like to go and lie down," Lucia said in a tired voice. She walked along the deck in her summery yellow frock and disappeared, ignoring a chorus of voices that had risen from the dock. Elizabeth watched her for a moment, and then went to the rail and gazed down onto the dock where forty or fifty men and women stood, calling out Lucia's name. One man started singing, *"Donna non vidi mai simile a questa,"* from *Manon Lescaut,* the voice strong but untrained, his smile wide as he threw his arms open and bowed to Elizabeth. She smiled and waved to him while watching the four men in their black suits march along the dock and climb into their limousine.

"What did those men want, Mummy?" Caroline asked as she and Gail and Brenda Leland ran along the deck toward Elizabeth. They were in their bathing suits, just out of the pool, and left wet marks and small puddles of water on the deck.

"They wanted your Aunt Lucia to sing at their opera house, darling," Elizabeth said, still looking down onto the dock.

"Here? In Naples?" Brenda asked.

"But she won't, will she?" Caroline watched Elizabeth sadly shake her head. "Maybe Aunt Lucia just *thinks* she can't sing anymore."

"Maybe if she'd try, she'd find out that she can," Gail said while trying to shake water out of her ears by hopping up and down.

"Perhaps you're right," Elizabeth said, watching them as they suddenly ran back toward the swimming pool, Brenda screaming in laughter as Gail snapped her towel at her, Caroline hopping on Gail's back and clutching her around the neck while Gail tried to shake her loose. Elizabeth was smiling at their antics when she saw Lawrence coming toward her. He had a cablegram in his hand and was reading it. Elizabeth saw the frown come over his face.

"What is it?" she asked.

For several moments they watched the girls running away, and then they slowly walked toward the garden salon, his arm around her waist.

"A cable from our offices in Washington. It looks as though Russia is going to refuse to consider the West's proposal for a four-power agreement for Berlin. There's talk of a blockade on all land traffic that goes between West Germany and Berlin."

"How does this affect Kendall?"

"The aircraft division. If there's a blockade on land, the West can retaliate with an airlift. Bring everything into Berlin by air."

"For more than two million people?" Elizabeth was amazed.

He grinned, and leaned down to kiss her cheek. "Haven't you heard, darling? We in the West can do anything." The grin disappeared as they entered the garden salon. She saw the characteristic tightening of his jaw, knew what it meant. Although he was in the port of Naples physically, his mind was already thousands of miles away in New York. "This means a step-up in plane production. They're going to need all the cargo planes they can get."

Elizabeth could see the limousine and the security car behind it, Lawrence between two of the yacht's officers, and several of Naples' plainclothes policemen hurrying in that direction along the dock. He kept turning around as he walked to wave at Caroline and Gail, who were calling out to him, "Goodbye, goodbye!"

"What a shame," Ellie said.

But Elizabeth laughed. "Wouldn't you have been surprised if he hadn't had to leave?"

Ellie smiled. "Yes, I guess so. In fact, this is probably the longest time he's been able to stay aboard, isn't it?"

"By far," Elizabeth said, while she waved. They waited and watched until the limousine pulled away and disappeared, then strolled off toward the stern deck, where it was coolest at this time of day.

But Caroline and Gail were still hanging over the ship's rail, eying the teeming dock below. The afternoon sun was hot, and the dockworkers, who were scurrying about loading cargo onto a ship across from the *Sapphire,* were calling out to each other and in a cheerful rush of Italian to Gail and Caroline, who laughed and waved and pretended they knew what the men were saying.

"We're going to be leaving soon," Caroline said, turning her head a little to listen harder as the yacht's engines began to hum.

"Oh, I like it here," Gail said with disappointment in her voice. "This is ever so much more interesting than some of those places we've been. Look! Look, Caro!" she squealed as a cage with a huge slinking black panther was wheeled along the dock on a wide cart. They shrieked and laughed and jumped up and down, their bright blue-and-yellow sundresses patches of color against the gleaming white of the yacht.

The first indication of trouble came with the figure of a man in uniform from the port's office running along the dock toward the *Sapphire* and shouting.

"What's that crazy man saying?" Gail said laughingly, as she and Caroline hooked their sandaled feet into the lower rung of the yacht's rail and hung on there.

From the corner of her eye, Caroline saw Conrad, one of the stewards, hurry out of the dining salon and lean over the rail. Suddenly, there were shouts and a babble of voices both from above on the captain's bridge and below on the dock as more official-looking men ran toward the *Sapphire.*

It was then that Caroline saw the crowd surging along the wide dock, a mob of mostly men. They were shouting, their voices angry, raised in a sing-song kind of chant. They were shaking their fists and moving quickly, several signs on tall poles waving above their heads, signs that neither Gail nor Caroline could read. Only the big, black, crudely drawn letters of the word *Communiste* meant anything to them.

Caroline saw Captain Morrison running toward them. His amiable features appeared almost fierce as he angrily shouted orders back over his shoulder. Beyond him, she saw her mother and Ellie hurrying along the deck. But none of them reached them before the first large stone clattered onto the deck near them. Both Gail and Caroline were aware that deckhands were running in all directions and that the *Sapphire* was slowly beginning to move away from the dock.

The crowd was almost below them now, Caroline saw. Both she and Gail, more curious than frightened, were still clinging to the rail, their feet on the lower rung. As Elizabeth and Ellie dragged them away into the nearest haven, Caroline kept shouting, "What is it? Who are they?"

Once inside the dining salon, shielded from the sudden rain of rocks and stones, Captain Morrison looked down at them and said, "Just a mob of protesters who apparently heard that the *Sapphire* was in the port here." He looked slightly shaken and pulled nervously at his small gray beard, as he knelt down and took both of their hands. "Are you all right?"

When they both nodded, he looked relieved and stood up again. Then, with a small salute, he left the room. "I have to get back to the bridge, Mrs. Kendall."

As the *Sapphire* gathered more speed and slid farther and farther away from the dock, they saw three small police cars with their lights flashing suddenly push through the crowd of several hundred people, who were still shouting and shaking raised fists toward the moving yacht.

Caroline looked up at her mother. "Why were those men so angry, Mummy?"

Elizabeth sat down, her knees almost buckling. She pulled both girls toward her, while Ellie still watched the dock, which was going farther and farther away. "Well, there's a political group called the Communist party—"

"I've heard of that," Gail said.

"And it's quite popular here in Italy. Particularly here in Naples, and—"

"But why were they shouting and throwing things at us?"

"Because they don't like rich people," Gail said bluntly.

Ellie and Elizabeth looked at each other, while Caroline murmured, "Oh, I see." She walked to a small upholstered chair that stood beneath one of the plate-glass windows and climbed up on it on her knees, pensively staring off toward the dock, her chin resting on her arms along the top of the chairback.

Soon the dock was so far distant it was a mere line on the horizon, with the stark outline of mountains dimly visible beyond. She gazed for a long time at the looming Vesuvius, which hung so menacingly over the bay. She could hear the soft humming of the *Sapphire*'s powerful engines and feel their throb.

Something . . . had happened back there by the dock that was making her feel very different. She didn't know exactly why. She only knew that the strange feeling was there, nagging at her somewhere, beneath the surface.

"Earlier . . . they were singing to Aunt Lucia down on the dock, and then—then more people came and started throwing rocks." She turned a puzzled face to her mother, who walked slowly to her and put her hands on her shoulders.

"I can't explain it, Caroline," she said softly. "I just can't explain it to you."

18
1952

"Where are we going, Daddy? Where are we going?" Caroline said excitedly as she flew across the main reception hall. He caught her in his arms as Nanny Grace came up to them, a half-frown, half-smile on her face.

"I'll tell you in the car," Lawrence said, laughing, as he put Caroline down, pretending to groan. "I guess, now that you're thirteen, I can't pick you up anymore."

" 'Ere now," Nanny Grace scolded in a good-natured tone. She tugged at Caroline's skirt to straighten it, bent down, and pulled her ankle socks up, then handed her a sweater. "Now take this, 'cause 'eaven knows where your father is takin' you, 'e's bein' so secret about it."

"I don't care, I don't care, I don't care," Caroline said in a sing-song as she skipped alongside him toward the vestibule where Ben stood waiting with Lawrence's hat, holding the big carved oak door open. "I ordered the Cadillac, sir," Ben said, pointing out to the black limousine standing beneath the porte cochere, Meacham beside it. "I thought it would be less noticeable."

"Good thinking, Ben," Lawrence said, taking Caroline's hand.

As they climbed into the car, Caroline noticed the usual black sedan just behind the limousine, with the two men in dark suits sitting in the front seat. When she waved at them the men laughed.

They were halfway through Central Park before Caroline again asked where they were going.

"To New Jersey," Lawrence said. "We're meeting your Uncle Warren there."

She snuggled up to him, and he tucked her hand in his arm and smiled down at her. "We don't do nearly enough things together, do we, sweetheart?" he said.

"Well, we ride together sometimes, when we're up at Kendall Hills," she said, trying hard to think. "And you went to a matinee with us last winter." Lawrence was smiling. "And sometimes you take Gail and me to lunch at your club when we come down to your office."

"You know what we're going to do from now on?"

"What?"

"We'll try to do something every week. Except when I'm away, of course. And I'll let you decide what it is each week."

"All right." She bounced excitedly. "But you decided this week, so you have to tell me where we're going."

They were speeding down the West Side Drive heading for the Lincoln Tunnel, the traffic rather light, as was usual for a Saturday morning. "Well, today is a little different, sweetheart. Today we're going to look at a newspaper over in Jersey."

"Oh, Daddy!" She bounced on the seat again. "Can I see where they print it?"

"Well, I certainly don't see why not." He watched as they entered the tunnel. "You see, it's one of a small group of newspapers here that we're thinking of buying. To add to our chain."

Her head was tipped to one side and she was thinking hard about something. "Maybe when I grow up, I'll work at a newspaper."

Lawrence laughed softly. "Well, you're going to be a very busy young woman. Last week you said you wanted to train horses when you grow up. The week before, your mother tells me, you said you'd like to go on the stage, and—"

Caroline turned and looked up at him with her clear blue-violet eyes. "Gail is the one who is going to be a star. I wish I could make up my mind, like Gail. She knows just exactly what she wants to do when she grows up."

As she chattered happily away, he watched her with a smile on his face, now and then saying Yes or No or I think so when an answer or comment was required.

When the car slowed, she looked up ahead and saw a narrow street with factories on both sides. A huge sign that said THE JOURNAL stood on top of a long, four-story, red brick building that stretched along one side. They drove through an open gate into a parking lot with a tall heavy wire fence around it. Inside, they went to the third floor in a small private elevator that opened into a corridor and a suite of offices. Warren Leland was waiting for them.

When he kissed her, she half-turned her cheek and tried to smile naturally at him, while in his usual hearty tone he said to a man standing beside him, "This young lady, Dave, is Caroline Kendall."

She shook hands primly with a somewhat cadaverous-looking tall man with smiling eyes but sunken cheeks.

"This is Dave Prentiss, Caroline, the publisher and editor-in-chief of the *Journal*."

She was then taken by a pretty young woman in the direction of the corridor door. Elsie Corwin was Dave Prentiss's secretary. "Oh, I'll show her everything, Mr. Leland," Miss Corwin said, as she rang the bell for the elevator. "The editorial department and the press room, and if you're still busy we'll have a little lunch in the cafeteria."

But as the elevator door opened, a young man burst through it. "Three carloads of guys from the night shift just drove up, Mr. Prentiss," he shouted as he ran toward the three men. Miss Corwin stopped, her hand on Caroline's shoulder. "And the day shift just walked out and joined them on the street."

Caroline felt her father's hands on her arms as he came around behind her. She saw first shock and then alarm on her Uncle Warren's face, and when she looked at Dave Prentiss she saw that his face had drained of all color.

"All right, Prentiss," her father was saying in a voice she had never heard before, "what's going on?"

But Dave Prentiss had rushed to the window and was looking down into the street. They all followed him. By standing on her tiptoes at the high window, Caroline could see men and women milling about in the street, carrying signs. One of them had large black printing on it that said "If Kendall, Inc., Buys the *Journal*, We'll Buy the Union Package." Caroline had a strange feeling in the pit of her stomach. It was like the afternoon in Naples.

"How did they know?" Lawrence said, his voice clipped and hard.

"News travels fast in this place," Prentiss said. "Obviously someone found out you were coming here this morning, and they've known for a week or so that the *Journal* was for sale."

Lawrence looked at Warren, almost accusingly. "Get the state police, Warren. I want an escort out of here in case we need it." He had looked down at Caroline meaningfully, and Warren nodded as he walked to a desk and picked up a telephone. Lawrence then turned to Prentiss. "Dave, you go down and tell them I'll talk to them, *if* they're willing to negotiate. But not here. They can send a three-person group of representatives to my office tomorrow morning."

"Righto," Prentiss said as he hurried toward a staircase door.

They waited until they heard the distant sound of sirens coming closer, and then they walked to the elevator, stepped in, and rode silently to the first floor. Caroline skipped along beside her father as they left the building and climbed into the long black limousine. Excitement shivered up her spine. She watched from the car windows as her father stood outside for several minutes and talked to Dave Prentiss, who ran up to him from out on the street where he had been talking to several of the men who had gathered around him, their signs waving overhead. She saw that the crowd had grown larger and had formed lines. They were marching around in a long circle in front of the building. But state police cars had parked in a row, end to end, across the street so that the people who were marching were closed into an area directly in front of the building.

When her father stepped into the car, she saw the black sedan that always accompanied them shoot out ahead and then watched as one of the police cars pulled in behind the limousine. Soon they were all speeding down the street away from the *Journal* and its shouting mob of people in the front. She looked at her father and saw that his jaw was still clenched hard and that the angry expression that had been there was just fading from his eyes.

"It's all right, Daddy," she said, reaching out to pat his hand, which was held in a fist on his knee. "I wasn't scared." He looked at her and chuckled, while his hand opened and closed over hers. "Good girl," he said admiringly.

"Are they doing something wrong?" she asked.

He took a moment to light a cigarette. "Well, it—it depends on the point of view." He drew deeply on the cigarette. "Your Uncle Warren—he's the president of our news chain, you see—he asked me to come over this morning to talk to the owners. It seems, however, that the people who work here want to join the union. That's the American Newspaper Guild. But we have to convince them that we . . ." His voice drifted off while he paused and thought about it for a moment, as the limousine sped along the road. "Well, I guess we're going to have to try to convince them that we can do more for them than a union can."

"But what do they want?" she asked.

"They want . . . higher wages, a shorter work week, and . . . job security."

She heard the hesitation in his voice. "Don't they have any of those things?"

"Well, that, too, I guess, is a point of view."

She thought about what he had said as she watched the flatlands spread out ahead of them, broken by the rows and rows of oil-storage tanks and tall chimneys spewing smoke. She wrinkled her nose at the odor, but her dark brows were drawn together in thought. "What's job security?" she asked.

"Knowing you have a job no matter what happens."

She nodded her head. "That would be good. If I were grown up and had a job, it would be nice to know it couldn't be taken away from me."

"Well, it's not as simple as that." He smiled. "A man—or a woman —might be inefficient, incompetent, lazy—"

"Maybe somebody only says that, for some other reason."

Lawrence stared down at her, while she watched the traffic on the outskirts of a town up ahead. "That could be true, I suppose."

"And maybe another man needs more money because he has lots of doctor bills, or his landlord raised his rent."

Lawrence still stared at her. "How do you know about things like that?" he asked, his voice soft with surprise.

"Ellie talks about it," she said, while peering around for a moment at the police car that was following them. "She said that sometimes people starved during the Depression. She said her father killed himself when he lost his job, and her little brother died because her mother couldn't afford a doctor or to take him to the hospital."

Lawrence let his gaze stray out the window. She had tucked her hand into his and after a moment he squeezed it hard. "You're quite a girl, Caroline Kendall," he said softly. "You're really quite a girl."

"Sit still, Caroline!" Gail suddenly shrieked. "Now, there you've done it again—and I've got fingernail polish all over my skirt." She was holding Caroline's slim foot and painting the toenails a deep blood red, while sitting on one of Caroline's twin beds.

"Well, it tickles," Caroline protested. She grabbed up the bottle of polish remover and a swab of cotton, and handed them to Gail. "Here, get it off quick before it sets."

While Gail rubbed at her skirt, Caroline hunched over her knee and finished painting the little toe on her left foot. Just then, Ellie burst in the door.

"Gail, you have two minutes to get downstairs for your voice lesson. Lucia is here and . . ." She stopped as she saw the pieces of cotton carefully placed between each of Caroline's toes on both feet. "Oh, don't tell me you're at it again?"

"Nobody can see it," Gail insisted as she wiggled off the bed and pulled her plaid skirt around straight. "Our stockings and shoes cover it up."

Ellie sighed and smiled. "Then what on earth is the use of doing it?"

"We're practicing," Caroline said, bending over to pull on her navy blue knee socks and loafers, the pieces of cotton flying in all directions.

"And pick up those pieces of cotton, both of you," Ellie said in a stern voice, even though she was smiling as she walked to the door. "Nanny Grace will have you across her knees if you don't. Hurry now."

They scooped up the cotton, dropped it in the wastebasket, and ran from the room into the corridor; then they raced toward the staircase, sliding as though on ice on the marble floor along the edges of the long red carpet. They came down the staircase the same way, sitting on the marble bannisters and sliding down, but only as far as the broad landing halfway. They saw Morgan, the butler, looking at them from the middle of the reception hall below, suppressing a smile and warning them with his eyes. Walking the rest of the way with decorous smiles but mischievous eyes, they hurried to the music room, where Lucia, who had heard Gail sing one day, now gave her lessons.

"Can I listen?" Caroline asked.

"What do you want to listen for? That's boring," Gail said

"I like to," Caroline said. "I love to hear you sing, Gail."

"Oh, all right," Gail said with an exaggerated sigh. "But all it is is those dumb scales, up and down, up and . . ." They turned at the sound of chimes and saw Morgan watch as Ben came from the rear and walked toward the vestibule at the front. When he opened the double-glass doors, they saw a man standing beneath the porte co-chere. They could hear the murmur of voices but that was all. Ben ushered the man into the vestibule, carefully closed the glass doors behind him, and conferred with Morgan, who said, "Go along, you two, on to the music room."

He watched them while they disappeared along the gallery leading to the music room, then followed at a safe distance, heading for the library beyond. "Miss Ellie," he said, standing in the doorway of her small office just off the library. She was working on some correspondence.

"Yes, Morgan?"

"A man to see you, Miss Ellie. Ben says his name is Emil Dukoff and that he came here from Prague in Czechoslovakia."

Ellie leaped to her feet. "Where is he, Morgan?"

"In the vestibule."

"Bring him here, please, Morgan, into the library."

She waited by the fireplace. It was early spring, there was a cold nip in the air, and she had asked Ben to build a fire for her. She stood there, hardly breathing, hands clenched hard at her side, knowing this tiny flicker of hope was foolish—but there it was, just the same. Perhaps Karl had somehow gotten out of Lidice just before the Germans arrived on that early-summer morning ten years ago. Perhaps he had been in hiding and had got word to someone who . . .

"You must stop this hopeless wishmaking, Ellie," Georges had said the evening before when they were sitting in the Bonat Café on West Thirty-first Street.

"But Anton knew only that Karl had gone to Lidice to see his parents and other brother. He didn't know whether he might have left or not—"

"Stop it, Ellie," Georges said quietly, putting his hand over hers. They had finished their dinner and were drinking their demitasse. She looked away, sudden tears in her eyes. He saw her try to blink them back and his heart went out to her, but he had to remain firm, he knew. His patience was wearing thin. No, not patience, he thought, looking at her, the soft blonde hair, curling from beneath the brim of her blue hat, the Renoir face with its delicate features and deep blue eyes, the graceful wrists and hands. No, not patience. He was beginning to doubt that she would ever accept the fact that Karl Wancek was dead and never coming back.

"I—I'm sorry, Georges," she had whispered. "I wish I could believe as you believe."

She remembered how she had said that as she stood by the library fire and watched the door. When the man appeared, he gazed at her for several moments before coming forward.

"Mrs. Wancek?" he said, his hand out. She waved him to a chair by the fire and asked Morgan to bring coffee. When she sat down opposite him, he looked around for a moment, seeing a massive fireplace, walls of books from ceiling to floor, rich wood paneling, and Oriental carpets.

"Such a big house," he said, searching for each word. "I did not expect—"

"I am the secretary here," she said with a sharpness that she hadn't intended. She saw him smile sheepishly. "I—I'm sorry. It's just that I become upset when I think there might be some word of my husband."

"Husband?" he said with surprise. "No, I not bring word of your husband." He was shaking his head.

"Oh. I see." She tried to hide the terrible disappointment.

"I been coming from Czechoslovakia for four months now," he said. "I go through Poland, to Baltic Sea, and then to Copenhagen. But take much time."

"Yes, of course," she said, as the old despair filled her once more.

"Things very bad in Czechoslovakia. Much suppression. People we know. They disappear in night. I am friend of Anton Wancek," he said with a smile. But the smile was short-lived.

"Anton?" Ellie said, leaning forward. "Is he all right?"

"No one who believes—who is for freedom—is all right," he said, shaking his head. "Even members of Communist party, but suspected of having pro-Western views. They are taken. Some executed. Three members of Philharmonic have disappeared. Anton and others, we belong to an underground organization. Someone may have talked. For now, he is safe. As conductor of Philharmonic. How long he is safe?" He shrugged. "No one knows that. Also, this year, there will be ceremony, for those, in memoriam, who assassinated the Nazi, Reinhard Heydrich. Suddenly, again, in this year of anniversary for ten years, your husband, Karl Wancek, he is hero. And Anton was his brother."

Ellie looked bewildered. "Then the government of Czechoslovakia believes he is dead?"

"I am sorry—yes. He has been legally declared dead. He was at Lidice when the Germans come."

Ellie stood up, walked to a window, and stared unseeingly out to the street. When Morgan came in with the silver coffee service, she returned to the fireplace, sat down, and poured their coffee.

"Thank you, Morgan," she said quietly as he left the room. When she handed a cup and saucer to Emil Dukoff, she said, "Is there any

260

way Anton can leave Czechoslovakia before—before something happens?"

He waited for a moment, then said, "I have thought of way. If you could go to Prague for ceremony, for memorial service for heroes who killed Heydrich, perhaps you could help."

"But how?"

"If you were to marry Anton Wancek, as husband of American, and with much publicity about famous conductor traveling to America for concerts, as your husband, perhaps he could leave. Marriage to American citizen will almost of certainty get someone out of Czechoslovakia."

"But—"

"It has been done before, I am told. Then marriage is dissolved in divorce."

Ellie thought for several moments, then looked up at him. "I would have to think about it, of course," she said quietly. When he nodded, she said, "Is there someplace I can get in touch with you?"

He wrote an address and phone number on a small piece of paper and handed it to her. Then she stood up and walked with him, out to the gallery with its long row of gold-framed portraits, and on into the main reception hall, where their footsteps echoed across the marble floor.

"You'll hear from me," she said with a sudden warm smile. He turned at the vestibule door to look back at her. She was standing just beyond the double-glass doors, slim and lovely in the pink wool frock. He nodded and walked out past Ben, who stood holding the big oak door.

"You are going to *what?*" Elizabeth said, aghast, as she suddenly looked up at Ellie. They were in the morning room arranging flowers in the low bowls and vases that Jessie and Edna had brought in to them. It was a task that Elizabeth loved and hurried to every third morning when the fresh flowers were delivered.

Ellie's lips tightened and she jutted her jaw out a bit, an expression Elizabeth knew indicated that her friend had become stubborn about something. "I'm going to Prague to marry Anton and bring him back here to the United States."

"But *why?*" Elizabeth sat down hard in a nearby chair.

"Because—because I want to. A man came here yesterday. His name is Emil Dukoff. He's a musician, a friend of Anton's who

261

managed to get out of Czechoslovakia. He said that Anton is safe at the moment, but the time will come when he will not be safe, that there are purges and executions and arrests going on—"

"Oh, Ellie." Elizabeth leaned toward her, hands out in a plea. "Ellie, please . . . And there's Georges. He loves you, Ellie."

"No, Elizabeth, I can't think of Georges now, and I won't let you talk me out of it. As the husband of an American citizen, they would let him leave Czechoslovakia, you see. I am going there and we'll be married there, right in Prague. Then I'll bring him back here." She was pacing the room, talking almost as though to herself. "This Emil Dukoff said that Anton belongs to some underground organization that works against the Communist government and that soon he won't be safe there—"

"Would you stop and listen to yourself!" Elizabeth rushed to her, grasped her arms, and began shaking her. "Do you have any idea what all of this sounds like? I realize he's Karl's brother, but—"

"No, Elizabeth," Ellie said, her face set stubbornly, "I've made up my mind, and no one is going to change it. I've already called the consulate and asked for a visa. There is going to be a ceremony, a memorial ceremony, honoring the dead heroes of the Heydrich assassination. As the wife of one of those men, the Czech Consulate said they would be more than willing to issue me a visa."

"Ellie, Ellie, for the ceremony, yes. Go. In fact, you must go. But not to marry Anton." Elizabeth was pleading, but Ellie pulled away from her and started toward the door, almost bumping into Honey and Enid as they came through, both wearing broad-brimmed straw hats and Chanel suits that almost seemed to match.

"Good heavens, what's this?" Honey was saying. "Do you know that we could hear you two all the way down the gallery?"

"Why—nothing," Elizabeth said, quickly recovering and turning to the flowers she was arranging, as Ellie waited by the door. "Ellie was just telling me she's going to Prague for a memorial ceremony they're holding there. It's for the dead heroes who assassinated Reinhard Heydrich, and the ceremony is to be held on the day Heydrich was killed. I'm afraid it upsets me, Ellie going there again, to one of those Iron Curtain countries."

"Who is Reinhard Heydrich?" Enid said, dropping her fur scarf over the back of a chair. She took a cigarette from a gold case and lit it.

"Why, he was one of the Nazis who killed all of those people,"

Honey said. She was standing in front of one of the long narrow mirrors that broke the stretch of apple-green paneling at intervals. She primped her hair beneath the broad-brimmed hat, then looked at Elizabeth and whirled around. "We're on our way to the hospital ball meeting, Elizabeth. Madge Devereaux made me promise I'd ask if you'd co-chair the ball with me and head the sponsor committee. I told her I would bring an answer today."

Elizabeth watched Honey as she turned back to the mirror and took a lipstick from her purse. She carefully outlined her lips, which were already a glistening red. Glancing quickly at Enid, who was sitting in one of the pale green bamboo chairs, examining her long coral-colored nails, she thought how utterly useless they were. Well . . . perhaps not entirely. They were the kind of wives that their husbands wanted them to be. And Honey was a whiz at running charity events, at getting other women, like Enid, to do the dirty work.

She pulled some ferns loose from the clusters of russet mums.

"Of course, Honey," she said, looking up from the flowers with a slow smile. "I'd be happy to help if I can."

Ellie stood in the sunshine beside Anton, listening to the drone of the official's voice, understanding only a word here and there, words that Karl had taught her. She looked around the wide square, where the platform in front of the Old Town Hall had been erected. The baroque splendor of the buildings that graced the square was unchanged. She was facing Zelezna Street, where she could see the Carolinium and the Tyl Theatre. And by turning her head, she could see the Malé Náměstí, the Little Town Square with its statue of Jan Hus, where she and Franceska had fed the pigeons. At the stroke of noon, she looked off in the distance to the fifteenth-century clock where first Christ and the twelve Apostles showed themselves at a little window above the clock face, then death as it tolled for lost time, then a Turk, a miser, a vain fool, and finally a cock.

The sun splashed brightly in long shafts across the square on this soft June morning, while back near the buildings the curious stood in pools of shadow, watching with some suspicion the ceremonies that were taking place. Suddenly the tall man with gray hair wearing a frock coat—the Mayor, Anton had said—was placing a medal in Ellie's hands. He leaned down and kissed her on both cheeks, and after a slight pause, a band broke into a dirge-like anthem.

When the ceremonies were over, Anton led her across the square to his small car and helped her in. When they passed Maislove Street, she peered down into its shadows. When she had first arrived a week before, she had gone to the apartment building where Franceska Corescu and her mother had lived. But they were gone, and no one could tell her what had happened to them.

"That happens, quite frequently now," Anton said in his slow, precise English. He looked at her with a sad smile. "So far, we go untouched. Even as they know there are dissidents among us. They want still to keep the Philharmonic intact." He turned the car onto the Charles Bridge, the historic royal trail, heavy with carved statuary and the massive towers at each end.

"Perhaps Franceska and Mme. Corescu simply moved to another place," Ellie said hopefully, as she gazed at the broad river.

"That is possible," Anton said, but he was unconvincing.

They passed the soaring gothic Cathedral of St. Vitus, the Royal Gardens, and the summer palace. They were headed for Lidice—or the place where it had once stood, a pilgrimage both felt they had to make. As they approached, they saw the beginnings of a new village. But where the old Lidice had stood were meadows. They walked about silently, tears sliding unashamedly down Ellie's cheeks. She stopped and picked a rose—the air was heavy with the scent of roses —put it to her lips for a moment, then folded it into a white handkerchief and put it in her purse. They walked there for perhaps an hour, finally turning back toward the car for the short drive back to Prague.

"We haven't spoken again about marriage, Anton," Ellie said in a quiet voice. She was watching the countryside fly by and didn't turn to look at him.

He glanced at her and then at the road again. "No, Ellie," he said. "How can I explain? It was astounding to me, your coming here for this purpose. And I am more grateful than you will ever know. But—"

"Your friend Emil Dukoff says you are in danger," she exclaimed.

"Emil makes much of little," he scoffed. They had entered the outskirts of the city, but he swept on at the same speed, maneuvering with skill through the winding narrow streets.

"That's not true. You said yourself that people are disappearing."

"I also said they wish to keep the Philharmonic unchanged." He smiled at her with confidence, his clear blue eyes calm. "It is—how do you say it?—a feather in their cap. We have worked hard to rebuild the orchestra. This has always been a city of music. The Philharmonic has always been one of the great orchestras of Europe. The authorities do not want to lose what they now have."

She listened to his voice, so like Karl's, studied his profile as he hunched forward over the wheel of the small car. Just the nose was slightly different, thinner at the bridge and coming to a sharper point. And when he smiled, his eyes remained serious, as though a part of him were afraid of too much happiness.

They were silent again until they reached Anton's apartment house, near the Václavské Náměstí, the old Wenceslas Square. He had convinced her when she arrived that she must stay there instead of going to a hotel, that his housekeeper, Hannela, would take good care of her. It was late afternoon when they arrived. The weather had suddenly changed, the sky turning gray and leaden. They hurried through a heavy spattering of raindrops into the lower foyer, a dark, damp hallway that was merely a receptacle for the creaking, open-cage lift that groaned to the five floors above. Anton pulled open the heavy wrought-iron door and let it close when they stepped in. With a shudder, the lift slowly rose, cables swishing above and below with an ominous sound. It clanged to a stop at the third story and they stepped out. Several moments passed after he pressed the bell before the door opened and Hannela's cheerful round face greeted them. She flapped her voluminous white apron excitedly, as though she hadn't seen them for months, a trait that Ellie had grown to expect in the short time she had been there.

"I bring tea, schnapps," she said, almost exhausting her supply of words in English, as she hurried down the long dark hallway toward the kitchen. Although she understood some German, Anton spoke to her in Slovak, her native language and dialect, slipping into it as fluently as he did into his own Czech, or English, or German, or French.

He called out some instruction to her, and as she disappeared, she smiled and nodded. "I bring tea," she said, settling that question.

When he had finished his tea, Anton hurried out to a late-afternoon rehearsal. Ellie realized he had only returned to the flat out of politeness to her. With a strange sense of loss and failure, she went to her room and lay down on the bed to rest. She would leave within a day or two, whenever Anton was able to arrange her departure.

That evening, at a concert of the Philharmonic, her first in Prague, she was transfixed by the beauty of the music. The crowded concert hall was brilliantly lighted, the massive chandeliers glittering on the ornately gilded interior, glowing down on the red velvet swags and swinging gold tassels, all in strong contrast to the rather drab appearance of the audience. As she watched Anton on the podium, conducting the Smetana program, she wanted to weep over a past that was fast slipping away; its rococo splendor remained only in the stones and architecture of Prague.

They rode back through the darkened streets, Anton silent and preoccupied. When she told him how much she had enjoyed the concert, he nodded and said, "I am glad you liked it." But that was all.

The gleaming white shirtfront and tie of his dress suit seemed almost incongruous in the dim light of the groaning lift as it rose through the silent apartment house. There was a faint odor of coal dust in the air, but the only sound was the creaking of the lift cables and the clanking of the wrought-iron gate when Anton swung it open. He slipped a large key into the lock, and the moment he pushed the door wide to let Ellie enter, they heard a scream. Hannela came running toward them, along the dark hallway that led to the front living room and the drawing room behind it. She was crying out incoherently, her hair disheveled and her white flannel dressing robe flying. Anton asked her a sharp question in Slovak, but she kept on babbling and ran back toward the front of the flat, with Anton and Ellie following.

Pools of yellow light from the lamps lit up a bizzare scene. Cushions from the deep comfortable sofas and chairs had been slashed and thrown to the floor, small tables lay on their sides, and at one long window, the drapes had been ripped off and tossed in a corner. A large blue and white jardiniere that had been filled with flowers was knocked over and broken, the water spilled onto the Oriental carpet.

Anton had quickly but gently pushed Hannela down onto a chair and was pouring her a cognac from a small glass-fronted cabinet, surprisingly untouched, that stood in the corner. Tears streamed down her lined face and there was dark terror in her eyes. She was still talking, with more coherence now, and Anton was nodding rapidly, his face a mask of cold anger.

"Men came, she says," he said to Ellie over his shoulder, pausing every few words to hear more of what Hannela was babbling. "Not in uniforms, but in dark coats and hats." He paused again. "They pushed their way in and started looking for something."

He suddenly ran to an adjoining door, reached in, and flipped on the lights of his music room. Ellie stared over his shoulder, her face aghast, at the large corner room with bare shining floors, a large grand piano, and floor-to-ceiling cupboards along one wall that held his music. All the small cupboard doors were open and the sheets of music lay scattered across the floor like a carpet.

Ellie followed him through the large comfortable apartment, but it was the same everywhere—bureau drawers open, the contents thrown about, mattresses slashed, cupboards and armoires in disarray, curtains pulled down, items from trunks and boxes in a storage room heaped in corners.

"It's madness," Anton whispered, as he sank into a chair in the living room and put his head between his hands.

"What were they looking for?" Ellie asked.

Anton slowly raised his head and looked at her. "There is an organization that prints pamphlets, literature that speaks to the people. It talks of freedom, of the uprising that is certain to come someday."

Hannela spoke sharply from where she was sitting, a few words. Anton quickly walked to a small radio on a table, turned it on, and as a news-reader's voice flowed into the room, he beckoned to Ellie. When she stood next to him, he spoke closely to her ear, turning the radio even louder.

"I am one of those suspected. This, I have known for a long time. But I have felt safe because of the music. Now—"

"Now, Anton?"

"Tonight I was told that Bregenza, a member of the Czech String Quartet, he was taken away from his flat this morning before dawn."

Ellie suddenly grasped his hands and pleaded, "You must leave, Anton, you've got to! We'll leave as soon as we possibly can."

"Yes," he said distractedly. "But, you, Ellie . . . ?"

"I came here with a purpose, Anton. I came here to marry you."

"No, Ellie, this is not fair to you—"

"If I hadn't wanted to do this, Anton, I wouldn't have come here. I was married to Karl and I loved him—I loved him from the moment I met him. At first, he couldn't think of anyone but Miriam, and I understood that. I was willing to wait. Then one day, I knew—knew he had begun to think of me in a different way. Soon, I knew that he loved me. Oh, Anton—" She suddenly stopped. She had almost said, *This could happen to us, too, Anton.* "Don't you see?" she said, quickly covering. "You're Karl's brother. I want to do this for you, but mostly for Karl."

"Ellie . . ." He was waving one hand helplessly and shaking his head.

She held her breath for a moment, aware her heart was pounding.

"And then, once you are safely out of here, in the States, it could be annulled, if you wish."

"That could be done?" he suddenly asked, looking at her.

She nodded, unable to speak. He turned to the radio and slowly turned the volume down, then stood there with his back to her, thinking. When he looked around at her, there was a slow smile spreading across his face. In that moment, he looked exactly like Karl.

"All right," he said softly. "If . . . if you are sure of this annulment?"

"I'm sure," she said, her voice faltering a little.

He nodded and started toward the music room, then paused for a moment. "Go to bed, Ellie. We will see about a marriage ceremony tomorrow."

They were married a week later. A friend of Anton's, high in the bureaucratic system of civil matters at the Town Hall, made the arrangements and put through the necessary papers. They were surprised at the ease with which it occurred. They had expected delays, questioning, perhaps even a denial of permission for the ceremony, which was performed in Anton's flat by a minor official whose sole duty seemed to be performing marriages.

Through the next weeks, Ellie grew to almost like Prague, even with the repressive atmosphere and constant reminders that it was a police state. She continued to sleep in the big old-fashioned bedroom, with cherubs carved into the plaster ceiling above. The eiderdown bed was big and soft, and gauzy white curtains blew at the long casement windows in gentle little puffs. Doves cooed on the stone ledge outside her windows each morning.

Each day, after Anton's rehearsal, she met him and went with him to one of the cafés frequented by musicians, writers, and artists. She came to love the late afternoons they spent with these talented people. Most of Anton's friends knew English and, in deference to her, they spoke it almost exclusively. There were always a number of attractive women present, mainly wives of some of his friends, but for the most part there were scores of men, all of whom delighted in paying compliments to "Anton's beautiful American wife."

"How can you sit here in café so late, Anton," Jiri Marshak, the well-known artist, was saying one evening with a wickedly teasing note in his voice, "when you have such a beautiful bride sitting there?" He had leaped to push his chair in next to hers when someone else moved slightly, bent close to her, touched her small glass of slivovitz with his, and drank it down in a toast to her. When she blushed, he and several others at the table sent up a shout of laughing approval. She glanced at Anton, saw a puzzled expression in his eyes, and looked away quickly, the blush rising higher in her cheeks. She quickly drank half of the slivovitz and felt it race through her veins, felt it glow and sing inside.

When they walked back to his flat through the soft summer night, he told her about how the negotiations for their leaving the country were progressing. She thought she heard a new tone in his voice. At one point he quickly grasped her hand to hold her back when an automobile suddenly raced around a corner. As they walked on, he kept holding it until, almost reluctantly it seemed, he dropped it. When they reached the flat, she turned to him in the darkened foyer. For several moments, as they stood closely facing each other, he looked down at her. Slowly he reached out and touched her hair, then let his hand rest against her cheek. She heard his breath as it grew faster, and pressed her cheek against his hand. When she looked up into his eyes, she saw that his were dark and seeking.

"Anton?" she whispered.

But slowly he turned away, his hand dropping to his side, and the moment was gone. "Good night, Ellie," he said softly, and she thought she heard a note of regret in his voice. She walked along the darkened hallway, turned into her room, and closed the door.

They had plane tickets to Amsterdam, where, Anton explained, they would change planes for Paris, then take a train to Le Havre. There they would board the *Liberté,* bound for New York. Negotiations, through underground channels, had also been underway with a concert booking service in New York. Two days before they were to leave Prague, Anton received a summons to appear at the Minister of Culture's offices.

Although he entered Kapockny's inner office with trepidation, he seemed to be completely self-possessed, a fact that annoyed the round and florid Minister of Culture no end. Fans whirled and whirred in the big high-ceilinged office, but while Anton looked cool and dry, Kapockny perspired, the beads of sweat running down the sides of his face and pouring uncomfortably underneath his collar and down his chest.

With no more than a grunted greeting, the sandy-haired minister eased his bulk out of his desk chair. As he came around to where Anton was seated, he suddenly held a newspaper up and spread it wide in front of Anton's face. It was the *London Times* and the headline read ANTON WANCEK, CZECH PHILHARMONIC CONDUCTOR, TO TOUR AMERICA. A small headline beneath it said LONDON PERFORMANCE TO FOLLOW.

Anton stared at the large black headlines.

"Would you care to say anything, Dr. Wancek?" Kapockny said.

"I am at a loss for words," Anton said coolly, while a great sigh of relief heaved within him. Publicity in newspapers such as the *London Times* could well pave his safe departure from Czechoslovakia. It would not do, in the eyes of the West, for him to disappear now. That would generate the kind of publicity those behind the Iron Curtain deplored.

"Oh, I am sure you are," Kapockny said with heavy sarcasm. He returned to his chair, leaned back expansively as he lit a long cigar. "I am informed you have married an American woman?"

"Yes, Minister, your information is correct." He smiled, almost enjoying the moment, his intense blue eyes never wavering from the perspiring man's flushed face. He crossed one sharply creased gray trouser leg over the other and touched the dark gray striped tie as though to make certain it was straight.

"Your brother's widow, I am told."

"Again, correct, Minister."

"Quite honestly, Dr. Wancek," the minister said, "I am delighted when I hear that malcontents such as yourself are leaving Czechoslovakia."

"Indeed? Malcontents?"

"I believe it is no secret you would prefer to see a quite different kind of government, a quite different philosophy here than the one that has brought us such great prosperity."

"I would simply like to see a less repressive government, Minister, one, for example, that would permit an unlimited choice of music that could be performed in its concert halls and theatres, one that would permit more freedom of expression and thought and—"

"Well, undoubtedly the decadence and turmoil of the country you are going to will hold a deep appeal for you, Dr. Wancek, and as I said before, I am always delighted when a man of your persuasion is leaving our midst. But I should warn you. There may be others who will not be so anxious for you to go."

Anton rose. "If that is all, Minister, I should like to go. I have my last performance tonight with the Philharmonic and I am running quite late."

The minister raised his arm in an airy wave, as though to say, *Get out, I've had enough of your impertinence.* Anton bowed, a cool smile on his lips, but when he reached the corridor outside, he began to tremble. Just two days, he thought, panic rising in his throat. *Just two days.*

Ruzyne, the airport, was a drab and dreary place, particularly at night. Dim lightbulbs overhead did little to relieve the depressing atmosphere of the dun-colored walls and small, crowded waiting rooms. People stood in docile lines, waiting their turn to be sternly interrogated, even if they were only taking a short trip to Brno or Karlovy Vary or České Budějovice. Ellie clasped her hands tightly together to keep them from trembling. A woman next to her was staring at her clothes, the soft summery blue dress and blue and white hat. "Such beautiful lady," Hannela had said, her eyes brimming as she hugged Ellie.

She looked up at Anton, standing in the line near her, and wondered how he could appear so calm. Then she saw the clench of his jaw and the tiny pulse pounding on the side of his neck. She was clutching her papers in her hand while trying to look casual and unperturbed, when suddenly a voice bawled out: "Dr. Wancek. Dr. Anton Wancek."

She stiffened, as Anton glanced around. They both saw the man who had called out standing at a half-open doorway up near the front. With a quick clasp of her arm, he said softly, "I'm sure it's nothing." And he walked away and went through the door.

For the next two hours, Ellie felt as though she were traveling in slow motion through a nightmare. The line moved slowly, but about an hour later she found herself in a small room where a man with features one would not remember asked her questions in an English she found difficult, if not impossible, to understand.

"But I must know where my husband is," she kept insisting. "We are traveling together and I haven't seen him for over an hour."

He ignored her plea and kept on looking through her papers, leaving dirty smudges on them from his hands and burning the edge of one with a foul-smelling cigarette. Abruptly he went out and left her sitting in the room for another hour, her heart thudding with a slow, irregular bumping and a nerve in one eyelid twitching. She turned at every sound and noise beyond the door, hoping it would be Anton or someone who had come to get her. From time to time, she could hear the roar of planes outside and once she heard a child screaming. When the door finally opened, she jumped to her feet and cried out, "Please, I have to find my husband!"

The young woman who came in would have been pretty if the uniform she was wearing hadn't been so bulky and ill-fitting, and if she could have learned to smile. The corners of her mouth were turned down in a permanent expression of unhappiness. She gestured to Ellie to follow her.

"But my husband . . ." Ellie cried out again in a futile attempt. She hurried after the young woman, out into the larger of the waiting rooms, toward a set of double doors with tiny windows set so high she couldn't see where they were going. On the other side of the doors was a long corridor that led, obviously, out to the tarmac on the airfield.

"Please," she shouted, the sound of engines beyond the open doors at the end almost drowning out her voice. Two dim lightbulbs swung from wires in the ceiling, casting weirdly moving shadows ahead of her. "I have to know about my husband!" But the young woman walked on in silence. Ellie ran after her, grasped her arm, and stopped her.

"My husband! Where is he?" she shrieked above the screeching noise of the engines.

"On plane," the girl answered, pointing ahead, and with relief Ellie followed her.

But when she boarded the plane, she could see Anton nowhere. The woman led her to a seat, told her to sit down, and handed her her papers. In moments, the plane began to move. Ellie frantically pushed her face against the tiny round window—all she could see was darkness alongside the runway as the plane gathered speed and lifted into the air.

Ellie was hopeful that when she arrived back in New York there would be some kind of information about Anton. But there was nothing. The Czech Consulate claimed to know nothing. She returned home one late afternoon after trying again to talk to someone at the Consulate. She paced the living room in her small apartment on the top floor of the Kendalls' Manhattan house and ranted almost incoherently. Gail sat watching her in hurt silence. She had just come in from school, where she and Caroline had been playing field hockey.

"We lost," she said, trying to get Ellie's attention. "Brearley lost, Mama." But Ellie didn't hear her, and kept pacing from the windows over to the high row of bookcases and back again. Gail bent her golden head and picked forlornly at her plaid skirt, smoothing out the pleats, then pressing them down again.

"Why did you do it?" she suddenly asked in an accusing tone.

"What—what did you say, Gail?" Ellie turned to her in confusion. She saw angry tears in Gail's eyes.

"Why did you do it, go off to some crazy country where they won't let anybody out and marry a man you hardly know?"

Ellie stared at her and, in a shocked voice, said, "He's your father's brother and he was in trouble."

"You don't marry somebody because he's in trouble."

"It was the only way to save him."

"But it didn't save him! He's not even here." Her voice was rising in bewilderment. "And it's as though *you're* not here anymore. Ever since that man Emil came and you went away, and you stayed and stayed. And then since you came home, it's all you've talked or thought about. Oh, Mama!" She ran to Ellie and threw her arms around her, sobbing.

For a long while, Ellie held her, smoothing her hair back, kissing away the tears on her cheeks. Finally she whispered, "Oh, darling, I'm sorry. I'm so terribly sorry. I haven't meant to hurt you. But I have to find Anton. Please, darling, give me a little more time. Just a little more time." Gail pulled slowly away and gently touched Ellie's cheek.

"He's not Daddy. Can't you see that, Mama? He's not Daddy."

But she left for Washington that night, and, with letters of introduction from Lawrence, got in to see the Undersecretary of State. For almost a week she waited. From the Undersecretary's offices she was referred to various agencies, including the Central Intelligence Agency, where a man sent her on to the Washington offices of the International Refugee Organization. She returned day after day until one morning she found herself sitting in the office of the tall woman who had first seen her almost a week before.

"Well, Mrs. Wancek," the woman said, as she shuffled some papers in front of her, putting them in order, "we've exhausted every avenue we have, and I'm just terribly sorry to have to tell you that we've come up with nothing." Her smile was sympathetic, but Ellie could tell that she was anxious to get on with her day.

"I see," Ellie said quietly, trying to hide the weary disappointment as she stood and picked up the suitcase at her side. She had already checked out of the hotel and was going straight to the railroad station. "Well, I am very appreciative of everything you've done." She hurried to the door, Mrs. Sidney following her, high heels tapping loudly on the bare floor. "Thank you again," Ellie said, turning briefly, then she ran along the corridor, pushing her way blindly past people coming in the opposite direction.

When Ben opened the vestibule door and took her suitcase from her hand, she heard through her weariness the grind of the taxicab's gears behind her. Lights flashed under the porte cochere as the taxi pulled away and out into the pouring rain, where the headlamps of automobiles glittered on the dark wet pavement of Fifth Avenue.

"Ellie?"

Elizabeth was coming toward her across the main reception hall. She was wearing an emerald green velvet evening gown, with the Kendall diamonds and emeralds sparkling at her ears and throat. Oh, yes, Ellie thought, they had tickets for Katharine Hepburn in *The Millionairess.* And Elizabeth and Lawrence would be expecting her to go with them. "Ellie, Anton is here. I tried to reach you at the hotel but you had left and—"

"Anton? Here?" She stopped halfway across the reception hall and stared at Elizabeth, who held her for a moment and kissed her cheek.

"He arrived late last night, went to a hotel, and then came here this afternoon." She took Ellie's hand and led her toward the gallery and the east wing of the house. "He's in the music room."

"Ellie!" He jumped up from the piano bench and met her halfway across the room, hands out to clasp hers.

She rushed to him, her face wreathed in smiles. "Anton! Thank God—oh, thank God, you're all right."

He put his arms about her and held her for a moment, then pushed her away a little to look down into her face. "I'm fine." He was laughing softly at the expression on her face, one of disbelief. "I'm not a ghost. It is really I, Ellie, and all in one piece."

She led him quickly to a couch and drew him down with her so that she was holding his hands once more. "What happened?" She sounded breathless, as she quickly looked at Elizabeth again, who was standing near the doorway. "Quickly, tell me. What happened?"

"I'll just find Morgan and ask him to bring tea," Elizabeth said, disappearing.

"Well—" His smile faded. "They detained me there, at the airport,

274

for many hours. No one would tell me anything. Finally, I was taken to a house on the outskirts of Prague and was left there, with just an old servant couple, and several men to watch me." He laughed ruefully. "As though I would try to escape." His voice grew bitter. "Escape to what? There is no escape in Czechoslovakia. No"—he shook his head, slowly—"no, my only hope was to wait, to see what they wanted, what they were going to do with me. Finally, one day, two men came, and asked me questions, over and over. Names. They wanted names. Names of members of secret organizations. Names of those in the Philharmonic they believed to be disloyal to the government. I told them I knew nothing. That all I knew was music. That all I cared to know was music. They went away and a few days later came again, asked the same questions, went away, repeated it once more a few days later. This went on for several weeks—" He shook his head, almost confusedly. "I started to lose track of time. But I think it was several weeks, perhaps only two—"

"It was one month ago today that I left Prague," Ellie said softly.

He nodded. "And then one night, two other men came. They seemed impatient, told me to pack my clothing, that we were leaving. In moments, it seemed, we were outside, in that long black car, speeding to the airfield. I knew then that someone, the American or British consul's offices—someone of imporance from the outside had been asking questions—"

"Lawrence had people making inquiries night and day." They looked up to see Elizabeth coming across the room, followed by Lucia, who was watching Anton intently.

"This is Lucia, Anton. You remember I told you about her—"

He was slowly rising and had his hand out. As he took hers he bent to kiss it, then looked up at her, smiling, his eyes filled with admiration. "Lucia Daniello," he said with something approaching awe in his voice. "I have recordings of you singing *Bohème* and *Cosi Fan Tutte*. Magnificent—"

"Please—" Lucia said graciously, her hands spread in apology. "We interrupted you." She and Elizabeth quickly sat down opposite them, Lucia's large dark eyes darting from Ellie's face to Anton's and back to Ellie again.

"Well," he said, as he sat down again. "There is not much more to tell. After the weeks of detainment I was rushed to the airport and put on a plane to Amsterdam. I knew the Americans or British had interceded"— he smiled at Elizabeth—"due, no doubt, Madame, to your husband. His name was mentioned when a Thomas Keneally from the American Legation in The Netherlands met my plane."

"Lawrence can be most persuasive," Lucia said with a silvery burst of laughter. Elizabeth glanced at her, hearing a new note in Lucia's voice, one that had been missing for a long, long time. Then she looked at Anton and Ellie again.

"And insistent," Elizabeth said with a smile, as he nodded. *Powerful* was a word that remained unsaid. Even in Czechoslovakia, with its closed borders and silenced press, the name of Lawrence Kendall had been heard. "Well, we're grateful and relieved that you're finally here." She smiled again. "And I hope that you'll remain here as our guest until"—she rose again, pulling Lucia by the hand up with her —"until you and Ellie know what—well, what you are going to do."

Anton glanced quickly from Elizabeth to Ellie and back to Elizabeth again. "I think it is only a matter of making arrangements—"

Elizabeth was walking toward the door, Lucia trailing after her. "I asked Morgan to bring you tea." She paused and looked back over her shoulder. "Lucia and I must hurry. We have a later afternoon meeting at the Metropolitan Museum, a benefit party we're running next month at the Waldorf." She ignored Lucia's questioning expression and took her hand to lead her out the door. "We're late as it is. See you at dinner."

Ellie and Anton were quiet several moments after they had left. He walked slowly across the room to one of the long windows and looked out to the Fifth Avenue traffic, while she watched him stiffly. A matter of making arrangements, he had said. Then he did want the annulment. She felt a bleakness steal through her as she watched him. He turned suddenly and started to say something, but stopped as he saw her face, saw the eagerness there, the slender body bent toward him, almost as though in a plea.

"I—well, that was very kind of Mrs. Kendall, asking me to remain as a guest here . . ." A gentle expression had come over his face. "But, I took my bags to the Pierre Hotel, Ellie. It is nice . . . on the park. And I didn't want to be a burden to anyone."

"Elizabeth meant what she said about you staying here—"

"I know," he said as he walked back to her, took her hands in his, and drew her to her feet. For a long moment he looked down at her. "It is better this way, Ellie."

"Yes, of course." She said it quickly, trying to smile. "And it will give us time, well, time to think about things. After all those weeks in Prague. It was so nerve-wracking, waiting, wondering what was going to happen, whether they would permit you to leave or not, never knowing from one day to the next—"

"Ellie." His voice was quiet. She stopped and slowly looked up at him. "We musn't . . . well, we musn't . . ." He studied her face for a moment, then smiled softly, as her heart seemed to catch in her throat. He looked so much like Karl in that moment. "I am very tired," he said, "and would like to get some sleep."

"Of course," she said. She walked him toward the door, one hand still clinging to his.

Ellie saw little of Anton in the next few weeks. He had become completely caught up in the music world in New York, planning a concert tour to introduce him to American audiences, a tour where he would be guest-conducting across the country. On the evenings he came to the Kendall townhouse for dinner, Sybil and Lucia were often there, and she heard snatches of conversation between him and Lucia, names such as Sol Hurok, Arthur Judson, or Columbia Artists Management, mentions of Spoleto and the Mozarteum in Salzburg, the Conducting Competition in London, the Cleveland Orchestra as compared to "the Philadelphia sound." His manner with her was solicitous, concerned, but it was when Lucia was present that he seemed to come alive. Their common love of and involvement with music had formed a bond between them, and several times Ellie heard him, in a coaxing voice, tell her that she must return to opera, that she owed it not only to herself but to her followers. And she saw how Lucia listened to him, raptly, hanging on every word, slowly nodding, still not persuaded but beginning to take an interest again in what was happening in the concert halls and the Metropolitan Opera House, at Hurok's office, and on tours across the country. But still, Ellie hoped.

But then one afternoon—the afternoon that Lucia came each week to give Gail her voice lesson—Ellie left her office near the library when Ben told her that Mr. Wancek had arrived. Ben had taken him to the music room to see Lucia. Ellie passed Gail running in the opposite direction as she walked along the gallery.

"Change for dinner, darling," Ellie called after her, and paused for a moment to watch Gail pull up her hockey socks while heading toward the center reception hall and staircase. She walked on then, smiling and shaking her head as Gail sang out over her shoulder,

"Which shall I wear? My black velvet Schiaparelli, or my Cecil Beaton gold lamé?"

Ellie stopped just outside the music room. She stood for a moment in the long shadowy gallery, and listened.

The shaded museum lights at the tops of the gold-framed portraits cast a soft glow, and she waited, almost afraid to enter. She heard the piano playing a Chopin scherzo, and when she finally entered the room, she stood and watched for a moment. The scene was one of such intensity that she couldn't seem to move. Anton was seated at the piano, playing, while Lucia leaned on it, listening. Their eyes were locked and, on Anton's face, Ellie saw the same expression she had seen on Karl's face that last time he had held her and said goodbye.

She sat in her compartment on the train until the last possible moment for some reason she didn't understand, dreading to step down onto the platform. She had been in Reno for a little over six weeks, but she felt as though she had been away for years. From the moment the train plunged beneath Park Avenue, she felt the tightening of her throat and the pressure of tears. But she forced them back. Elizabeth had prepared her in a phone call.

"I think you should know, Ellie, before you get home . . . Anton and Lucia plan to be married."

She had paused for a moment before answering. "I—I'm glad, Elizabeth. They are so right for each other." And strangely enough, she realized she meant it. "It's just that—I feel so adrift."

"Your life will come back together again, darling," Elizabeth had said softly. "Just come home, Ellie, come home where we love you."

She walked along the dimly lit platform, the redcap up ahead of her with her luggage. I feel nothing, she thought, nothing at all . . . just a terrible emptiness. As though I have no name, no identity.

"You want me to carry these to the taxi stand, Miss?" the redcap said, looking over his shoulder.

"Thank you, but someone is meeting me." Elizabeth had said she would send Meacham with one of the cars. She glanced at a newspaper in the hands of a man walking near her. STALIN DIES AFTER 29-YEAR RULE, she read. Who had thought that Stalin would ever die? she mused dully. She paused for a moment, then started walking again. Life *does* move on, she thought. The world keeps changing, even our lives . . .

278

"Mama!" She heard the joyous shout and looked up toward the gate leading into Grand Central Terminal. Gail was dancing about excitedly, her gold curls bouncing in the bright light, and . . . Georges, smiling, was standing beside her.

BOOK
IV

19
1956

As the next few years passed, Caroline and Gail were graduated from the Brearley School, and Caroline went on to Vassar College, while Gail flung herself headlong into vocal and dancing lessons, acting classes, and fencing. The two young women managed to spend at least one weekend together each month either in New York or in Pough-keepsie, usually on campus for some college-sponsored event or on dates with young men from West Point or Yale.

Ellie and Elizabeth found themselves more and more involved in volunteer work—"the curse or blessing of an idle woman, I'm not certain which," Elizabeth always said laughingly—and in the running of benefit parties and balls. When Anton left on a tour of Europe in 1955, Lucia returned to the Metropolitan Opera Company in a new production of *Madama Butterfly*. Even before her marriage to Anton, she had begun vocalizing and studying again, flinging herself into her work with a fierceness that stunned even Anton.

Out of breath, Gail dropped to the floor with the others in the class, hitched up her white leg warmers, then flopped onto her back with a loud "Ahhhhh." As the girlish voices and laughter rose all around her in a crescendo, she moved her head to see the clock on the wall. Another ten minutes of dance class, then she would have to run to her voice lesson on Central Park West. This was a new vocal coach and she didn't want to be late.

"Lunch, Gail?" Anna Dahlstrom said, turning her head toward Gail.

"Sorry. After my voice lesson, I'm going to a matinee of *My Fair Lady*. Caroline's down from school, and she got tickets."

"But how?" Anna sat up suddenly, her pale hair streaming down her back in a pony tail. "It's sold out already for months and months."

"Well—Lucia knows the producers." She yawned. "She's the one who actually got us the tickets." She explained. "Lucia Daniello."

"The opera singer? How do you know her?"

"Lucia's—well, sort of a relative," Gail said, sitting up and stretching from side to side. "And she's Caroline's aunt by marriage. Her husband was killed in the war and now she's married to Anton Wancek, the Czech conductor who is doing guest performances all over the country."

"His name is the same as yours," Anna said, as though making a huge discovery.

"He's my uncle."

With their legs crossed in front of them and arms raised *en haut* for fifth position, fingertips touching, they were bending from side to side in unison. They then rose, tall and slim as reeds in their black leotards, and carried on the routine on their feet. Gail's hair was piled high on her head in a loose golden knot, with curls trailing down on her forehead and neck.

"Didn't I read that he coaxed her back to the Met?" Anna asked as they bent from side to side. "That she stopped singing for quite a long time, but now she's going to do *La Bohème* and *Madama Butterfly?*"

"*Madama Butterfly* and *Il Trittico,*" Gail said, correcting her.

"All right, girls!" the instructor shouted, clapping her hands for attention. "Back on your feet. Ten more minutes to go!"

They asked Meacham to drop them off at the Plaza after the matinee, so they could have chicken sandwiches and tea in the Palm Court, a favorite place of theirs, particularly on a damp, gray autumn afternoon.

"Well, what did you expect?" Gail was saying, as she bit into the sandwich. "That you'd be treated like Mary Nobody from Kalamazoo, Michigan?"

"Well, I didn't expect the silly professor to make an announcement," Caroline said. She stirred some sugar into her tea and took a sip, all the while glancing around, her gaze moving cautiously, as it always did, anticipating photographers and reporters or gushing women who recognized her from newspaper pictures. She listened for a moment to the music from the string quartet, then looked at Gail, who was eating hungrily, and let her eyes wander back to the musicians again. She stared glumly at one of the violinists, who had a long lock of dark hair bobbing about on his forehead, but she hardly saw him. "Now I'll have someone following me around again, everywhere I go. Just when I'd persuaded Mother and Dad I didn't need anyone."

"Oh, yeah, baby!" Gail said, lapsing into one of her slang moods, as she reached over to Caroline's plate. "You through eating?" When Caroline nodded, she took the sandwich half on her plate. Caroline giggled as she saw Gail bite into the sandwich. "By all rights, you should weigh a ton."

"I work it off," Gail said airily. "Five dance classes a week." She put the sandwich down on her plate and leaned forward conspiratorially. "Can you keep a secret?"

"Have I ever told one you asked me to keep?" Caroline's blue-violet eyes widened in anticipation beneath the navy blue French beret pulled low over one eyebrow.

"I tried out for a musical yesterday."

"You what?" Caroline's mouth dropped in surprise.

"*Damn Yankees.* A road tour."

"Oh, Gail, how exciting." She grasped her hand. "Do you think you'll get it?"

"I think I stand a good chance. It's just in the chorus—"

"Don't say *just* in the chorus. That's the most exciting thing I ever heard." Suddenly her face clouded. "But that means you'll be going away." As she turned her head away, the glossy dark hair slid over her shoulders.

"Well, what do you call what you did?" Gail laughed. "You went away."

"But just to Poughkeepsie. That's only eighty miles."

"You went away," she said stubbornly.

"But you'll be going miles and miles and miles away. I won't see you for months."

Gail nodded slowly. "That's the worst part about growing up." Her smile was sad as she watched the musicians. "You have to leave people you love."

Caroline was hesitant. "What will Ellie say?"

Gail looked at her for a moment, then back at the musicians. She was wearing a green angora sweater under her tweed suit, the color turning her eyes to an even more brilliant color. "She's going to be

285

upset. That's why I won't tell her until the last minute, if I get the job."

"She'll be proud of you."

"But she won't want me to leave." She shifted uncomfortably in her chair and laughed tonelessly. "Well, maybe Georges will get a break."

Caroline looked around to make certain none of her mother's friends were in the Palm Court, then took a cigarette out of her purse and asked curiously, "Is that really why she's never married Georges?"

"In a way, I think she's still holding onto my father through me."

Caroline's eyes widened in that peculiarly attractive way she had. "I wish I had a talent like you and could be doing what you're going to do."

"You'll do something else when you finish at Vassar."

"What?" Caroline said with scorn. "Get married, have children, join committees, attend museum board meetings, dedications of hospital wings, listen to lawyers read boring annual reports? Oh, I *want* to get married, Gail, I want to fall in love and get married. But I want to do something with my life, too, something with some meaning."

Gail grinned. "Well, you could become interested in archaeology and go on digs, or take up flying and be the next Amelia Earhart, or try to climb Mt. Everest, or—"

"You're making fun of me." The violet of her eyes darkened with hurt.

Gail grasped Caroline's hand. "There are loads of things you could do. All of them good, even exciting. But finish college first." She leaned toward her, her expression curious. "What do you like? What do you *want* to do?"

Caroline looked at her shyly, not certain what Gail's reaction would be. "Well . . . I like to write."

"Write?"

"I'm taking a creative-writing class. My instructor thinks I . . . well, that I have talent as a writer."

"Oh, Caro, how wonderful!" Gail said, clasping her hands again.

Emboldened by this, Caroline leaned forward and said in soft excitement, "Ever since that day, years ago, my father took me over to the newspaper in New Jersey—I don't know what it was. I stood there in that big newsroom and looked all around. There were just a few people there. It was almost empty, because it was a Saturday, and then they called a strike. I looked down at one typewriter. There was a

286

piece of paper in it, with just one paragraph written. I read it, and I've never forgotten it. . . . 'She was elderly and wrinkled and her eyes were an old faded blue. She was sitting in the living room of a cold-water flat. . . .' I can't remember the exact words. But it was about this elderly woman who was on welfare and how no one cared about her anymore. How no one came to see her and all she had was her cat. It just stopped in the middle of the sentence. I was reading it and it just stopped there, Gail. I guess the reporter had gotten up and walked out onto the street to strike. And when I read it, I think that was when I knew I wanted to be a writer . . ."

"Oh, Caro," Gail said softly, smiling. "I'm going to miss you."

Caroline answered her smile with one of her own. "Remember that day in the playhouse at Newport? When we made a pact that we would never let anyone separate us?"

"Even our husbands," Gail said, laughing softly. "Can't you just see one of us getting married and saying to her husband, "Sorry, but she has to come along on the honeymoon.' How marvelous!" *Marvelous* was Gail's word for this year. She smiled at Caroline. "And we decided to write the pact out and sign it in blood, but when it came time to stick our fingers with a pin for the blood, neither one of us had the nerve." They laughed hard, remembering. "Caro, it's been such heaven," she said, her voice soft, as she touched Caroline's arm. "All the marvelous years behind us." Her face clouded for a moment. "A girl in dance class the other day asked me a funny question. She asked me what it had been like growing up with a Kendall but not being one." When Caroline frowned, she hurried on. "I said, 'I never really thought about it before.' And so I went home and thought about it."

"And . . . ?"

"The same schools, the riding lessons, summers at Kendall Hall and on the *Sapphire.* All of it just as though—well, as though we were sisters." She laughed shakily. "It's an awful lot for someone whose mother just happened to be walking along a dusty road in Rhode Island one summer day and was given a ride in a big Pierce-Arrow." Her eyes were far away when she smiled again. "She said her whole life changed in that single moment."

"All of ours did. Our mothers, such close friends, and . . ." She put her hand on Gail's. "And now us. We *are* like sisters."

But Gail's gaze wandered to the outer lobby near the Plaza's front entrance. She saw one of the guards in his unobtrusive dark suit and unmemorable face hovering near the revolving door, his glance wandering occasionally to their table in the Palm Court, and she knew, irrevocably, what the difference would always be. Caroline would inherit massive wealth one day. Gail would always live in its shadow.

When *Damn Yankees* ended its tour, Gail joined a review that traveled to Washington and closed there. "But everything turned out all right," she wrote to Caroline that late spring of 1957. "I'm working with a small instrumental group in a very posh little club here, a place that a lot of the young congressmen come to, and sometimes even a senator or two. The thing that's so great about it is that I'm singing, not just in a chorus, but as a solo, and they like me. Oh, Caro, *they like me.* Both the *Washington Post* and the *Star* wrote reviews and one of them raved, actually raved about my act. As you know, I'm using the name Halloran. . . ."

She finished the letter, put it in an envelope, addressed and sealed it, and dropped it into her purse. When she turned back to the dressing room mirror, she heard a knock on the door and looked up.

"Come on in," she called out.

It was one of the waiters with a long white flower box. "It just came, Miss Halloran," he said, as he handed it to her and left with a smile on his face.

She put the box down on the dressing table, slid the top off it, and stared at two dozen red roses. Her face was covered with cold cream and she had a towel tied around her head. She lifted the card and read it.

"For three nights in a row I have sat and listened to you. Would you have dinner with me tomorrow night before you go on so that I can tell you how much I enjoy your singing?" There was a telephone number and his signature below it . . . Senator Richard McHale Belden. Yes, she remembered. The handsome man sitting at one of the front tables.

She sat down hard on the chair and gazed around her, as though seeing the place for the first time, the bright makeup lights framing the mirror, the telegrams and notes she had stuck around the edge of it, the lumpy chaise where she stretched out to rest, the rug with its cigarette burns, the curtained window that looked out on an alley.

She lifted the roses from the box and breathed their fragrance. Pulling a large imitation cut-glass vase from beneath the dressing table, she filled it from the small wash basin and slid the flowers into it. They seemed to fill the room, their aroma heavy and sensuous, the blood red of the petals brilliant against the white wall. She picked the card up again and touched the signature, liking the way the letters flowed. *Richard McHale Belden,* she whispered.

"Well, what more can I tell you?" he said, looking at her for a long moment, then letting his eyes wander across the restaurant. Everything seemed muted and soft, the lighting, the music, the velvety banquette where they sat, the flickering candlelight, the pale roses in the crystal vase. He saw that they had both merely picked at their food and he smiled. The charge of electricity between them had been instant. "I'm the oldest of five children. My mother is quiet, pretty. You'd like her. She comes from Baltimore. My father, Patrick, is from Wales and was shrewd enough to do well in shipping and trucking. I'm from Philadelphia."

His eyes crinkled at the corners when he laughed, making the blue seem bluer, the bronze skin glow. His features were sharp and clean, his brown hair carefully cut and groomed. She watched his hands as he cupped a match and brought it toward her cigarette and wondered how they would feel . . . touching her. They were strong hands, well-shaped and expressive, the fingers long.

"More," she demanded.

"Greedy." He laughed, blew out a column of smoke, and leaned his head back. "Well, let me see—I was a fighter pilot during the war and was elected to the House of Representatives in 1952, the Senate last year. And even though I'm the oldest of five, I'm the only unmarried one of the bunch." He looked at her again. "You are much more interesting. I would much rather hear about you."

"It's really terribly dull," she said. "Born and raised mostly in New York." The small crystals on her white gown glittered in the soft light, glittered as brilliantly as her eyes.

"Mostly?"

"Oh—summers occasionally in New England, a friend's boat sometimes, no college but grueling days of vocal and dancing lessons, a road tour last season of *Damn Yankees.*" She wailed. "Oh, it's even duller than I thought."

"I think it's fascinating," he said softly. "I think you're fascinating." His eyes devoured her and a shiver ran up her shine. "Why can I think of nothing but clichés at a time like this? Like, I've never met anyone like you before. Like, I want to see you again and again and again. Like—"

"Where have you been all my life?" They laughed, then he took her hand and held it, and he whispered, "I want to make love to you."

He came to the club each night, waited until she was through, then took her home to her tiny apartment in Georgetown. They stopped along the way for breakfast in an all-night restaurant where they drank cup after cup of coffee, looking into each other's eyes, hands always touching. For three nights, she made him leave her at the door, but on the fourth night, as they left the club, she said, "Why don't I make breakfast for us?"

She made coffee, scrambled eggs, and bacon and served jam with the toast. But when they sat down to eat, he reached out and touched her, leaned closer as they kissed, and then he slowly picked her up and carried her into the bedroom. When he put her down on the bed, he knelt in front of her and started to undress her. "Stop me now, Gail, if you don't want it to go any further," he whispered. But she shook her head from side to side, her eyes never leaving his.

He lay down alongside her, then raised himself on one elbow and looked at her. She felt her heart racing wildly. His mouth was hungry and filled with magic. When he held her closer, his arms pulling her against him, she thought her bones would melt. Her hair had come loose from its topknot and flowed over the pillow in a shower of pale gold.

"You're so beautiful," he said, "and I'm in love with you."

She shivered with excitement as his hand trailed down her throat and slowly unbuttoned her blouse. Dawn was coming thinly through the windows, and with her hands cradling his face, she sought his eyes.

"I want to love you, but I'm afraid we'd be separated, that you'd leave me." Her voice was a whisper.

"No," he said, as he pushed the blouse from her shoulders, his fingers caressing the bare skin. "That could never happen. I love you too much." And he lowered his head and kissed her again, and she knew that what he said was true. All doubt vanished, as a joy and wildness rose in her. Nothing was real anymore except the feeling of his mouth, the hardness of his body crushing down on her, the exultation crowding into her throat, and then the soft laughter mixed with tears. "I want to stay here forever," he murmured, as the windows lightened with a rosy glow.

All through that spring and summer of 1957, they were together almost every night. He made occasional short trips to Pennsylvania,

290

but other than that they spent every moment they could with each other. Ellie visited twice and was charmed by Richard Belden, but returned to New York worried. It was obvious to her that they were deeply in love, but when she questioned Gail about marriage, Gail shrugged it off and said they hadn't discussed it.

"Besides, Mama," she said, as they waited for Ellie's train at the railway station, "I have my career." But although she wouldn't admit it, her career didn't seem as important as her feeling for Richard.

"A woman should be married and have children," Ellie insisted.

"Mama, I'm not even twenty," Gail said, laughing, as she watched the crowds of travelers swirling around them.

"How do you know there isn't someone else back in Philadelphia?"

"Mama!" Gail scolded, still laughing.

"I'm sorry, darling," Ellie said, smiling. "It's just that I—"

But Gail quickly changed the subject. A voice on the loudspeaker was bawling out Ellie's train and track number, and as they started toward the gate, she said, "What about you and Georges, Mama? When are you going to marry him?" She watched her mother closely. "You're still so young-looking and pretty, but he may not be willing to wait forever."

"I want to see you settled—"

"No, Mama." Gail's voice was firm, her mouth set. "I'll never be settled. I have a career and someday I want to go on Broadway."

"Gail—"

"Please. Don't put the burden on me." Her voice was gentle but unyielding. "If you don't want to marry Georges, that has nothing to do with me. But if you love him, Mama, then marry him before it's too late."

Ellie stared through the gate opening, past the conductor who was checking the tickets as travelers went through on to the train. She watched the steam hiss from underneath the carriages. "I—I don't know, Gail." She stood there, slim and pretty in a blue silk suit and tiny straw hat.

"He loves you so much," Gail said softly. "Don't keep him waiting any longer."

She watched her mother hurry away, moving gracefully through the slower-walking crowds, her golden hair short and perky beneath the white hat. She turned once and waved. When Gail could no longer see her, she walked out of the station and stepped into a cab.

* * *

"You're pregnant, aren't you?" Rick Sheldon, the pianist, said. She was leaning on the piano, studying the sheet music he had given her, and looked up at him. The group had moved to a larger, more expensive club, but they had a limited engagement and she was becoming concerned about where they might find work next. She started to deny it, but realized it was useless as she looked up at the slight, sandy-haired young man who rarely tried to hide the fact that he was in love with her.

"How did you know?"

"I know you, Gail, as well as I know the arrangements I do for you." They were alone in the club, with several hours of rehearsal behind them, and he was putting his sheet music into his briefcase. With a touch of sarcasm, he added, "Apparently better than your friend, the Senator, does." When she didn't answer, he came around to her, gently ruffled her hair, and, when she wearily laid her head against his chest, held her. "I'd marry you in a minute, even with you carrying someone else's baby," he said softly.

She reached up and touched his cheek. When the tears came to her eyes, she turned away, picked up her jacket, and started across the darkened dance floor toward the exit, her hair a bright splotch of gold in the shadows.

Rick, she thought, and brushed at one eye with her hand. He was so vulnerable . . . emotions so close to the surface. Talented, sensitive, a lonely kind of person who was completely involved in his music.

She looked back over her shoulder to where he still stood by the piano. "I'll see you tonight, Rick," she said softly and hurried on. He watched her until the darkness swallowed her up.

Gail threw the windows open wide and for a moment just stood there, breathing in the soft air. The moon was a sliver, but the sky was clear and starry. She felt his hands on her shoulders and then his arms coming around her. She sank back against him, holding his arms against her, the shivery magic rising in her, as always. When she turned in his arms, she said it softly and quickly.

"I've been wanting to tell you for a week, but I didn't quite know how, Richard."

"Tell me . . . ?" His lips were against her brow.

"It's a baby. Well—I mean, I'm going to have one."

She felt him stiffen. It was almost imperceptible but she froze in his arms, her heart suddenly pounding. After a moment his arms drew her closer.

"A baby," he whispered. "A baby . . ." His voice was hushed with wonder.

They stood for several long moments in silence, looking down into the narrow street. A milk truck came around the corner and slid up to the curb. They watched as the driver, with his rack of bottles, ran into the building across the street, the bottles clinking softly, his footsteps padded and cheerful-sounding.

"We'll go to Elkton," he suddenly said.

"Elkton?" she said, confused.

He grinned in the darkness as he held her away a little and looked down at her. "A quick-marriage place, in Maryland. We'll leave Saturday right after the club closes and be married there. Then we'll go to Philadelphia to tell my father and mother. We can phone your mother from there, darling."

While her heart raced with excitement and relief, she felt a slight foreboding. He had talked about his father, but she had never met him. He sounded overwhelming, a man who had come to this country at the age of fourteen, built a trucking business that became nationwide before he was thirty, then bought lines of freighters, shipping coal, iron ore, and scrap metal throughout the world.

"Richard," she said, "couldn't we keep it to ourselves for just a little while? We could go to Philadelphia in two or three weeks."

"Can't," he said, slowly shaking his head as he sat in the small boudoir chair and pulled her down onto his lap. "I'm on the committee for that investigation into racketeering in labor-management relations this fall and we start meeting Tuesday." He suddenly threw his head back and laughed, like a child exploding with joy. "A baby! You know, the truth is I've known for a long time that I wanted us to be married. But I guess I wouldn't admit it, even to myself. The Bachelor Senator, they call me. Thirty-five and still not married. And my mother and sisters have given up. They don't even ask me about it anymore. Only my father. He keeps ranting, 'Who is going to carry on the Belden name and business?' Oh, darling, wait until he meets you!" He suddenly stood up, and carried her across to the bed, where he put her down and lay beside her. "And he hears about the baby."

Gail didn't dare look at Richard. She knew they would both burst into peals of laughter. They had stopped at the first sign on the long road of signs in Elkton that advertised quick and inexpensive marriages. The house was a small, ugly one-story cottage. The justice of the peace was bony, tall, and stooped; his wife was short and round and insisted on playing the wedding march, although there was no room to march and no one marching. The justice's arm, as he droned out the words of the ceremony, kept bumping a tall and ugly floor lamp, knocking the tiny mismatched shade sideways. The house smelled of corned beef and cabbage, and the second witness, in addition to the justice's wife, was the woman next door, who held a Pekingese throughout the ceremony.

They climbed back into Richard's car, only then permitting themselves to laugh. But Gail suddenly sobered as Richard put the key into the ignition.

"Is he going to like me, Richard?"

"How could he possibly help it?"

He took her chin in his hand, kissed her softly, then turned on the ignition. "And my mother and sisters are going to adore you."

The Belden house was a stately red Georgian brick with gleaming white trim and shining brass, and a tall black iron fence in front. A black manservant grasped Richard and hugged him, then shook Gail's hand warmly and took them through a wide hallway to a library at the rear of the house. A man who looked the way Richard would when he was sixty rose from a deep wing chair by the hearth.

"Well, this is a surprise," he said, dropping the newspaper he held to the floor and embracing his son. He smiled at Gail as though he had always known her and when Richard said, "Dad, this is Gail," he took her hand and clasped it between both of his hands.

Grover, the manservant, brought in a tray of drinks, all the time exclaiming how nice it was to have Mr. Richard home again, how he kept reading about him in the newspapers. When they were sitting before the fire, Patrick Belden raised his glass and said, "Cheers!" It was at that moment that Gail saw a flicker of warning in his eyes and she felt something cold form around her heart.

"Well, Gail—I don't think Richard mentioned your last name—I'm delighted to meet you. You're from Washington?"

"No, just working there, Mr. Belden," she said, trying to sound normal, but feeling her hands tremble. She suddenly put her glass down. "I'm from New York." She still had her left glove on, hiding her new wedding band.

"Working on Capitol Hill?" His voice was warm and coaxing.

"No, Gail is a singer," Richard said. He was leaning with one elbow on the mantel. "You'll have to come to hear her. She's an absolutely spellbinding performer."

Gail saw the flicker again. Patrick Belden was polishing his steel-rimmed glasses with a large white handkerchief and glanced at her for a brief second as Richard talked.

"I'd like that. I expect to be in Washington next month for a day or two on business."

"Well, I'm afraid our engagement at the Jockey Club will be finished at the end of this month—"

"Perhaps I can get down there earlier," he said jovially, as he reached with the whiskey decanter to refill Richard's glass. Gail watched the liquid spill over the ice and felt a sinking sensation at the pit of her stomach.

"Dad . . ." Richard said. He stepped over to the wing chair opposite his father where Gail sat and clasped her hand. "Gail and I were married this morning. We drove here to tell you and Mother."

The silence was suffocating. For a moment, an expression of shock crossed Patrick Belden's face and Gail thought, surprised, *He didn't even suspect that we were married.* In moments he regained control and, in a voice that masked whatever he might be thinking, he said, "Well, congratulations are certainly in order." He stood up and walked over to Gail, bent down and kissed her on the cheek, then turned and shook Richard's hand, pumping it slowly up and down as he clapped him on the shoulder with the other hand. "I'm sorry your mother isn't here for this news. But she's up in Wrightstown. Your sister Joan, you know, is expecting her baby at any moment."

"Well, I'll phone her this evening," Richard said.

"You're staying, of course," Patrick said, as he walked to the library door. "I'll tell Grover to let the cook know you'll be here for dinner and breakfast. Will you be able to stay longer?"

"No, we'll have to leave first thing in the morning."

"Well, at least I'll have you here for a few hours," he said as he went out of the room.

Richard pulled her to her feet and took her in his arms. "We'll let him get used to that for a while, darling, before we tell him about the baby. We'll break that to him after dinner."

Gail bent close to the mirror and carefully brushed the pencil over her brows, darkening them ever so slightly. She leaned back and studied her face with a detached kind of scrutiny. Satisfied her makeup was correct for the lighting on the bandstand, she pulled out the pins and the terrycloth band from around her head and let her hair flow down over her shoulders. I'll wear it down tonight, she thought with a smile. Richard would be coming later with some friends from the Senate and he liked her hair down.

"Come in," she called out at a tap on the door.

"Gail, we've hit it," Rick said excitedly, as he rushed into her dressing room waving a telegram in his hand. "An agent from New York, a Jack Gordon, was here last week and heard us. He wants to represent us, guarantees he'll have us working the best clubs in New York by the first of the year. He has an opening for us in a club in Chicago starting the first of November at a thousand a week."

"Rick, stop joking!"

"No. Look." He spread the telegram out in front of her. She read it carefully, jumped to her feet, and threw her arms around him. "Oh, Rick, how fabulous!"

He slowly held her away from him. "What about the Senator? Is he going to let you go to Chicago?" She heard the old thread of sarcasm and sighed.

"Of course he'll let me go," she said, sitting down again and brushing her hair after glancing at her wristwatch. "I was a singer, you know, before I was Mrs. Belden." Suddenly her hand stopped in midair and she turned around. "And besides, Richard's father feels we should keep things quiet for a few months, about our marriage and the baby. He thinks Richard's career is at a critical point at the moment. A certain faction in the party is beginning to push someone else for the Senate position in the next election. The next six weeks will tell, he said. So, if I'm in Chicago, that will help matters some."

"And having a singer for a wife would give them a target, I suppose." The sarcasm was heavier.

"Don't, Rick," she said gently, looking up at him in the mirror.

"Sorry, hon," he said, running a hand through his sandy hair. "But just who the hell do these people think they are?"

"It isn't easy staying on Capitol Hill," she said, "not with a constituency that is as fickle as voters seem to be. And Senators do not make a habit of marrying singers, you know, darling."

"Why couldn't it have been me instead of Belden?" Rick said, his face contorted with anguish as he went out, slamming the door behind him. Gail stared at the door for a moment, then slowly began arranging her hair.

* * *

"Wonderful, Gail," Jack Gordon said, grasping her hand and kissing it as she came off the brightly lit bandstand into the backstage area of the supper club. The group was no longer the Rick Sheldon Quintet. Gordon had reshaped it into a floor show act, starring Gail Halloran—and Rick had assured Gail the quintet would stay with the act until she had to stop working because of the baby. "Listen to them out there," Jack shouted over the roar of applause. "Go out and take another bow."

When she came off for the last time, the suave Latin dance team of Alicante and Bijos brushed past her in the half darkness with murmurs of congratulations. She fell into Jack's arms, softly excited, her eyes glittering like stars. He whirled her around and around and, holding her hand, walked with her back to her dressing room, where she flopped onto a long couch and kicked her shoes off.

Jack leaned back against the dressing table and folded his arms, smiling down at her. He seemed so unlike what she had imagined agents to be. He had a lanky elegance about him, with trimly cut and groomed dark hair, and piercing dark eyes that could become heavy-lidded and vague when he didn't like someone. "And he wears Brooks Brothers suits," Gail giggled over the phone to Caroline when she phoned her about the Chicago engagement.

"Well, that must mean he's successful, Gail, so you've probably landed yourself a good agent."

"He wasn't even upset when I told him I would have to stop working for about eight months." She started giggling again. "Another three or four weeks and the seams are going to bust on my clothes."

"But Richard, Gail? What about Richard? How does he feel about your engagement in Chicago?"

"Well, he's not too thrilled, I mean about my being that far away. But he's being wonderful about it."

"I'm coming down this weekend. I want to meet him before you leave."

"Oh, Caro, I'm dying to see you."

They met at breakfast two mornings later at the Shoreham, where Caroline was staying. She liked Richard Belden on sight, and when Gail was called to the lobby for a phone call from Rick, they both watched her as she walked away from them, still trim in spite of her pregnancy, the green and gray tweed jacket of her suit swinging from the broad gray fur collar, golden hair catching the wan November sun that fell through the tall windows.

Caroline toyed with the spoon on her saucer, then picked up her coffee and sipped it. She looked at him over the rim of the cup. "It's none of my business, really, but I"— she laughed apologetically— "usually poke my nose in where it doesn't belong—"

"Where Gail is concerned?" he asked softly.

She nodded. "Where Gail is concerned." She looked into the cup for a minute before she put it down. The pale blue wool suit with its mink collar and cuffs molded to her slender figure as she leaned toward him. "We've been friends since I was born, you see. Close friends. We're . . . like sisters, really."

"I know." He smiled, then nodded at the waiter who refilled his coffee cup. When the waiter walked away, he said, "Gail has told me." He lifted the cup to his mouth, while she leaned back and watched him, liking the sharp, clean features, the direct gaze of his blue eyes, the way the brown hair grew thickly over his forehead.

"I've been wondering—when you're going to announce it. Your marriage."

He smiled again. "I would have done it right away. But both Dad and Gail talked me into waiting until after the election." He grinned this time. "Voters, it seems, like the status quo. Before an election, that is. Afterwards, it doesn't seem to matter what you tell them."

"Short of murder, I guess," Caroline said, laughing.

"And a few other things," he said, laughing with her, then turning to watch as Gail came back toward them.

"Nothing important," she said, sitting down again. "Just a change in rehearsal time."

Gail glanced at Jack Gordon now and then in the mirror as she creamed off her stage makeup, her head wrapped turban-like in the white towel, eyebrows furrowed worriedly.

"Look, don't worry about him," he was saying as he leaned back against the wall and lit a cigarette. "Sure, small combo groups like Rick's are on their way out, but he's a talented guy and he'll probably go back to what he really wants to do. Most all blues and jazzmen do. I've lined up some work for him, probably even some recording."

She looked at him gratefully. "Thanks, Jack. I knew you would. And maybe someday we can team up again."

He raised his eyebrows, then drew slowly on his cigarette. "Well,

298

that would depend—on what we decide we're going to do with you." She whipped off the towel and started brushing her hair. "The age of record buyers is going down. Teenagers are buying about seventy percent of the records and rock 'n' roll is taking over. *The Hit Parade* is off the air. It's Elvis Presley and Little Anthony. Big expensive supper clubs like this will start fading, Gail. So will the big bands. We can go one of two ways with you—once you've had the baby and are back in business again. You can go for jazz and small clubs, or we can make a run for Broadway."

She thought about it for a long moment, then nodded. "I'm a dancer, too, you know." She was silent again, but finally she looked up at him. "I'd like to think about it, Jack."

"You mean . . . you'd like to talk to your husband about it," he said quietly, with a smile. But she had seen the quick tightening of his jaw. "All right. I can wait." He walked to the door and stopped with his hand on the knob. "I have to go to New York tonight. But I'll be back before your run is finished here." He held his hand up in a kind of salute. "You know where to reach me if you need me."

Gail had just finished her last show a week later and was walking to her dressing room with the sound of applause still echoing along the corridor. She opened the door and stopped short.

"How are you, Gail?" he said with an airy wave of his hand. He was sitting on the far end of the couch, while a theatrically handsome young man with light blond hair stood leaning against the opposite wall, his hands in his trouser pockets. "Come in, come in. This is Garry."

Gail nodded, came into the dressing room, and closed the door, walking warily as she saw the hard clamp of Patrick Belden's mouth and the cold expression in his eyes. It was an expression she had briefly caught a flicker of when she first met him, one that had made her stop and wonder.

"How are you, Mr. Belden?" she said. She walked to the dressing table and leaned back against it, her hands clamping the edges.

"Oh, not bad. Not bad at all for a man getting on to sixty." He glanced over his shoulder in the direction of the young man. "Garry here tells me that he had an affair with you last summer and early fall."

Gail stared at Patrick Belden, then she let her gaze slowly turn to the young man leaning against the wall. There was a smirking smile on his face. She felt shock flood through her, then a stab of fear lodged at the base of her skull, prickling icily at the hairline.

"I've never seen him before in my life," she said in a low, trembling voice, looking directly at Patrick.

"No? That's strange. Because he swears to it. He says this baby is his."

"That's a damned rotten lie," she cried out.

"I don't think so," Patrick said. He slipped his hand into his jacket pocket and pulled out some flat items. He singled out two and showed them to her. "Here are some pictures showing Garry coming out of your apartment building in one instance and going in in the other."

She bent down and looked at them. "They could have been taken anytime, after I moved out—"

"And a letter." He held up a white envelope. "Oh, only one of several. Love letters." He started to take the letter out of the envelope, but she grabbed it from him.

Suddenly she felt terribly cold. A nausea was rising up in her throat. "This is a forgery," she said, her voice shaking.

"That is what you claim." He glanced over his shoulder again. "Tell her, Garry."

"Sure," the young man said, pushing away from the wall and walking over to her. She cringed away from him and put the dressing table chair between them. "I waited for you at your apartment, oh, maybe twenty or thirty times. You'd come from Senator Belden's apartment and I'd be waiting for you. It would be four, five, sometimes six in the morning and we'd go to bed—"

"You're disgusting!" Her voice was low and filled with loathing.

"Well—" He laughed lightly. "You say that now, Gail—"

She whirled around to Patrick. "You've paid him to say all of these things!"

"Here, now." Patrick's eyes were cold and gray behind the steel-rimmed glasses. "You had better be careful what kind of accusations you make, young lady."

"—and you always laughed," the young man went on, just as though he hadn't been interrupted. "You told me you wanted to marry Senator Belden only because of his position, because of what he could do for you, but that you really were in love with me and—"

"Stop it!" Gail cried out.

"You can go, Garry," Belden said as he rose and gestured with his head toward the door.

300

When the young man had left, Patrick turned to her. "I've made arrangements for everything. First an annulment and—"

"Annulment?" She was shaking her head, laughing in a strangely disbelieving way, as though this were all a crazy dream. "I can't believe I'm hearing this." And then she stared at him. "Richard and I are in love. And more than anything I want this baby." Bewildered, she shook her head again. "Please go, Mr. Belden. I'll pretend you never came here, that none of this ever happened. Just get out quickly, before I have to call someone to have you *put* out."

He walked to the door, but when he turned to look back at her, his hand on the doorknob, there was an unpleasant smile on his face. "I'll let you think about it, Gail. Until tomorrow."

"That won't be necessary." Her expression was cold, her face set hard.

"Oh, I think it will," he said. "I meant every word I said. I want this marriage annulled. I have plans for Richard and they don't include you. I don't intend to have his career eclipsed because of marriage to a singer."

"I haven't made a decision about my career," she said, her voice as cold and hard as his. "Whether to go on with it or to stop and just be Richard's wife—"

"No, I'm afraid it won't do. You see, I want him to make the right marriage, the kind that will further his career. Even if you gave up this —this *singing*, it wouldn't matter. Your reputation—"

"Please go, Mr. Belden. This is getting us nowhere."

"Not only as a performer, but also this connection with Garry, the affair with him, having his baby—"

"*Get out!*" Gail was clenching her fists at her side.

"And with his prison record and protecting you from the authorities when he was being questioned before his trial—"

She watched him in growing bewilderment.

"Well, certainly you remember that. The drugs charge. When Garry was picked up by the police, they knew he had been involved with a woman in his drug dealing. A woman he was in love with and in the same business, nightclubs, I believe he said. He refused to give them her name. But he told me the woman was you and that he can prove it, which, of course, I realized is true after I saw the pictures and the letters. He's prepared at this point to go back and tell the truth to the authorities. Says he doesn't like the way you've been treating him in the past months, secretly marrying my son and pretending the child is Richard's." He started to open the door, but stopped again. "Oh, yes, I almost forgot. I found out about Garry when the people I hired started investigating your friend out there." He gestured with his head. "The young fellow who leads your combo."

"Rick?" She felt a premonition of disaster.

"Yes, the investigation led to some pretty shady characters, all in the music or theatre business, among them Garry."

Something nagged in Gail's memory, something Rick had once told her, a raid on some little jazz spot in Greenwich Village where he was working. He'd spent the night in the Tombs. He was among four or five who had been picked up. But he was one of two they let go the next morning.

"Garry played the drums at one time, until he decided he wanted to be an actor. But he did some drug dealing on the side, and spent some time in the Tombs while this Rick was trying to make bail for him. He got a suspended sentence, but he has a record nevertheless."

"I told you. I never saw this *Garry* before. Never!"

"The involvement is obvious, you, Rick, Garry. . . ." He was slowly rolling the soft felt brim of his hat as he spoke. "In fact, Garry made some mention of how you and Rick—before he knew you . . ."

That week. In the beginning. Before she met Richard, when she had the bronchial thing. Rick hadn't left her side for days and nights, nursing her through it.

"—which all sounds fairly sleazy. Promiscuity in a wife isn't exactly what I had in mind for Richard when he went to Washington." The sarcasm in his voice hung in the air.

"Rick and I are good friends, that's all. Just good friends. I was terribly ill one week when I first joined the combo, and he helped me through it." She heard the pleading in her own voice, and clutched hold of the edge of the dressing table even harder. "Everything you're saying is a lie! Richard will be back from this campaign trip in a week. I'll tell him that you came here, what you said, and why—"

"This story and all of its sordid details could be broken in tomorrow morning's newspapers and on every television news spot by seven-thirty A.M. All I have to do is have someone pick up the phone." He let it sink in, watched her face as she realized just what could happen. When he spoke again, his voice was low. "How long do you think his career would last then? What do you think would happen in this upcoming election?"

She stared at the floor for a long moment, then slowly raised her eyes. Her face was ashen. "You'd do that? Ruin him? Ruin your own son?"

"If you leave me no other alternative. If it's the only way to get this annulment through." His tone was soft and insinuating. "Yes, it would mean years and years of rebuilding his character, years of work to make the public forget. And maybe it would never work. Maybe he could never make it back. But in any event, you would lose him. How long do you think your marriage to him would last under this kind of a cloud? At first he might believe you, might *want* to believe you. But in time he would begin to wonder, wonder if any or all of it could be true. In the end, you would have nothing anyway. So . . . why not step out now? For a while he will be hurt. But in time he'll be able to forget you, and he will still be Senator Richard Belden."

She had turned toward the wall, back rigid. He couldn't see her face, couldn't see the tears that were blinding her.

"I've made the arrangements for the annulment." His voice was almost toneless as he put a card down on her dressing table and alongside it a thick white envelope. "There's a card there with the name of a law firm on it. Contact them. They will take care of everything. When Richard returns you will tell him you've had an abortion—"

"No!"

"—and that you want an annulment, that you want your career . . . Oh, I'm told you have one of the top agents in New York, Jack Gordon. He's one of the best, I hear." He pointed to the envelope. "There are tickets for Switzerland in there. The child will be raised in Switzerland. And more than enough money will be provided for its care, more than enough to hire some competent woman to raise the child over there. A house will be found and furnished—"

Somehow, she held back the tears, determined that he should not see her weeping.

"Contact the law firm on that card there. They will take care of everything." He started to open the door, but she stopped him.

"Wait!"

"You will do exactly as I have instructed, Gail Halloran, or I will destroy you. Make no mistake about that. You will lose Richard *and* your career. You'll have nothing. Other men can be bought to swear they've had affairs with you. What a shame for someone with such a promising career." He opened the door and looked over his shoulder.

"I'll stop at nothing. Richard is my only son."

When the door closed, she didn't move, the horror of it flooding through her. She turned back to the dressing table, picked up the telephone, then slowly held it away from her. She put it down, the clicking sound it made when it touched the cradle cutting into her like a knife.

20
1957

A week before Christmas, Gail returned to New York. The annulment had been granted, and Richard had made no attempt to see her after she called him on the phone from Chicago. She had gritted her teeth, made her voice hard, and said, "You're going to despise me, Richard, and you should. But I had to do it." She made her voice harder. "I didn't want to be tied down to a baby. So I—had an abortion."

For a shocked moment he didn't speak. "Why?" was all he said, his voice echoing through the telephone and over the miles like a ghost of the voice she remembered. "Why, Gail?"

There was a long pause as she fought back the tears and tried to gain control. "Because . . . because I thought the publicity of—of being married to a Senator would help my career."

"But instead," he said bitterly, "one of the top agents in the business discovered you and you didn't need me after all."

She heard the phone click and go dead. And with the sound, something died inside her.

She hadn't let anyone know she was arriving. On the train, she sat in her compartment over the long miles watching the small towns and cities go by. Each time the train passed a road crossing in the darkness, she would hear the clang of the warning bells whine past and see the flashing red of the lights. Off in the distance loomed the occasional dim lights of a farmhouse and beneath her the wheels clicked in a kind of comforting sound, while up ahead the engine's whistle floated back, a lonely cry in the night.

The terrible despair that plagued all of her waking hours and caused her to start up from a fitful sleep all through the night had taken its toll in her face. Her eyes were haunted and circled with shadows.

When her train pulled into New York, she wandered through Pennsylvania Station as though she didn't know where to go. At last she walked out onto Seventh Avenue, stood there for a moment, then stepped into a cab, tipping the porter without even looking at him. She told the taxi driver to take her to the Plaza.

In her room, she sat on the bed by the telephone. For more than an hour, she didn't move, but at last she lifted the phone and told the operator the number she wanted to call.

"What's wrong, Gail? What is it?" Ellie asked, alarm in her voice.

"I—I couldn't come home. Not yet, Mama. I . . . I want to talk to you here."

"Where is here, darling?"

"I'm at the Plaza."

"I'll be there just as soon as I can get there, Gail."

"Yes, Mama."

They sat in the waning afternoon light, the lamps in her room still not turned on. Ellie had ordered tea and some small sandwiches. She tried to make Gail eat something, but the effort was futile.

"It's over, Mama," Gail finally said. "Our marriage is over."

"Over?" Ellie was shocked, but she controlled her voice. "Why, Gail? Why is it over?" Her blonde hair, smoothly drawn back into a French knot, delicately etched her face in line and shadow.

"I . . . can't tell you any more than that. All I can tell you is that it's ended." She stood up and walked to the wide window looking out to Central Park in the snowy twilight. She could see the traffic on Fifth Avenue, the lights of the vehicles just coming on. The sound of horns and brakes screeching was distant, muted, and the doorman's whistle below pealed softly.

"Did Richard decide . . . ?"

"We both decided," Gail said harshly, then bit her lower lip, until she almost exclaimed with the pain. "It's over. There's nothing left."

"But, Gail, I don't understand. I wish I could, but—"

"Please, Mama!" Her tone softened as she turned around and leaned back against the sill. "I can't talk about it anymore. Not that part of it. All I can tell you now is that I'm going to Switzerland to have the baby."

"Switzerland? But why Switzerland?" Ellie was bewildered.

Gail suddenly walked to her, knelt down on one knee, and grasped her mother's wrists. "You've got to promise me you won't tell anyone anything, not that I was ever married to Richard, nothing!"

"Gail, I—"

"You've got to, Mama. I can't explain why. You'll just have to believe me when I tell you that everything is at stake here. Everything!"

"But, darling, you were so in love with him—"

"Oh, my God, Mama, please!" Tears clung to her lashes.

"Just tell me why Switzerland, Gail," Ellie pleaded.

Gail rose and walked back to the window. She could see Christmas tree lights up Fifth Avenue a little way in front of the Pierre as the traffic inched in the early-evening crush. She felt like a tiny boat, drifting helplessly from the shore.

"Patrick Belden—Richard's father—he insisted the baby be born and brought up there. There will be a house and a woman to take care of the baby. He will pay all of the expenses." She laughed bitterly as she turned. "Oh, he's being most generous—"

"Then he is the one behind all of this," Ellie said softly, shaking her head. "Gail, whatever it is that has happened, Lawrence Kendall is a powerful man and will help—"

Gail whirled around. "No!" She grasped her mother's hand. "You must make them understand it's as much my own decision as Richard's, and that the baby's father is paying for the expenses in Switzerland. I'll explain it to Caroline in my own way. But no one else must know." They were silent for a moment.

"I must tell Georges," Ellie finally said, "because, you see, Georges and I are going to be married. I only waited until you came home."

Gail ran to her mother, knelt down again, and kissed her. "Oh, Mama, I'm so happy for you." The tears she had been holding back began to roll down her cheeks.

"And I must tell Georges, because I've just decided that he and I are going to Switzerland to take care of the baby."

"What—what on earth are you talking about?" Gail was slowly rising. She shook her head in a moment of confusion.

"He has often said he would have gone back to Europe years ago if he hadn't kept hoping the day would come when we would be married. He's always wanted to return there to live. He could get a job in some small school, teaching English perhaps."

Gail's eyes brimmed. "Would you? Would you really?"

"I'm sure Georges will think it's a wonderful idea." Ellie stood up. Walking to Gail, she put her arms around her and held her. "And I would love it, darling, taking care of my own grandchild."

"Oh, Mama," Gail sighed. "I think I'm ready to go home now."

"You're not telling me everything, Ellie," Elizabeth said, "and I'm not going to press you for any more information. But I *am* going to miss you. Terribly." She pressed her friend's hand, her eyes brimming with tears.

They were riding in the Rolls to Kendall Hills, where everyone would gather for Christmas. The seat beside Meacham was heaped with gaily wrapped packages and the trunk was crammed with more gifts.

"When were you planning on leaving?" she asked Ellie, an oddly probing note in her voice.

"The baby will arrive in May sometime. We thought we would leave in February or March. Georges will go soon, to look for a place for us to live. And a teaching position that could start in the autumn."

"Ellie," Elizabeth said, lighting a cigarette. She pushed her furs back from her face, then looked around at Ellie. "I've been doing some inquiring. I have some money that I want to invest, quite a lot of it, money that Lawrence has been giving me over the years. It's amazing how it has mounted up. I decided I wanted to invest it in a private school that Kendall, Inc., became interested in. Many of their pilots at TransGlobal are based in Switzerland and put their children in private schools. It's near Basel, overlooking the Rhine, a lovely place, and just recently a search firm we hired learned that the owners had it up for sale."

"What are you thinking?" Ellie said, almost afraid to guess.

"It would be something that you and Georges could do together. This is a school attended mainly by children of American business-men, diplomats, pilots who fly the overseas route and live in Europe. And of course people who simply want a European education for their children. It's a fair-sized campus, with the usual school facilities and dormitories, and several houses on the property. Lawrence had Henry Winters go over there and look at it. It sounds perfect for you and Georges. And Georges would make a marvelous headmaster."

"Oh, Elizabeth," Ellie said breathlessly. "Georges would be so flattered and thrilled. I can't think of anything he would love more."

"Then once we've talked to Georges, if he likes the idea as you think he will, why don't we go ahead with it? Henry Winters—you know who he is, Kendall, Inc.'s, troubleshooter and part of the acquisitions team—well, he gave Lawrence an excellent report. He said it's in fine condition, solvent, with a smallish but full enrollment. And it has a very good reputation among Swiss schools. It's co-ed and although it's not Le Rosey, which is probably the most expensive and exclusive prep school in the world, still it's almost as prestigious. It's . . . well, quiet. Avoids any kind of publicity and discourages a certain kind of glamour and notoriety that a few of the schools in Europe seem to thrive on. You know, children of film stars, that sort of thing. Academic excellence is its best quality. They even give some scholarships at Bellone. That was the name of the man who first started the school."

"Bellone," Ellie murmured. Then she looked around at Elizabeth. "You decided this after I told you about Gail, didn't you?"

Elizabeth acted as though she hadn't heard her. "Well, let's see what Georges has to say about it when he gets to Kendall Hills tonight."

"Oh, we don't have to wait. I *know* what he will say. And it sounds like the perfect place for us to bring up Gail's child after it's born." She turned to Elizabeth, almost sternly. "Are you certain you want to go into this?"

Elizabeth smiled and patted Ellie's hand. "I've never been more certain of anything in my life."

Brenda Leland climbed the stairs carefully, pausing before she lifted each foot, then moving it with as little extra motion as possible. She knew she looked ridiculous, but she didn't care. Four of her school books were placed, one on the other, on top of her head, and she was trying desperately to keep them from sliding off as she neared the top of the stairs.

"Everything is terrific about you, Bren. Men absolutely love your gorgeous curly red hair and especially that milk-and-roses complexion. Even your nose," Caroline had said the evening before when they finished studying. She had teasingly pinched the end of her upturned nose. "But your posture is awful. You have to do something about it before the dance tomorrow." She had showed her how to pile books on top of her head and walk across their dormitory room without letting them slide to the floor. "After you've made it across the room ten or twenty times, try the stairs."

"I'll never make it on the stairs," Brenda had wailed. But here she was, almost to the top, and the books were still on her head.

Although Brenda was a year older than Caroline, they had become roommates in Brenda's junior year, when Caroline became a sophomore at Vassar. Where Brenda was small, several inches shorter than Caroline, petite but well rounded, Caroline was tall and willowy. Brenda was giggly and mischievous, Caroline more controlled and deliberate. In fact, they were the closest of friends. While growing up, with Gail completing the "gruesome threesome," as Jamie laughingly called them, they were almost inseparable.

At the top of the stairs, she let the books slide from her head, catching them with a "Whoomph!" when they hit her arms and hands. Then, whistling off-key, she swung along the corridor toward their room with a little smile on her lips. She and Caroline were going to a hop that night. They had been dating young men at West Point and would be staying at the Thayer Hotel for the weekend. She had met someone that her mother finally approved of who wasn't a stiff, stuffy bore. Bill Trumbull was related to the Cabots, and his father had made his money in stocks and bonds.

She pushed open the door of the room and suddenly stopped, surprised to find someone there.

"What are you reading?" she demanded angrily.

Her sister, Katherine, was standing by Caroline's desk, reading something that looked like a telegram.

"Well, that's a nice greeting," Katherine said, folding the piece of paper. She slipped it back into the envelope and, licking the flap, pressed it until it stuck again. "Here I drive all the way over here on my way to Boston to ask you if you want to go with me—I can get you a blind date with a friend of a man I've met who goes to Harvard. But you—"

"I have a date tonight," Brenda said bluntly, going over to the desk, where she picked up the envelope and looked at it. "You have some nerve! Opening Caroline's cable."

Katherine strolled over to the chintz-cushioned windowseat and sat down. She crossed her long silken legs and carelessly swung one slim foot back and forth. "Oh, it's just some very unimportant news." She smiled with carefully reddened lips, lips exactly the same color as her long nails. She was taller than Brenda, with hips that were too large for her small breasts and narrow shoulders, a flaw she disguised cleverly with well-designed and flattering clothes. "News about *Gail's baby* arriving." She said the words with an unpleasant innuendo that was unmistakable.

Brenda's eyes lit up, but she hid the excitement before Katherine could see it. "You can be so rotten sometimes, Katherine," Brenda said, as she dumped her books on her own desk and stood there watching her sister. "One of these days somebody's going to knock you on your butt!"

"Really, Brenda, your language or use of it, has deteriorated to a loathsome level. If Mother could hear you—"

"I don't give a damn what you think of my language, *or use of it.*" She mimicked Katherine, who simply smiled in an exaggeratedly patient way that was designed to drive Brenda into a frenzy. At least it always had.

But Brenda managed to control herself. She started throwing her clothes in every direction as she peeled them off. "I'm going to take a bath, Katherine. I don't know what you're going to do. But I'd suggest, if you plan to go to Cambridge tonight, you'd better get going."

She walked to the bathroom in her tiny lace panties and bra, her derrière wiggling in a way that she knew would anger Katherine. But Katherine was too pleased with herself to be upset. She smoothed back the reddish hair—several shades darker than Brenda's—then took a compact out of her purse and, looking in the mirror, lightly powdered her already perfect nose. Artfully applied makeup each morning turned a somewhat sharply featured face into that of a striking-looking young woman. She was wearing her hair in the new beehive style, a style so new that even the magazines and society pages of the newspapers hadn't begun to feature it yet. Katherine had just brought it back from France several weeks before, where she had been studying painting.

"Studying painting," Brenda had said to Caroline with a sarcastic little laugh. "She throws different colors of paint at the canvas and calls it painting. All she's there for is to have something to do that sounds clever and interesting until she meets someone who will marry her."

Caroline had laughed in spite of herself. "You shouldn't talk about your sister like that, Bren."

"She's lucky, that's all I can say," Brenda had answered, rolling the last curler in her hair, a ritual she performed each night while drinking hot chocolate and smoking an ill-smelling cigarillo.

Katherine heard the water running in the bathtub and waited for Brenda to come back into the room.

"You really should break your date for tonight, darling," she drawled in her lazy voice. "Because Franco's friend is certain to be someone terribly important and attractive."

"*Terribly important and attractive,*" Brenda mimicked again as she dug into one of her bureau drawers looking for fresh lingerie. "And who in the hell is Franco?"

Katherine winced at the *hell,* but regained her composure. "Franco, my dear little sister, is the Count Franco di San Nicola. I met him at their Paris apartment when he flew to meet his parents there."

"A real count?" Brenda asked bluntly as she turned to look at her sister. "Or a phony one like that dope you brought to Newport last summer?"

"Dieter's grandfather was a real baron. Just because the Germans eliminated titles of their nobility after World War I doesn't mean he—"

"He was a dope, title or no title. But what about this Franco?" She had found a bra and panties and padded halfway back across to the bathroom when she stopped and looked at Katherine again.

"He's in his final year of the business school at Harvard. His family is old Venetian nobility. They have a magnificent palazzo in Venice." She lit a cigarette. "I've seen pictures of it. They're terribly rich. Dripping with it. Oh, not like Uncle Lawrence. But *dripping* with it, nevertheless."

Brenda continued her walk to the bathroom door again, then stopped. "You know something, Katherine? You are a crashing bore. All you talk about is money." She smiled triumphantly at the flash of anger in Katherine's face.

Katherine stood up, whirled about so that her navy-and-white-pol-ka-dot silk dress fluttered prettily about her legs, picked up her purse from the windowseat, and hurried to the door. "And you are still a grubby little monster," she said, almost bumping into Caroline, who was just coming into the room.

"Katherine!" she exclaimed, leaning over to kiss her cheek. "Leaving already? I saw the new driver Meacham's been training, downstairs with the Lincoln, and he told me you were here."

"I'm on my way to Cambridge and I have to rush. Uncle Lawrence didn't want me driving my own car, so Gilmartin drove me."

"Who'd kidnap *you?*" Brenda scoffed.

"You *are* a grubby, vulgar little monster," she spat out at Brenda. Then, trying to compose herself, she smiled archly at Caroline, waved her hand, and disappeared out the door. "Bye, Caroline."

"Honestly, Bren," Caroline said, trying not to laugh as she walked to her desk and put her books down. Brenda ran up behind her, grabbed the cable, and pushed it into her hand.

"Open it! It must be from Gail, and I'm dying to hear what it says."

Caroline ripped open the envelope without noticing it had been tampered with, then let out a happy shriek. "Gail's baby. She's had a boy. Everything is wonderful, Ellie says, and his name is Richard Karl Wancek."

Brenda reached sleepily over to the phone on the bedside table, fumbled in the dark finding it, and finally said, "Hello," as Caroline suddenly sat up in the other twin bed, turned on the lamp, and looked anxiously at her roommate.

"It's the overseas operator," Brenda said as she handed the phone to her. She sat up with an expectant expression on her face, listening.

"Hello?" Caroline said, barely controlling the excitement in her voice. She listened for several moments, then shouted, "Gail!" She glanced at the small bedside clock. "I finally fell asleep. It's hours since I first put this call in. Oh, Gail, what wonderful news!"

Brenda hugged her knees and grinned as she listened.

"He's beautiful, Caro!" The faintness of Gail's voice through the overseas connection couldn't disguise the joy. "Gosh, this is exciting, being a mother. I wish you could see him."

"I'll be there at spring vacation, even if I can only stay for a few days."

"I can't wait. I'm staying on for a while. Believe it or not, I'm nursing this child. I know, I know"—she was giggling deliciously— "smart-mouthed Gail, turned into an old-fashioned mama. But the doctor says it will give him a good start and God knows"—there was a brief flash of bitterness in her voice—"that's the very least I can do for him. I can't produce a father for him."

"Gail . . ." Caroline cried out softly.

"Look, nobody said that life was going to be perfect." Her voice had hardened again, then she laughed and rushed on. "I cabled Jack Gordon, told him to hold anything on the back burner that he might find for me."

"He phoned me a few hours ago when he got your cable about the baby. He thinks you're very special. Did you know that?"

Gail ignored it. "Mama and Georges said to send you their love. And wait until you see this little mutt I have here. You'll adore him."

Her voice seemed to be fading and Caroline pressed the phone harder to her ear. "I'll be there soon."

"Can't wait, darling."

"Bye, Gail. And hug the baby for me."

She put the phone in the cradle and slowly slid down onto her back again, arms crossed behind her head. Brenda watched her for a moment.

"Who was the father?" she asked softly. "I never asked . . ."

"Oh . . . a man Gail met in Washington," she said vaguely, then snapped the light off. "It—it didn't work out. They were going to be married. Then something happened." The silence deepened in the darkness, and then in a soft voice, she said, "But she loved him . . . desperately."

Gail stared up at the ceiling of the hospital room. Everything was so white, so pristine, even to the starched white curtains at the long windows, and beyond the glass the glaring white snow that iced the rooftops of Basel, covering the winding streets and sloping hills. She slowly blinked back the tears. Hearing Caroline's voice had opened a healing wound. Here, thousands of miles away from hurting reminders, there were long periods when she could almost forget. But Caroline's voice, spilling excitedly through the phone, meant . . . *home.* And brought it all rushing back.

Roughly, with the back of her hand, she brushed the tears away. *Richard . . . oh, Richard . . .*

"There they are!" a reporter from the *Chronicle* screamed. She was a tall gawky woman of about thirty, her hat suddenly askew when the photographer who was with her pulled up his camera and bumped her head with his elbow as he started shooting pictures of the couple coming out of the vaulting entrance, down the cathedral steps toward the waiting limousines. The reporter was scribbling in a notebook as she followed the photographer into the street.

The couple paused for a moment halfway down the steps as half a dozen photographers knelt and took picture after picture.

"Senator Belden! Senator Belden!" the *Chronicle* society page reporter screamed, her voice getting hoarse. "Would you look over here so we can get a picture of you from the front for the *Chronicle?*"

Richard Belden and his bride smiled into the camera, then finally continued down the steps. Two small boys in black Eton suits were lifting the long train above the stone of the steps, while the bride held the flowing skirt of her white satin gown a little aloft as she stepped daintily down toward the limousine's open door. The twelve brides-maids, all in shades of blush pink, the gowns like inverted tulips, their floppy-brimmed straw hats blowing in the light breeze, crowded along behind the bridal couple, the ushers and groomsmen in their cutaways laughingly towering over them. Two flowers girls had scattered rose petals over the steps and sidewalk.

"Mrs. Belden?" the *Chronicle* reporter screeched as she shoved through the crowd of onlookers who had overtaken the photographers and reporters. "When you broke your engagement to Victor Palmer, did you—?" But her question was lost in the crescendo of voices and traffic sounds. For a brief moment, the San Francisco socialite glared at the reporter from out of the misty cloud of tulle about her face. The former Frances Williston Morehead wanted nothing to mar this day when she became the wife of Senator Richard McHale Belden of Pennsylvania.

As they stepped into the limousine and the flashbulbs popped through the windows, the *Chronicle* reporter heard a middle-aged woman say to anyone who cared to listen, "Well, they both got what they wanted, I guess. He's the one with the money and glamour, and she's the one with the family tree. A cousin of mine who lives in Washington said he was running around with some trashy singer, but he sure dumped her fast when he met Frances Morehead."

21
1958

It was exactly as Caroline had pictured it, only more breathtaking. The gondola, gleaming black with a coat of arms on each side of its graceful bow, slipped through the water of the Grand Canal like a gliding swan. The two gondoliers, unlike those they saw with their white or blue-and-white-striped T-shirts and red-banded straw hats in passing gondolas, wore summer livery, their splendid figures drawing the fluttering attention of tourists' cameras as they drifted by.

For long moments, Caroline felt completely detached from Mark Rumsey, the bodyguard who went everywhere with her. A big, pleasant, sandy-haired man of forty-five who had never married and seemed content with his life the way it was, he was given a two-month-long vacation each year to make up for the grueling responsibility of accompanying her from morning till night. He, too, was gazing about in a kind of surprised awe, occasionally glancing at a passing *vaporetto* with a practiced eye, checking the occupants, watching for bulging jackets or bulky packages.

"How did we happen to miss this in all our travels?" he asked, teasingly, with a smile.

"Brenda and I came here once on the *Sapphire* when we were small," Caroline said, still looking ahead, her eyes unblinking as though she might miss something. "But we were on our way to Mykonos and Athens, I think, and didn't stay here long."

Again they were silent, trying to absorb the silvery beauty of the water, winding its serpentine course through the heart of Venice from the railway station to the Piazza San Marco. Lined on either side with magnificent palazzi, their gondola moorings reaching from the water like leaning peppermint sticks, the canal seethed with motion and color from the churning *vaporetti* and *motoscafo,* a hurtling fireboat and the skimming gondolas. Awning-covered cafés and terraces did not detract but added to the lacy gothic beauty of the palaces that rose in graceful splendor at the water's edge. Colors, blending and running into each other like an artist's pastel palette, embellished the plaster walls and marble balustrades, and the sun showered it all with a sheen of glittering gold.

"I can't believe it," Brenda said in a breathless gasp. "We're really here and"—she leaned close to Caroline—"actually *almost* alone. No nannies, parents, aunts, or uncles." As the gondola drifted toward the left and slowed somewhat, she looked up at the nearest row of palazzi and said, "I wonder which it is."

"Well, whichever one, Katherine must adore living here," Caroline said. She turned her head, trying to catch the words of their two gondoliers as they jabbered between them and gestured to the driver of the motorboat that followed slowly behind with the luggage.

"There she is," Brenda said in a low voice with a warning note in it, then muttered, "and *why* Franco married her I'll never know. He's really a dream."

"Oh, come on, Bren," Caroline laughed softly. "It's just because she's your sister—"

"You can't stand her either, and you know it," Brenda said in a hissing stage whisper.

"Well, she *is* hard to take at times," Caroline admitted, with a slow shake of her head. She was studying the facade of the di San Nicola palazzo. The delicate apricot walls with gilded pilasters and gothic balconies were like something from a fairytale. Katherine and the tall, slim young count who was her husband of two months waited at the top of six white stone steps leading up from the narrow landing. He wore a white linen suit and she stood framed by white marble walls within the shadow of a recessed entranceway, her pale green gown blowing a little in the breeze.

"That we couldn't have stayed at a hotel, instead of where we'll be under *her* thumb, is just plain sickening."

"You're lucky they let us come at all, without at least Nanny Grace."

"Good Lord, Caroline, we *are* a little old for that! And besides, she was determined to go visit her sister in London, you said."

"Well, you two, you really made it," Katherine called out in her drawling, cool tone that echoed across the water, the tinge of sarcasm as evident as ever.

"Oh, shut up," Brenda muttered under her breath.

"*Ple-e-ease,* Bren," Caroline said softly, then smiled at Katherine and Franco as the gondola glided closer and came to a stop at the landing. "How are you, Katherine? Franco, it's so good to see you again." She was stepping onto the landing with Franco and a manservant helping her.

"Caroline," Franco exclaimed, then kissed both cheeks, repeating the gestures with Brenda. "My parents are so pleased you consented to come." He spoke English with almost a British accent, the result of an education in English schools before Harvard.

"And we're so excited to be here, Franco," Caroline said.

"We have wonderful plans for your visit," he said, leading them through the entranceway into a center courtyard with marble flooring and a wide staircase that led to the reception hall of the palazzo itself. "Parties, receptions, and even an English tea that my sister has arranged for you to meet her friends."

Caroline leaned her head against the gracefully contoured pillar of the balcony and closed her eyes for a moment. The air seemed perfumed, touched with the fragrance of jasmine and gardenia drifting up from the courtyard. Stars glittered across the sky, and from far below she could hear the gentle lapping of water against the palazzo walls. She felt drugged by the heady sights and sounds and aromas of this astonishing city. She and Brenda had spent three days roaming from one narrow winding *calle* to another, browsing through the shops and wandering alongside the canals. They had watched the pigeons soar upward and away in the Piazza San Marco when the noon gun rang out. With Mark Rumsey pacing behind at a distance, they had become lost in the crowds of tourists in the piazza, had capucino at the Florian Café, and stared in awe at the frescoes by Tiepolo and the pastels by Rosalba Carriera.

Now, almost satiated, she stood on the long balcony as the slim moon caught brief reflections of ghostly black gondolas gliding along the canal. Above the softly bleating noise of a *motoscafo* she heard the distant notes of the American-type dance band in the ballroom of the palazzo. One hundred guests had been invited to the sumptuous dinner and dancing later that evening. But needing to be alone for a few moments to try to reabsorb the crowded hours of the past few days,

Caroline had stolen to the balcony, where she watched the drifting quality of motion on the broad canal below.

"I hope I am not intruding," the voice said, and she turned. In the moonlight, her pale blue gown looked almost white. A strand of creamy pearls at her throat shone in milky iridescence, while her long hair tumbled over her shoulders. There was such promise in that lovely body, he had thought earlier, the moonlight now confirming it.

She smiled. "No. It's just that we've seen so much in these three days I can't quite believe it's not only a dream." He laughed as she added, "I think I came out here to make certain it wasn't really Fifth Avenue, after all."

"Venice has this effect on everyone, even sometimes the Venetians themselves," he said. He lounged back against the balustrade and lit a cigarette, his white dinner jacket gleaming in the darkness, his profile a handsome outline. Although she had met him briefly that evening and danced only once with him, she remembered how the dark eyes had probed hers, how she had wanted to reach up and touch the softly waving blue-black hair that swept back from his brow.

"Perhaps that is what makes them so delightful," she said. "The fact that they can be part of this beautiful fantasy."

"What a charming thing to say," he said, his accent more European than Franco's. Massimo di Cavelli, she later learned from Katherine, had been educated in Florence and Siena, and had studied commerce in Zurich. For many generations, his family had been leading merchants in Venice, and his father, an art connoisseur, was possessor of one of the most important art collections in Europe.

"Franco said that you are his closest friend," Caroline said, also recalling that they were in some way distantly related. "And cousins?"

"My mother is first cousin to Franco's father."

Caroline then remembered that Katherine had said Marisa di Cavelli was a principessa. They chatted easily, finding common interests immediately. When he asked her to go to the Lido for swimming and lunch the following day, she didn't hesitate to accept. They danced only with each other the rest of the evening, and when he said goodnight, she watched from the balcony above with a quickening of her heartbeat.

With his hand in hers, leading her, Caroline walked up the broad marble staircase in the palazzo's courtyard, marveling at how the day's intense heat seemed to have fallen behind in this cool haven of green-ery, gothic-arched windows and doorways, carved stone, and priceless statues. She looked up and saw Marisa di Cavelli, the principessa, waiting at the top, the sleek lines of her still youthful figure caught in the quiet elegance of tailored white linen, her handsome, almost beak-like face made sharp by dark hair that swept back into a smooth French twist. She smiled when Caroline looked up.

"Well, at last we meet," she said in lightly accented English. "I have asked Massimo for days now when he would bring you here for luncheon. Each morning he has rushed off, saying, 'Caroline and I are going to the Lido today' or 'Caroline and I are going to Torcello this morning' or 'Caroline and I are going to the glassworks at Murano.' And I say, 'Caroline, Caroline. When are we going to meet this Caroline?' So at last he brings you to Ca' di Cavelli."

They had reached the top and Caroline found her hand in the principessa's. "How lovely she is!" Massimo's mother exlaimed in her low musical voice as she turned to her son, Caroline's hand still in hers. She laughed softly, seeing Caroline blush. "But, my dear, you must not blush at what is true." And before Caroline could answer her, she was leading them through a wide entrance into the cool, dim interior of the palazzo, her slim heels tapping on the marble floor.

As they walked down endless marble corridors lined with priceless paintings and frescoes, through chambers filled with stiffly formal but exquisite Byzantine-style furnishings of gold and richly varied colors gleaming out of the half darkness, she felt Massimo's hand tighten over hers and looked up at him with a smile.

Like his mother, he was dressed in white linen, the soft blue shirt casually open at the neck. The flash of his smile against bronzed skin made something flutter violently inside her. And when they sat at a table on a shady terrace, he touched her hand and she trembled.

Enrico di Cavelli was an older version of his son, Massimo, tall and darkly handsome. He joined them hurriedly for lunch and talked almost incessantly about his exporting business that was now reaching out "to Fifth Avenue, State Street, and Wilshire Boulevard," all said with a beaming smile and in an English that was much more difficult to understand than his wife's or son's.

"I liked them very much," Caroline said to Massimo an hour later as his motorboat skimmed across the lagoon, heading toward the colorful fishing village islands of Burano, Massimo behind the wheel.

"And they liked you." Massimo looked at her with a smile. "I could see that immediately." His eyes behind the dark glasses said far more than his words, and she shivered a little in the hot sun.

"Franco said that you are in business with your father?" She was letting her hand trail over the side in the cool rush of water. Her pale yellow dress fluttered in the wind, a wind that swept her hair back and caught it into a funnel-shaped mass.

He grinned and made a comical face. "Yes, he has caught me at last and chained me to a desk. Only this week he permitted me to take the days away from the business for myself, which I find quite wonderful." He threw his head back and laughed. "I am really a playboy at heart."

"Playboy!" she scoffed with a laugh. "Franco has told us all about your *playboy* period, when you worked for two years with a mobile medical unit, visiting isolated areas in Africa, mostly in Tanzania."

"Franco talks too much," he said with a frown. He had cut the motor back on the engine and was letting the boat drift toward a long narrow canal with brightly colored ancient houses hovering along each side. She saw men shaking out their fishing nets to hang in the sun, women pulling clotheslines from windows and plucking off the vividly shaded garments.

"He said you had wanted to be a doctor." She spoke softly.

He chuckled. "The idealistic dreams of boyhood. And perhaps a certain amount of rebellion. I came back from Tanzania, finished my schooling, and was persuaded by my father that it was my duty as the only son to carry on the di Cavelli business."

"But he said that you still go back to Africa from time to time, that you were in Algeria during the nationalist uprising two years ago and that you worked with a medical team—"

"Yes, Franco *does* talk too much," he said, but he grinned down at her, then called out in Italian to a young boy running over to the quayside. The boy grasped the line that Massimo threw out and quickly pulled the boat close to the quay. *"Prego,"* the boy said, dark eyes merry beneath a thatch of brown curls.

"Ci fermiamo solo per poche ore." Massimo explained to him that they would be gone only a few hours, and told him to take care of the boat. The boy grinned and jabbered excitedly when Massimo pressed some lire into his hands and promised more when they returned. Taking her arm, he led her toward a narrow street where she could see lace stalls set up and the lace-makers busy at work in the sun with their small velvet cushions.

They wandered for an hour or more, then sat in a small café on a quay, where Massimo ordered a bottle of wine. Caroline watched in fascination as the quayside bustled with life, children running in play, dogs barking and circling them, the fishermen with their boats and nets, and women standing in clusters, gossiping. When Massimo purchased a bouquet of riotously colored blossoms, she buried her face in them, then held them to her, so that the pink and red of the roses stole into her throat and cheeks. For a moment he gently held her face between his hands. "You're lovely," he half-whispered. "I'm glad— so glad you came to Venice."

The next week passed in a haze of happiness for Caroline. Brenda protested only mildly that she was having to go sightseeing alone or with Katherine. While spending most of her waking hours with this tall, slender young man, simply sitting in cafés or standing hand in hand in darkened churches or quiet museums, feeling the sea spray in her face as his motorboat roared through the water to Murano or Lido, she knew she had gone through a profound change. It was like a low charge of electricity, constant, never leaving her. There was a brightness about them that made people smile when they passed them; everyone and everything else seemed to fade away. They had found something, this brightness seemed to say, that no one else had ever possessed. It shimmered in her eyes, like the eyes of a child gazing up at a lighted Christmas tree, and sharpened his face with the look of a man who will share nothing of the prize he has found.

He was amused at first at the slightly distant sight of Mark Rumsey's figure, discreetly following them or sitting quietly in the rear of the bronze-hulled speedboat. But after a few days, he asked in a concerned voice, "Is there really danger?"

She thought about it for a moment. They were walking along a *calle* leading to the Rialto Bridge, where he insisted he must buy her a gift, anything she would like to have. "The family receives threats from time to time," she said reluctantly.

"If you lived in Venice, you would be safe," he said softly. She glanced at him, then quickly away, her cheeks flushing and heart leaping. She selected a miniature, one of little value by an obscure artist, and painted on vellum, but of such delicacy and beauty that she insisted this was what she wanted.

He walked her back to the di San Nicola palazzo and told her he would come for her that evening at eight. He was bringing a friend who would escort Brenda. With Katherine and Franco joining them, the six were going to a small outdoor nightclub where they would first eat and then dance.

She dressed in a gown of white crepe touched with delicate peacock sprays of tiny brilliants. It hugged her figure but flounced out at the knees and plunged daringly at the back to her waist. Carrying a scarlet taffeta cape over her arm, she met him in the reception hall, where the Count and Countess di San Nicola, a handsome couple, waited to see the three young couples off for the evening of dancing.

Massimo and Caroline stayed through dinner and for an hour or so later with the other two couples, but then, on the roof garden of the hotel, he drew her to the side, snapped his fingers for an attendant to bring her cape, and they left. For the next two hours, they drifted through one narrow, winding canal after another in the di Cavelli gondola, with Mark slumped back and dozing in the stern, the gondolier seemingly quite oblivious to the way the young couple sat closely holding hands. They could hear the singing of a voice echoing around the bends of the canals ahead of them. Softly, Massimo told her what living in Venice was like, of the subtle, intoxicating hold the city had on its inhabitants, of how it was never quite a normal way of life, but always touched with the holiday spirit, with the joy that one feels surrounded with beauty. She yearned for him to kiss her, felt a kind of desperation in wanting him to know she had fallen in love with him. She felt that time was beginning to run out, for she had heard his father mention that Massimo was accompanying him on a business trip to Paris in two days.

"I feel we have so little time," he was miraculously saying, and she turned her face up to him in the half darkness. "But if, by chance, you feel even in the smallest amount what I am feeling for you, time doesn't matter."

"Oh, Massimo," she whispered, and he touched one finger beneath her chin and lifted it. When he kissed her, she felt the universe had tilted, stars tumbling from the sky.

"That, my darling, should tell you how I feel about you," he finally said, lifting his head away a little, his eyes glittering down into hers. In that moment, she knew how deeply she loved him. Their love was perfect, she thought, coming so quickly, the first moment they met, really, that initial wave of recognition, and then the long, slow, sensuous building of intimacy, the thrill when touching by chance. There in the darkness, he kissed her once more and she felt her innocence vanish.

"I love you, Caroline," he said, in a voice so low that only she could hear it, and yet she felt it echoing and reechoing across the water. The gondola had swung out into the Grand Canal now and was passing other gondolas in the darkness. "It is happening so quickly, I know, but with both of us leaving . . . Will you marry me?"

She hesitated only a moment. "Yes, Massimo," she whispered, her mouth against his cheek, and he held her tightly until they stepped onto the di San Nicola landing.

Low lights glowed in corners of staircases and corridors. They quietly bid Mark Rumsey good night and watched him walk away toward his room in the rear of the palazzo.

"Don't leave me now, Massimo," she pleaded. They walked up the staircase into her suite of rooms, on through into the bedroom, where a single small lamp burned in a corner.

A crystal loop held her gown on one shoulder. He watched as she slowly unfastened it, letting her gown drop to the floor. While she slipped to the center of the large canopied bed, he threw his clothing off and came toward her, tall and gracefully lean in the shadowy light.

When he lay across her, his mouth crushing hers, she let her hands slip over his back, felt the beauty of his muscles, and wanted him desperately. But his lovemaking was slow and gentle in the beginning, a tender, tentative brushing of his lips across her mouth, then sliding across her cheek and down her throat with a feathery softness.

She knew, no matter how long their life together, she would never forget these moments, the sounds from the canal that drifted through the long windows, a snatch of silvery laughter spilling across the water from a distance, a gondolier's voice calling out to another.

Her perfume enveloped them in a kind of mist as the cool sheets became warm and damp. The gentleness of their lovemaking had given way to a fiery excitement, rolling and writhing in a wild abandonment. When he rose above her, she clung to him, and when he sank within, she cried out sharply, but pulled him to her again, feeling the tensile strength of his body stretched above hers, becoming a part of her as they raced in unison toward the core of their passion.

For a long, long time, they didn't move but lay frozen in a deathlike grasp where they seemed to float in a soft, warm nothingness. She cradled his face between her hands and looked into his face. "I always wondered what this kind of love would be like," she whispered. He saw tears on her cheeks and kissed them away.

"And what did you discover?" he asked.

324

"How deeply I can love someone. How exciting love can be. How it changes from moment to moment and yet stays the same, how it grows, but is always constant. I feel I've known you since the very day I was born." Her fingers were tracing his nose and lips.

"You are leaving in three days?" he asked, and she could hear the disappointment in his voice.

She nodded. "We promised Gail—my friend—that we would come to Switzerland where she's visiting her—visiting relatives at the moment." No need for explanations now, she thought, plenty of time for that later. "And then we go back to New York."

"I will arrange to come to New York in September," he said softly, as his body began an urgent need for hers again. "To talk to your father about our marriage."

"Yes . . ." she murmured, smiling into the darkness, smiling at the incongruity of his formality while they lay in her bed. He made love to her once more, their passion pulsing, surrounding them, engulfing them. Then, in the darkness, he rose and dressed, whispering, "Tomorrow evening?"

After watching as he stole through the door and disappeared, she pulled on a light robe and walked to the small balcony. A single *vaporetto* chugged along in the faint moonlight. She smiled as she let her head fall back against the pillar. Tomorrow, she whispered, *tomorrow.*

They stopped for coffee in the Florian Café, sitting where they could watch the passing Venetians, the groups of milling tourists following their guides who held furled umbrellas aloft, and the impeccably dressed *carabinieri* walking leisurely up and down in twos and threes while their eyes searched for pretty young ladies. The Piazza San Marco was still the heart and soul of the *Serenissima,* Caroline thought, watching a young magician perform his tricks. She tossed him some coins and he walked on, his place taken by a small grimy-faced boy who stood on his head for her, a wide grin on his mouth.

"I could sit here all day watching this craziness," Brenda said, as pigeons from all directions swooped down to one end of the square at the strike of the clock in the tower. She was snapping her camera wildly.

Caroline looked at Katherine, who was repairing her lipstick in a small mirror. "How lucky you are to live here, Katherine," she said, trying to keep the excitement out of her voice. Brenda had questioned her earlier about her disappearance the night before, but Caroline had sworn her to secrecy after revealing only that she and Massimo had been attracted to each other. Let her think only that, she thought, until after Massimo comes to New York in September. For the moment, she wanted to keep the breathless wonder of it to herself.

"Well, it's absolutely marvelous this part of the year. But winter can be miserable, rainy and damp and cold. And there are so many things about New York that I miss—"

"Oh, you'll never be satisfied," Brenda grumbled. "Imagine living in a place like this. It would be like going to the circus or a party every day of the week." She suddenly darted a short distance away to get a snapshot of some tourists feeding the pigeons.

Katherine turned and stared at Caroline, her eyes filled with curiosity. "I gather from what I've been seeing that you and Massimo di Cavelli have been hitting it off. You want to be careful there, Caroline," she said, looking in her compact mirror again and dusting a bit of powder across her nose.

"Careful?" Caroline said, her voice striving for a casual tone, as she handed the small grinning boy a few coins. "Careful of what?"

"Oh, Venice has its share of fortune-hunters," Katherine said, snapping the gold compact shut and sliding it into her white antelope purse. "The di Cavellis had a great deal of money once. Huge money, in fact. But the import-export business almost went under during the war, of course. It's been struggling ever since, but according to Franco's father, it's a losing battle. Massimo's father has been trying to raise capital in massive amounts recently, but I understand he's counting on Massimo making a *good* marriage, if you know what I mean—"

"*Good* marriage?" Caroline picked up her cappuccino and sipped at it, trying to hide the sudden surge of fear she felt.

"Why, marrying a pile of money, of course." She was signaling to the waiter to bring the check. "*Cameriere!*" she called out. "*Posso avere il conto, per favore?*"

As the waiter rushed toward them, Caroline said in a low voice, "I don't believe that, Katherine. He doesn't seem like the type who—"

"Type? It doesn't take any type, darling. All it takes is needing a hefty shot of capital in the business. If Signor di Cavelli doesn't get one soon, he'll have to start selling off that art collection he's so proud of. Even that would be a mere drop in the bucket." She threw some bills onto the check on the small tray the waiter had put down and called out, "Come along, you two. I have a gown I want to pick up at Signora Pegrino's salon."

For a moment, Caroline stared down at the small tray of lire without seeing anything. She nodded absently at the bowing waiter and slowly stood up. Brenda and Katherine were looking at the statues of the Moors in the clock tower. For a moment, she wavered, standing there by the table in her pale violet linen dress and wide-brimmed matching straw hat. She quickly slipped dark glasses on, as her heart plunged and then thudded sickeningly, a strange kind of nausea rising in her throat. She wanted to run—somewhere, anywhere. But she stood there, not knowing what to do, stunned and sick at heart. She wanted to lie down in a dark place. She wanted to die. But when Brenda called out, "Come on, Caroline," she followed a little way behind them, not trusting herself to speak or look them directly in the face as yet. When they reached Signora Pegrino's salon, not far from the Piazza San Marco, Caroline touched Brenda's arm just as she started to follow Katherine into the shop.

"Oh, Brenda, I forgot to tell you that I promised Evalina I would meet her for lunch."

"Evalina? For lunch?" Brenda said, looking a little surprised. The young Countess Evalina di San Nicola, Franco's sister, was curator of a small art gallery in a seventeenth-century palace on the Grand Canal.

"She's going to help me with some art purchases. I want to get Christmas gifts for Mummy and Daddy and I haven't the vaguest idea what to look for."

She walked off with a wave of her hand, her smile a hard bright slash of red beneath the dark glasses. "I'll see you both at dinner."

Only a few servants seemed to be in the palazzo when Caroline entered, Mark Rumsey just a few steps behind her.

"You can take the afternoon off, Mark," she said with a stiff smile as she ran up the staircase, looking down at him briefly. "I have an awful headache and want to lie down until dinner."

"Right," he said, looking up at her. "Well, if you're sure . . . ?"

"I'm sure," she called down.

"I'd like to pick up a few little gifts for my sister and her kid, while I've got the chance."

"That's fine," she said, disappearing, her voice floating down the stairwell. She walked along the dim wide corridor, feeling strangely unsteady. Her hand trembled a little as she pushed the door to her suite open. She knew that everyone was gone for the day, the Countess di San Nicola visiting her aged mother, Franco and his father in Mestre, and Evalina at the museum.

She picked up the telephone and asked for the overseas operator, putting a call through to Henry Winters at Kendall, Inc. When the operator said she would call her back when she had put through the call, Caroline paced the room nervously. She glanced at her watch. It would be early morning in New York, just about the time Henry would be arriving at the offices.

She stepped out onto the balcony that looked down on the Grand Canal, again caught by the exuberance and color of Venice, by the everyday bastle and hustle of modern life entangled so skillfully in the ancient setting. She stood there for almost an hour, waiting tensely. Then the peal of the telephone pulled her running into the vast room with its silk hangings and woven tapestries.

"Henry!" she said, with a gasp when she recognized his voice. "Thank heaven you come to work early."

"What is it, Caroline?" he asked. She heard the alarm in his voice. She had known Henry Winters all her life. As one of her father's most trusted employees, he had come to the various houses over the years whenever there was any kind of trouble that Lawrence Kendall wanted handled discreetly.

"I need some information on the exporting business in Venice owned by the di Cavelli family. Enrico di Cavelli is the principal owner. I believe there's a brother or cousin also involved on that level. And then there's a son, Massimo—he has also become one of the officers, I think." Her voice faltered a little.

"Are you all right?" Henry asked quickly, his voice distant but clear as he picked up on her tone. She could almost see him, silvery head bent close as he sat on the corner of his desk, nervously pushing the horn-rimmed glasses back on his nose.

"Yes." She controlled her voice, forced it to sound normal. "Just curious. About its solvency."

"How soon do you need to know?"

"As soon as possible."

"Give me a few hours."

"I'll wait here by the phone." She gave him the number of the private line to her suite.

He sounded hesitant. "Caroline—just for my own information—does the son figure in this somewhere?"

She paused, swallowed hard, and said, "Yes." She felt tears crowding into her throat.

"I'll get back to you as soon as I can."

She hung up the phone slowly and walked again to the balcony, where she stood beneath one of its narrow gothic arches and looked down onto the canal. She would not see Massimo until nine that evening. He was taking her to the Florian Café, where they would listen to a concert. The Piazza San Marco would be crowded. It would be safely impersonal . . . and yet, also so very personal, the lavender twilight and the lights flickering on, the music from the orchestras on each side of the square. She clenched a fist against her mouth . . . remembering the first night Massimo had taken her there. Hours passed, the afternoon light waned, but still she waited there.

When the telephone finally rang, she simply stared at it for a moment.

"Yes?" she finally said into the mouthpiece.

"Caroline?" It was Henry Winters's voice.

"Yes." She held herself rigid.

"Well—it's not very good news." She could imagine him, one leg swinging nervously, the other braced on the floor as he sat on the corner of the big walnut desk with its shining surface. "The business was a very successful one prior to World War Two. Huge, in fact, by the standards those days. The war almost destroyed it. They've borrowed up to the limit in Zurich and Paris, even New York. There isn't a bank left that will touch them."

She had been holding her breath until her chest hurt. When her legs felt as though they would buckle, she sank into a chair, the hard carved edges cutting into her thighs through her thin dress.

"As for the son? Well—" He seemed to be riffling through some papers. She could tell he was reading. "Graduate of the University of Bologna. Some graduate work in economics at Oxford . . . accomplished horseman, fairly well known in tennis. Got to Wimbledon two years in a row. Engagement broken about eighteen months ago to a young woman in the Scarpi family. Great wealth. Homes in Rome, Cap d'Antibes, and Venice. Automobile manufacturers, with plants in—"

"What was her name? Do you know?" She felt an iciness on her skin, crawling up her bare arms.

"Yes, er—Elena. Elena Scarpi. She was about twenty-two at the time. Educated here in the States. Sweetbriar. While her brother, Eduardo, was at M.I.T. She broke the engagement. There was evidently talk that he was . . . well, that he was in the market for an heiress, very eligible young bachelor, important family and all that, and the Scarpi family—well, old man Scarpi, her grandfather, evidently started out as a machinist—"

"That's all I need to know, Henry," she said wearily.

"Are you okay, honey?" he asked anxiously.

"Yes. Yes . . . I'm fine. It's just someone I met here, a young woman, who wanted to know."

"Oh. Well, fine." She could hear the relief in his voice.

When she hung up, she kept looking at the ivory telephone in its gold cradle, amazed that something so devastating and shattering could have come out of such a delicate-looking instrument. Slowly, she walked into the bedroom and threw herself face down on the bed, where she lay motionless for hours.

She could feel Massimo's eyes on her as she watched the pigeons swoop upward and fly over the spires and domes of St. Mark's. They were sitting at one of the small tables, cups of espresso in front of them. The orchestra was playing Gershwin's *Rhapsody in Blue* and Caroline tipped her head as though listening, while her heart was filled with turmoil. She felt his hand slowly clasp and hold hers at the edge of the table.

"Funny . . ." she said, "the song reminds me of something, a concert I went to several years ago, the Boston Pops. I was on a date with a student from M.I.T." She laughed softly. "First and last time. Let me see, what was his name? He said his family lived part of the year in Venice. You might know him." She pretended to think for several moments. "Oh, yes. Eduardo. Eduardo—Scarpi. That was it. Eduardo Scarpi."

She was watching Massimo's face. He moved his head casually and looked down. There was just the barest change in expression, so faint that she couldn't be sure it had changed at all.

"Scarpi?" he said. He was thinking hard. "Well, there are many Scarpis in Italy. But the only ones I know about are the automobile people." She watched him intently, her heart seeming to stop. "They may live part of the time in Venice. But, no, I do not know them."

Her heart plunged and she turned away quickly, as though to watch

330

some people who were noisily pulling out chairs as they sat at a nearby table. From that moment on, she stared at the orchestra, pouring all of her concentration into it, afraid to look at him, knowing her eyes would flash accusingly.

She waited through several more musical selections before she trusted herself to speak. She turned to him and said, "Massimo, I have the most dreadful headache. I wonder if you would take me back to the di San Nicolas'. I really feel ill."

"Darling!" he said, with alarm in his voice. "But of course."

She let him kiss her as they said good night, but insisted he come no farther with her than the boat landing below the palazzo, still pleading that she felt terribly ill. When she was out of his sight and he had stepped back into the bobbing gondola, she ran, the tears beginning to stream down her face, praying she wouldn't meet anyone. She could hear the taffeta of her black cocktail dress rustling as she flew through the corridors and up the staircases. She had taken off the black satin pumps and was running in her stockinged feet. After climbing the final staircase, she raced along the corridor and let herself into her suite, locking the door behind her.

Her mind flailed about in a jumble of disconnected thoughts, all of them whirling in a humiliation so deep that she couldn't face herself in the mirror. Moving quickly, she changed to a navy blue linen suit and deep-brimmed straw hat, then crammed her toothbrush, nightgown, passport, and extra stockings and lingerie into the largest purse she had. She had a small amount of cash. Her travelers' cheques would be enough, she thought. Carefully scribbling a note to Brenda that she was going to sleep early with a sick headache and would see her at breakfast, she slipped it under the door next to hers as she ran past. She watched along each dim corridor and staircase with care to make certain no one saw her, reached a small street entrance that was used by the servants, and hurried out.

She walked for perhaps a mile through the winding byways, the late-evening life of Venice swirling about her in a cheerful bedlam of sounds. A smiling shopkeeper called out to her to come inside and see the Venetian glassware, but she hurried on. Near the Ca' D'Oro, at Vaporetto stop six, she ran down onto the landing platform and stepped aboard the vessel just as it was about to pull out. It was crowded with tourists, but she found a corner, and with her heart pounding fiercely, she watched the traffic on the canal as the boat plowed on.

At the Piazzale Roma, she ran up toward the railway station, her head lowered, in fear of passing someone she might have met at one of the many parties and dances held in the past week. She purchased a ticket to Milan, stood on the platform for more than half an hour waiting for the train, and finally collapsed into a seat, turning her head to the window and staring out with dull eyes into the darkness. It would be several hours until dawn.

When the train arrived at Milan, she hurried through the crowded Stazione Centrale and flagged a taxi.

"Dove vuole andare, Signorina?" the young driver asked, jumping out to open the door for her, his eyes appreciatively skimming her face and figure. "You go to where, Signorina?" he repeated in English as he climbed back behind the wheel.

"I want to catch an international flight at the airport." She slid back into a corner of the seat.

"Nessuno valigia?" he asked, puzzled, looking around at her. "No suitcase?"

"No—they're at the airport," she blurted.

With that explanation, which he only partially understood, the taxi took off, its wheels screeching on the road below. Scorching heat from the pavement and the low-setting afternoon sun made the air in the taxi almost suffocating. She wiped at her neck with a hanky, absently watching from the window. Her mind had dulled and yet she still felt the terrible urgency to flee, to leave Italy far behind her. At an airport money booth she changed a number of her larger travelers' cheques and warily approached the Pan Am ticket counter. TransGlobal flew in and out of Milan, but she purposely avoided it. As the reservations clerk processed her ticket, she looked up at the wall clock. She wouldn't be missed yet—not for another hour or so. And by that time, the plane she had requested a first-class ticket on would be winging its way toward the United States. But she still kept glancing around, her eyes nervously scanning the crowded terminal. The ticket clerk didn't appear to recognize her name. And when she handed her the envelope containing her ticket and returned her passport, Caroline smiled at her briefly and hurried away. At the *Ufficio Telegrafico,* she quickly sent a telegram to Brenda, telling her she was all right, but had to spend some time alone.

It wasn't until the plane taxied onto the runway less than an hour later that Caroline felt she had gotten safely away. Then and only then did she put her head back, close her eyes, and sleep out of utter exhaustion.

When she wakened, the flight attendant was bending over her to ask if she wanted something to eat. Caroline mumbled her thanks but shook her head. It was dark beyond the small windows, and still drugged from an uneasy sleep, she thought back over the previous hours with a dulled kind of apathy. The feeling of shame and humiliation returned, and she closed her eyes. She was in a state of shock, shock from learning the truth about Massimo di Cavelli and from her daring flight from Venice. She had boarded the first plane leaving for the United States, not even caring that its destination was Boston.

Boston, she thought. Yes, that was it. She would go to Newport, to Kendall Hall. Her parents were in Buenos Aires, where her father was attending an Inter-American Conference, something to do with trade and investment in Latin American countries. Nanny Grace was in London visiting her sister, Larry and Avery and their families were off on the *Sapphire,* Jamie and Barbara were in the Berkshires, and the staff at Kendall Hall had been given a month's vacation. Only the caretaker, a new man she had never met, would be there. She would tell him she was Nanny Grace's niece and had come to stay in her cottage back by the playhouse until Nanny Grace returned.

She registered at a small hotel near the bus terminal in Boston under the name of Catherine Kramer, to match the initials on her purse. As it was early morning, she was the first customer in a luggage store, where she bought a medium-sized suitcase. After leaving it in her hotel room, she took a taxi to Filene's and purchased clothes— several pairs of slacks and blouses, two summery dresses, and some lingerie—and then bought two pairs of shoes at a shoe store. After quickly packing everything into the suitcase, she went to the lobby, checked out, and walked the block and a half to the Greyhound terminal, where she caught a bus to Newport.

The taxi driver in Newport hardly glanced at her as she stepped into the back of his cab.

"I want to go to Kendall Hall," she said, as she settled back in the seat.

He had started to pull away from the curb, but stopped and turned around in his seat. "Kendall Hall's all closed up for the month," he said. "Ain't nobody there but the caretaker."

"I know," she said, wishing he wouldn't stare at her in that way. "But my aunt—Grace Philby—she's on the staff there, and has a cottage—"

"I know Grace Philby," he said, peering at her again.

"Well, I'm her niece and she said I could use her cottage until she gets back from London." Her heart was pounding hard as she fought to keep her voice normal.

He turned back to the wheel slowly. "That's right. She went to England 'bout two weeks ago." He pulled out into the slow stream of afternoon traffic. "Didn't know she had no American nieces."

"Oh, yes, her brother—my father—he came to the United States before she did."

He seemed satisfied with her explanation and lapsed into silence, for which she was grateful. When he pulled up to turn in to the gate at Kendall Hall, she leaned forward with money for the fare and said, "You can drop me right here."

When he turned the taxi around and drove away, she walked up to the high black iron gate and rang the bell. It was several minutes before a man appeared, walking along the circular driveway from beyond the massive stone and marble house. He was middle-aged, wearing paint-spattered dungarees and a blue workman's shirt. "Yes?" he called out. His grayish hair stuck up in wisps and he had paint on his rather large nose.

"I'm Grace Philby's niece," she said.

He stopped on the other side of the gate and peered through at her. "Grace Philby?" he said, peering harder. "You mean the nursemaid?"

"Yes. They call her Nanny Grace. She said I could use her cottage until she gets back from London."

He stared at her for a moment or two more, then apparently satisfied she was who she said she was, he opened the grilled door in the high brick wall, let her come in through it, and then locked it again. "You got a key?" he demanded.

"No," Caroline said, walking along beside him. "But I know where she hides one. I can use that."

He took her suitcase from her and smiled down at her. "Well, it's kinda nice to see someone around here. I'm new here, y'see, an' don't know much of anybody in town. An' since everybody went off on vacation, even my cousin—"

"Your cousin?" She tried not to sound alarmed.

"He's the head chauffeur for the Kendalls."

"Oh, Meacham's your cousin."

"You know Bill?" He grinned down at her.

"I've heard my Aunt Grace speak of him."

He stuck his hand out as they walked toward the cottage, a small

334

white four-room house with green shutters and a tiny front porch, nestling next to the playhouse, which was similar but had a wide veranda around two sides. They stood in the shadowy center of a deep grove of trees. It had always been Caroline's favorite place at Kendall Hall.

When she shook his hand, he said, "I'm Dan Gorman."

"It's nice to know you, Mr. Gorman. My name is—Carol Philby." She hid the initials on her purse just as they came up onto the small porch of Nanny Grace's house. Reaching above the doorframe, she edged her hand along it until it touched the key.

"Well, you surely did know where the key was," he said, a twinkle in his eye as the last glint of doubt left. He saluted as he backed down the three steps. "Have to get back to my painting." He was walking away with a wave. "Promised to have the garages all finished by the time everyone gets back here September first. Anything I can do or get for you, just yell. You can leave a list of groceries you want outside the door, and I'll pick 'em up in the morning."

She watched until he disappeared, and slowly went into the little house and closed the door.

For the first day or so, Caroline wandered about the estate, spending most of her time at the gazebo near the low stone wall that looked down on Cliff Walk and the ocean. It was here she sat and brooded over what had happened, how she had so innocently and stupidly believed Massimo had fallen in love with her, how she had trusted him, totally, and had let herself be led into the beginning of an affair . . . an affair that was to have ended in marriage. How could I? she kept whispering to herself. How could I?

She remembered the night they had spent together and felt the agony of its memory sweep through her, leaving only a terrible emptiness in its wake. At night, she often walked along the seawall, her loneliness reaching out across the empty expanse of dark ocean. She felt numb at first, but gradually the numbness gave way to a kind of silent anger. On the second night, she stole into the long row of two-story garages. A stairway there led to an underground entrance to the main house, coming up into the kitchens, a route the servants used on rainy days from their quarters over the garages. She walked through the house with a flashlight, her sneakers making a soft squishing sound on the marble floors. It seemed ghostly and strange, the cavernous ceilings of the first-floor rooms lost in the darkness above, sheeting covering much of the furniture, just the trickling of the fountain from the lion's mouth in the main reception hall seeming familiar and somehow comforting. She let the water spill over her fingers, cool and sweet, the sound like soft music in the crushing silence. It was then that the tears began to slide down her face. She hadn't wept a tear since the morning that she and Brenda and Katherine had been sitting in the Piazza San Marco. But now they came, sobs rising up from her throat. She slid down to the floor and leaned against the base of the fountain, her body heaving. Finally she got to her feet and returned through the underground passage to the garages and quietly stepped out into the still night.

She lay watching the ceiling in the small bedroom of Nanny Grace's cottage that night. It was almost dawn when she finally drifted off to sleep. But she slept—at last—without the fitful rousings of the three nights before.

The following morning, after giving Dan Gorman another small list of groceries to get for her as he had offered, she set off toward the farthest corner of the estate, along the seawall, a spot hidden from the house and outbuildings by a long line of trees. She had brought a pad of paper and some pencils with her and sat up on the wall, leaning back against a pillar with her knees hunched in front of her. She sat there writing for long periods of time, then lifting her eyes and staring out at the sea, her face almost hard, except for the trace of hurt and self-doubt in the blue-violet eyes.

Her pencil raced over the pages, writing about a young woman meeting a man in Venice and falling in love . . .

Lawrence Kendall paced back and forth in front of the French doors leading to the balcony, the long wire of the telephone trailing over the carpet as he walked. Elizabeth watched him from where she stood by the doors, coffee cup in hand and nervously sipping, her long white silk robe rippling a little in the soft wind.

"No—she's all right. Do you hear me, Brenda?" He was almost shouting and shaking his head at the poor connection. "She's all right. Rumsey followed your suggestion and found her in Newport. *In Newport!*" He raised his voice again and enunciated slowly, suddenly standing still for a moment. From where he stood he could look down on the wide, tree-lined Plaza de la República and to the soaring obelisk that had been erected to commemorate the founding of the city of Buenos Aires. "Yes, he flew directly to Boston and went to

Newport, but I took your suggestion, Brenda . . ."

Elizabeth smiled briefly, the change in expression breaking the tension in her face for a passing moment. He had wanted to send Mark Rumsey and the other bodyguard storming into Kendall Hall, if they found her there, but with added persuasion from Elizabeth, he had heeded that first transatlantic call from Brenda, begging him to let Caroline have some time to herself, to let her think no one had yet discovered her.

"Something must have been bothering her terribly, Uncle Lawrence, for her to leave the way she did. Please, *please* give her a week, even two weeks, to just be by herself," Brenda had pleaded, and he had finally listened. When he put in another long-distance call to Mark Rumsey, he had said, "Just keep an eye on her. Keep your distance and give her room to work out whatever it is that's bothering her."

He and Elizabeth returned to New York ten days later—and waited. Henry Winters, his troubleshooter, assured him it had never gotten into the newspapers or onto the television news. "We were lucky on this one," he told Lawrence, as the Rolls Royce sped across the Triboro Bridge from the airport and cut west toward Fifth Avenue. "Your niece kept it quiet over there, once she received the wire from your daughter. And the newspapers never picked it up here."

"Thank God," Elizabeth breathed.

"And Mark Rumsey said she seems to be fine. Never goes anywhere, just sits out by the seawall much of the time, reading or writing on a pad of paper."

When Elizabeth put her hand in Lawrence's, he smiled down at her and said, "I promise, darling, I won't interfere."

Caroline had been there for several hours one morning when she looked up from her writing. She heard something and then she saw him. He had scaled the high brick wall from the other side and was sitting on the top of it, one hand over his eyes, looking out over the water and then toward the Kendall mansion. His hair was sun-bleached and blowing a little in the soft wind. He wore a faded blue shirt and pants and his skin was bronzed to the color of a peach. She started to slip down from the low wall, but he saw her and waved. When she didn't return the wave, he slid to the ground and, with a slight limp, loped toward her across the velvet-like grass.

"Hi," he called out as he drew near.

She had known his eyes would be blue, but not that they would have drained the blue from the sea. They blazed at her from out of the golden tan of his face, and there was a laughing quality in them that made her smile in spite of herself. She sat with her white-sneak-ered feet dangling down, watching him as he approached her.

"My father said no one was here," he said, as he suddenly sat down on the ground, his legs crossed, elbows resting on his knees. "He said the family was in Europe or someplace and the servants were all given the month off. I wanted to see how people live who are this rich. Who are *you?*"

"Well, I'm a relative of one of the women who works here. Her niece. She told me I could stay here until she gets back from England."

He gestured with his head. "My father is one of the gardeners for the estate next door. My name is Jeff Collier." He looked around him. "I've never been here before. My mother sent me down to bring him his lunch. He forgot it this morning." He made an unpleasant face. "You won't catch me ever working in a place like this."

"Oh? Why not?" she asked.

He looked at her as though she didn't know anything at all. "I have more ambition than that, being somebody's servant!" He pulled a package of cigarettes from his shirt pocket, held it toward her, and, when she shook her head, lit one and puffed on it for a moment. "I go to college," he said, swelling a little. "To Boston U. On the G.I. Bill." He looked off to the ocean, and his eyes seemed faraway, remote. "I was in Korea."

She heard the hurt and bitterness in his voice, and something inside of her reached out. "I didn't know very much about the Korean War. I was only about twelve when it started." Her voice was soft, inviting confidence.

"I was seventeen," he said, still looking off toward the ocean, where a large sailboat skimmed low over the water, heeling as it came about. "I lied about my age to get into the infantry." His laugh had an empty sound. "I'd always wanted to be in the infantry, ever since I was a kid and watching those World War II movies, John Wayne and Alan Ladd."

"What happened?" she asked in a low voice.

"I got hit when the U.S. Eighth Army retook Seoul. They called it *Operation Killer.* It was a killer, all right."

"Were you discharged then?" Her voice was hesitant.

He laughed again, tonelessly. "Sure. Into a hospital. I guess I've been in more veterans' hospitals than you could count. For five years,

they kept pushing me from one to another and on to the next one."
He pulled one pants leg up a little, and then the other one, and she
saw the long angry red scars. "I had to learn to walk all over again.
That is, after they got through chopping me up and putting me back
together again." He suddenly looked at his wristwatch and stood up.
"I have to get going." The hardness in his eyes softened when he
looked at her again.

She slid down from the wall and stood looking at him, slim and
lovely in her white slacks and deep blue blouse. She was holding the
notebook against her, as though it contained secrets.

"Writing your boyfriend?" he said, teasingly.

She blushed a little. "No—only scribbling."

"Scribbling?" he asked, a soft curiosity in his voice.

"Just . . . thoughts."

"You're a writer," he said softly, a ripple of excitement beneath the
words.

"Well . . ." She laughed with a mild self-disparagement. "I love to
write. That doesn't mean I'm a *writer.*"

"You can be anything you want to be," he said, his eyes that blazing
blue again. "I started writing, too, when I was in one of those hospitals. I want to be a reporter. On a newspaper."

Something leaped in her. A newspaper reporter. Perhaps she could
help him . . .

"I'm taking journalism courses at B.U." She saw the tight line of
his jaw, heard the determination in his voice. "And I made up my
mind, nothing is going to stop me."

"I think that's wonderful," she said, breathlessly. She felt an exhilaration, a kind of renewal, and when he looked at his watch again, she
wanted to take hold of his wrist and tell him to stay and sit with her
some more. She wanted to listen to him, and talk and talk and talk.

"My job . . ." He had turned and was starting back toward the brick
wall, the limp a little more evident as he hurried.

"Where?" she called out. Suddenly it was important she know.
"Where do you work?"

"I work at Burnham's, jerking sodas," he called out, "from noon
to eight." At the base of the wall, he stopped and looked back at her.
"Would you like to go out sometime? A movie, or just someplace
where we could talk?"

"I'd love to," she said.

"How about tonight?" He smiled, and it was like the sun breaking through clouds. "At eight-thirty? I'll pick you up outside the front gate." He grinned again. "Unless you want to go over the wall, like I did? The Drexels are away, just like the people who live here. Why they bother having these places when they never come here!"

"Over the wall," she said. "That way I won't have to ring for the caretaker."

He waved as he scaled the wall, and she stared at the place where she had last seen him, the smile slowly disappearing from her face, the hurt coming back into her eyes. For half an hour, he had helped her forget Massimo, helped her forget the path of moonlight that spilled across a bed in Venice, forget the shadowy lines of his face as she held it between her hands, the touch of his mouth on hers, his fingers trailing down over her throat and her breast . . .

She walked back to the little white cottage. Perhaps, as they talked, she could tell him . . . tell him how she hurt inside. She nodded, as though he had answered her, and walked up onto the tiny porch.

For the next three nights, they sat for hours in coffee shops or in his old roadster with the top down, parked close to the beach, the moon trailing across the water and music pulsing through the dark. They talked about Korea again, his voice thick with pain, and then she listened as he told her about growing up in a family of six children, of a father who used a thick strap that hung in the kitchen whenever one of the children did something wrong, of a religious mother who seldom talked, and of the sister named Marie who was never punished because she was born with a caul, something that his mother believed made her different from the others. "My mother always said Marie was 'singled out by God for some special mission.' When I learned in biology class about those things, I told her it was only part of the afterbirth, but she hit me!"

They sat in silence for a while. When he looked up at her, he said, "You know, you're awfully pretty." He stared at her for several moments, then asked, "What do you do?"

"Why, I—I go to school. Like you."

"You do?" He seemed surprised. "Where?" He got up, pulling her to her feet.

"Well, I—I have a scholarship. I go to Vassar."

He whistled appreciatively. "You must be pretty smart for them to let you in there." He was just paying for their coffee and grinned at the young cashier, who giggled and blushed a little when he told her she was too pretty to be working in a coffee shop punching the keys on a cash register. Caroline felt a swift rush of jealousy, then turned away, chiding herself. They were just friends, friends who liked to sit for hours talking about writing, about faraway places, and about what he was going to do in the future.

She wandered out to the sidewalk, the hot summer night suffocating, even there near the docks and the water. Traffic moved slowly along the street, Newporters out trying to get a breath of air, one carload of young people calling out noisily to some friends walking past the lighted shops. She smiled, suddenly feeling a part of it. There was no danger of anyone recognizing her, she thought. None of her friends came near this area in the evenings. Nevertheless, she kept her face turned toward the shop while waiting for Jeff to come out, her eyes clouding a little as she saw him still teasing the pretty cashier, while pushing his change into his pocket.

When he finally came out, he said, "You like to dance?"

"I love it," she said eagerly, looking up into his face.

He grasped her arm. "Then let's go."

They drove in his old roadster to what had once been a roadhouse on the road to Fall River. "It used to be a speakeasy back during Prohibition," he explained, as he led her across the crowded parking lot toward the entrance. The building was outlined with what looked like Christmas tree lights, and the crash of music, with a thumping drum and a slightly out-of-tune piano and saxophone, spilled into the night. Caroline felt strangely light and exhilarated as she hurried along beside him, liking the feel of his arm across her back.

They sat in a booth, one of a row that ran along one side of the big bare room with its low ceiling and winking beer signs over the bar. One of them had glass tubes all around the edges with some kind of colored liquid swirling through them. It was noisy, with several groups of men talking at the bar, the stools in between them filled with couples. The three-piece combo played every song alike, with the same thumping beat of the drum and the wailing saxophone, always a note or two behind the melody banged out by the piano player.

Jeff ordered rye and ginger ale for them without asking her what she wanted, and when the drinks came, she made a face at the first sip.

"Drink it down," he said, laughing. "I always order a double on the first round. The next one'll go down easier."

Smiling inwardly, she thought of the dry sherry she usually had and then only when someone insisted she have something. Somehow she managed to get the drink down, disliking the taste of the liquor—and the sweetness of the ginger ale even more. But Jeff was right. The second drink was easier; it even tasted better. She felt a pleasant, almost weightless feeling as she drifted about in his arms out on the dance floor, his limp barely noticeable. After the fourth or fifth song, they sat down. There was a fresh drink at her place, and she drank it while they talked and talked. He ordered more drinks and they talked on. Then he pulled her out onto the floor again. Some of the brighter lights had been turned off and the big room took on a kind of mystery, the neon lights from the bar painting the shadows with leaping flashes of red and gold. The three musicians were out in the parking lot smoking, and someone had put money in the juke box for a pulsing Harry James record.

He was holding her close, and when she looked up at him, he kissed her, their bodies still swaying slowly to the music. When they pulled away a little, she tried to look down or off at the other dancing couples in the half darkness, but his eyes held hers and she clung to him.

"Let's get out of here," he muttered, a huskiness in his voice.

"Jeff," she said, about to protest. But he kissed her again, and she melted into the closeness of his arms. She was only vaguely aware of his putting money down on their table and of the walk from the roadhouse to the car. One arm held her strongly against him and at every few steps he stopped to kiss her. She heard soft laughter from the direction of three glowing cigarettes across the parking lot and she smiled into the darkness. When he put her into the right side of the roadster and slid in behind the wheel, she leaned her head back on the seat and watched the stars as the car sped down the dark road. He had turned the radio on and soft music flowed from the speaker.

When the roadster finally pulled off the road and he switched off the motor, she heard the sound of breakers on the sand. They were on a stretch of Ocean Avenue near the State Park where the only lights were a rising moon and the scattering of stars across the sky. Taking a blanket from in back, he pulled her from the car and led her down to the beach.

"I think I should go home, Jeff," she started to say, but he eased her down onto the blanket and silenced her with his mouth crushing down on hers. When he raised his head, she looked up at him with half-closed eyes, something singing in her blood. She felt his hands unfastening her blouse, but she seemed powerless to move as his mouth came down to hers again. When his hand touched her breast, she felt herself arch toward him.

She heard the waves rush from the sea and crash across the sand, pulling her with them into the center of his passion. When something whispered *Turn back,* she knew it was too late. His hands had moved swiftly, while his kiss moaned deeper and deeper. Her cotton skirt and panties were flung aside and he had slid on top of her.

"Jeff—wait—" she tried to say, but he stopped the words with his lips. She felt weightless, tingling, with something low inside aching, reaching out for his touch. His mouth and hands and the sinuous movement of his hips made her gasp and move against him. She felt herself sliding away, giving herself to him, wanting him, wanting more and more and more, and finally abandoning herself as she felt his rough strength and power inside of her, and then the waves of pleasure, one on top of the other. They became rigid and still in that burst of wild and frenzied pleasure, and then at last he slid down beside her and pillowed her head on his shoulder.

"Christ!" he muttered softly. "How did I get so lucky?"

She clung to him, trying to sort out her feelings. The memory of Massimo's gentleness passed through her consciousness like a fleeting shadow, but she pushed it away. Jeff was here. To him, she was simply Carol Philby, niece of one of the Kendall family's retainers. Whatever he felt for her, it was because of herself and nothing more.

She knew it was only a matter of days before someone would come to Kendall Hall on the chance that she might be there. But she savored each day that passed, reveling in her newfound freedom and looking toward each evening with breathless eagerness when she could be with Jeff Collier. They swam in the moonlight, went dancing, held hands in movie theatres, walked on the beach, and made love. The hurtful memory of Massimo di Cavelli drifted further and further away. Over and over, Jeff told her that he loved her; when she asked herself if she was in love with him, her thoughts went astray. For the moment, it didn't matter. Whatever it was she felt, it was enough. If suddenly like a thunderbolt, some morning when she awoke in the sunny yellow and white bedroom, it came to her and she knew she was in love, somehow she would convince her parents that Jeff Collier was the man who was right for her. Until then, she only wanted to feel what she was feeling, the intoxicating excitement of knowing that she was wanted for herself. Only herself. Because she was pretty and young and desirable.

"I wish I could figure you out," he said one evening when they were sitting in the malt shop near the movie theatre.

"That's easy," she said, tossing her hair back and laughing. "There's nothing to try to figure out. I'm just me."

"No," he said slowly, shaking his head back and forth. He was twisting the straw in his glass and watching her intently. She looked away after a moment, trying to avoid the penetrating stare. "I don't know what it is. But you're . . . different."

"That's ridiculous," she said with a short laugh. She looked around at the noisy, bright shop. A long line of young people stood near the counter, waiting to be served. At the rear six or seven boys were clambering about the booth where they were sitting. The owner, an older man in a peaked white soda jerk's hat, shouted at them, "Hey, pipe down or get out of here." She watched them snigger and poke each other. They had duck tails and wore baggy pegged pants, and made faces when the owner turned his back, but she noticed they quieted down.

"No, that's why I think I—well, that I wanted to take you out. You're different from any other girls I've known."

"Different?" she asked carefully. "How?"

"I don't know. Your voice—it has a quiet sound to it. And you—well, you dress differently and say things that most girls don't say. I suppose it's because you go to college. I mean, I never went out with anyone who went to a college like Vassar before." He was staring at her still and asked curiously, "Don't you feel kind of funny? You know, strange? There on a scholarship, when most of the girls come from families with a lot of dough?"

"No," she said quietly, forcing herself to look straight into his eyes. "No, I don't. Most of the friends I've made are marvelous. They treat me no differently from the way they treat everyone else." She thought of Florence Meighan, the sophomore in her dorm from Providence, going through Vassar on a full scholarship, how popular she was, a close friend of hers and Brenda's. "It's not important, you see. How much money one has, I mean."

"That's what you think," he said with an abrupt laugh. The group of boisterous boys shambled past, laughing and whistling as they saw Caroline. He reached out and grasped the wrist of one, and said, "Watch it, man!" His jaw was tense and his eyes turned to blue steel.

344

"Aw, I was just kidding," the boy said, pulling loose and running after his friends as they piled out through the door.

"They didn't mean anything," she said, touching his hand. But he pulled his arm away, as though he resented the gesture.

"I don't like anyone edging in on my territory. Even some stupid kid."

She watched him, puzzled, as he walked to the counter to pay for their malts. But when he turned, he was smiling. She rose when he reached out and pulled her to her feet. "Let's drive out to State Park," he said, huskily, put his arm around her waist, and drew her toward the door. And as they walked out into the hot night, she felt the familiar tingling at the base of her spine, shivering upward, then shattering like a skyrocket when his hand brushed her breast. It lingered there for a moment when he helped her into the car, and she smiled softly as he walked around and slid beneath the wheel.

"You're beautiful," he whispered, his hand running teasingly from her knee to her thigh as he turned on the ignition. She half turned to him, her body in immediate response. He was like a fever in her, she thought. She still didn't know how she felt about him. All she knew was that he filled the terrible emptiness when she was with him. And that was enough for now.

She left for New York on the night that Jeff packed his car and drove to Boston. His goodbye, earlier that evening, came without warning. She had thought he would be in Newport at least another week, and when he kissed her and said he was going, he seemed to have left her already.

"My address," he had said, handing her a small piece of paper. "If you happen to get to Boston, give me a ring." She stared at him in the darkness, then climbed out of the car and watched the taillight disappear down the long winding driveway on the Drexel estate. She had seen Mark Rumsey's car parked a discreet distance beyond the main entrance to Kendall Hall. She walked out to the road slowly, dreamlike, as though in a trance. When she leaned down and looked in the window of his car, she said, "Would you take me to New York, Mark?" If he was surprised to see her outside the Kendall compound, he didn't show it, but simply told her that as soon as she was packed they would leave. Half an hour later, she left the cottage with her suitcase and climbed into the sedan.

"How long have they known I was here, Mark?" she asked as he drove the car onto the ferry that crossed to Jamestown.

"Long enough." He grinned at her through the half-darkness. "But they wanted you to work out whatever it was that was bothering you."

She nodded and looked out the open window just as the ferry churned away from the dock and plowed across the dark waters, the sea spray caressing her face.

22

Autumn came swiftly that October, with the trees a flaming gold and red before the month was a week old. A crisp wine-like fragrance mixed with the faintly acrid aroma of burning leaves hanging over the campus. But the golden light and the exuberant laughter of the hundreds of students ringing across the green were lost to Caroline.

Gail had come from New York for the weekend at the end of the month. They were curled up in the cushioned windowseat of Caroline's sitting room, watching from the open casement windows as students hurried by below, their voices a cheerful babble in the waning light. They had been silent for several moments, as smoke spiraled lazily upward from Gail's cigarette.

"You shouldn't smoke," Caroline said.

"You, too?" Gail asked, smiling. "Everybody picks on me."

"Well, dammit, Gail, *singers* shouldn't smoke."

"Okay, singers shouldn't smoke. I'll quit next week."

"You always say that."

"I mean it this time. Next week for sure."

But Caroline simply smiled and shook her head while watching four brightly dressed students walk out of the dormitory door below and head noisily toward the dining hall. "Really, Gail—"

"Because next week I start rehearsals for a show." Her voice rippled with excitement.

Caroline turned and looked at her, her mouth open in surprise. "A show?"

"The second lead in *Girls of Spring*. Peter Weymouth's new musical."

Caroline grabbed her and hugged her. "Oh, Gail, how wonderful!" Then she sat back and looked at her. "But you just got back from Switzerland. How did everything happen so fast?"

"I don't know. Jack Gordon called me almost the moment after I stepped in the door and told me to get myself down to the Shubert Theatre for a casting call. When I got there, they took me off to a separate room—Weymouth and the director, a man named Felix Goldmeier. They had a pianist there and asked me to sing something, right off the top of my head. Good God, it was awful. But they seemed to think I was the new Mary Martin, the way they treated me. And they told me they were giving me the second lead and . . ." Her voice trailed off. After a moment, she looked at Caroline, the blue eyes disturbed. "It's Patrick Belden behind all this." She was shaking her head in a helpless kind of way.

"Richard's father?" Caroline asked warily. She watched Gail for a moment. "What really happened between you?" There was a pause. "Can you talk about it yet?"

Gail stared out the window. "There've been so many times I've wanted to tell you." She turned tear-filled eyes to Caroline. "Everything." She began then, her voice in tight control, all of it from beginning to end. When she finished, Caroline, in a shocked, angry voice, said, "Patrick Belden is the kind of man whose children probably have to make an appointment to see him."

"You must never tell anyone. Only Mama and Georges know what really happened."

"This is crazy," Caroline raged. "You've got to tell Richard." But Gail cried out, "No!" and shook her head hard. "Gail . . . !" Caroline started.

"Mr. Belden owns half of Philadelphia. He buys and sells people the way he buys and sells ships and trucking lines. He sold me and bought a San Francisco socialite for Richard, someone *who will be good for Richard's political career.*"

Caroline squeezed Gail's hand hard. "I'm sorry," she whispered.

Gail laughed bitterly. "Well, at least Mr. Belden kept his promise to me. He said he would see to it my career opened up. I just found out he got Jack Gordon for me as my agent, without Jack knowing what was behind it all, thank God. At least he accepted me as a client on what he considers talent."

"But you have the baby. You're happy about that, aren't you?"

Gail turned shining eyes to her. "Wait until you see him. He's the most beautiful child you ever saw." She peered at Caroline closely. "What is it, Caro?"

When Caroline shook her head and tried to look away, Gail put her finger under her chin and turned her face toward her again. "Tell me. Ever since I got here this morning, I've known something was bothering you." There was a long silence, while Caroline's dark lashes shadowed her cheeks, then she looked up, her face stricken.

"I'm pregnant, Gail," she said in a strangled voice.

Gail's mouth fell open, dumbly. "Pregnant?" She stared at her. *"You?"* Shaking her head back and forth, she tried to find words and failed. Finally she said, "Who? I mean, who is the father?" Suddenly she lunged forward on her knees. "Brenda told me something yesterday, when I called on the phone to say I was coming up. She's been trying to understand why you suddenly ran away, left Venice. She said there was a man there, someone you were—"

"No," Caroline said sharply. "No, that's not it. He has nothing to do with this." She was silent for a moment, fighting for control. "It's —it's someone else, someone I met when I got to Newport."

"Does he know?" Gail finally asked.

Caroline slowly shook her head. "No—not yet. He's at school in Boston. I—I'm going up there this next weekend to tell him."

Suddenly Gail clasped both of her hands. "It's going to be all right, honey. I'm sure of that. When you tell this man, he'll probably go crazy with happiness. Who is he? Not one of those stuffed shirts from the Casino, I hope." When Caroline slowly shook her head, her gaze frozen unseeingly on some far point down on the campus, Gail said, "Well, if it's Johnny Campion, wonderful! He's a very decent sort and your parents like him. Or Russ MacKim, the one you played so much tennis with summer before last."

"It's none of them, Gail," Caroline said, looking at her, the violet eyes dark with unhappiness. "His father is one of the gardeners on the Drexel estate, next door." There was a long silence.

"Good God!" Gail breathed. "What a hell of a mess."

Caroline started up fiercely. She was standing, with one knee still on the cushion. "If we're married, they'll have to accept it. They'll have no choice."

"Of course, darling," Gail said. "It might take time, but . . ."

"And they'll grow to like him."

"I'm sure they will." She grabbed up her purse. "Let's go and get some dinner." She walked to the door and turned around. "Come on,

Caro," she said softly. "Everything is going to be all right." But she saw something that she suspected was doubt in Caroline's eyes. "He knows who you are, doesn't he?"

Caroline stared at her, then slowly shook her head. "I told him Nanny Grace was my aunt. He thinks my name is—Carol Philby."

"You'll have to get an abortion."

Caroline was sitting on a lumpy couch with cushions thrown against the wall. There were worn spots in the cover and a spring right under her right thigh was jabbing into her. She looked at the crooked picture of the Acropolis on the opposite wall. The glass was cracked and one corner of the frame was broken. He had mumbled an introduction to his roommate, then asked him to leave them alone for a little while, and Caroline had listened to the tall redhead clatter out of the room and down the dorm stairway. When she looked back to Jeff, she felt as though he were a stranger. He seemed remote and nervous, and kept pacing up and down the cluttered room. When she told him she was pregnant, he had stared at her for a full minute, then turned and slammed his fist against the wall.

"... It's the only way," she heard him saying. She pushed her hands into her coat pockets to keep him from seeing them tremble, then walked toward the door, where she had stopped when she first entered. He had not asked her to sit down or to come further into the room, but she had sat down anyway.

"Only way?" she murmured.

"To get an abortion. *Christ,* Carol. I don't even have any money I can spare."

He leaned against the scarred desk, then slid back and pulled his legs up, hunching his knees and leaning on them. A goose-neck lamp on the desk was the only light in the room, and rain slashed down the single window. He suddenly jumped off the desk and ran from the room, calling out behind him, "Wait here a minute." When he came back, he had a slip of paper in his hand that he gave to her.

"This guy is supposed to be good. Not one of those butchers in a back alley. He's a regular doctor and he does this on the side to make some extra money." Caroline was staring at him, shock on her face. "Well, he's not exactly a doctor yet. He's a med student. But he'll do a good job for—"

She turned and ran from the room, down the three flights to the dingy vestibule, where she stopped, gasping for breath, sobbing and turning her face to the scarred, grimy wall.

She waited there for several minutes until she had become calmer, then looked up the stairwell and listened. She hadn't really expected him to follow her, but a thread of hope had gone down the stairs with her. She finally turned, pulled the heavy door open, and walked the half block to where Mark Rumsey was parked with the car where she had convinced him to stay, insisting she would be all right.

She opened the door and climbed in beside him. "Could you drive me right back to school, Mark?" she said in a strange voice. "My friend wasn't there and I don't want to wait."

Caroline had made her plans carefully. She had called the medical student by telephone from school and asked him if she could come to the apartment he shared with two other students some evening late. They settled on Tuesday of the following week at nine o'clock in the evening.

She and Mark arrived at the Copley Plaza late in the afternoon. "I'm meeting some friends I went to school with at Brearley," she had told him, when proposing the Boston trip several days earlier. "They go to Radcliffe and Boston U. now." After checking into the hotel, Mark right across the corridor from her suite, she insisted she was tired and would order dinner from room service. He could do whatever he wanted with his evening, she insisted, "because I'm going to bed," she said.

She listened at the door of her suite, heard him leave at about seven-thirty, and knew he would be going to dinner and then probably a movie. Shortly after eight, she hurried down to the lobby and out to St. James Avenue, where she climbed into a taxi and gave the driver the medical student's address. She huddled back in the dark corner of the cab, shivering with both despair and fear. It was raining and she had worn a raincoat with a hood, which she pulled closely about her face. With sinking heart, she watched the reflection of lights on the wet pavements as the taxi sped toward Cambridge.

When the driver slowed along a narrow street and stopped in front of an old, shabby-looking building, she paid him and climbed out, then looked at the row of small apartment houses, typical of the kind that students lived in off campus. She found the name on the discolored and tarnished brass mailbox and bell in the tiny vestibule and pushed the bell. When a buzzer rang, she pushed open the lower door, walked to the darkened stairwell, and looked upward fearfully.

Closing her eyes for a moment, she held her breath and clenched her hands in the pockets of her raincoat. "Please . . ." she whispered. "Please let it be over with quickly."

"Someone down there?" a young male voice called out from above.

"Yes," she said, her voice faltering. Then clenching her hands harder, she forced her voice to sound calm. "My name is Carol Philby."

"Come on up."

She stood with her arms resting on the stone wall and gazed out to the ocean. The sky and water were a clear crystalline blue, high clouds scudding across the sky, tiny whitecaps whipping up the sea, the wind cold and brisk for early May. She had asked Mark to drive her to Kendall Hall on a sudden whim the afternoon before, with a three-day weekend from school facing her.

Almost six months had passed since she had gone to that dark street in the rain in Cambridge one late-autumn night. But she still felt a deep sense of loss, a terrible kind of mourning. The two medical students had made it as easy for her as they could. Both fiercely believed that abortion should be legalized. Afterward, one of them, a dark-haired young man from Detroit, took her back to the hotel, gave her a small vial of antibiotics, and insisted that if she had any unusual bleeding, she should get herself to a hospital quickly.

She smiled sadly, remembering how kind they had been to her.

"Ready to go to lunch?" She turned and saw Mark far across the green lawn, next to her father's Lagonda, which he kept at Kendall Hall and laughingly asked Mark and the Kendall drivers "to exercise for me." She and Mark chatted aimlessly as they drove through the cold sunshine and deserted streets to the wharf area of Newport to eat at a new seafood restaurant she had heard about.

After a leisurely lunch, they left the restaurant and were at the car parked in front when a voice stopped her. Holding herself rigidly, she looked up the street.

"Carol! Hey, Carol!" he was calling.

She saw the puzzled expression on Mark's face as Jeff Collier came loping toward them. Mark had opened the door to the Logonda and Caroline had just been about to step in. Suddenly pretending she hadn't noticed Jeff and quickly slipping her dark glasses on, she turned away, but his voice stopped her again.

"Hey, Carol! Carol Philby!"

Mark stepped protectively in front of her, his right hand going toward the holster she knew was inside his jacket. She saw Jeff stop a few feet away and stare at her clothes—the beige suede coat with the dark sable lining and collar—then at the Lagonda. She saw the confusion in his face.

"Look, fella . . ." Mark started to say, edging toward him menacingly, when Caroline turned around and spoke.

"Hello, Jeff," she said, her voice expressionless.

He laughed sharply, the uncertainty gone, but there was still confusion on his face. "Hey, I was pretty sure it was you, but—"

"But the name isn't Philby." She was aware that Mark was watching her with slight puzzlement. "It's Kendall. Caroline Kendall."

Jeff stepped back one or two steps, as though he had been slapped. She watched the change of expressions on his face, from confusion, to sudden awareness of what the name Caroline Kendall meant, to shock.

"Kendall? You're Caroline Kendall." He was laughing and shaking his head, the laugh one of utter bewilderment, but threaded with a new interest. "Hey, that's something. I mean, what a surprise." He looked around at Mark. "Carol—I mean Caroline—and I became good friends last summer, and . . ." He was taking a step toward her when she suddenly stepped into the car and Mark barred him from coming any closer.

"But not anymore," she said coldly, then looked away when Mark slammed the door and walked around to the other side.

As they drove away, Mark, in the rear-view mirror, saw Jeff still standing there, his mouth hanging open and staring after them.

After a block or so and without looking at him, she said, "Questions, Mark?" He heard the tremor in her voice, sensed the anguish.

"Not a one." He paused for a moment, then reached out and squeezed her hand reassuringly. "Whatever it was"—he chuckled—"he looked like he had it coming to him."

23
1960

As the last roar of applause began to die down, Gail hurried from the stage. The crowded backstage was first caught in that mysterious glow of lights filtering from the stage, then blazing with work lights that flashed on when the final curtain call was taken.

"Great performance, better than usual," Ray Petrie, the stage manager, called out as she passed.

"Thanks, Ray," she shouted over her shoulder.

"Terrific, honey," Connie Bing, a member of the chorus line, said, squeezing her arm as she ran past. Gail smiled at her. Connie was her favorite of all the cast. They often went out for supper together after the show, sometimes Gail treating at Sardi's or "21," and sometimes Connie treating at a Chinese restaurant or all-night coffee shop. When he was in town, Jack Gordon would more often than not take them both and pay the bill. And Connie always teased Gail the following night or matinee with, "That guy really goes for you, Gail. Why don't you give him a break?"

"Why don't you mind your own business?" Gail always said good-naturedly and they would drop it until the next time. She was trying to get an understudy spot for Connie in the show, insisting to Mark Hancock, the director of *If the Show Fits,* that there was a lot of talent beneath Connie's long strawberry-pink hair, high-kicking legs, and pretty face. But Connie had rebuffed his blunt advances and he was still annoyed with her, although he knew it was only a matter of time before he would have to give in. Gail Halloran had become a big star almost overnight. She had caught the attention of the critics in her first prominent role two years before with a voice that couldn't be ignored.

354

But he would delay as long as he could, his ego still ruffled by Connie Bing's flat "No!"

As Gail approached her dressing room, she noticed that the door was ajar. When she pushed it open and started in, she suddenly stopped. For several minutes they stared at each other.

"Hello, Gail," he said. Her heart plunged wildly.

"What—what are you doing here, Richard?"

She walked a wide circle around him until she reached her dressing table, where she turned and leaned against it. His skin was as deeply bronzed as ever, his hair as carefully cut and groomed. If he had smiled, she knew she would have had to turn away. She tried to find a flaw in the clean, sharp features, in the tall, lean figure. But it was all as wonderful as ever and she dropped her eyes, unable to bear looking at him. She suddenly felt his hands on her shoulders, slowly turning her around. Then his mouth was on hers and they were kissing each other wildly.

"My God, my God, how I've wanted this," he muttered as he kissed her eyes and brow, as he cupped her face in his hands and kissed her mouth again. Tears were running down her cheeks, and he took out a handkerchief to wipe them away. "Why?" he asked "Why, Gail? Why, darling, did you send me away?" But before she could try to find an answer, he held her a little away from him and said, *"He* got to you, didn't he? My father?" She heard the terrible anger in his voice and grasped him hard.

"Don't, Richard," she cried. "What possible good can that do now?"

"I stopped off to see him last night, before coming here to New York on business, a political meeting I had to attend today. He said something—let it slip—and I realized he had been the cause of all this." He pulled her to him again and buried his face in her golden hair. "That's why I had to come and see you tonight. I watched the show and you were glorious. Everything else fades when you're on that stage! And while I watched you, I realized how much we have lost—"

"But you're here now." I don't care, she thought exultantly, I don't care what happens, because we're together again. Exhilaration raced through her, wildly singing, as though lifting her from the ground, as though she were floating. The familiarity of his body against hers was almost more than she could bear. *He's mine,* she thought fiercely. *He was mine before he was hers.* She touched his face and kissed it, and

355

it was as though he had never left. She felt him hard against her, and she whispered, "Let's go home, Richard."

A limousine waited at the stage door, and in the darkness of the rear seat he kissed her. She melted against him. When they finally reached her apartment, they didn't even stop in the living room, but walked, holding each other, into her bedroom. They flung their clothes aside and fell onto the bed.

And then it all settled into place . . . the first searching gentleness, the soft kisses and drifting hands, his mouth on her throat, on her breasts, fingers touching in secret places, exploring as though it were all new. Her hands were finding him, slowly, then insistently pulling him onto her. There was the stretch and feel of his long body and then the sweet joining of flesh and the drowning sensation as his strength pulled at her, drew all life out of her and sent it soaring back inside until she cried out and thrust against him, hearing sighs and sighs and murmurs, hers blending with his. When she sank back onto the bed, he spread across her, his face buried in her neck.

"We lost the baby," he said sadly, "but thank God we found each other again."

She heard the sorrow in his words, *We lost the baby.* Then he didn't know. His father hadn't told him—not that much. She put her hands on either side of his face and tried to see his eyes in the darkness. "I didn't have the abortion, Richard," she whispered. "His name is Richard and he's the image of you."

She felt his arms tighten about her and heard the almost inaudible gasp. For a moment he buried his face against her throat and she felt tears on her skin. "When can I see him?" he asked.

"He's in Switzerland with my mother. Whenever you can go there."

If the Show Fits went out on tour in mid-August, but with a replacement for Gail, who had two weeks before rehearsals started on her new show, *The Girl From Tulsa.*

"Come to Basel with me, Caro," she begged, over and over, until Caroline finally agreed. Caroline was going to graduate school that autumn of 1960, and had decided on Columbia and living at home. "To study journalism," she had told her father. "I want to do something useful with my life. And I want to stop being followed. Please, Daddy," she begged. "Call off the bodyguards."

Lawrence had finally seemed to agree, although Mark Rumsey's replacement, Pete McGonigle, who was young enough looking to be able to pass as a student, had already been hired to roam the Columbia campus, following her at a long distance, unknown to her, then to trail her little sports car until she reached home, where all other excursions, by agreement with her father, were to be taken with Kendall drivers or Mark at the wheel of one or the other of the family cars.

Caroline and Gail flew to Zurich on TransGlobal; one of the male flight attendants was a new bodyguard who had just been hired. "Three new threats last month, as you know," Henry Winters had told Lawrence, "so, much as she wants it, I don't think we can let her go off completely on her own. He speaks a good French and German, both, so he'll be the driver for the car we've ordered for them in Zurich." Lawrence had nodded his satisfaction with the plan, well aware that the older she grew, the greater the risks, for she was beginning to slip away from them, avoiding the bodyguards whenever she possibly could.

When they landed in Zurich and got through Customs, there was a brief delay while they waited for the car and driver that had been hired. A TransGlobal official waited with them and, with great relief, handed them into the car when it arrived and the driver identified himself.

"What's your name?" Gail said, leaning foreward so the young man could hear her.

"Rolf," he said with a slight accent, turning his head and smiling broadly. He was young and blond and apparently European. But Caroline had detected something about him. Something oddly American. As the car sped away from the airport, she sat on the edge of the seat and tapped his shoulder.

"Just so we keep everything straight," she said, and he heard the amusement in her voice. "Were you hired by a man named Henry Winters back in New York?" They saw his neck tense and exchanged smiles. "It's all right." She patted his shoulder and sat back in the seat. "I promise not to tell Henry we guessed, and we'll try not to give you a hard time. Or too much of a chase."

"Thanks, Miss Kendall," he said, looking over his shoulder with a relieved smile.

Caroline was true to her word to Rolf. She spent most of the first week simply roaming about the grounds of the school and the tiny village of Grenzenwald on whose edge the school nestled. The moment of their arrival had been the hardest for her. She had been certain that seeing Gail's little boy would be a difficult and painful experience, but she had not been prepared for how easy the child made it for her, himself. He was a serious-eyed, handsome little boy of two who lovingly put his arms about her neck and kissed her as though he had known her all along, and for the next few days he went everywhere with her and Gail, clinging to their hands, skipping along between them.

As the school year had not started yet, Ellie and Georges left in their little car after several days for a long weekend in Lyon, where Georges' sister lived.

"I was so happy to be able to spend these few days with you, Caroline," Ellie said, hugging her again as Georges cheerfully tooted the horn for her. They were standing in front of the headmaster's house, a pretty, rather formal structure of chalet roof and clinging ivy over weathered stone, with a terrace on three sides and long French doors opening to the terrace from each room. It sat on a green where all of the buildings of the school faced—the chalet-style dormitories and classroom building, and a number of other picturesque houses where some of the teaching staff lived.

"Well, for heaven's sake, she'll still be here when you get back," Gail said, laughing.

But as Ellie hugged Caroline again, she knew better. She had seen an urgency, a restlessness in Caroline's eyes, an expression she knew well and remembered from her childhood. "Of course," she said, waving her hand to Georges, as he tooted the horn again, that she would be right with him. "It's just that it's been so long since I last saw her."

"How wonderful you look, Ellie," Caroline said, standing back a little to admire the trim figure in a pale blue suit, the hair as light golden as ever, but curling slightly about her face in a smart new fashion. She had always had a fairytale look about her, with her perfect features and dainty bone structure. "Oh, Ellie, you're as pretty as ever," Caroline said as she hugged her, then pushed her along the walk toward the car. She laughed. "But now you look like the fairy godmother."

They drove away in a flurry of goodbyes, Dickie waving as hard as Gail and Caroline and calling out to Ellie and Georges in his piping little voice, echoing Caroline and Gail. "Have a good time, Grand-mère and Grandpère."

He was still standing at the edge of the road as the car drove off and disappeared through the distant gates.

"Come along, Dickie!" Gail called to him as she and Caroline, arm in arm, started toward the car where Rolf stood waiting. "We're going to Basel for the morning."

They drove to the Münsterplatz and wandered through its cobbled streets and across the great square to the fourteenth-century Münster Cathedral, then stood high above the Rhine and watched the boats glide gracefully beneath the bridges.

They turned back and bought Dickie ice cream from a man in the square who had a trick dog, and then sat in an outside café drinking coffee, while Dickie's ice cream melted and trickled down his chin. On the drive back to Bellone, Dickie slept with his head in Caroline's lap. Caroline and Gail both started forward a little when they entered the gates and saw a long Mercedes limousine parked in the gravel driveway in front of the headmaster's house.

"Good lord," Gail said, "somebody's brought their kid a week early."

She hurried in the direction of the house, while Caroline lifted the sleeping child from the car. Just as Gail reached the terrace steps, Caroline saw a tall man come through the doorway, and watched as Gail and he suddenly embraced. She saw his gaze wander to her, as she approached, holding the child, and heard him say to Gail, "I only have twenty-four hours. I came with a group from Congress visiting NATO installations in Europe."

Gail had tears in her eyes, but her face was wreathed in smiles. "How are you, Caroline?" Richard murmured as he bent and kissed her on the cheek. Nodding and smiling at him, she let him take Dickie from her arms and watched as he gently held him, careful not to wake him. She had read in the newspapers not long ago that he and his wife had had twin daughters. She circled him quietly, and walked to Gail, who stood in the path, tears sliding down her face. She grasped her hand and squeezed it hard as she passed on the way into the house. Once in her room, she began packing her suitcases. Gail found her there an hour later.

"Where are you going?" she asked, her voice and face still filled with the wonderment of Richard's arrival.

"Back to New York," Caroline said, folding a skirt and placing it in a suitcase. She turned and took hold of Gail's shoulders. "You and Richard need this time alone, before Ellie and Georges get back."

But Gail had only half heard her. She was standing with her back against the closed door of the bedroom, a lovely cool room with overhanging eaves and a balcony beyond the French doors. "I can't handle it any other way, Caro," she said, defensively. "I love him too much."

"Darling," Caroline said softly. "I just don't want you to be hurt."

"I'll take that chance."

Caroline placed the last garment into the suitcase. "I'm glad he came here, Gail, glad that he knows about Dickie." She snapped the suitcase shut, the clicking sound breaking Gail's reverie.

"Don't leave, Caroline," she said, following her to the door where Caroline had placed her other bag. Caroline turned and put her arms around her for a moment, then pulled away.

"I have to go, Gail. Oh, it isn't only because of Richard's arrival. But being here, coming with you because I just seemed to be drifting in my life, made me realize I have to start working toward something. I have to find a goal to reach for."

"But you're going to graduate school—"

"I've simply been using it as an excuse for existence and that isn't good enough, Gail. Look at you." She began pulling on the gray silk jacket to her suit, the lilac blouse beneath making her eyes brim with color. "Already an established Broadway star—"

"With Patrick Belden's help," she said bitterly. She was leaning against the wall, her hands behind her like a small child, the linen dress a dazzling sheath of white against the rosy tan of her skin. The pale golden hair fell in soft waves around her face, the features as delicate and pretty as Ellie's.

Caroline grasped her shoulders. "Don't ever say that again. You got where you are because you're brilliantly talented and damned good-looking besides."

"Oh, Caro, no wonder I love you," Gail said, hugging her. Then she pushed her away. "So, what is it? Columbia?"

Caroline nodded. "And really working at it." She smiled, a sad kind of smile. "Is it wrong of me to sometimes hate who I am, to wish I could be someone else? Ever since I was a little girl, I've been so aware of who the Kendalls are, and I began to wonder about who and what lay outside those gates at Kendall Hills or beyond the windows of the house in New York. When we were at Newport, I used to watch you leaving with your mother when she took you to Fall River sometimes to visit relatives. I remember Mummy would let me ride in the car with you to where you got on a bus in the center of town. It was so exciting, watching all the people climb on the bus—and then you'd wave to me from inside, after you'd sat down. I used to dream that you and Ellie took me with you. And when we were at Kendall Hills and were being driven to school through Rijksville, I thought how wonderful it would be if we could go to the schools those children were going to, if we could stand at corners and wait for school buses, or just run across streets the way they did, shouting at each other, riding bicycles. And in New York, I used to stand at my bedroom window and watch people walking up and down Fifth Avenue. Just walking. All by themselves, with no one following them."

Gail smiled and said, "And all the time, those children on the streets of Rijksville were probably looking up to see a long Rolls Royce glide by. One little girl probably turned to her friend and said, 'I wish I could be that little girl in the big car that drives in through those black iron gates and disappears up through the trees to the top of the hill where there's a big mansion . . .' " Her voice drifted off, and they smiled at each other, then in silence held each other close for a moment.

"Kiss Dickie goodbye for me," Caroline said, and Gail nodded, unable to speak.

Gail and Richard stood on the steps of the terrace, waving, as Caroline and Rolf started to drive away. Then the car turned through the gates and roared off in the direction of Zurich.

Richard didn't tell her his news until he was almost ready to leave the next day. His bags packed, he stood with her in the big corner bedroom, the tangy fragrance of geraniums from the window boxes on the balcony drifting in through the wide French doors.

"I've been asked by Harvey Everett to be his running mate for Vice President in the coming election," he said, as he held her by the shoulders.

She suddenly looked like a child, bewildered, torn between surprise and fear of loss. She had wound her hair into a big golden topknot on top of her head, with strands that had escaped drifting about her face, the effect changing her Dresden doll beauty into that of a gamine. She tried to smile, but when she spoke, her voice faltered. "Congratulations, darling."

There was a long pause as they simply looked at each other. "That means it is going to be much more difficult to see you . . ."

Already, she realized, she had begun to assume a new role. She put her arms about his waist and, as he went on talking, leaned her head against his chest. "So, I've taken a house near New York, up in a rather remote area of Westchester." He took a small folded map and key out of his pocket, and handed them to her. "I'll let you know, from time to time, when I can be there."

"I'll be there, too," she said, standing on her tiptoes and kissing him. Again she tried to smile.

Holding her around the waist, he turned then and walked her to the door. "It isn't going to be easy," he said. "Nothing is going to be easy from now on."

"I know," she said, not trusting her voice.

Suddenly, he pulled her arm from around him and, turning her to face him, held on to her wrists, held them so hard that she twisted them to try to break away and said, "Richard, you're hurting me."

"I'm sorry," he said, "but I have to make you understand." Since his arrival he had looked relaxed and happy. He had lounged about in white duck trousers and polo shirts and sneakers; they had played tennis, gone swimming, and with Dickie walked through the hills surrounding Bellone or wandered through the winding streets of Grenzenwald. But now he stood before her with a grim expression on his handsome face, the dark gray suit suggesting Washington rather than a small village in Switzerland. "I *can't* divorce her."

"I never asked—"

"It would mean the end of everything now, if I did."

"I just want us to be together whenever we can, darling."

"She may even know there's someone else, but she doesn't care, as long as we go on as things are."

"I'm not asking for anything more," Gail suddenly cried, as she grasped the lapels of his jacket and tugged at them. Suddenly he put his arms about her, and in the long shafts of sunlight from the afternoon sun falling through the French doors, he held her, swaying gently, back and forth, back and forth. "Gail, I love you," he whispered. "I'll always love you. Don't ever believe anything else. No matter what happens, darling, you must always believe that."

And at last they left the room, both silent, arms about each other. They walked downstairs, through the cool, high-ceilinged house, and out to the terrace where the limousine waited.

He kissed her, a long kiss, looked up to the bedroom windows where his son was napping, then climbed into the car and drove away.

BOOK
V

24
1962

Caroline's job at the *Madison Hill Bulletin* meant long hours and being on call twenty-four hours a day, seven days a week. Lawrence Kendall, once he finally agreed to let her try working as a reporter, had insisted that starting on a small newspaper would give her the best experience. It was near Detroit, he told her, very small, a good place to learn.

"They'll put me on the women's page," she had wailed. "Writing articles about club meetings, church bazaars, and fashion shows." But he had been insistent and she had sighed, then giggled. "I never knew there were such tiny papers. Only four reporters?"

"Counting the city editor," he said with a grin. "He covers the police beat, writes the obituaries, and sets type for the front page."

She started using the name Carol Kramer, and was surprised at how little emotion she felt about becoming "Carol" again. Jeff Collier's face and the sound of his words had faded into a distance she found beyond conscious reach. It was only at odd moments when she heard a man's voice with the cultured accents of the Continent—or saw a tall man swinging gracefully down a street, his dark, burnished head tipped to one side—that she thought about Massimo, with a feeling of pain that was almost as new and fresh as ever.

But he was far from her thoughts the morning she reported for work at the *Madison Hill Bulletin.* With her heart feeling as though it were in her throat, she stood in front of the one-story building and stared up at the sign. She finally walked inside and crossed to Phil Rowan, the city editor. "Mr. Rowan? My name is Carol Kramer. I was told you'd be expecting me here this morning." He sat behind the desk, a gnomelike little man with beetling reddish eyebrows and an intelligent high brow, which at the moment was frowning. Squinting, he studied her from head to toe.

"You're too pretty to be a reporter," he said in a nasal voice. "My experience in the past with women reporters has been that they'd never win any beauty contests. Never even come close. I'm talking about the good ones." He picked up a chipped white mug and sipped at the coffee.

"I'm a good reporter, Mr. Rowan," she said quickly, sounding more confident than she felt. She sat down quickly when he motioned her into a battered chair.

"And I don't like being told I have to hire someone."

"I'm sorry, but—"

"This was one of the best little independent newspapers in this state when Kendall came along and swallowed us up five years ago. Until then I could hire anybody I pleased. Now—"

"Mr. Rowan, I'll work very hard, and I'll do the very best I possibly can," she said all in a rush. "I don't like this way of being hired any better than you do."

"Then why'd you use whoever you used to get yourself this job?"

"Because—well, because it was the only way I could get one," she said miserably.

He stared at her for a moment, then burst into laughter. "Well, I'll be damned. Not only pretty, but straight-out honest as well."

Through the pall of smoke pouring from the windows of the building, she saw figures running around in black slickers and the scooped helmets of firemen. She left the car in a spot across the street where one of Madison Hill's four policemen had indicated as he directed the traffic, then grabbed her notebook and her camera. She could hear the growing wail of sirens as fire trucks from nearby Oak Grove approached. She leaped from the car and stepped up onto the hood.

Through the uproar she heard someone calling, "Carol! Carol Kramer!" She looked down from the roof of her car, where she had scrambled to get a better angle for her camera shots. She was down on one knee with the camera up at her eye, snapping it fast as the firemen pushed one wheelchair after another out from the black pall and choking clouds of smoke that rolled upward from the nursing home.

"Just a minute!" she shouted as she kept clicking away, rolling the film faster and faster as screaming from the swelling crowd behind the barriers drowned out her voice. She looked away from the camera long enough to see the teenager with his big red earmuffs and freckled face running toward her car.

"Oh, good, Billy!" she called out, her voice hoarse from shouting against the roar of the crowd, the sirens, and the general pandemonium that had seized Payhune Street, where the Payhune Nursing Home was located. "I need some more film. Get it, will you? In the glove compartment of my car."

Billy worked at the *Madison Hill Bulletin* afternoons after school, helping out in the composing room and doing other odd jobs, sometimes even writing a story when the other three reporters were all busy on other assignments.

Billy handed the film up to her and watched her as she put it into the camera, fingers now grown skillful after six months of work in Madison Hill. He liked Carol Kramer. She treated him like a grownup and encouraged him with his writing. And she was different from most women he knew. Look at her now, he thought, her face grimy from the drifting smoke, blue jeans tucked into high boots, the big heavy jacket slung back, her bare hands on the camera red from the bitter cold.

"What do you want me to do, Carol?" he shouted.

"Start getting the names of survivors," she said without looking up from her task. "The Red Cross from Flint has set up over there on Mrs. Haskins's front porch. They're screening the people there." She had the camera up to one eye again and was aiming it at a stretcher that was being rushed toward one of the ambulances. As she looked up for a moment, she saw Billy running in the direction of the Haskins' front porch, hopping over the coils of hose from the fire engines, splashing through the puddles and slush.

Six months ago, she couldn't have done this, she thought. She'd almost fainted the first time Phil Rowan sent her out on an assignment to cover an accident at the railroad crossing where a train had hit a bus. At the sight of her first dead person, and one who had been horribly maimed in the accident, she had thought she would faint and had run behind some bushes, where she had vomited violently. But when she saw Bert Masters, the reporter who the city editor always gave the plum assignments to, laughing grimly at her when she came out from behind the bushes, she had gritted her teeth and forced herself to watch and take pictures for Bert, even though waves of dizziness kept sweeping over her and tears were running down her cheeks.

"Look, kid," the veteran gray-haired reporter had said, when they were finally driving in his beat-up old Buick back to the newspaper on Main Street, "you were okay. Not bad for your first assignment like that. I'll let you write the sidebar, if you'd like."

She smiled widely, wanting to hug him. But she held back her excitement and, almost primly, said, "Thank you very much, Mr. Masters." The mixture of horror and happiness was a combination she soon became accustomed to, horror from the accident she had seen with bodies of the dead and wounded laid out on the ground near the railroad tracks, and happiness at the feeling of accomplishment and the excitement of writing a story on deadline, then seeing the prints of her camera shots hanging up to dry and finally making their way onto the front page of the *Madison Hill Bulletin.*

"Why do you stay in Madison Hill, Mr. Masters?" Caroline had asked him that evening when the press in the back part of the building was finally quiet, just she and Masters and the city editor still there, drinking coffee and waiting for the latest casualty figures that they would use in the second-day story the following afternoon.

"The name is Bert, Carol, and I stay"—he scowled at Phil Rowan, who was grinning at him—"because I like a small newspaper and I like being a big frog in a little puddle. And what about you? What are you doing here?" The dark brown eyes were piercingly relentless as he peered at her over the rim of his cup.

"Well—experience. My journalism professor said the smaller newspapers are the best place to get good experience."

She remembered how she had begged her father to let her start out working on the Kendall paper in Boston or one of the other larger cities where they had newspapers. But, when he had finally relented about her working on *any* newspaper, he had told Warren Leland to find her a spot on one of the smaller ones.

"Does it have to be the smallest?" she had wailed, when Warren phoned several days later and named the *Madison Hill Bulletin.*

Actually, she was glad it had happened the way it did. Like each of the three reporters on the staff, she had been taught how to use a professional camera and often took her own pictures for her stories when not working as photographer for either Bert or Willy Comstock. And her writing was improving every day. Both Phil Rowan and Bert had told her so. In addition, she got a chance to write everything—obituaries, features, news stories, whatever she wanted.

"Your journalism professor knew what he was talking about," Bert was saying, pulling her back from her reverie. She saw that he and Phil

368

were grinning. " 'Course, my journalism professor said to me, 'Masters, most of my students are now working for the *New York Times* or the *Washington Post.*' "

Their grins had widened and she smiled sheepishly. She remembered that Bert Masters had said he started right out of high school working for Phil Rowan's father on the *Bulletin.*

"That's okay, kid," Bert said, reaching out with the battered coffee pot and pouring her more coffee. She smiled. "Even if you did go to journalism school, you're pretty good." She had gotten so she liked the camaraderie, even the occasional teasing. She knew they were still curious about her, but they had stopped asking questions since those first few days, when she simply told them that her name was Carol Kramer and she had come from New York, where she'd been studying at Columbia University.

With Gail helping her, she had gone to Macy's and some of the other department stores to buy some clothes off the racks so that she could avoid bringing anything from her own wardrobe. She had rented a small apartment in a house, on the second floor, and for the first time in her life her father had let her go off without a bodyguard. At least, that's what she thought. Unknown to her, a new taxi driver in town was there to keep as close an eye on her as was possible, under the circumstances.

She jumped down from the top of her car, a small blue sedan she had bought shortly after arriving in Madison Hill. She saw Billy running toward her, a sheet of paper in his hand.

"Here it is," he said, panting a little as he handed it to her. They stood then and watched as more wheelchairs were pushed across the street to the Haskins house. Caroline kept shaking her head back and forth. "I don't get sick like those first few times I saw something like this, Billy, but—" She paused as her voice caught a little. "But, seeing people like this . . . some dead, others badly hurt or unconscious, these old people, I . . ." She was shaking her head again. "I don't know, Billy. Maybe I'm not tough enough to be a reporter."

"Tough?" Billy looked at her with admiration. "I don't think you could be a very good reporter, Carol, if you were tough." He smiled a little. "And you're a terrific reporter."

She looked around at him, slowly. There were tears in her eyes that she roughly brushed away with the sleeve of her jacket.

"You mean that?"

He smiled up at her. "Heck, yes."

They watched quietly as two stretchers with sheets covering them were wheeled along the middle of the street in front of them, then were lifted and pushed into the back of an ambulance.

When it had rolled slowly through the crowds and disappeared around the corner, Billy looked at her again.

"I even saw Mr. Masters cry once, the time they pulled the bodies of two kids out of Craymore Pond." He smiled at her tremulously. "Heck, I think you're the best darned reporter on the paper."

Caroline heard the sirens and shuddered. She stood by the library door, where she could see across the vast room with its ceiling-to-floor rows of books and dark carved paneled walls. Firelight and lamps glinted brightly on the rims of brass high above in the coffered ceiling. Her mother was kneeling beside her father, who lay without moving on one of the long sofas. Larry was talking quietly into the telephone, and Avery stood by the windows, looking down the long curving driveway that led to the gates a mile away. She glanced along the gallery that stretched the length of the wing. Jamie and Barbara stood with Brenda and her fiancé, Kip Stevens, while Faye and Honey huddled together whispering beneath one of the tall mullioned windows, their backs to the row of gold-framed family portraits. The first Lawrence Robertson Kendall had been painted with his white side-whiskers and old-fashioned stiffly pointed collar. Next to him was Samuel Kendall, the grandfather she had never known; then came Margaret Reid Kendall, her grandmother; and finally, the portrait of her father as a young man of twenty-two.

From where she stood, she could see the portrait of her mother and father over the fireplace of the library, the tones of her mother's skin like a pale peach in the firelight, her green velvet gown and long strand of pearls casting her in the role of queen—or certainly princess.

When the sirens became louder, she ran along the other end of the gallery to the main reception hall, past the towering Christmas tree, its lights still blazing, in the center of the huge hall. Just half an hour earlier, the entire family had been seated in the large dining room for Christmas dinner. Lawrence had carved the turkey at one end of the table, while Larry hovered over the prime ribs of beef and Yorkshire pudding at the other end. Katherine had arrived with Franco and their pale three-year-old son, Luciano, and two-year-old daughter, Adriana.

The house at Kendall Hills had blazed with light from early Christmas Eve on, and carols played almost incessantly, ringing through the vast house as a soft but persistent reminder that this was surely Christmas. But then, not more than fifteen minutes after they had sat down at the long shining table, just moments after Abbott and Ben had poured the bubbling champagne, Lawrence looked up from his carving knife and fork, his eyes frantically seeking those of Elizabeth, who sat at his side.

"Ohhh," he said, slumping down into his chair, the cutlery clattering down onto the large silver platter, his hand reaching out toward Elizabeth.

"Lawrence," she cried, jumping to her feet. As she grasped and held him, she looked at Caroline, seated halfway down the table. "Call the Rijksville Hospital. And then the gate." As Caroline, her face stricken, darted up from the table and out of the dining room, Elizabeth looked at Larry. "Get the doctor on the phone. Ask him what we should do until they get here." When Larry ran from the room, she knelt beside Lawrence and held him against her, while she said to Abbott and Ben, "Let's get him into the library."

For days, Lawrence's life hung by a fragile thread. Elizabeth and Caroline hardly ever left his side. They spelled each other, one of them always there, the other going back to Kendall Hills for a few hours of sleep and a change of clothing. At first, neither of them noticed that the others—Larry, Avery, and Warren Leland—seemed more concerned with emergency meetings with other officers of the various companies and with lawyers who handled the Trust, the financial behemoth that had been set up as a holding company for the vast corporate ventures, than they were with Lawrence Kendall himself. But as the days passed, Caroline became aware of the situation. She was stopped by Payden, the elderly butler at Kendall Hills, one afternoon.

"Mr. Jamie is in the west wing bar, Miss Caroline, and said to tell you when you came back from the hospital that he wants to see you." She hurried across the reception hall and into the corridor leading to the west wing, where she found Jamie playing with one of the novelty games her father had had brought in when the boys were in prep school. He was leaning over the pinball machine, jamming at the knob with one hand, a highball in the other.

"Jamie?" she said softly from the door.

They walked to a low couch and sat down. Just the lights for the

371

long mahogany bar were turned on, giving the English-type paneled room with its deep leather couches and chairs and dark oak tables a heavy look.

"They're upstairs, you know, in the library with the doors closed, divvying up the spoils. You and Elizabeth have been so preoccupied running back and forth to the hospital, I thought you might not have noticed what's going on."

She put her hand on his. "You've been doing all right yourself, getting to the hospital." She walked to the bar and poured herself a Coke, then sat on a bar stool and faced him. "Yes, I'd begun to notice *something.*" She smiled tiredly. "But, you see, Jamie, he's not going to die."

Jamie smiled his lopsided grin. "I hope you're right, Caro. First the heart, and then a stroke on top of it."

"I talked to Dr. Hopkins this morning, and also that specialist they brought in from Vienna. They feel certain he's not only going to pull through, but that he'll be almost his old self again."

Jamie laughed softly. "That should give Larry's ulcer something to celebrate about."

Caroline stared at him. "Do you really believe that, Jamie?" she asked softly. "That Larry wants . . . ?"

"I really believe that, little sister." He raised his glass. "In fact, I'll drink to it. Larry is a man who wants power and lots of it."

She took another sip of her Coke, then slipped off the bar stool and headed toward the door. "I just came home for a hot bath and a change of clothes. I want to get back by four, because all of the doctors will be in consultation until then and they said they'd tell us how his condition is as of this moment."

"I want to go with you," he said. When she frowned a bit at him, he walked to the bar, reached over and poured his drink into the sink, and lifted her almost-full glass of Coke. "Switching to the Good Stuff right this second." And when he grinned, she smiled, and left him sitting on the bar stool, making a face at the glass in his hand.

Caroline lay back and let the water lull her into a dreamy state, the fragrance of the bath crystals rising in the steamy air. Gail had been at the hospital that morning, and they had had an argument, one of the few they had ever had. It had left Caroline even more exhausted than usual during these hard days. She had been disturbed at how much Gail was smoking, almost chain-smoking, and she had paced nervously up and down the hospital corridor. There were circles under Gail's eyes and she was painfully thin.

"Why do you do this to yourself?" Caroline had asked softly.

"Do?" Gail said sharply. "What am I doing to myself?"

"You know what I'm talking about, Gail," Caroline said, leaning back against the windowsill in the corridor where they were waiting. "Pushing yourself so, from one show to another, rushing to Grenzenwald whenever you can get a few days, waiting endless hours and even days for Richard, just to have him never show up. Oh, Gail, Jack is so in love with you. If you'd just give—"

"Don't you think that all of that is my problem and not yours, Caroline? And don't talk to me about Jack. He's my agent. That's all!" she said hotly, wondering where the sharp words were coming from, but unable to stop them as they tumbled from her mouth. She turned away, seeing the hurt in Caroline's face. Then in a low voice she said, "You don't just fall out of love."

"You know that I'm right, Gail," Caroline persisted, her voice taking on a pleading sound. "Please, darling, start thinking about yourself and what it's doing to you. Do you have any idea what you're fighting against? This isn't just some politician, or even a Congressman or Senator anymore. Good Lord, Gail, he's the *Vice President*. You're not only making yourself miserably unhappy, but you're playing with very dangerous fire. If someone should find out—"

"No one is going to find out," Gail hissed in a low angry voice. "You and my mother are the only ones besides Richard and myself who know." Her voice took on a note of sarcasm. "And I don't think you're going to turn us in. And least not yet."

Caroline looked as though she had been slapped. "You know I would never do anything to hurt you, Gail."

Gail suddenly turned and threw her arms around Caroline, and while Caroline held her, she sobbed out her anguish. "I saw him this last weekend, the first time in four months. The two days were gone before I knew it, and then just as he was leaving, he told me Harvey Everett is already talking about a second term and he would want Richard as his running mate again. I had hoped it would all come to an end with this term, and then maybe, just maybe . . ."

Caroline had wanted to say, *No, Gail, not maybe. Not ever. Never, Gail. It will never happen.* But she said nothing. She simply walked to the elevator with her, holding her hand tightly, sensing the pain Gail was feeling, wanting somehow to reach out and console her, then turning to her at the elevator. "Gail, somehow everything is going to be all right." She leaned over and kissed her cheek, held her for a moment, then whispered, "I'm always just a phone call away, if you need me."

Gail hugged her, then holding onto Caroline's hands, she said in a strange voice, "Thank God for you. I know that at any moment everything could suddenly come to an end with Richard." She smiled with a tinge of bitterness. "That's what happens with affairs, you know."

"Don't, Gail!"

The elevator door opened, and with a forced but brilliant smile, Gail had stepped into it. "Don't worry, darling, I'm okay. Really I am." As the elevator door closed, Caroline had seen a brief wave of Gail's hand.

When Caroline finally stirred from the bath, stepped out, and toweled herself, she felt through her whole body how tired she was. Quickly slipping into panties and a bra, she combed her hair, ran a lipstick over her mouth, and lightly touched her eyelids with shadow.

She pulled on her stockings, smoothed them over her long, slim legs, then walked into her dressing room and took down a gold and brown tweed skirt and a pale yellow sweater. She slipped them on, pushed her feet into plain, brown high-heeled pumps and went into her bedroom, where she sat down at the dressing table and stared at herself in the mirror.

When she had called Phil Rowan the night before and told him he had better not hold her job for her any longer, that she didn't know when she would be able to get back, he had said, "Well, I wish I could hold it, Carol. Because you turned out to be a damned good reporter. But, the trouble is, I just can't keep the other two here covering for you much longer."

"Please, Phil, I understand," she had said. "And thank you for giving me everything that you did, a chance to really learn my job."

"Come back to see us someday," he had said with a little catch in his voice.

She leaned close to the mirror, rubbing away the mistiness in her eyes with a tissue, then put some perfume behind her ears. Wonderful, crazy, funny Phil Rowan, she thought. He had let her do more and more as time went on, not just women's page stories, but the robbery at the First National Bank, the explosion out on Route Nine, the Mayor's funeral—and he had even sent her in to Detroit when the auto workers threatened to strike, and to a state mental hospital where employees had been accused of resorting to violence in treatment of patients.

Pulling a warm fur coat from her closet, she left the room and hurried along the corridor, then down the stairs. Jamie would be waiting to go to the hospital with her to hear from the doctors what they wanted or did not want to hear.

"Well, if it's a case of not making it or making it," her father had said weakly the evening before, when Caroline bent down to kiss him on the forehead, "you and your mother and Jamie have worked hard at trying to see that I *do* make it." His left hand still lay useless on the sheet and his speech was still a little slurred.

"You're going to make it," she said softly. "I promise you."

He had looked away toward the window and she saw the familiar clenching of his jaw. In spite of the gaunt and weakly pale look about his face, at sixty-eight Lawrence Kendall was still a handsome, virile-appearing man, she thought. She had gone to the door, looking back at him across the shadowy room, and when he smiled, she repeated, "I promise you."

And he did. Over the next weeks his condition improved almost dramatically. Therapists were brought into the small hospital to work with him, and slowly the speech improved. He learned to use his left arm all over again, forcing the muscles to work. When he was first allowed out of bed, his left leg dragged somewhat, but within weeks he had also mastered that, and by the time he left the hospital, he had only the slightest limp.

"It's that damned determination of his," one of the doctors had said with an admiring laugh to Elizabeth and Caroline. "Between that and the new methods of therapy we have, he's about as good as new."

While Lawrence was recuperating at Kendall Hills, Caroline spent hour upon hour with him. Almost daily, limousines from the city arrived and left, carrying executives and lawyers and secretaries from the lower Manhattan offices to and from the estate up the Hudson River. The doctors had limited him to two hours of time devoted to work periods, but soon the two hours stretched to three, and then four, and by late spring he announced that he was going back to work, "doctors or no doctors," he exploded to Elizabeth. It was then that Caroline decided she, too, was ready to leave.

"I want to start working again," she said to him one evening as they sat on one of the awninged terraces where they had had their dinner.

Candles still flickered in the tall hurricane lamps, spilling over a crystal bowl filled with fragrant roses. The snowy cloth and shimmering wineglasses caught the light, while fireflies winked across the dark lawn and a dog down by the gate bayed, the sound carried on the light breeze. Elizabeth had moved to a grouping of summer lawn chairs at the other end of the terrace with Enid Leland and Jamie and Barbara; Caroline sat next to her father, still at the table. Warren, with his long cigar clenched tightly in his mouth, stood at the edge of the terrace, blowing the smoke off into the darkness.

"I've been hoping you had gotten that out of your system." Lawrence said. "Your mother said you've been doing a lot of work with the Junior League these past few months, working in the hospital clinic and also with one of the League projects in a children's nursery school."

"I want to go back to what I was doing," she said stubbornly. She was wearing a summery white frock with pale lavendar flowers on it and had pulled her dark hair back behind her ears so that it flowed across her back. Her eyes were wide with the eagerness and excitement he had first noticed when she visited once or twice from her job in Madison Hill.

"Well, if that oddball character that you told me about back at the *Madison Hill Bulletin* will take you back—"

"No," she said abruptly, and he looked up at her. "I want to go to Boston, to the *World Inquirer*."

Lawrence looked at her long and hard. "That's one of the biggest papers in the group."

"I want to work in a city and not on the women's page. Not that there's anything wrong with the women's pages, but I want a different kind of reporting. I got a little taste of it at Madison Hill and that's what I want." He saw that her mouth was firm.

Warren had wandered down near the others at the far end of the terrace, where he was bent toward Elizabeth, lighting her cigarette.

"Before you go any further, I think there is something you should know, and then perhaps give all of this more thought." Lawrence put his hand over hers at the edge of the table for a moment, while she watched him quizzically. He glanced for a long moment toward Jamie, an expression of sad affection in his face. "With this—this *episode* I've just been through, I've been doing a lot of rethinking and I've come to the conclusion that I must do some rearranging. I've made some rather drastic changes in my will." He was still watching Jamie. "He'll be all right." He added softly, "Jamie will always be taken care of so that no one or nothing can touch him." He looked around then at Caroline. "Larry and Avery chose the wrong route. I've watched them at every turn—oh, with great skill and subtlety, of course—go against you and Jamie. They chose to perpetuate a division in this family and that is something I will not tolerate." When Caroline started to protest, he waved his hand to indicate he wished to go on. "Oh, yes, I recognize that Larry is a bright and talented young man. And he will continue to be useful to Kendall, Inc., as well as to benefit from it. As will Avery. But . . ." He paused for a moment. "The division of assets will remain as is. The holdings you will inherit—the petroleum and refining companies, the airline, and Kendall newspapers—will still be under your direction and for you solely. As will Larry and Avery's for them. But Jamie's, held in a trust, a separate trust from the Kendall Trust, will be placed in an interlocking directorate with your interests." He stopped to sip at the small glass of amber liqueur, then held it up in front of one of the flickering candles to see its color. "By creating this interlocking directorate, I've left you and Jamie—" his voice became even softer and he leaned a little toward her—"in control of more than fifty percent of the Kendall, Inc., interests, and you, as the principal trustee of Jamie's trust, will, in actuality, be sitting in the driver's seat, through a private holding company called Stuart Securities."

"Daddy, I . . ." Caroline was shaking her head. But Lawrence grasped her hand.

"This is the way it's going to be, Caroline. With you, I feel certain Kendall, Inc., will not resort to public ownership. That is something that will be inevitable further down the line as the heirs of all of you —and their heirs—multiply. But I would like to see sole ownership remain in the family, with dilution of control delayed for another generation or two. Time enough through the multiple erosion of death and taxes and absence of talent."

She thought about it for a long time, her face serious, engrossed with the magnitude of what he had said. Just as she turned back to him, from the corner of his eye he saw Warren wandering back.

"I still want to go to Boston. To the *World Inquirer,* Daddy."

"You can have both." His voice was quiet. "You're my daughter."

He smiled as he looked at the set of her mouth. Just like me at that age, he thought, ready to conquer the world, and he remembered the day at Yale when they had come to tell him that his mother and father were gone, lost on the *Lusitania* in 1915 when it had been sunk by a German submarine.

"Then I can go to the *World Inquirer?*"

"Did you hear that, Warren?" he asked, and Warren came closer, but still at the edge of the terrace to keep the cigar smoke away from Lawrence.

"I heard it," he said with his broad but bland smile, the one that Caroline always thought of as coming out of a package or sliding out of a machine—the even rows of white teeth and round, almost expressionless blue eyes behind the steel-rimmed glasses.

"Well, what do you think?"

Warren looked at Caroline as though he were about to give her a gift, but wanted to hold her in suspense for just one moment longer. "I—er, I suppose it could be arranged."

"All right," Lawrence said, looking back at Caroline and patting her hand that lay on the table near him. "And I must say, it will be nice having you a little closer." He leaned over and kissed her cheek. "But *do* come home once in a while and give a father a break, will you?"

Caroline sat and watched Gail take the makeup off, lathering her skin with cleansing cream, then gently wiping it with tissues, until she looked almost as she had when they were in their early teens, before they were permitted to use makeup. The lights around the large dressing room mirror blazed unmercifully onto her face, and Caroline shook her head admiringly.

"I must say, you look wonderful with or without it. And on that stage tonight, you were marvelous."

"Like the show, huh?" Gail said, as she brushed her hair out and twisted it up into her usual topknot.

"Well, who am I to go against the critics?" Caroline smiled impishly, then ducked when Gail threw a towel at her.

"You are in an awfully good mood tonight," Gail said, watching her through the mirror as she put on her lipstick and dusted some powder over her nose. "What's up?"

Caroline smiled again, her face aglow. "I'm going to work for the *World Inquirer* in Boston."

"Oh, Caro!" Gail turned and hugged her.

"That's why I had to see your show tonight. I'm leaving tomorrow."

"With or without the bodyguards?" Gail asked drolly, as she stood up and they started toward the door.

"We-ell," Caroline said, making a quirky face. "They pretend and I pretend. I've given up trying to convince Daddy I don't need them".

Gail snapped off the light as they left the dressing room and walked toward the stage door. "Honey hates it because she doesn't have anyone following her about," she said with a catty little laugh.

"Well, she can have mine anytime," Caroline said, smiling at two of the young women from the chorus line as they pushed past her in the narrow corridor.

" 'Night, Joe," Gail said. The elderly man was pushing the stage door open for them and saluting as though tipping his hat.

"See you tomorrow, Miss Halloran." They stood out on the sidewalk in the muggy summer night, Caroline pretending she didn't see the black sedan at the curb and the young man standing beside it, showing some identification to a policeman who nodded and moved on.

"Well, where will it be? Sardi's or '21' or a new little Italian joint that I discovered right around the corner?"

"The new little Italian joint right around the corner," Caroline said, laughing, and they set off down the street, arm in arm, jostling past the crowds of late-night theatregoers spilling out of the theatres.

At a tap on her dressing room door, Gail called out, "Come on in." She had taken off her makeup, put on her street clothes, and was pinning her hair up when the door opened and Old Joe stood there. "A man by the name of Ralph is waitin' outside, Miss Gail, and there's a limousine at the door."

Gail froze, hands over her head just as she was about to push the two pins through her hair. *Ralph.* It had been almost three months since Ralph and the car had come for her.

"All right, Joe, and thank you," she said with a calmness she wasn't feeling. When he closed the door, she picked up her purse and hurried out, brushing by cast members in the corridor and by the stage door with a quick good night to each one. Jack Gordon was just coming through the stage door when she approached it, half running.

"Hey," he said softly, clasping hold of her arm and stopping her. "I thought we had a supper date?"

"I—I'm sorry, Jack," she said. "But something's come up."

"Yes, I know," he said, gesturing with his head toward the street, and slowly dropping his hand from her arm. "I see *the limousine* is there."

"Please . . ." She stepped away from him. "I don't want to start anything now, Jack."

He grasped her arm again and said in a low voice, "Just who the hell *is* he, anyway?"

"I have to go." She pulled away, but he held her arm fast.

"Two—three months go by, then all of a sudden that damn limousine is there, and you run off like a scared rabbit."

"Please let me go." She pulled loose, then faced him with blazing eyes. "I don't owe anyone on this earth an explanation."

"Please, Gail," he said in a pleading tone. "Please, honey—"

"Not even you!" She turned and ran out the door, and he watched it as it slowly closed, the black and white sign on it coming into view again: PLEASE MAKE CERTAIN THIS DOOR IS LOCKED BEHIND YOU.

Gail undressed by the moonlight, then watched him come across the room to her, tall and straight, his body gleaming in the soft, hazy light. She lay back and he stood looking down at her for several moments.

"You're beautiful," he whispered. "So beautiful."

Slowly he stretched out beside her, his eyes caressing her, slowly moving from her face, all along her body. Then he gathered her close to him while he kissed her, making it last and last and last.

The bed was wide. Patterns of light from a pale moon fell across them like a mantle of snow. Their heads were in shadow, but he could still see the glitter of her eyes.

"How can I say it—tell you what this means to me?" he whispered.

Their love was something that grew and grew with time. She had put a record on in the long, low living room where only the light from a fire on the hearth flickered up the walls and across the beamed ceiling. The Rachmaninoff *Second Symphony* flowed across and into the bedroom, growing like their love, thrusting, soaring . . . slowly and insistently until they were caught in a hard and relentless rhythm that sang with hungry, voluptuous desire fulfilled.

They lay silently without speaking, their bodies damp and warm and clinging closely. After a while, he pulled them up against the padded headboard and lit cigarettes for them, the tips glowing in the half darkness. He finally spoke. "This is so damned unfair to you—"

But she didn't let him finish. She put two fingers over his lips, and said, "If I didn't want it this way, Richard, I wouldn't be here."

They lapsed into silence again and then he said, "I'm going to Europe tomorrow, a goodwill tour." He grinned into the darkness. "One of those useless things that Vice Presidents do. To France, West Germany, Belgium, and Italy. I'll finish in Switzerland and see Dickie for a day or two. I'll have Georges bring him to the hotel, the Bellevue Palace in Berne, to avoid any problems. Georges will take a room on another floor as a precaution."

"I'm so glad," she said softly. They were silent again for several moments and then she spoke. "When I was there the last time in July, he asked me who you were." She felt his body tense. "I told him that you were a very old and dear friend of mine."

He squashed their cigarettes out and, sliding down, pulled her down with him, then turned her to him and began softly kissing her. "How right you are, my darling, a very old and dear friend."

"Kramer!" a voice bellowed and Caroline looked up from her typewriter. The metro editor was staring at her across the city room, his bushy brows drawn together in an expression of annoyance. Severe annoyance, she thought, as she jumped to her feet and ran to his desk.

"Yes?"

He shoved a piece of copy paper under her nose. "Did you write this brief on the garbage strike?"

"Yes." She couldn't quite bring herself to say *sir.* "Er, yes, I did."

"Well, it's a piece of crap." He slung it at her and it floated lazily to the cluttered floor. She tried to catch it, just as she heard a snicker behind her, but it floated out of her reach and she had to walk over near Ray Purdy's feet to pick it up, while he kept on snickering. She started back to her desk, but the metro editor roared at her again. "Come back here, you. I'm not through with you."

She bit her lip hard as she walked back to him.

"Don't you think it might be a good idea to find out what's wrong with it, Miss Kramer?" he asked, his voice heavy with sarcasm.

"Yes, Mr. Ashford." She stared at the thick dark hair on his arms beneath the rolled-up shirt sleeves instead of at his eyes, for fear she would cry.

"All right," he said gruffly, yanking the piece of copy paper from her hand and looking at it. "The lead's at the bottom down in the fourth paragraph and your chronology's all screwed up. And you've got the name of the union boss misspelled. Jeez, that's all we need, to misspell that bastard's name."

"I'm sorry, but I didn't know how to spell it—"

"Well, *ask* somebody, dammit. If you don't know something, *ask.*"

"Yes, Mr. Ashford," she said, starting to turn, when he called out to her again. "Look, Miss Kramer." He suddenly dropped his voice to a low pitch that only she could hear. "I don't know who it is that got you this job, and what's more, I don't care. All I care about is that you pull your weight around here like everybody else."

"Yes, Mr. Ashford," she said, barely able to speak, forcing back the tears. She walked to her desk and sat down, grateful it was at the rear of the vast room with its glaring overhead lights, sea of battered desks, clattering typewriters, and overflowing wastebaskets. Up behind the metro editor's desk in a small penned-off area was the news editor's desk. And behind it were the wire machines, clacking away in a stuttering rhythm, bells clanging occasionally to indicate that a special bulletin was coming over.

She stared at the piece of copy paper, while her heart stopped pounding and the aching tears in her throat slowly melted. Suddenly she felt a hand on her shoulder and looked up.

"Hi," the pretty girl said. She pulled up the swivel chair from a nearby empty desk and sat on it next to Caroline. "My name is Patty Dunbar. First of all"—she was printing out something on a piece of scratch paper—"here's how you spell the union boss's name."

"Oh, thank you," Caroline said, slipping a fresh piece of copy paper into her typewriter.

Patty had picked up the garbage strike piece and was studying it. "And let's see what Big Mouth was screaming about."

"Big Mouth?" Caroline asked.

"Ashford," Patty said with a grin. "He's never very agreeable about anything, but when he gets like this, it's usually because his wife has left him again."

"His wife leaves him?" Caroline said, her eyes wide.

"Well, wouldn't you if you were his wife?"

Caroline giggled. "I guess I would."

"Okay," Patty said, "all you need to do is bring this paragraph up to the top, and switch these two graphs right here and you've got it the way he likes it, on the line, with no cute stuff like unnecessary quotes or incidental anecotes. 'Nothing that is not organically related to the nut of the story,' as he always says."

"What does that mean?" Caroline asked in amazement.

"Damned if I know," Patty said, and they laughed.

"He's tough and he's nasty at times, but he's a good editor," Patty was saying as they lingered over coffee. She had asked Caroline to go to dinner with her that night in a pleasant little restaurant just off Boylston Street. "And most of the time, he'll leave you alone if you do your job, even though he does seem to hate women."

"Because of his wife," Caroline said knowingly and with a laugh.

"Because of his wife, no doubt." She smiled up at the waiter, who stood poised with the coffee pot. When he had finished refilling their cups, she said, "Where are you from, Carol?"

"Well—from New York, originally," Caroline said. "But I've been working at a small newspaper out near Detroit."

"One of ours?" When Caroline nodded, she said, "God knows Kendall has a pile of them. Thirty-four at last count, I think it was."

"Tell me more about the *Inquirer*." Caroline leaned forward eagerly, but just as anxious, as well, to change the subject from the acquisition policy of Kendall Newspapers. "Does that Ray Purdy always snicker when Mr. Ashford bawls someone out?"

"He's a creep. Got his job because his father's somebody at one of the big banks. Runs it or something."

"You mean they do that kind of thing?"

"Not really. But I think his father, or maybe it was his grandfather, was on the board of directors of the *World Inquirer* when it was still independently owned. Actually, the policy on the paper is pretty fair and square. No stars. At least that's what they always say. The top reporters and correspondents sit right out in the newsroom with the rest of us, no private offices or cubbyholes." She smiled. "Of course, reporters like Ab Streitner and Steve McCallum and Ed Pinckney, they're pretty straight shooters and don't play it like Hollywood."

"Who are they?"

"Pinckney writes the column "On the Street," and McCallum and Streitner are sent out on all the special stuff. In fact, there's talk that Streitner might be the one to replace Dale Milligan in Washington when he retires next month. And McCallum was sent to Vietnam three months ago when they began the escalation of troops there."

"Is that where he is now?" Caroline asked with curiosity. "This McCallum?"

Patty nodded as she sipped at her coffee. "Sending back some good stuff, too. He doesn't fool around or worry about anyone's feelings. His stuff is tough, all the blood and guts right out there. Steve's anti-war, anyway, and especially *this* war. Super-liberal, I guess you'd call him." Caroline smiled as she listened. It was obvious Patty was half in love with him. But Patty saw the implication in the smile and laughingly shook her head. "Sure, every gal falls for him. He's John Wayne with brains. But you get over it when you see his dedication to singlehood. Boy, is he single!"

Caroline laughed and stirred some cream into her coffee as she gazed around the restaurant, liking its coziness, the Chianti bottles hanging on the walls and in the low archway, the tiny, glowing oil lamps on the tables, and the long mural of the harbor in Ischia on one wall. "Came up from nothing, someone said. First-generation American. Practically born on the boat from Ireland. Claims his big regret in life is that he wasn't old enough to vote for Norman Thomas when he ran for President on the Socialist ticket."

"That's good," Caroline said eagerly. "I mean—this newspaper is so conservative, it needs someone like that to give it depth."

"He'd agree with you there," Patty said. She yawned, squashed her cigarette out, and began trying to catch the waiter's eye so they could pay their bill and leave. She was a medium-height young woman with a rather plump body but a pretty face. Her brown hair was cut in straight bangs across her forehead and slightly turned under at her shoulders.

"I'll drop you off," she said sleepily, and Caroline smilingly remembered the wild ride to the restaurant in her little MG. Pete McGonigle must have lost a few years off his life over that one, she thought. "Where do you live?"

"Well, a friend of my aunt went south for the winter and is letting me use her house in Louisburg Square," she said limply, hoping the tale rang true. Actually—and this was a concession to her father—she had agreed to live in one of the townhouses there, which he had purchased for her, with Nanny Grace installed as housekeeper and Pete McGonigle living in one of the third-floor rooms.

"Louisburg Square?" Patty said, her eyes round with surprise. "Well, *my dear,* what a fancy address!"

"It's only borrowed," Caroline protested.

384

"Even so," Patty said, deeply impressed. "I wish *my* aunt had friends like that."

For the next year and a half Caroline dug hard into the newspaper and her job, volunteering for every assignment she could, eager to learn everything as quickly as possible. The Vietnam situation was something she watched with a somewhat oblique eye, so involved was she in the political workings of Boston, the intrigues and behind-the-scenes maneuvering, then the wider picture as she was moved to the state desk. She knew that Prime Minister Diem had been murdered and that General Nguyen Khanh had seized power in Saigon. She read about the Vietcong terrorist bombing of an American military billet there, flinching at the horror of it while admiring the style of writing under Steve McCallum's byline.

By the time 1965 arrived, she wondered where all the months had flown to, and looked back on her eighteen months or more at the *Inquirer* with a sense of some accomplishment and pride.

The day that Harvey Everett died of a heart attack was the day that Steve McCallum came back from Vietnam to a rousing party in the newsroom. When the story came over the wire that the President of the United States was dead, Scotty Blankenship, the city editor, started shooting out assignments, right over the paper plates of Ryder's Delicatessen sandwiches and the paper cups filled with cheap red wine, while the party went on all around him, though somewhat more subdued than would occur normally.

"Kramer!" he shouted over the noise. "Get out to Brookline. He has a cousin who lives there. She's an old lady with a lot of dogs, the eccentric of the Everett family. Talk to her if it means going down the chimney. I want local angles on this story."

Caroline grabbed the address and ran. By the time she got back, the party was over, it was dark, and the newsroom was back to its normal clattering state. She wanted to call Gail, but knew she had to write her story first. A big young man with wavy brown hair, a rumpled tweed suit, and a battered brown felt hat over his face was flung backward in her swivel chair, his feet in a drawer of her desk, sound asleep.

"Here," Patty half whispered, "use my desk. I'm just leaving to interview the attendant in the ladies' room of the Ritz-Carlton. She went to school with President Everett in Hartford." She made a face and rolled her eyes upward. She started toward the stairway, but stopped and looked back, pointing. "That, in your chair, is Steve McCallum. He thought it would be quieter back here. He just found out he's been nominated for a Pulitzer for the story on the troop escalation in Vietnam, and he drank a little too much wine."

Caroline worked quietly for fully an hour, took the copy up to Scotty's desk, and dropped it into the basket, then went back to Patty's desk and put in a phone call to Gail at the theatre.

"My God, Gail," she gasped, "I wanted to call you when I heard, but I was being pushed out the door on an assignment."

"Do you realize what this means?" Gail said and Caroline heard the shock in her voice.

"Yes." Caroline gathered her courage, then putting her mouth as close to the mouthpiece as possible, she spoke in a soft voice. "Yes, I think I do, Gail, and it isn't going to be easy for you." She waited through a long silence. "Are you there, Gail?" The "yes" was hollow, quiet, a dead sound. "You're going to have to face it, darling. You won't dare take a chance on trying to see him. Not from now on."

"Caro . . ." It was a cry, coming from her deep anguish.

"Gail!" Caroline made her voice hard. "You've got a performance to do tonight." She looked at her watch. "In less than half an hour—"

"I can't do it."

"You can, and you have to, Gail. Dammit, you're an actress. People in the theatre make a vow. You told me that once. They go on no matter what has happened to them. They put everything personal aside and go on, no matter how much it hurts." There was another silence, and then she heard sounds in the background. Voices. "Gail?"

"It's—it's all right, Caro. I just told them I'd be ready in fifteen minutes." Her voice sounded wooden, strained. "It'll be a lousy performance. But then I guess you're entitled to a few of those in a lifetime." She was even beginning to sound more normal.

Caroline laughed softly. "I guess you are." She quickly looked at her schedule on her desk calendar, then said, "Gail, I'll come down for the weekend, if I can."

"Please, Caro. I *have* to see you. I think I'll go mad if I don't have someone to scream at."

"Well, save your screaming until then." After she hung up, she stared at the phone for a moment.

"How does one save screaming?" a voice asked. She looked over to her desk, where the coolest blue eyes she had ever seen were watching her. He had tilted the chair back to an upward position and was picking his hat up from the floor, where it had fallen.

"Hello," she said, a bit awed by what she had heard about him. "I'm Carol Kramer. I already know who *you* are."

"Who am I?" he asked, as though confused, and then grinned. His smile was crooked, lifting at one side, and one eyebrow shot up when he asked questions. He was good-looking in a big, rumpled way.

He suddenly stood up and stretched, buttoned his collar, and retied his tie. Just as suddenly he sat on the edge of Patty's desk and looked down at Caroline.

"Would you do me a favor?"

"What?" she asked, thinking that it didn't matter what it was, no matter what, she would do it.

"Would you have dinner with me? In spite of all the party-time this afternoon and all this hoopla about my coming home, just about everyone else suddenly ran out on assignments and left me all alone."

He sounded so pitiful, she burst out laughing.

He was laughing, too, but he stopped, and as his laughter drifted off, hers did as well, and they were simply looking at each other.

"No," he said softly, "that isn't why I want to have dinner with you. I want to because I haven't seen anyone as beautiful as you in a long, long time."

They had dinner and then sat in the restaurant talking for hours. He took her to her car and said, "I want to do this again."

"I, too," she said. He hadn't touched her through the long evening. But she had seen an expression in his eyes and had felt something shiver along her spine. As she drove off, she saw in her rear-view mirror that he was standing beside his car, watching the tail-light on her own car disappear.

When she arrived at work the next morning, she heard someone mention that Ab Streitner and Steve McCallum had been sent to Washington to cover the President's funeral. And then Steve would fly to Rabat, Morocco, where border skirmishes had broken out again with the Algerians. She sat at her desk as a strange emptiness filled her. She had driven to work in a light, almost excited frame of mind, but now the feeling was gone. She looked at her desk calendar and idly pushed it away. At eleven she had to go with a photographer to Logan Airport to get a picture and some quotes from the Governor, who was returning from Florida, where the nation's Governors had been meeting.

Just as she stood up to go over to the coffee machine, her phone rang. When she picked it up, the voice said, "Are you the reporter who has been working on the Randy Keane case?"

She had to stop and think. *Randy Keane.* Oh, yes, he was the Hollywood actor who was coming to trial in his wife's death. The year before, they had been registered at a Boston hotel where he was making personal appearances in connection with a film. His wife had been found dead early one morning at the bottom of an air shaft of the hotel. He claimed she had been depressed in the few months preceding her death and had apparently jumped while he was sleeping. But the grand jury had asked for a trial when the suggestion had been made that she had been trying to get a divorce from him.

"No, I'm not the reporter," she said. "But if you'll wait a moment, I'll—"

"No!" the woman's voice said. "I don't want to talk to that reporter. I want to talk to someone else—to you."

"All right," Caroline said, slowly sitting down and picking up her pencil. There was something in the woman's voice that piqued her curiosity. "Do you want to tell me something?"

"Yes, but not over the telephone." She heard a thread of fear in the voice. "Could you meet me somewhere?"

"Ye-es. Where?"

"In the Public Garden? Where they sell the tickets for the swan boats? Don't tell anyone I called or that you're meeting me. I beg you."

"In an hour?" Caroline asked. "I'm wearing a tan polo coat, with a red plaid scarf."

"In an hour," the woman said.

The woman was in her late fifties, well-dressed but wearing a droopy-brimmed hat and dark glasses. She kept the collar of her coat up around her face so that Caroline couldn't see too much of it. She seemed frightened and hesitant. Because of this, Caroline left her notebook and pencil in her bag. They walked a short distance, then sat down on a bench in a somewhat hidden spot. The woman looked all around and began to talk.

"Deborah Keane didn't jump to her death. She was"—she looked around her again, and dropped her voice—"she was pushed or thrown down that air shaft." Caroline's heart began to thud. Something in the woman's voice told her she was speaking the truth.

"How do you know?" she asked.

The woman opened her purse, hesitantly took out a white envelope, and handed it to Caroline. Inside were color snapshots of a pretty young woman who had been badly beaten. Her eyes were black, and large bruises and cuts were obvious on her face and arms. The pictures had been taken with flash bulbs and through a mirror by the young woman herself. On the borders someone had printed the date, August 1964, and on the backs were the words "These pictures were taken just a few hours after Randy beat me. This isn't the first time this has happened. It happened once before when I told him I wanted a divorce. No matter what I do or don't do, he goes into these uncontrollable rages. And when I mention divorce, he threatens me. Please keep these pictures, in case I need them. Deborah."

Caroline stared at the snapshots. "Can I keep them?"

"If you promise not to say where they came from." When Caroline nodded and said that she promised, the woman asked, "How do I know I can trust you, believe you?"

"I can't do any more than promise." When the woman seemed satisfied with that answer, Caroline asked, "Can you tell me anything more?"

She looked off in the distance. "Deborah had to finance his last three pictures. His career was sliding. When she finally told him she was through and wanted a divorce, that's when he began to threaten her."

"She had that kind of money?"

"Her father had left her everything when he died. You can find all of that in the records." She smiled faintly. "She was a wonderful girl."

They sat in silence for a few moments. "Was—was Deborah your daughter?" Caroline finally asked. When the woman didn't answer her, Caroline slipped the envelope with the snapshots into her bag, stood up, and looked down at her. "I'll do what I can," she said, and she walked away.

25
1965

When Steve McCallum walked into the city room, he waved at several of the reporters and at Scotty Blankenship as though he had just walked out an hour or so before. When they crowded around him, he pointed to the glass wall at one side of the room where the editors for the national and international desks sat talking into phones. "Just don't let those guys see me. I'd like to hang around, at least for a few days to get my suits pressed."

After they all drifted away and he sat going through the pile of mail in front of him, he suddenly looked around toward the back of the newsroom. Patty Dunbar saw him staring at the empty desk beside her and she smiled. He got to his feet and wandered back, then sat on the corner of her desk.

"Where's Carol Kramer?"

"That's right," she said, looking up from her typewriter. "You'd have no way of knowing, would you?" She sighed and leaned back in the swivel chair. "Carol's in jail."

"She's what?" He got to his feet. "What are you talking about?"

"She got pulled into the Keane case. You know, Randy Keane, the Hollywood star who was on trial for his wife's death. Somebody gave Carol snapshots of the dead woman, showing how she had been beaten by him a few weeks before she was found dead here at the bottom of a hotel air shaft. When the defense insisted she reveal her source, she refused. She was ordered to reveal her source, and the *Inquirer* took it to the U.S. Court of Appeals last week. We argued she had the First Amendment right to refuse to reveal confidential sources. But we lost and she was sent to jail for fourteen days."

Steve turned and strode toward the front of the big room. Patty saw him leaning on Scotty's desk and talking to him, an urgency in the way he was leaning forward. So that's it, she thought with a smile, without any surprise. Half of the men in the city room were in love with Carol Kramer.

"Empty everything in your pockets and put them in this basket," the woman guard said, "and don't go waving that press card at me, because you're still going to be treated like everybody else."

He looked at her hard face and grinned, as he pulled his wallet and other odds and ends from his pockets and put them in the basket. He looked around the small room and grimaced. A long counter ran along one wall, with three women guards standing behind it, stony-faced and telling everyone the same thing, to empty their pockets. Visiting hours had just started and there was a long line behind him. After he had signed his name and let the guard stamp an invisible number on the back of his hand that would show up when necessary under ultraviolet light, he was told to follow a group of ten that was just going through a door.

Steve had been in jails and prisons before in the course of his job. But never to see a slim, violet-eyed young woman with animated but precise speech, shoulder-length dark hair that fell in waves about her face, and features so exquisite he had gasped a little when he first looked at her.

They had gone through several sets of locked gates within the building and then came into a large day room, where women of all ages sat at small tables talking earnestly to visitors. He was relieved to see that their conditions were somewhat better than on the men's side. The cell blocks they had passed were long corridors with small enclosed rooms, or cubicles, in rows on either side, and solid doors that were locked from the outside at night. Something cringed inside him when he thought of Carol in one of those rooms. Then when he saw her sitting at one of the tables in a corner, he watched her until she turned her head and, with a leap of surprise and pleasure on her face, smiled.

"I couldn't believe what I heard when I walked into the city room this morning," he said, taking her hands in his, then sitting down beside her. She was wearing the plain blue blouse and skirt that all the prisoners wore and a white cardigan.

She laughed, but it was a shaky little laugh, and he squeezed her hands tighter. "I was just walking across the room to the coffee machine," she said. "I shouldn't have turned back to answer the phone." She explained what had happened, and when she finished he was shaking his head.

"How much longer do you have to stay here?" he said. He was looking around them with an angry expression on his face.

"Five more days." She smiled and said softly, "It's not as bad as I was afraid it would be. I was terrified at first. I have to admit that. But then, when I saw it here, I realized that somehow I'd manage to get through the fourteen days without screaming." She tried to laugh again and he saw how pale she was and the toll it had taken on her already. "Oh, but, Steve, how awful it would be to have to stay here for years and years and years. I think I would die. I would *want* to die."

On a sudden impulse, he put his arms around her and held her to him. They had walked over to one of the barred windows and it was just as though she belonged in his arms. When he spoke, his voice was low, almost a whisper, and his arms tightened around her. "On the day you leave, I'm coming to get you."

She felt the strength in his arms, and as she leaned against him, again it seemed a perfectly natural thing to do. He looked down at her and nuzzled his chin against the top of her head. "And I'll take you out for the biggest damned steak you've ever seen."

Before going down in the elevator, he had watched for a moment from the windows of the large suite on the fourth floor of the hotel. State Street, as far as he could see both north and south, was a swaying sea of people, but directly down in front of the Palmer House a cordon of police was holding back the crowd. He could see the line of black limousines, the fluttering pennants on the fenders of the second car, and mounted police pushing the line of people even farther back across the broad street.

"Your coat, sir. It's chilly outside. Almost November."

He turned, smiled at the man, and took the black chesterfield from him, then walked swiftly across the suite's living room and out through the foyer, flanked on all sides by Secret Service, Hank Phillips, his press secretary, and a scattering of others who traveled with him. As he stepped into the elevator, which was being held for him, he hunched into the coat and watched the floor signals light up as the elevator hummed. He had thought of having her come here for the two days, but at the last moment changed his mind. Too risky, he thought . . . never knew when some reporter might manage to get on the floor and get wind of something.

They were hurrying toward the entrance, and beyond the revolving glass doors he could see the swirl of police and wall of faces watching the front of the hotel. He paused just outside on the sidewalk and raised his arms in a double salute, as the swell of voices grew, a deafening roar above the sound of motors as the line of limousines edged forward. He stepped toward the curb, arms still raised and waving, when he lurched with the impact, then felt his body pitch forward and heard the screams . . . but farther and farther away . . . fading . . . fading . . . fading . . .

Caroline was standing at the AP wire machine, ripping off the stories and putting them on the news editor's desk, when the bell started clanging. She stared at the purple type on the sheet that was just ticking through.

"No!" It was a cry. Repeated as a whisper.

Several people near her looked up, including Scotty. "What's up?" he said. He stared at her, puzzled, for a split second.

"The President . . ." She gasped, held her hand to her mouth as though she were going to be sick.

"What the hell?" Scotty leaped to the machine, hearing the shock in her voice. He pulled the wire story out straight and read it rapidly. "Jesus!" he said. "The President has been shot!"

A terrible pervading silence rolled through the city room, while Caroline stood leaning against the wall. Her head was shaking back and forth and she was saying, "No . . . no . . ." She started to walk to Scotty, started to say, "I have to go—" But she stepped back, leaning against the wall again and shaking her head, helplessly. Somehow, she had to get some time off and go to New York. She had to be with Gail. She walked quietly back to her desk, where she sat in her chair, huddled and shivering. Finally, she picked up the phone and asked the operator to get her a number in New York.

Gail watched the television screen with dull, glazed eyes. Caroline had called her doctor and obtained a sedative that made Gail feel as though everything had faded to a distance.

"Please, Gail," Caroline was pleading. "Don't watch it."

"I have to," Gail said, slowly, ploddingly, as though her tongue had become thick and heavy. "I have to feel what he felt, know what it was like when it happened . . ."

Helplessly, Caroline sat down and watched. Over and over it had been shown, the terrible moment when it all had come to an end. Richard Belden had been in Chicago, making a speech to the Teamsters' Union there. He was coming out of the Palmer House entrance on State Street, where he had been speaking, when the shots rang out, three of them. For a moment, the figure in the black chesterfield coat, hat in his hand and upraised, waving, had stood perfectly still. And then he had pitched forward, while screams rang out and the sidewalk in front of the hotel became pandemonium. As they watched the replay of the now deadly familiar television scene, they saw the Secret Service men leap and grab hold of a man who was trying to push through the crowd out onto the street. They saw them drag him toward the hotel entrance, while others knelt over the fallen President. They heard the screams, the screech of sirens, the shouts of the police, police on the street and mounted on horses, racing toward the ambulance that careened along State Street and shrieked to a stop.

Caroline watched Gail's face. It was expressionless, dry-eyed, the shock so deep that she couldn't drag herself up from its depths even to weep. She rose to turn off the television set, and Caroline watched her as she walked in her white velvet robe across the living room to the rosewood desk. It was a pretty living room, high above Central Park on the West Side, with deep chintz-covered chairs and sofas, soft beige carpeting, and wide bay windows looking out over the park.

She picked up the phone and told the long-distance operator she wanted to place a person-to-person call to a Mr. Patrick Belden in Philadelphia. "Tell him Gail Halloran is calling."

"Gail . . ." Caroline half-whispered, caution in her voice.

But Gail ignored her. She waited several moments, moving her head slightly as she finally heard a voice at the other end of the line.

"Mr. Belden, this is Gail." She waited, then clasped the phone with both hands. "Please listen to me very carefully. I want Richard's son to be at his father's funeral." She swayed a little.

"Gail . . ." Caroline started toward her with one hand out.

"I'm having him brought to the United States tomorrow, and he and I will be at the Shoreham Hotel in Washington on the following day." There was silence as she listened. "Yes, I'll expect you, or someone, on the morning of the funeral to come for Dickie." She quietly put the phone down, stood there for a moment, then walked in her bare feet toward the bedroom.

Dickie sat on the edge of the chair in silence, watching his mother, who kept walking to the windows with her coffee cup in her hand, nervously tapping the window glass with her long fingernails. He was wearing a new dark blue suit and his hair was slicked down so that the cowlick wouldn't stick up.

He never took his eyes from his mother, wondering why she had been so quiet since he first arrived the night before with Grandmère Ellie, who was sitting in the bedroom beyond watching the television screen. He could hear the distant sound of a man's voice from the television set, deep and sad sounding, and sometimes there was music, the kind of music he'd heard in church when Grandmère and Grand-père had taken him there. He looked around the hotel suite and frowned a little. There hadn't been any toys here for him to play with or deep puffy sofas or chairs for him to bounce in. Everything was stiff and hard to sit on, and when he looked out the window he saw they were high above the streets and other buildings.

At a soft tapping on the door, his mother walked across the room and swung the door open. Dickie stared at the man who came in. He was wearing a black coat and carried a black hat and his hair was a smooth thick thatch of white. He nodded to Dickie's mother, walked slowly toward him, bent down a little, took his hand, and said, "Dickie, my name is Patrick Belden. I'm going to take you with me for a little while." He picked him up from the chair, held him to him for a moment, then slowly put him down on the floor and pointed toward the corridor. "We're going to a church," he said. "And when we get there, you'll go in the church with the two men who are outside the door. They are friends of mine, Dickie."

Dickie nodded, as a flutter of fear trembled inside of him. But when he looked at his mother, she said softly, "It's all right, darling. I'll be waiting here with Grandmère for you."

He remembered for years and years afterward going down in the elevator with the man holding his hand tightly, and in front of the hotel climbing into a long black car with the two men, who smiled and patted his head. The man named Patrick Belden got into another long black limousine that they followed, driving along wide streets and past gleaming white buildings.

When they arrived at the church, he saw thick crowds of people all along the sidewalks and lining the long steps up to the entrance, while men with cameras kept running along the edge of the crowds and taking pictures. He lost sight of Patrick Belden and walked between the two men up the steps. Halfway up he heard a woman call out, "Who do you suppose that little boy is?" The woman was clutching a newspaper in her hands, and he caught a glimpse of a big picture, the picture of a man's face, and the man was waving his hand over his head and smiling. Dickie looked back over his shoulder for a moment and stared. The man in the picture was the man he faintly remembered who came to Bellone, the man who picked him up and hugged him so hard it almost hurt, who held him and played games with him, and who made his mother laugh but with tears in her eyes. Somehow he knew that the man in the picture on the newspaper had something to do with his walking up the steps and into the big, cavernous dark church, where candles burned up on the distant altar and music echoed down from above, voices singing the kind of hymns that he had heard in the church at Grenzenwald. And then he saw the flag-draped coffin just below the gleaming white altar.

He looked up at the man beside him, who was staring straight ahead of him while piously holding his hat in his lap. Dickie touched his arm and whispered, "Did the man in the picture die?"

The man beside him stared down at him, his expression puzzled. Then he put his finger to his lips and said, "Shhhh," as a procession of men and boys in white robes came onto the altar from the sides and the music soared upward, filling the great cathedral with a sadly triumphal sound. There was the heavy fragrance of incense and flowers, and his feet felt cold as they dangled above the stone floor.

He sat forward on the limousine seat, his chin just even with the bottom of the window. All along the streets as the limousine slowly inched forward, he saw crowds of people, just like back at the big cathedral, some of them openly weeping, most of them dressed in black, and all of them staring at the passing black limousines. He was sitting beside the man named Patrick Belden again and soon they passed through the gates of a cemetery. He watched from a long distance while seated in the limousine with the two men who had taken him to the church, watched as many people clustered near a wide canopy and then after a while drifted away in clusters of twos and threes.

And once again the man named Patrick Belden was in the car with them, clutching his hand hard, his eyes looking grimly ahead as the limousine drove through the wide streets once more. He walked with him through the lobby of the hotel, having to skip a little to keep up with his long strides, and then they were back with his mother in the suite where lamps glowed softly, and he smelled the faint fragrance of her perfume.

"He's . . . a wonderful child. Richard would have been proud of him," the man said.

"Richard was proud of him," his mother said. "He saw him in Switzerland, you see."

Steve met Caroline's plane when it arrived, insisting, as it was a Sunday, that he cook them brunch at his apartment. In the car driving from Logan he asked her a dozen questions. She was relieved he had to keep his eyes on the road when she answered, shame creeping over her as she repeated the lies. She had told him her mother had the flu, and as her father traveled a great deal—he was a traveling salesman, she had explained—she didn't want her mother to be alone and ill.

"It was only a heavy cold," she said, pretending to look at something out the window of the car. "And—and my father came home last night."

"Where did you say they lived?" he asked in idle curiosity.

"Well, they have a little place up in the East Seventies."

He whistled. "Expensive territory."

"Well—they've lived there a long time. And with—with rent control . . ." She squirmed inside, especially when she glanced over her shoulder and saw the black sedan following them.

"Hey, I promised my mother and father I'd come home next weekend. How about going with me?"

She looked at him in surprise. "Why, I'd like that, Steve," she said. They were pulling up in front of his apartment building.

"They live in Providence." He turned and looked at her, and added softly. "I'd like them to meet you."

They sat on the floor in front of the fireplace, eating eggs Benedict and drinking Bloody Marys. He read her the comics and they laughed like children, carefully avoiding the front section of the newspaper, where all of the stories about the assassination and the funeral were. Like most of the nation, they needed a respite from tragedy. Caroline closed it all from her mind for the time being, and when he leaned over and kissed her, ever so softly, she wound her arms around his neck.

He picked her up then and carried her to the bedroom. Hovering over her on the bed, he whispered, "I've never met anyone like you before, Carol." He had undressed her, while kissing her, and when she lay naked beneath him, he sat up, pulled off his clothes, then lay beside her and kissed the cleft between her breasts.

"Darling, darling," she murmured, and his mouth teased her skin. The wonder of his touch, his hands roving across her body, was like magic. Every nerve in her body throbbed, came alive. Her hands were stroking him, pulling him closer, and when he slid on top of her, she moved beneath him, slowly, sinuously, the motion a new language, one of desire. She thrust upward, feeling his strength as he pushed against her. He had lowered the blinds, but light seeped through and she saw his face above her. "Steve." It was a whisper while she rose to to him, again and again, the small cries fluttering from her mouth, until suddenly he held her hard against him, and she wanted it to stay that way forever and ever as languorous waves of pleasure swept through her, a pulsing tide sweeping her to the edge.

They lay beside each other, closely drifting in a sweet silence. His leg lay across her and she burrowed deeper against him. When he kissed her again, it was gentle, lingering. She sighed and closed her eyes, and in moments, they were both asleep.

When they woke, it was dark. He drove her home and raised his eyebrows at where she lived. "A friend of my aunt's owns it. She went south to live and asked me to live here and take care of it until she decides if she wants to sell or keep it. An older woman, her housekeeper, still lives here, so she—well, she kind of takes care of me." She hoped the explanation didn't sound as feeble and limp as it felt.

"Not bad," he said, and she wondered if she detected suspicion in his voice. She saw him glance at the dark sedan that pulled past them and slid up to the curb two houses ahead. But then he looked back at her again, pulled her to him, and kissed her the way he had kissed her earlier, all of her nerve endings suddenly tingling. "If I let you do that again," she whispered breathlessly, while opening the door, "I'll never leave." She ran up the steps and disappeared into the house.

A week later, on a cold early November day, they visited his parents in Providence. It was a workingman's neighborhood, the three-story frame houses called tenements divided into three flats. He made no apologies for the cramped rooms, the overstuffed plush-covered furniture with crocheted antimacassars and doilies everywhere, and she admired him for that. Meals were eaten in the spotless old-fashioned kitchen, and his father, in a blue workshirt, sat down and began to eat before she or Mollie McCallum had even pulled out their chairs. The white-haired couple never seemed to address each other. Tom McCallum was perpetually silent, while Mollie talked incessantly, and Steve became more and more glum as Sunday wore on.

They were halfway back to Boston before he spoke, and then he muttered, "It would never work."

"What would never work?" she asked carefully.

"Just who the hell are you, anyway?" he asked brusquely, looking over at her in the darkness of the car. "My mother acted like she was scared to death of you—"

"That's ridiculous," she protested hotly.

"And my father said to me under his breath, 'She thinks she's too good for us.' Maybe he's right." He was ranting angrily.

"That's not fair!" She, too, was raising her voice.

"Fair? What's fair?" he shouted. "You were just too damned sweet to be true! Condescendingly sweet."

"Stop," she cried, her hands over her ears.

"Christ! You acted like you'd never even been in a kitchen before." His fury had reached a new peak, while she huddled in the far corner, tears running down her face. "I said, who are you anyway? Where the hell did you come from? My mother laughed at the way you made your bed this morning. Haven't you ever even made a bed before?"

"Stop it!" she lashed out, angry and hurt and confused. "I don't want to hear any more. Just because I made a rumpled bed, just because I don't happen to like kitchens. Maybe you're right. It would never work."

He suddenly pulled the car off the road, put his arms around her and held her, his arms tight, almost hurting her. "I'm sorry," he whispered miserably. "It's just that . . . sometimes I feel as though I don't really know you, as though there's something you aren't telling me, Carol."

She laughed shakily and pulled away. "That's crazy. There's nothing to tell." He stared at her in the dimly lit interior of the car, then turned the ignition on and drove back onto the highway.

One or two weekends a month she visited her parents, usually evading the truth when Steve asked her questions, inventing visits to friends. She was torn—torn between spending the time with him and having to lie about where she had been. Several times during the winter she flew to Palm Beach, where her parents were spending the winter, Lawrence still recuperating. Once at Logan Airport, when she was being escorted by one of her father's pilots out to the Kendall jet on the tarmac, she suddenly ducked her head and ran. She had seen Steve coming across the tarmac in a stream of passengers from a commercial airliner. He had been in Detroit covering a United Auto Workers' strike and she was afraid he might have seen her being led to the big private jetliner.

In the spring, when Gail's musical came to Boston, they sat up late into the dawn after opening night. Gail was staying with her at her townhouse in Louisburg Square. Like the old days, they were drinking hot chocolate and then tea as the night wore on.

"I can't talk about my parents to him, because I'm tired of the lies," Caroline ranted. She was lying face down across one twin bed while Gail sat up in the other, putting polish on her toenails. "And I can't tell him the truth about them. He would hate everything there is about the Kendalls. His politics are—well, they're different. He doesn't believe in the same things, he—"

"You mean he's a socialist?"

"Well, he's certainly not a Republican!" Caroline blurted, and Gail exploded in laughter, but when she looked at Caroline's face, she grew quiet again. "He's told me he doesn't understand me, that there's something about me that puzzles him. The last time I admitted going to my parents, he said he wanted to go with me the next time, and when I told him it wouldn't be for a long, long time, he became angry and walked away."

"Do you love him, Caro?" Gail asked.

There was a long silence, and finally Caroline looked at her. "We've never even spoken the word *love*. I—I've been so afraid—so afraid I'd lose him if I told him the truth about myself, and so I've held back from him, held so much back that he knows something is missing, something is wrong."

"What is it?" Gail asked, reaching over and touching her hand.

"He's going away. He's going back to Saigon."

"Odd," Gail said with a slow smile. "I'm going there in October with a USO troupe, when this show closes."

Caroline stared at her, and then she said softly, "When you see him, tell him I love him, will you, Gail?"

* * *

400

"I won't ask another favor of you, Uncle Warren," Caroline said, "if you'll just do this one thing for me." She looked beyond him in the tall leather chair behind his desk, on to the broad sweep of the lower Hudson where huge ships and barges headed upstream. "I want to do a series on a USO group entertaining in a war zone, doing shows for the advisers who are there."

Warren was lighting one of his long cigars and Caroline mentally wrinkled her nose. She sat opposite him in a trim navy-blue suit, the frilly white collar of her blouse framing her face. "But Vietnam, Caroline. I can hardly condone a jaunt like that."

"I won't be where there's any fighting. I'll be in Saigon. That's where Gail is going with the USO. It's like going to Paris. About as dangerous."

"But your father—"

"I'll tell him, I promise, once I'm given the assignment by the international desk. But I can't get the assignment unless you have someone speak to Grant Mason, the publisher."

Warren pulled at the end of his long nose, thinking it over. He swung his chair around as though to gain insight from the sky and the view below his window. When the chair swung slowly around again, Caroline held her breath. "Well, as long as your father is to have the last word . . ." He smiled expansively and boomed, "Always happy to do something for you, Caroline."

Caroline felt the same discomfort she had always known in his presence. His grandiose manner annoyed her. Best to take a business-like approach, so she stood up and gripped his hand. "I'm really grateful."

He got to his feet, grumbling, "You kids! All of you. Never settle down. Katherine wanting a divorce, now that she's met a member of the British peerage. Brenda and her husband off to a ranch in Wyoming, Jamie getting the drying-out treatment again . . ."

A fleeting trace of hurt touched her eyes when he mentioned Jamie, but then she leaned toward him again and said eagerly, "I think that's wonderful about Brenda. She's always adored horses and the outdoors—"

"Damned nonsense. Next year it will be something else." He came around the desk and, taking her arm, led her across the deeply carpeted office to the door. "Well, run along, and I'll have someone give Mason a call." At the door he gave her a fatherly hug.

She bravely bore his kiss on the cheek. "Thank you again, so much."

He nodded and watched her hurry through the outer office and disappear into one of the many reception areas and then corridors of the Kendall building, where a private elevator with beaten brass doors would silently carry her down the twenty-three floors to the lobby.

She gazed down from the large military aircraft to the sea of green foliage bordering the long shoreline that was the lower end of South Vietnam. The calm brillant blue of the sea and the vision of green from twenty thousand feet looked as peaceful as the rolling green hills of Kentucky. In moments, the plane would touch down in Saigon, and she felt a moment of doubt. What would she do if Steve became angry when he saw her? She knew she was a big part of the reason why he had left the States.

As the wheels shrieked along the runway, she clutched Gail's arm. "He's going to hate my coming here."

Gail looked at her. "What kind of a jerk is he, anyhow?"

"He's not a jerk," Caroline said hotly. "It's just that he—well, he doesn't trust me. He knows—feels I'm keeping something from him."

"Caroline," Gail said with exaggerated weariness. "Why don't you just tell him the truth about yourself?"

"He'd detest me." She sounded frantic. "You don't understand. He despises people like the Rockefellers and Du Ponts and—and us. He thinks that anyone who has that kind of money had to get it in some crooked way and at the expense of poor people, by exploiting the workingman. Everything is wrong—nothing matches between us—"

"We-e-ell! Something certainly does!" Gail said, with a wicked little grin.

"And he suspects something."

"Look, darling, it's too late to worry about that now," Gail said cheerfully as she peered out the small window. "Because we're here."

A military bus was waiting for the group. As the excited singers and dancers clambered on and fell into the seats, laughing and shouting, the army sergeant and driver who had met them counted heads, then the bus lumbered off through the countryside and into the streets of Saigon. There was a faintly familiar air about the city, and then Caroline recalled being told that the French, who had colonized Vietnam, fashioned the cities in their colonies to suit themselves by exporting the atmosphere of Paris, with Saigon as one of the best examples. Tree-lined streets with rows of handsome shops and sidewalk cafés still bore the strong imprint of France. Luxurious villas in the residential districts stood behind high walls and tropical gardens. The fragrance of jasmine and mimosa was everywhere, and life seemed very placid and pleasant indeed.

"This seems about as much like a war zone," Gail muttered, "as New York or Los Angeles."

Gail was relieved to see that the Continentale Palace Hotel was handsome in appearance and size, and matched almost anything in New York. It had an Old World European charm and luxury about it. The long covered terrace with its high arches, snowy-clothed tables, and tropical foliages quickly became a gathering place for the USO troupe. Their room was high-ceilinged and cool, with a wide-blade fan lazily turning overhead and the ever-present fragrance of flowers drifting in through the deep casement windows. They quickly unpacked and hurried down to the lobby, where Caroline inquired if Steve McCallum was anywhere about.

"Ah, yes, Mr. McCallum just returned last evening from Da Nang," the brightly smiling clerk at the desk said. "I will have the operator ring his room." His English was as precise as his brass-buttoned uniform.

"Thank you," she said nervously. "Just tell him a friend from the States is here, please."

She turned and walked toward Gail, who had suddenly become surrounded by four or five young men in uniform who had been walking toward the bar and, recognizing her, had stopped to ask for her autograph. She stood among them, laughing and chattering brightly, every inch the actress in the green linen dress, big-brimmed green straw hat, and matching sandals. Smiling, Caroline detoured and crossed the lobby.

She stood by a small kiosk where newspapers and other periodicals in many languages were sold. She read the headlines in an English newspaper: CURRENT TROOP STRENGTH IN VIETNAM BELIEVED AT ALMOST FOUR HUNDRED THOUSAND. She started to pick the paper up to read the story more closely when she heard a voice.

"What the hell are you doing here?"

She turned slowly as her anger suddenly flared. Then nothing has changed, she thought, but when she looked up into his face, she saw that he was glad to see her. Hungrily she drank in the blue eyes, handsome face, and bronzed skin. "I guess I mean *how* the hell did you get here?" he said. He was holding her arms and shaking his head in what looked like a combination of annoyance and admiration, while his gaze raked her carefully from head to toe.

"I convinced them I should do a series on a USO group entertaining here." She was laughing excitedly, little flecks of gold dancing in the violet eyes. She pointed to Gail. "When Gail said she was coming over, I got the idea." She looked cool and beautiful in a trim white suit and pumps.

He pulled her into his arms and held her against him, murmuring into her hair, "I should spank you for it, but if you must know, I'm damned glad you're here." His voice was husky as he said, "Do you think we could leave Gail to the six advisers who look like they're headed toward the bar with her?"

"I think so," she said softly, as she smiled at Gail, who was waving over her shoulder before disappearing beyond the marble pillars and bank of ferns. With his arm about her, they walked across the lobby and mounted the wide staircase, oblivious to everyone they passed, their eyes saying what they had never dared say aloud.

She lay in his arms, watching the fan turn lazily overhead. He had half closed the tall inside shutters on the windows and a pale green light filtered into the room. The hours of the afternoon had passed as they made slow, sensual love, exploring each other, their clothes scattered across the floor, the bed in a disarray. He rose and walked to the big, airy bathroom. She heard water running in the tub and felt the core of desire flare anew. She knew he would call her to come to him and when the sound of water stopped, he said, "I'm waiting for you."

He was lying full-length in the tub and held out his arms. She stepped in and slowly lowered herself to him, as a moan rose from her throat. It was the most sensuous thing she had ever known, the slow soaping of their bodies, as though music played and they followed its rhythm, then the almost imperceptible starting of motion, his body moving up to hers while she gently swayed. Everything that was unimportant slipped away. There was only that core, throbbing and aching, and the smoothness of their bodies, the stroking of hands, mouths coming together, the beauty of skin and rippling muscles beneath water, two bodies that were one, and then the shuddering, clutching wonder, the water becoming still. So very still.

404

"I love you," he suddenly said as she knelt to dry his legs. He pulled her to her feet and when she turned a tremulous smile up to him, he grinned and said softly, "I don't give a damn who or what you may be. You could be a reincarnation of Lizzie Borden, for all I care. All I know is that I don't want to live without you."

"Steve," she whispered. "Oh, Steve."

"Tell me, dammit," he demanded, tilting her chin up so he could see into her eyes.

"I love you," she said, and he closed his eyes and smiled as he pulled her into his arms.

The following morning, Steve and several other newsmen flew with a congressional fact-finding committee to the Mekong Delta and Hue on an inspection tour. His assignment was to stay with the Congressmen until they left Vietnam five days later to fly back to Washington. While he was gone, Caroline stayed close to the USO troupe. She had brought her camera and took countless pictures of the performances. It was an exciting production group, the twelve young men and women pushing themselves to put on the best shows they possibly could. Caroline marveled at Gail, at her energy and the magic she projected, the captivating voice and the way she moved on the stage. The afternoon Steve was due back, the troupe was performing on an outdoor stage. The audience, seated on long benches in the splashing sunlight, kept roaring its approval and shouted for more. Whenever Gail came onto the stage, they jumped to their feet and whistled. She wore a dazzling white beaded costume with a short fringed skirt that whirled and sparkled in the sunlight. Caroline had already interviewed most of the young dancers and singers and had taken copious notes for the color pieces she would write. She was moving around the audience area in her tan slacks and shirt, a second camera and other equipment hanging on a strap at her side, while she kept snapping shots with her Nikon, kneeling or sometimes standing on the end of one of the benches for different angles. At one point she stopped and glanced over her shoulder, quickly. Some distance behind her was a big, broad-shouldered young man in uniform with short, curly hair. He was somewhat nondescript, but looked familiar. And then she knew. She smiled grimly, as she knelt down once more and took another picture. She had begged her father to let her make the trip without a bodyguard following her. Obviously, someone at Kendall, Inc., had used his influence to have her watched by someone from the

Intelligence Command while she was in Saigon. Undoubtedly there had been someone on the plane as well.

She sighed, pushed her Nikon down into the leather camera bag, sat down on a bench at the end of a row, and started taking more notes. There was no escaping it . . . no escaping her father or the fact that even as Carol Kramer, traveling with a USO troupe to the Pacific, she was still . . . *Caroline Kendall.*

Back at the hotel in the late afternoon, while Gail was having a drink down in the bar with a young army officer, Caroline lay back in the tub in the big, airy bathroom and let the scented water lull her into a half-sleep. The leaves of an acacia tree rustled softly at the long open window. Steve had told her he would probably be back in time to meet her at six, for dinner. She let the steam and fragrance rise all around her, then after ten minutes or so, she stepped from the tub, toweled herself, and began to dress. By five minutes to six she was ready. She looked at herself in the long mirror. The lilac linen dress molded to her figure in one artful sheath. Matching high-heeled sandals and a short jacket of the same material as the dress made her feel extremely feminine again. The khaki slacks and shirt and short-sleeved jacket she had been wearing almost constantly since leaving the United States had been comfortable but robbed her of something. But now she felt it again. She had applied a soft touch of lipstick and wore small pearls at her ears, and in the lobby, all eyes turned to her as she passed, the dark hair swinging on her shoulders.

When she saw him coming into the lobby, her heart began pounding. His skin was burned to a dark bronze, and in the short-sleeved bush jacket he seemed to tower over the other two men he was with. The moment he saw her and smiled, she took a step back. The man to his left was also smiling at her and hurrying toward her with his hand out, the silver head tipped to one side a little in quick recognition. There was a déjà vu about the moment and she felt a nausea rise in her throat.

"Why, Caroline," the voice boomed out and she recoiled inside as she saw a puzzled look come over Steve's face. "Caroline Kendall! What are you doing here, of all places?" Steve stopped and stared at her, while the Senator kissed her cheek and bumbled on. "Why, Caroline, I just had lunch with your father at the Union Club last week." Steve was standing a little to one side, staring at her, while the Senator began introducing her. "This is Caroline Kendall, Steve," he said, glancing at Steve and then the man beyond Steve. "Steve McCallum and Brad Gallagher, Caroline, two young men who were of incomparable help on this fact-finding tour." He rushed on without pause. "And what on earth are you doing here in this godforsaken place?"

She looked at Steve, whose face now reflected both confusion and anger, and without answering the Senator, she slipped her hand through Steve's arm and gently began tugging him away.

"I know Steve, Senator," she said, trying to smile naturally. "We're old friends from the States."

The Senator looked surprised, but then he smiled and glanced at Steve with new respect. "Well, then, you must know Lawrence Kendall as well, Caroline's father."

"Lawrence Kendall?" Steve said with a tight voice. "*The* Lawrence Kendall?" Caroline felt him recoil, his arm pulling away from her. "Are we talking about Kendall, Inc.?"

Somehow they managed to conclude the conversation and say goodbye to the Senator and Brad Gallagher, who strode away toward the elevators. Grim-lipped, Steve led her to the bar. It was cool and dim, for which she was thankful. The murmur of voices and occasional burst of laughter went unheeded as they sat at a small table and ordered long, cold gin drinks. For several moments, they didn't speak. The silence continued even after their drinks were put down. Absently she pushed the swizzle stick around.

"I don't fall in love easily," he said in a hard voice, his eyes trained on some distant object, the lids squinting as though sunlight had penetrated the dimness. "So I suppose I won't fall out of it any more easily."

"Steve . . ." It was a soft cry. She touched his arm, but he pulled it away.

"I despise liars and frauds," he said. He turned and looked at her full in the face. "And I have very little use for those who accumulate fortunes that are so vast they cannot even be measured, who have done so at the expense of others who are far less fortunate."

"Please let me—"

"There's nothing you can say, Carol," he said, his voice cold and unrelenting. He took a long swallow of his drink, almost finishing it. "Or should I say Caroline?"

"You're got to listen to me, let me tell you why I did it—"

"What difference does it make why you did it? It wouldn't change

407

anything. Nothing you could say now could change anything." He threw some money on the table and rose. "And at least let me pay for the drinks, our last drink together."

He strode from the room, the anger flushing his face to a deep red beneath the tan. She sat there for a long time, not moving, her face almost expressionless. Finally, she got to her feet and walked out of the bar, crossed the lobby to the elevators, and disappeared through the door when it opened.

Even Gail couldn't coax her from the room that evening. She lay on her bed with her face to the windows, fully dressed, her eyes wide and staring. She kept hearing his voice and the words, over and over in her mind, and yet she didn't move, she didn't cry; she just kept watching the motion of the tree branches beyond the windows as a gentle breeze stirred them, the tiny white flowers among the leaves trembling.

That was where Gail left her when she went to her evening performance, still bewildered about what had occurred. But when she returned at almost midnight, Caroline was sitting by the window in a long white silk robe. In a strangely distant voice, she told Gail what had happened and Gail nodded her head, understanding. She undressed in silence, then, lighting a cigarette, sat on the floor beside Caroline. Clasping her arms about her knees, she looked up. "If I were as much in love with Steve as you seem to be, then I certainly wouldn't take what he said this afternoon as final. Sure, he was mad. Mad as hell, and I can't say I blame him. Where you thought you were going with this masquerade, I never *did* figure out. But let him sleep on it, Carol. He's bound to realize in the morning how much he still loves you, once all this righteous indignation has worn off."

Caroline looked down at her. "Do you really believe that?"

"Sure I do." Gail took a long drag on her cigarette. "He probably felt like a perfect ass when that Senator blurted everything out. I would have, I know." She saw tears beginning to appear in Caroline's eyes and roll down her cheeks. Good, she thought. First remorse, then a little self-pity, and finally hope. Was it ever any different?

They sat in silence for a long while. Just one lamp in a corner of the room created a cool and restful feeling. Gail drew again on the cigarette, and closed her eyes for a moment. She hadn't thought about Richard in a long while. It was too painful. Still. But as she thought about him, while sounds from the distant streets of Saigon drifted in

408

through the long open windows, she realized that much of the sharp pain had left her. It would never be completely gone, she knew. She had loved him too much for that. But their long separations had given her strength and endurance, and their child had given her hope and kept her from being too deeply bitter. She thought of Dickie and smiled. And she thought of Jack Gordon, back in New York, and her eyes softened.

"Go after him tomorrow, Caro," she said softly. Caroline looked around at her, a flicker of hope in her eyes. "First thing in the morning. Wait for him downstairs and make him listen. Tell him how much you love him and how nothing else should matter. *Nothing!*"

Moments later, Caroline reached down, clasped Gail's hand, and squeezed it. Then she rose and walked over to her bed. When she looked at Gail, there was a ghost of a smile on her lips. "I actually think I might be able to sleep now," she said, and as she slipped beneath the sheet, she sighed and closed her eyes.

She had been waiting for an hour when she finally approached the desk and said to the concierge, the older of the two men who were putting mail in the boxes, "Mr. McCallum, please. I wonder if you would ring his room for me?"

The two men looked at each other and then the concierge leaned a little over the high desk. "Mr. McCallum, he leave last night."

"He left?" It was a small gasp.

"He leave. Take everything with him," the concierge said, while the younger man nodded in concert, and then they turned back to their mail sorting.

Caroline and Gail began looking for him within minutes. Following every lead, they tried to discover where he had gone. At that time there were less than twenty-five newsmen in Saigon, most of them more concerned with the political turmoil and the South Vietnamese Army-led coups that had continued through the summer and fall than with anything else. So it wasn't difficult for them to learn that Steve had flown with a helicopter crew to Da Nang.

"He won't be coming back for a while," the sandy-haired young Brad Gallagher told them. "He said he was fed up with the obsession with nothing but political agitation and army coups. I'm heading for the Mekong Delta myself, where some combat troops are digging in, and he said he may end up there."

Caroline's short-lived hope disappeared. She tried to get permission to fly to Da Nang, but was refused. Suddenly the handsome city of Saigon began to take on a shoddy, impermanent look. She started to wander frantically about with her notebook and camera, trying not to think, to cram her mind and the three days left with an observer's trivia and wartime notations.

Flimsy modern office buildings, native stall markets, piles of garbage, choking traffic, and smog plagued the streets. Away from the luxury of the Continentale and Caravelle hotels, from the embassies, the theatre and outdoor garden where the USO shows were put on, the city took on a sleazy, sordid look. There were shrieking street vendors everywhere, children hawking American cigarettes and black-market American liquor. She took rolls and rolls of pictures— of pimps and prostitutes, the tiny street peddlers, the garbage and filth, the military vehicles choking the streets, pretty Vietnamese women in their pastel *ao-dais,* and the signs and banners that were everywhere, welcoming Americans to Saigon.

And then the day came that they had to leave.

Caroline watched from the plane window as it taxied to the runway, through narrow paths between arriving and departing planes, her heart heavy. And Gail, watching, remembered what her mother had once told her. Well, she thought sadly, Caroline hadn't had to wait long to begin inheriting the burdens of wealth. And as the plane winged skyward, she reached out and clasped Caroline's hand.

26
1966

When Caroline and Gail returned from Vietnam, Lawrence Kendall immediately summed up the situation and decided Caroline needed a diversion of some kind.

St. Moritz was the one place that Lawrence Kendall permitted his wife or daughter to go without bodyguards. "The security is built in, mountain-locked," he often commented. And so he insisted they stop off there, before going on to Bellone for a visit.

It was Gail's first trip to St. Moritz, and she gazed with open mouth up at the amazing sight before them. Sitting high above the frozen lakes were the turrets and towers and gables of Badrutt's Palace Hotel, a mere suggestion of the sumptuous surprises that waited within.

"It looks absolutely crazy," Gail said, as they arrived at the entrance in a horse-drawn sleigh. "And I love it already." She jumped from the sleigh in her red fox coat and boots, blonde hair flowing over the collar, and began to whirl about on the snow, while people in ski clothes stopped to watch and laugh. She flew through the high-ceilinged lobby and across the Persian rugs with the abandon of a child, while Caroline in her lynx coat followed at a more sedate pace.

It was still difficult to smile or to indulge in small talk, hard to carry on any kind of conversation. Most of her thoughts were still filled with Steve McCallum. But she made the effort, skating on the Palace Hotel rink, taking the funicular to Corviglia-Piz Nair for skiing, watching the horse races on the frozen lake, and swimming in the Palace pool. She even accompanied Gail to the King's Club disco, but excused herself and left when a young man who introduced himself as the Baron Helmut von Dorfmueller insisted on dancing with her, as his friend whirled Gail off across the floor.

She sat impatiently through a dinner party the following evening in one of the elaborate chalets of Suvretta, browsed in Cartier's the next morning while Gail bought earrings and a necklace, and listened with amusement on the sunny terrace of the Hotel Chantarella while Helmut pointed out Mohammed Riza Pahlavi, the Shah of Iran, and his empress standing in casual conversation with a Hollywood film director and a London banker.

When the young baron had learned that Caroline was *the* Caroline Kendall, he became even more attentive.

"If it ever happens when it's someone I might really be interested in, Caro, you had better fall off the mountain or make a fast disappearance of some kind." She grinned as they dressed for dinner that evening in the huge bedroom of their suite, which overlooked the mountains. "And I have to admit, Helmut is kind of adorable."

"Really, Gail! He's an empty-headed fool," Caroline snapped while pulling the zipper up on the pale green silk jersey gown. "Not one of them is worth the pencil in Jack's pocket."

"Mmmmm, he is nice, isn't he?" Gail said lazily. She was sitting at the dressing table, finishing off her makeup, her silvery gown glittering in the soft lamplight. "But as long as I'm here . . ." She let it trail off. Since the majority of the guests were European, they had both been surprised at how many people at the Palace and in St. Moritz had recognized her.

"Well, we do get to New York every once in a while," said the baron's friend, a bronzed and blond young man from Stockholm whose family was in steel and who looked born to both ski and dinner clothes.

Somehow Caroline managed to get through that last evening, but finally had to tell Helmut that no, she wouldn't see him again, in Paris, London, *or* New York.

"Ugh, why are they so persistent?" she said as they walked to their suite later that night. Gail had taken off her shoes and was padding along in her stocking feet, carrying a flimsy little high-heeled sandal in each hand.

"Because, my darling, dear but simple little friend . . ."

Caroline closed her eyes and held her breath. She didn't want to hear it. That men were attracted to her because she was Caroline

412

Kendall, *heiress to one of the largest fortunes in the world.*

"You are gorgeous, bright, witty, have a smashing figure, and—well, it helps that you're Caroline Kendall."

Caroline smiled at her, as they walked into the suite. "Thanks for leaving that to the last," she said with sarcasm.

They left for Basel the next morning. Mark Rumsey met them with a car at Zurich Airport and they arrived at Bellone just in time for tea. As they pulled up before the big stone house, Ellie and Georges, with Dickie between them, came out and down the terrace steps. With tears and laughter, Gail swooped the little boy into her arms.

"Caroline, oh, Caroline, I'm so glad you came with Gail," Ellie said, putting her arms around her. Caroline softly touched the pretty blonde woman's cheeks, then turned and kissed Georges. She knelt down to hug Dickie, who immediately informed her, "I'm eight years old!"

Bellone was beautiful in the snow, taking on a feverish gaiety as the students hurried from building to building in their bright ski jackets and stocking caps. Caroline and Gail walked to the village with Dickie, where they bought him hot chocolate in the coffee house and gifts for Ellie and Georges. They sat before huge fires and talked about the old days with Ellie and Georges. But after three days, Caroline's restlessness and conscience sent her to her room, where she quickly packed her suitcases.

"Why?" Gail pleaded. "We just got here."

"Because I have to stop acting like a spoiled brat and get back to my job."

"But you—"

"I know." Caroline smiled. "If I don't feel like going back, I just pick up the telephone, call my father's offices or Warren Leland, and . . ." She turned and started closing her suitcases. "That's just what people expect me to do. Because of who I am. And that's exactly why I can't do it." She looked over her shoulder at Gail with a smile. "I have two weeks' vacation coming to me. I've taken exactly eleven days of it. I'm going home and on to Boston. I'll be back at my desk on Monday morning."

Gail suddenly laughed. "What a crazy lady. When you can do just exactly what you want."

"That's why." Caroline straightened up, just as Georges and Ellie came into the room.

"Ready for those bags to go down?" Georges asked. He took

Caroline's face between his hands and kissed her forehead. "We wish you would stay, chérie."

"I know." Caroline smiled. "But I must go."

"We understand," Ellie said, as they each picked up a suitcase and crowded toward the door.

They all stood on the steps and waved as the car with Mark Rumsey and Caroline drove away and disappeared through the gate.

"She's finally *really* grown up," Ellie murmured as she linked her arms through those of Georges and Gail and they walked into the house.

27
1970

The city room at the *Inquirer* had changed little over the years. More paint had peeled from the walls, the wire wastebaskets were more battered than ever, the letter *P* on Caroline's typewriter was still chipped, and the hot-water faucet in the ladies' room still produced cold water. But she looked across the city room each morning with fondness as she sat down at her desk, a carton of steaming hot coffee beside her adding that special early-morning fragrance to the blend of pencil shavings, dust, ink, and last night's pizza. The high grime-covered windows filtered the morning light as she sorted through her early mail, feet up on her wastebasket, which the night staff had stuffed to the rim with discarded story leads, Chinese take-out containers, hamburger wrappers, and coffee cartons.

"God, I'm tired," Connie Winslow complained as she leaned back dangerously far in the old swivel chair and stretched her arms above her head. "I sat on that damned stake-out with Dan Staley until three A.M., and nothing!" She yawned. "I think I'm getting a sore throat."

"Uh-huh," Caroline said, slitting a letter open. Patty Dunbar had long since left for a job on a California newspaper, and Connie, with her fuzzy blonde hair and hypochondria, had inherited her desk next to Caroline.

"Carol, I really love that skirt," Connie said as she slid a piece of copy paper into her typewriter with one hand and probed the glands in her neck with the other. "When you're ready to dump it, will you dump it my way?"

"Who said I was going to dump it?"

"Well, my God, you dumped that purple wool two weeks ago and it hardly had any wear in it. I don't care what you say, *that* was a Rudi Gernreich or I'll eat my hat." She looked around at her with her usual curious stare. "How anybody can afford clothes like you have on *these* salaries, I'll never—"

"Bargain hunting, Connie, I've told you. I'm very good at it." She pushed the last piece of correspondence down onto a sharp spindle and quickly rolled some copy paper into her typewriter. She didn't even cross her fingers anymore when she told her white lies.

"Yeah," Connie muttered under her breath, while Caroline simply smiled. "Or maybe a sugar daddy—"

"Hey, Carol," Billy Samuels, the copy boy, yelled as he ran toward her waving an envelope in his hand. "A cable."

She took it from him with a quick smile of thanks and ripped it open, while Connie leaned a little toward her. When she read it she smiled again. "Oh, how wonderful!" she said.

"Well, what? My God, we don't get cables every day here."

"Remember my friend Gail Halloran?"

"Well, of course. She's the musical comedy star."

"She's getting married in Rome, where she's making a film. To her agent. And she wants me there for the wedding."

"Rome," Connie said dreamily. "Imagine getting married in Rome."

"Well, I guess that means I'll take my vacation early," Caroline said, getting up from her desk and walking up to Bob Ashford's desk at the front of the city room.

"My God, some people get all the breaks," Connie grumbled to herself as she began pounding on her typewriter.

Rome in May was warm, but made up for the heat with its golden domes and towers and crumbling but magnificent ruins. She stayed at the Hassler, where both the wedding and reception were held.

"I still can't believe it," Jack Gordon said to her under his breath as they stood together in the high-ceilinged drawing room of the spacious suite overlooking the city. It was crammed to the big wide double doors with babbling guests, talking in all languages, everyone sipping champagne and laughing and shouting congratulations at the bride and bridegroom. Caroline gazed up at him with fondness and said softly, "Well, I guess from the expression on your face that she was well worth waiting for."

He smiled his response, and as he did, she noticed the fine wrinkles at the corners of his dark eyes, silvery streaks at the temples. He was still gracefully lean and lanky and in the cutaway and gray-striped trousers there was a certain elegance about him. They stood together in warm silence, sipping their champagne and watching Gail in her long white chiffon gown as she talked to guests. Suddenly Dickie broke away from her and with a broad smile on his face came toward them. He was tall for twelve and already revealing the good looks of his father and the charm and humor of his mother. He edged between them, clasping both by the arms, and said, as he looked up at Jack with a brimming smile, "She said, after your honeymoon, that you'll both come to Bellone for a month." He quickly turned to Caroline. "Come and stay with us, Aunt Caroline."

"Well, maybe for some weekends," she said with a smile. "I've fallen so in love with this city since arriving, that I've managed to get the international desk to assign me to Rome for a while." She looked over near the doors and frowned a little. Mark Rumsey was still very much a part of her existence, and at the moment, he simply looked like one of the guests as he stood by the white and gold doors talking to a paunchy-looking man with white hair and a monocle.

A cable two days before to Warren Leland had brought the response that he would see what he could do about the Rome assignment for her. The following day another cable had arrived, this time from the international desk of the Inquirer, giving her permission to stay "until reassignment."

She ran with the other guests through the Hassler lobby throwing rice and confetti at the newly married couple, then rode to Fiumicino Airport with Ellie and Georges and Dickie, only to be solemnly told at the plane gate by the boy, "I'd rather be called Dick now, if you don't mind, Aunt Caroline."

Ellie smiled and said, "I guess when a young man approaches his thirteenth birthday, that's the very least we can do."

Caroline looked at him with misty eyes, then hugged him to her. "Well, as long as I can still do this, I don't mind losing the little boy we once knew."

He smiled at her and with the back of his hand wiped a tear away, then, looking back and waving, started through the gate. Georges was the last to go. He wore his customary rakish white panama hat, and she realized he would never lose the look of the Paris boulevardier. He leaned down and kissed her cheek. "Come to see us often," he said. "Ellie misses you. We all do."

She waved until they had disappeared, then walked with Mark out of the huge terminal and climbed into the car.

They drove to the southern strip of the Amalfi Drive, where sun flooded the jagged cliffs and sandy beaches along the brilliant blue waters of the Tyrrenian Sea. Jack had been driving with one hand on the wheel and one hand clasping Gail's, but when they first began encountering the hairpin curves on the road that wound through olive and lemon groves along the cliffs, he grinned and said, "Have to pay a little more attention here." With that, he put both hands on the wheel.

Gail watched from the window of the Mercedes, enthralled as suddenly on a sharp curve and dip in the road stretches of the coast far below would suddenly appear like some mirage, the sapphire blue coves and rocky peaks that soared above making her catch her breath.

"What a perfect place for a honeymoon," she said an hour later as she stood in the middle of their suite at the San Pietro and looked around her. Flaming bougainvillea from the terrace crawled across the ceiling of the lovely salon, bringing the outdoors in through the wide doors. She walked to the terrace and looked far down to the beach, breathing deeply. The fragrance of lemon blossoms blended with the briny aroma of the sea. She felt Jack's hands on her shoulders and leaned back against him. "Thank you for bringing me here," she whispered, and he touched his lips to her hair, as his arms circled her.

They lunched on ripe melon and huge shrimp, then wandered through the village of Positano with its Moorish-style buildings that clung step-like to the steeply rising hill. Gail shopped for gifts in the smart little boutiques while Jack trailed along, watching her in amusement as she struggled with her Italian phrasebook, much to the delight of the shopkeepers, several of whom recognized her from her films. She wore a yellow and white dress that fluttered about her knees in the caressing little wind that blew from the sea, the golden hair caught in its distinctive top-knot and wisping about her face and over her ears.

"I must write and tell Caro about this place," she bubbled, her hand in his as they swung along toward the beach with its red-and-white candy-striped cabanas. Crowds of bathers in brightly colored bikinis and trunks dotted the water. "She must come here. She would absolutely love it."

"You two are never far apart, if only in your thoughts, are you?" Jack said, and she looked at him sharply, then broke into a wide smile, as she saw the warmth and humor in his eyes.

"Far enough that we don't intrude," she said, tipping her head as she thought about it, "but close enough that we've always been there when the other one needed someone."

They dined that evening in the candlelit dining room that seemed to hang in space, its massive windows pulling in the flaming sunset and then the lavender haze of twilight as it drifted over the sea. He held her close as they danced on the terrace, the tiny crystals on her pale yellow gown sparkling in the candlelight against his dinner jacket as they glided and bent like a flame in the wind. And when the moon cut a path across the water, he led her through the hotel to their suite.

They stood close, but without touching, facing each other, the dark blue of the sea and sky filling the universe beyond them through the wide terrace doors of their bedroom. He pushed the narrow straps of her gown from her shoulders and it shimmered to the floor, leaving her bathed in moonlight. Slowly, she unfastened the studs on his shirt.

"God, you're beautiful," he whispered.

He had tossed the dinner jacket on a chair, and with both hands she was pushing back the shirt until it slithered from his arms. "I was just going to say the same about you." Her smile was secret, as though others were in the room and it was only for him.

"Women are beautiful. Men are—are—"

"Delicious," she murmured, her lips roving over the skin on his chest.

With one swift movement, he picked her up and carried her to the bed, where he lay down beside her and gazed the length of her. She pulled him down to her and let her lips wander and whisper over his face. With infinite patience, they explored each other's bodies, holding back the storm of passion, measuring each sensation as his hands roamed across her flesh.

She saw him above her in the faint stream of moonlight that filtered into the room, saw the dark hair falling on his forehead, the wide sloping outline of his shoulders, his head in strong silhouette. The sound of the sea beyond the windows and walls was like music, coming closer, then falling away in rhythmic waves that lay at the edge of their consciousness. Her hands circled him to pull him down to her, and she shuddered deliciously at the feel of muscles rippling across his back.

But patient exploration deserted them, and in its place came abandonment. It roared into their senses and swept them on. And when finally they lay back, her head on his shoulder, she felt caught in a drifting trance.

"I love you," she whispered. "So very, very much."

He smiled into the darkness, and pulled her close. He had never stopped loving her.

Caroline took an apartment with a wide canopied terrace overlooking the Spanish Steps, where she could see the very last view that the poet Keats had seen before he died, from his windows of the house at the foot of the steps. She never tired of the constantly moving scene around the Bernini fountain at the bottom, or the waves of people as they moved up and down the stairs where the flower vendors and sellers of curios and souvenirs mingled with the tourists in a vivid mosaic.

Once settled, she began covering everything for the newspaper, from a sit-down strike of airport workers in the main airport terminal, to a first-person story on her audience with Pope Paul VI at the Vatican. She traveled to Anzio and wrote a moving piece on the cemetery at Nettuno, which held the graves of 10,000 American soldiers killed in the days after the landing during World War II. She wrote of the contrast, the Anzio of 1970 with its waving palm trees and pleasant promenades, and few signs of that fateful January day in 1944 when landing craft slid up on the beaches.

Her life in Rome drifted almost pleasantly, when she could force herself to stop thinking of Steve McCallum. She learned the language rather quickly, finding her fluency in French a help in picking up Italian. She made friends, a small circle from the news media from many different countries, and others from an interesting international set. But she was close to no one. It was almost as though she were afraid of any kind of intimacy. Steve was almost always in the back of her mind, like a deep and open wound that never seemed to heal, but that she kept far enough from her conscious self to deflect and disseminate the pain.

As her experience in covering large events grew, she began receiving assignments in other cities and countries within a fairly short flying distance. When Egypt's President Gamal Abdel Nasser died of a heart attack, she flew to Cairo for the funeral. Then in 1972, when the Israeli Olympic team was taken hostage in Munich, she arrived at the airport just hours before the massacre took place.

She spent that Christmas at Bellone and lingered on for a time while

Gail and Jack visited, but left suddenly for Paris to cover the Vietnam peace pact that was to be signed on January twenty-seventh, in the Hotel Majestic. Although she knew that Steve was still in Vietnam, her eyes darted from face to face of the closely packed press corps during the morning ceremony, just on the chance that he might be there. With a mixture of disappointment and relief, she saw he was not. In the plane returning to Rome, she felt a saddening of spirits.

"Chin up," Mark said softly. He had been idly thumbing through a news magazine at her side in the first-class section, glancing at her from time to time with concern. He knew her well enough to read her thoughts, knew enough about her relationship with Steve to be sympathetic, and had guessed at her disappointment.

She tried to smile at him, picked up her glass of wine and slowly sipped it, then, while looking out the small window at a bank of clouds they were floating through, she said in a soft voice, "I'm such a fool, aren't I, Mark?"

He put a hand over hers. "Foolish maybe. Foolish in love. But certainly never a fool." He smiled at the flight attendant, who had bent down for a moment to peer at their glasses to make certain they weren't empty. When she walked on along the aisle, he said in a careful voice, "Maybe you should go back." He said it almost hesitantly. "To Saigon. Talk to him."

Swinging her head slowly from side to side, she said, "Even if it were possible, with credentials becoming harder and harder to get, I —I couldn't. I couldn't face the hurt of it again—of seeing him walk away from me."

Soon after returning to Rome, she took some of her vacation and joined Lawrence and Elizabeth on the *Sapphire* as it cruised through the Greek Islands. She came back to her apartment on the Piazza di Spagna with a renewed interest in her job. For months she plunged into covering every kind of story she could find, the filming of an American movie in the Trastevere section, the terrorist kidnapping of three Italian officials, a fashion show in an ancient grotto, the running of the *Contrade* in Siena, and then the film festival in Cannes.

Mark, always from a distance when she worked, watched with amusement as she rebuffed most male interest in her. There was the second secretary from the Spanish Embassy, a startlingly handsome man in his mid-thirties "who most women would die for," said Margery Contegni, a casual friend of Caroline's, whose husband was in the American Embassy. But Caroline simply smiled, and drifted off through the cocktail party with a polite but slightly bored expression on her face. And there was the Venezuelan oil magnate she had interviewed when he arrived in Rome on business. He had followed her about for days and was finally dislodged from the fringes of her life only when Caroline flew to Israel in October—the Egyptians and Israelis had begun to battle along the Suez Canal and on the Golan Heights.

She spent much of her free time reading the newspaper accounts of what was happening in Vietnam. The last American troops had left early in 1973, and with that the Communist buildup of supplies and armaments and soldiers accelerated in South Vietnam. By March in 1975, they had captured Banmethuot, then Hue, and finally Da Nang. A letter from Ed Pinckney told her that the publisher Grant Mason was talking about retirement, that conditions at the *Inquirer* were slipping badly, that Ab Streitner had gone to the space agency control center in Houston, and that—Steve was going to the Middle East.

She put the letter down slowly, and looked off across the golden rooftops of Rome. She could see the dome on St. Peter's, gleaming in the sun. *The Middle East.* She was going to the Middle East herself. In 1973, a news communiqué from Cairo had reported that Egypt's President Anwar el-Sadat and Colonel Muammar el-Qaddafi of Libya had proclaimed the birth of "a new unity." She had wondered at this at the time, having found qualities in Sadat that were admirable. He had ousted the Soviet advisors and technicians and signed trade agreements with the European Economic Community, in spite of his close alliance with Libya and Syria, both of which advocated all-out guerrila warfare with Israel. There were contradictions in him that she found interesting, and so she had begun a long series of steps that would, she hoped, permit her an interview with the Egyptian head of state. Finally, permission came.

She and Mark flew to Cairo that September of 1975. Once through the security entrance area, they proceeded into the main hall of the terminal to claim their luggage. Mark saw him first. He grasped Caroline's arm, almost knocking her folded trench coat to the floor, and muttered low, "Watch it! Someone's coming toward you with a big smile and his hand out to shake yours, and there's a bunch of reporters and photographers behind him."

She tried to turn around, reverse her steps, but the man called out, "Caroline! Caroline Kendall."

At first she didn't recognize him, but then realized it was Dwight

Goss, a friend of her father and member of the State Department. Since the United States and Egypt had resumed diplomatic relations two years earlier, members of the State Department had been shuttling back and forth at frequent intervals. As she shook his hand and mumbled something, while trying to walk on, a photographer suddenly jumped in front of her and snapped her picture. Goss and an aide beside him appeared confused as she backed away. She almost felt sorry for him when one of the reporters gathered close asked him, "You mean *the* Caroline Kendall? Lawrence Kendall's daughter?"

Goss was nodding and trying to catch her eye, wondering why she was behaving in such a curious fashion. When they began pelting her with questions, she again tried to walk away, with Mark pulling at her arm and attempting to shoulder his way through the crowd. But one reporter, with reddish hair and cynical gray eyes, grasped her other arm and said, "Wait a minute. I met you in Rome, during that airport workers' strike. We shared a sandwich. Remember?" He turned around to the others and said, "Hey, you guys, she may be Caroline Kendall, but she's been working as a news correspondent in Rome under the name of"—he scratched his head, trying to recall—"of Carol Kramer. That's it. Carol Kramer." His face had become angry.

He turned and looked her full in the eyes. "Christ! With all the money you've got, do you have to take this job away from somebody else who really needs it? What a lousy thing to do."

Caroline stared at him for a moment, stunned into immobility. It was as though he had slapped her. She turned and ran, Mark Rumsey following her at a fast clip.

The following morning, with Mark getting her through the hotel lobby without incident, she went for her interview with the Egyptian President. Forcing herself to concentrate only on him, and keeping her thoughts in the background about the altercation at the airport the day before, she spent the allotted hour with President Sadat, finding him completely charming and cooperative.

Back in the hotel she kept to her suite until the newspapers were delivered to her. While waiting, she looked down onto the Nile. A graceful *felucca* was swooping along the river, its wide sail looping out in the gentle wind. When the knock came on the door and Mark walked in with the papers, she asked him to join her on the balcony for lunch, while she sat down and gingerly opened the *International Herald Tribune*. The story, on an inside page, was brief, since little

423

information had reached Paris. But the *Egyptian Gazette,* the English-language newspaper of Cairo, had her name in one-inch headlines. The story was probably already traveling by AP or UPI wire to New York. She could feel the slow pounding of her heart.

"You know, it was really only a matter of time," Mark said, as he sipped at his coffee and looked off to the curious blend that was Cairo —the graceful minarets, shady parks bordering the Nile, wide boulevards, and flower-filled gardens all vying with modern buildings reaching to the sky. "I'm really surprised that someone hasn't spotted you before this."

She nodded, knowing he was right, but she resented it anyway. Tears of anger and frustration filled her eyes.

"I've already been in touch with New York," he said, breaking off a piece of croissant and putting it in his mouth. "The *Sapphire* has been in Sardinia. Your two older brothers and their wives were there. They've left, but the *Sapphire* has gone on to Nice and is waiting for your parents there. They'll be arriving from New York in about a week. Your father wants me to get you there. I've already booked a flight. We have to be at the airport in two hours."

She nodded again, rose, and walked to the balcony door. "I'll pack right away," she said, looking at him. He saw the deep hurt in her eyes.

"Look," he said softly, "you've worked as a reporter long enough to know how stories are slanted."

She shook her head. "But I never savaged anyone, Mark. I never deliberately set out to try to hurt someone."

"But, honey," he said, standing up and taking her by the shoulders, "that guy really believed what he said to you."

They flew directly to Nice, where Caroline insisted on staying at the Negresco, when they saw reporters and a photographer lurking near the *Sapphire.* It was a seafront hotel that Caroline recalled from her childhood, built in the French château manner; with a great sweep of mansard roof and domed tower. It somehow gave her comfort, just knowing that it was still there.

"I don't want to go on the *Sapphire,*" she said, knowing Mark would be disappointed. He had his own quarters there and friends among the large crew and staff. "Not until Mummy and Daddy arrive."

She rented a Mercedes and insisted on driving herself. For the first two days, they visited the seaside villages along the lower road—

424

Villefranche, on a big blue bowl of a bay, Cap Ferrat with its long promontory of luxurious villas amid sheltered coves and beaches, and Beaulieu with its casino. She drove on to Monaco, the second smallest state in Europe and just nine miles east of Nice.

The third day, this time with the top down and Mark driving, they chose the Upper Corniche and headed for Vistaero. It was a glorious morning, the sun drenching the high rocky coast, the sea stretching off to the horizon like a bright blue carpet in the brilliant light. They passed olive groves and vineyards as they climbed, villas smothered in bougainvillea and mimosa, lemon and orange trees, roses and laurel. She looked down on the graceful harbors and picturesque towns and felt the turmoil and hurt inside lessen. Mark glanced at her from time to time, but was quiet. He knew her and knew it was best to let her work it out herself.

"He was so angry," she said softly, as though they had been talking about it. "Why was he so angry?"

Mark hid his surprise as he looked at her again. "The reporter in Cairo?" He thought about it for a moment. "Political rebel, I suppose. Red hot on social reform. Probably hates capitalism in all its forms. Or—maybe it's as simple as something like having a friend who can't get a job on a newspaper, and with some crazy kind of logic, he blames you." He paused. "You know, maybe you should try to prove to that guy in the airport that he was wrong about you."

She gazed at him, as though he had opened a locked door. He was tanned and fit-looking from just the few days they had been in Nice, the white polo shirt he wore turning his tan an even deeper bronze. At breakfast that morning, he had told her, with an engaging grin about how he and some friends from the *Sapphire*'s crew had gone out on the town the night before. He looked happy, contented. Mark was the most uncomplicated person Caroline knew and she at times envied him and his ability to keep his life free of the complexities and problems that others seemed to have. "When you steer clear of marriage," he often said cheerfully, "you reduce the possibility of calamity in your life by about seventy-five percent."

He was looking at her again as the car purred swiftly past two boys on bicycles, who waved as they passed. "Feeling better?"

"Oh, Mark," she said, throwing her arms wide, as though embracing the sun and warm wind and the vast blue sky above the treetops, "yes. Feeling better."

"Atta girl, kiddo! Ready to tackle the world?" He grinned down at her. "You're beginning to sound like your old self, I'm happy to say."

"I've been thinking things out." She smiled at him. "Anyway, who could feel badly on a day like this?" But then she turned her head sharply.

It all happened so quickly. She was only briefly aware of what lay ahead of them. Mark had swung the car around a hairpin curve on a downgrade, and coming at them in the wrong lane was a gardener's truck, chugging up the road. She heard the screech of tires and Mark's string of shouted oaths, and knew, as he attempted to swing around the battered truck, that the car was going to turn over. She felt herself being flung through the air and, before blacking out, heard a terrifying explosion. Then there was nothing . . . nothing but a swimming darkness that rushed up to meet her and closed out the melting sunshine and brilliant blue of the sky above them.

She opened her eyes slowly. For several moments, everything seemed blurred, out of focus. She heard a man's voice, with a strong accent, talking and then fading, as though he had gone away. She smelled the odors of a hospital before she could see that she was in a hospital room. Then she felt a hand touching hers.

"Oh, darling," she heard. It was her mother's voice, soft, trembling but filled with relief. "Oh, darling . . ."

She saw her mother and father, standing beside the bed. "Sweetheart," he said, almost brokenly. She felt pain and realized her shoulder and arm were encased in a cast, felt more pain and found she couldn't move. "What is it?" she whispered.

"Well, you were badly hurt, sweetheart," her father said. He had pulled a chair up and was sitting beside her.

"How badly?" she asked, the words rasping from her throat. When neither of them answered, she said insistently, "How badly?"

"The spleen was damaged and had to be removed. You have a broken shoulder and arm, and bruising lacerations." He wasn't looking at her.

She stared at him. "And . . . Mark?"

"I—I'm sorry, sweetheart. Mark is dead."

Caroline's free hand came up to her face and covered her eyes. Tears slid down her cheeks and both of them reached out to touch her again. She heard her father murmuring to someone on the far side of the room, then felt the prick of a needle and began to slowly slide

426

away, slowly, slowly . . . until just a corner of her mind clung to consciousness. Then there was nothing.

A month later the *Sapphire* was steaming south toward Santorini. Caroline lay back in the green-and-white-striped lounge chair, her long dark hair flung back, her eyes closed to the sun. Elizabeth sat under the canvas, dark glasses on her eyes and a book in her lap. She kept glancing at Caroline, who had lain perfectly still for almost half an hour. Somehow she knew she wasn't sleeping. When she saw a tear slip from the corner of her eye, she reached out and gently touched her hand, and Caroline's eyes opened.

"You have to begin to believe, darling," Elizabeth said softly, "that it wasn't your fault."

It was several moments before Caroline spoke. "He was looking forward to that evening so much. He had just seen his friends and they planned to go out together again that evening on shore." She swallowed hard and looked off toward the placid sea. "Mark was my friend," she said. "And I loved him as my friend."

For several moments neither of them said anything. Caroline looked off at the sea, at the whitecaps dancing in the sun. "He taught me something," she said quietly. "He taught me that I shouldn't sit in a corner and feel sorry for myself."

Elizabeth smiled. Caroline had told her what Mark had said about the red-haired young reporter at the airport in Cairo. "Meaning?"

Caroline looked at her. "Meaning that I want to go home and"— she smiled, remembering—"start tackling the world." Her voice became soft. "And I want to hear Mark say, *Atta girl, kiddo* . . . if only in my heart."

28

They spent that Christmas at Bellone, much to the delight of Ellie and Georges. Gail was already there when Caroline and Elizabeth arrived, along with Dudley Coombs, the soft-spoken North Carolinian who had taken Mark's place. Lawrence and Jack Gordon flew over for the holiday, just for three days, then returned to New York, taking Elizabeth with them, while Caroline lingered on.

"I just finished a film that doesn't seem to have any name as yet," Gail had explained when Caroline and Elizabeth first got to Bellone. "And I have about twelve days before I have to start rehearsals for a new musical in New York. But I was half crazy, Caro, when I couldn't get away to go to you when you were in that hospital."

The evening Lawrence and Jack left, Caroline and Gail were sitting in the library, a huge fire leaping on the hearth. Before retiring, Georges brought hot toddies to them, and when Gail put them down on the low coffee table, he took Caroline's hands in his and said, "Thank God you are all right, chérie." His hair had silvered and was getting thin on the top, but he was still as slim and handsome as he had been years ago. As always, his warm brown eyes seemed to dance when he laughed or smiled. "Ellie paced the floor nights until Elizabeth phoned and said you were finally on the road to recovery."

"The school looks wonderful, Georges. You've done such a marvelous job here."

"Well, yes. I think we always make progress. Now with the new gymnasium and the enlargement of the stables, we're growing a little, but not too much to lose our intimacy and personal attention, our hallmarks."

He kissed them both and, with a wave of his hand, left them before the fire. They sat for a long moment watching the flames leap, finding comfort in the warm silence.

"All right," Gail said. "What is this wonderful secret you want to tell me?" She sank to the floor and started pulling her boots off.

Caroline curled her legs beneath her in the corner of the low couch and sipped at her hot toddy. "This isn't just a visit back to the States." She pushed her hair back from her face.

"Oh?" Gail said. "What exactly is it?"

"I—I'm going home to stay."

Gail gazed at her, wide-eyed. "Go on."

"Warren Leland, in addition to heading Kendall Newspapers, is interim publisher of the *World Inquirer* in Boston. In absentia, mostly. I want to take over."

"As publisher?" Gail was startled.

"As publisher. Grant Mason retired."

It took several moments for Gail to absorb this. And then she smiled. "Well, bravo, my darling, bravo.

"Ed Pinckney has written me that it's in a shambles, been going downhill for the past few years. The morale is at its lowest point. Nothing's been done to improve the physical layout—broken type-writers, peeling plaster, antiquated wire machines. And now there's still another new managing editor, a woman, one of those types who thinks she has to be tough, ride everybody because she's a woman and in management, tall, red-headed, good-looking, never married. There was another one, just before her, a man who belittled the ability of everyone, anyone who had been there before he arrived. Said they were all inferior quality, a bunch of amateurs. That, of course, made him feel superior. He then proceeded to create his own fiefdom, by rewarding those who showed a sick kind of loyalty to him. He pushed them into key spots where they were to inflict humiliation on others who wouldn't join the team."

"Sounds like a snake pit. Those against them. Setting one side against the other. The old division trick. Together we stand, divided you fall."

"You've got it." Caroline stretched her legs out. "There's a lot of cleaning up to be done, and I don't mean just broken bathroom fixtures and water fountains. I want to make it a place again where people like to come to work, where they admire their bosses, and

where they're treated like human beings, like the talented profession-
als they are.

And what about Steve?" Gail asked with a sudden bluntness that
made Caroline stare at her.

"What—about Steve?" Her voice was barely above a whisper.

"He's back in the U.S., Caro. He was in Washington, covering the
Senate's investigation of the CIA role in the overthrow of President
Allende in Chile. Two weeks ago, he suddenly popped up in New
York. I'd just gotten back from the coast. Jack and I had dinner with
him."

Caroline was sitting forward, the hot toddy grasped hard in her
hands. Her face was stricken. White. The blue-violet eyes were deepening to a purple in the firelight.

"Honey"—Gail reached out and touched her arm—"he's still so in
love with you."

Caroline said something unintelligible and lunged to her feet. She
laughed with bitterness. "What a strange way he has of showing it."

"He doesn't even understand it himself."

"And I understand it even less." Gail heard the hurt and anger and
bewilderment in Caroline's voice. "I can change how I think, how I
walk, talk, dress, eat, the books I read, the political columnists I
follow, I can even change some of the ideas and ideals that I grew up
with. But I can't change who I am. I can't be the person he wants me
to be. I can't walk out of my skin and be someone else."

"He went on up to Boston. Then he leaves again for the Middle
East. I thought you had to know."

Caroline put her drink down and walked to the door, the long,
narrow gray flannel slacks accentuating her slenderness. She stopped
at the door and, with unhappy eyes, looked back at Gail, the dark hair
a cloud about her face. "I don't want to talk about him anymore, Gail.
I *can't* talk about him anymore. It hurts too much." And she was
suddenly gone.

The following evening, Dick took Caroline to the school's small
theatre, where he showed her Gail's latest musical film, *Marissa,* the
movie version of her Broadway production. "Isn't she terrific?" he
exclaimed over and over. "I keep forgetting she's my mother."

"You've never seen her perform in person, have you?" Caroline
asked as they walked back across the small campus, lights from the
windows of the dormitories and the house glittering through the
night.

"One of these days I will," he said with a smile. "My mother wants me to come to the States to go to college," he said.

"And how do you feel about that?" she asked.

"Well, I would miss everyone here," he said. "Grandmère and Grandpère, the friends I've made here at Bellone. But I would like to see my mother and Jack more often." She felt more than saw his smile in the darkness. "I like Jack. I'm glad my mother married him." And then she heard the wistfulness and looked around at the tall teenager.

"But I *did* have a father, you know."

Caroline sighed inaudibly. So it was to be an inquisition. She remembered one of several years before, which finally ended when Gail had said to him, "I'll tell you everything, Dick, when I feel you're old enough to know."

He stopped in the path just under the low chalet eaves of the house. "I want to go to Princeton," he suddenly said, gazing into her face. "Like my father did."

Caroline stiffened. *Like my father did.*

He slowly turned his head and looked away. "That day of the funeral. In Washington. When my mother and I waited for the man to come to the hotel and take me in the long black car. I was little and didn't really know what was happening. But I saw a woman in the crowd on the cathedral steps and she was clutching a newspaper." His voice took on a curious tone. "I saw a man's face, a picture in the newspaper, and it was the same man who came here twice. My mother called him Richard." His voice became soft. "And they were very much in love."

"Then . . . you know who he was," Caroline said slowly. And he nodded.

They walked into the house in silence. Just inside, she leaned over and kissed him on the cheek. "I guess the time has come," she said softly, "that you're old enough to know everything." She touched his face gently, feeling the cold from the outside. His eyes, beneath the touseled brown hair, were bright, inquiring, eager. "I think she's up in her room, writing letters. Why don't you go up and talk to her?"

She watched until he had disappeared into the shadowy reaches of the upper floor. So the time has finally come when we must go home, she thought, pulling off the heavy tweed coat. She glanced again up the staircase, but there was only darkness up there. With a slight shiver, she turned toward the library. There would be a fire on the

431

hearth and the momentary comfort of a deep easy chair pulled up close beside it.

They all stood on the wide stone steps of the house, watching as Georges swept the Citroën around the circular driveway and up to the entrance of the chalet-type house, Dudley Coombs sitting beside him. Ellie was hugging both Gail and Caroline, one arm around each, her blue eyes misted with tears. "It's been so wonderful, having both of you here," she said in a husky voice.

Gail then turned to Dick. They looked at each other, hands clasped in front of them. Then he threw himself into her arms and whispered, "I'm glad you told me everything." For several moments they were silent. Caroline climbed into the car and waited, the collar of her fur coat held close against her cheeks.

"When the school year is over, darling," Gail whispered to Dick as she pulled back a little and looked at him, "you'll fly to New York."

He smiled brightly, and she climbed into the car, then blew him a kiss as it pulled away and down the long driveway toward the main road of Bellone.

29
1975

There was a slick of rain on Fifth Avenue. It dimpled the tinted windows of the long black limousine with tiny diamond-like drops and threw back reflections of the street lamps and headlights from the rush of cars and buses flowing south. They had just dropped Gail off at her apartment on Central Park West and had come out of the park into the surge of southbound traffic.

Caroline gazed at the back of Han Powell's head. His full name was Hannibal, her father had explained in a recent letter, and he was one of two new drivers Meacham had hired. "A sharp kid," her father's letter had said. "Drives for us at night. Goes to Pace during the days, studying to be a teacher. He took that new kind of course to foil kidnappings; you know, the three-hundred-and-sixty-degree turns at fifty and sixty miles an hour. I just hope if he ever has to do one that I'm not in the car. I don't think my old bones would take it." *Old bones,* she scoffed silently. Her father was hale and hearty for a man in his early eighties.

She smiled into the darkness of the Rolls. Han looked like he could make those kinds of turns. His visored black cap was set jauntily to one side on his head, and when he had smiled broadly, introducing himself to her and to Dudley Coombs at Kennedy Airport, then preceded them through the terminal to the waiting car, he had a spring to his step and a quick, watchful turn of his head from side to side, which let her know he would be swift in an emergency.

Dudley, sitting beside him up ahead, was chatting away as though they had always known each other. And then they were finally pulling off the avenue and beneath the wide porte cochere.

"Good night and thank you, both of you," Caroline said as they all stood just below the broad marble steps.

"It's a pleasure to finally meet you, Miss Kendall," Han was saying as he tipped his hat. The usual dark sedan had pulled up behind the Rolls beneath the porte cochere, and the two security men were unloading her luggage and carrying it past Morgan, who stood in the open doorway, gray and frail-looking, but still erect.

"Thank you, Han," she said, shaking his hand, then she hurried up the three steps and, crossing to the door, put her arms around Morgan, who had tears in his eyes.

"Miss Caroline, he said, his voice trembling. "Miss Caroline, it's so good to have you home again."

She kissed his cheek. "And it's good to *be* home." They walked across the massive reception hall, her high heels tapping on the marble floor. Morgan had taken her fur coat and was watching her with a soft smile as she ran toward the staircase.

"Your mother and father are waiting for you," he called out as she flew up the stairs.

She found them in the living room of their suite, watching the late news on television, both in robes, the room soft and rosy with firelight and low lamps. Caroline ran to her father before he could get up from the chair and threw herself into his arms.

"Well! Well, isn't this nice, having you home again," he said thickly, not even trying to disguise the tears in his voice.

"Oh, Daddy, how I've missed you," she said against his cheek, half-laughing, half-crying. Then they pulled back and looked at each other.

"He's asked me what time it is every five minutes since nine o'clock," Elizabeth said, as Caroline rose and walked to her, then knelt down and held her mother close. "And every day since a week ago, when I arrived home, he's worried out loud each hour or so, afraid you were going to change your mind and stay."

"No," Caroline said, slowly shaking her head, as she walked back to her father and sank down in front of him. "I'm back to stay. But . . . I have a very large request to make."

Lawrence smiled. His hair, completely white now, framed a face that was only lightly lined. The deep-set gray eyes, always penetrating, seemed to have grown even wiser with the years. But her accident and the passing decades had taken their toll. In the last year, his hands had developed a slight tremor. "A fair bargain, for having you home

434

again." There was a long pause. "Well?" he said.

"I want to go back to the *Inquirer,* Daddy."

"That's no great problem." He and Elizabeth smiled at each other.

"But—as the publisher." There was a long silence.

He hunched forward a little, his eyes peering deeply into hers. "You know, Caroline," he said softly, "I've been wondering how long it was going to take you to get around to that."

Caroline walked into the city room and stood off at the edge, watching the activity, reporters pounding typewriters, people milling about with wire copy in their hands, copy boys dashing along the aisles.

"It looks the same," she said to Ed Pinckney, who stood at her side. "Only worse. If that's possible." She loosened her coat collar.

"Then I didn't exaggerate," he said with his quirky smile. She had her arm through his and was hugging it closely.

"No, you didn't exaggerate," she said. "In fact, you didn't even begin to describe how awful it looks." She stared at the peeling paint and broken plaster. Someone had patched a broken window with a piece of cardboard. One of the clanking old elevators was out of order. Probably had been for months. Everything looked old and worn, the desks, the chairs, the typewriters, even the wire wastebaskets. It was depressing. Insulting to the people who worked here, she thought angrily.

"I'm going to raise some hell," she muttered.

"Around here?" Ed said wearily. "Honey, with St. Edna raising her own particular brand on a daily basis—"

"Not here. With my father. With Warren Leland. This place is a disgrace."

He grinned. "Want to meet anyone?"

"Not today," she said through a clenched jaw.

"Come to my office, then," he said. "I'll give you a cup of coffee and tell you all the sorry details." They walked along the far side of the room and went into his small cubbyhole, which was just large enough for a desk, a typewriter, and two chairs. He waved her to a seat and turned to pour water from a small Silex on a hot plate into two Styrofoam cups. He added some instant coffee, then handed her one. "Ashford is gone. You won't be sorry to hear that. He went to a Philadelphia paper. Scotty Blankenship retired—"

"I liked Scotty," she murmured over the rim of her cup.

"Braggiotti's gone. So's Everhard, and Wilkinson, and Michaels. They couldn't take the chill from the boss lady."

Caroline's eyes narrowed, but she said nothing as she slipped the beaver coat off.

"Ackerman bought a small weekly in New Hampshire. Connie Winslow got married, and started raising a family. Ab Streitner's in Houston at the space agency control center. Oh, yes . . ."

Caroline stiffened.

"And—well, I told you in my letter that Steve's in Washington."

"On temporary assignment, or what?" Her jaw suddenly felt tight and her heart started pounding. Then it hasn't lessened, she thought, it was worse than ever. She sipped the coffee, feeling small comfort in the stream of warm liquid seeping down her throat. It's supposed to get better, she told herself as feelings of loneliness and hurt rose within her. With an ocean separating her from Boston, she had managed to keep it in check, but now, as she looked out over the huge newsroom, it all swept over her in a deluge of memories—her old desk where she had found him sleeping that day, stretched back in her swivel chair, his hat over his face . . . the north elevator, where he always leaned against the wall, evenings, waiting for her, that lopsided grin on his face, a cigarette hanging from the corner of his mouth . . . Scotty Blankenship's desk, where Steve used to push the papers aside to sit on the corner and, to Scotty's deep annoyance, with his feet on the upturned wastebasket, begin an hour-long argument about an assignment.

"Once he got a load of St. Edna, he told her he preferred Vietnam to Boston, so she sent him to Washington—oh-oh," he said. "Here she comes."

Caroline saw a tall, red-headed woman in a smart-looking green wool dress coming toward Ed's office from across the newsroom. She was attractive, extremely feminine-looking, rather heavily made-up.

"It's Caroline Kendall, isn't it?" she said, smiling, as she walked into his office, her hand outstretched, a slim hand with carefully groomed nails of a coral shade.

Caroline took it briefly, then shoved her hands into the pockets of her camel's hair suit jacket. She had stood up and was leaning against the wall next to Ed. Edna Hutchison stood on the other side of the desk, facing them.

"I've been looking forward so much to meeting you," the woman said, and for a moment Caroline could almost believe that Ed's de-

436

scription had to be of someone else. But then she saw a flicker of something in her eyes that was gone in a second.

"Edna Hutchison," Ed was saying, and Caroline smiled briefly.

"Yes, Miss Hutchison. I'm glad I had a chance to see you in the few minutes I'm going to be here today," she said as she sat down again and began sipping her coffee. "I want you and the editors to make a master plan that will involve working conditions in the newsroom while a major remodeling job is under way. It will begin on the first of next month."

"Why—ye-e-es, Miss Kendall. Remodeling? How wonderful," she said, while her expression said that she thought it was anything *but* wonderful.

"And starting Tuesday—I'll be here on Monday, occupying my office, Miss Hutchison—I want to begin a series of private sessions with each and every one of the employees in the editorial department. I want to get to know all of them, on a one-to-one basis." Out of the corner of her eye she saw Ed Pinckney grinning. His collar was askew, the tie hanging limply; a button was missing from his shirt, and the expensive corduroy jacket was unpressed and lumpy-looking.

"That sounds—like an excellent idea," the woman said, her voice faltering.

"I want to find out why they're so unhappy, why the morale is in the condition it's in, why—"

"Well . . ."

Caroline suddenly stood up, grabbed her coat, and walked to the door. She looked around at Ed. "How about that lunch you promised me, Ed?"

"You bet," he said, his grin ever wider as he took his trench coat and followed her out of the office.

"Very nice to have met you," Caroline said, glancing her way for a moment.

"See you at the four o'clock news meeting, Edna," Ed said, without looking back.

"Ye-es. The four o'clock news meeting," Miss Hutchison said with some confusion. Then she quickly called to Caroline, "Perhaps you can be there, too, Miss Kendall." Her expression said that she rather hoped otherwise.

"Perhaps I can," Caroline said, smiling sweetly over her shoulder. "I'm certainly going to *try.*"

But the smile slowly disappeared as she stepped into the elevator ahead of Ed. A sports columnist with a nauseous-looking green jacket and a shock of red hair was asking Ed if he would like tickets to some sporting event. She had nodded to him as she started pulling on her gloves, then blocked their voices out. She was thinking about Edna Hutchison and then she was not thinking about her at all. She was thinking about Steve and how those last moments with him had colored everything that she had done and said since. For moments, while parrying with Edna Hutchison, she had been able to forget. But the memory kept coming back, and the terrible sinking feeling returned, the bleak, gray emptiness. She closed her eyes, giving in to memories . . . memories of how it felt when he touched her, the way his voice murmured across her cheek and lips when he made love to her . . . memories of his eyes in those last moments, the hardness of his voice, the coldness, the way he stood up and walked away . . .

She opened her eyes and pulled the second glove on, lips tightening, as Ed took her arm to leave the elevator.

It was raining outside, a cold, sleety rain that had brought the traffic on the street almost to a standstill. "Wait while I get a cab," Ed said, dashing off, and she nodded, gratefully. It would give her time to push the memories away. *No more, Caroline,* she told herself, *no more memories. Put them away with the past, where they belong. No more . . . no more . . .*

30
1979

Caroline was on her way to Washington toward the end of March to conduct her second interview with Egypt's Anwar el-Sadat, who was in the United States to sign the peace treaty with Israel's Menachem Begin.

"As publisher, I occasionally permit myself the luxury of writing an editorial or doing an interview," she said with a smile to her father. She had stopped in Manhattan en route to the nation's capital to see her parents, and was disturbed at how pale and thin Lawrence Kendall seemed. They were in the library, with firelight dancing across the shelves of books, and a drizzling rain slashing against the windows. Caroline had seen the worry in Elizabeth's eyes when she arrived an hour earlier, but now she was alone with her father while Elizabeth left the library to tell Morgan that Caroline would stay for dinner.

Caroline and her father sat for a moment in a comfortable silence. He was sitting in a deep chair before the fire, with his legs up on a hassock and a light robe over his knees. She pulled a small chair up close and took one of his hands in hers.

"You're too thin," she said. "I worry about you—"

"Worry about your mother," he said softly, looking toward the door with caution in his voice.

"Mother—?"

"I don't want to alarm you, Caroline." His hand trembled a little in hers and she clasped it harder. "But she had some bleeding. I only found out about it yesterday. She told me then. I insisted she call the doctor, and she did. She made an appointment to see him tomorrow. She wanted to wait until after you had been here."

"Oh, Daddy," Caroline said with soft alarm in her voice. "I'll cancel my trip and go to the doctor with her."

He smiled and patted her hand over his. "I knew you'd say that. Good girl! I feel better already." He grinned, and she saw a glimmer of the younger Lawrence Kendall in that smile, the handsome, tall man who ruled a financial empire, but who had always had time to stop and answer a little girl's question, to hold her close, to kiss the top of her head and whisper how much she meant to him. "She's going to give me hell when she hears that I've told you, but . . ."

Caroline smiled. "We'll somehow survive her wrath." They grinned at each other. Elizabeth's wrath was an old joke between them.

He touched her cheek then. "And what about you, my girl?"

She looked deeply into the fire. "The *Inquirer* is finally in good shape. We've just about completed our four-year plan of remodeling, and our computer system is one of the best and most up-to-date in the country."

"Warren showed me the pictures of the newsroom you sent him." He smiled. "He took it gracefully, backing out of the newspaper operation, but I knew he wasn't happy about it. Kept saying, of course, that he knew you'd make a big success of it."

"Well, I'm not showing much of a profit in this first year of taking over the entire group, but in the long run we'll catch up. By streamlining the newsrooms and making working conditions better for the employees, we'll begin to take it out of the red within three or four years."

"I'm not worried," he said. He was watching her carefully. "And your personal life?"

She laughed softly. "No, nothing serious, I'm afraid."

"Caroline—"

"Darling, much as I know you and Mother would love to see me married, settled down, there's no one in my life worth mentioning."

"No one?" He picked up the glass of pale, diluted scotch on the small table beside him and sipped it. She knew he wanted to ask about Steve McCallum, but would not.

"Well, let me see," she said, pretending to try to think of someone even the least bit suitable. "There's Clay Williamson. He inherited the Williamson factories outside of Pawtucket. And there's Andrew Fisher. Up-and-coming attorney. You'd like them both." They were grinning at each other again. "Trouble is, I don't."

For a moment, the old camaraderie had returned. For a moment, they had been able to put Elizabeth's problem at the back of their minds, but as she came through the door, the heavy gray satin dinner dress gleaming dully in the firelight, Caroline stood up and walked to her with her hands outstretched.

"You are not to say a word," she said all in a soft rush. "But Daddy has told me about the bleeding and about your—"

"Lawrence, you shouldn't have!" Elizabeth looked at him in reproval.

"Yes, he should have, and I'm glad he did. And I'm staying right here and going to the doctor with you tomorrow."

"Caroline—" Elizabeth said, protesting.

"There's nothing more to be said," Caroline said firmly. "It's all settled."

Lawrence Kendall died in his sleep of a heart attack the night before Elizabeth was to come home to the townhouse from the hospital. Her surgery, a hysterectomy, had been successful, according to the surgeons. "If you are going to have cancer and you're a woman, it's just possible that's the safest place to have it, if safe is the proper term to use in this case," Dr. Newbard had told Caroline after the surgery.

Caroline was wakened before light that morning by her mother's maid, Emily, a pretty young woman of about thirty who had been with Elizabeth for the past five years.

"It's—it's your father, Miss Kendall," she said tearfully, one hand twisting in the other.

Caroline sat up sharply, eyes wide. Something in Emily's tone told her the worst.

"My father?"

"Armand, his valet, found him. You know, Miss, the new valet Mrs. Kendall hired for him just two months ago—"

"Yes, yes," Caroline had turned and pushed her feet into mules at the side of her bed. She pushed her hair back distractedly, then reached for her robe at the end of the bed. "Yes, Emily—"

As she stood up and pulled on her robe, she knew she was afraid to hear any more. "What—what is it?"

"Oh, Miss . . ." Emily was dissolving in tears. She turned and ran from the room, just as old Morgan appeared at the door.

Caroline and Morgan stared at each other, and then Caroline rushed to him, and he put his arms about her as she sobbed.

"There, there," he said. "There, there, little girl. Just cry as much as you can. Then you must get yourself dressed and go to the hospital to be with your mother."

And now, six months later, she was sitting in that same library where she had sat with her father on those last evenings before his death. But this time it was Ellie sitting next to her, and Morgan was standing at the doorway far across the room.

"Yes, Morgan?" she said, and made a small gesture indicating he could take the coffee cart away.

He came across the room and turned the cart around to start toward the door with it. "Meacham would like to know what time you want the cars brought around for the drive to the church in Rijksville for the services."

Caroline thought for a moment, the terrible sense of loss sweeping through her again. "Oh. Yes. Eleven. Yes—eleven."

He nodded and murmured, "Yes, Miss Caroline," and disappeared through the door, the cart making a soft swishing sound over the thick carpet. Caroline stood up and put the screen closer to the fireplace.

"When she wrote to me six months ago," Ellie said softly, "I had hoped the surgery she had then would be the end of it."

Caroline sadly shook her head. "We all hoped." She shrugged in a helpless kind of way, and turned around. "But then, with Daddy's death, little seemed to matter to her anymore."

"I know." Ellie rose slowly, the folds of her pale blue velvet robe falling into place. "She missed him so terribly. Every letter she wrote said how much."

They stood for a long moment with their arms around each other. "Their love was so special," Caroline whispered. "The kind of love I always wanted for myself. Perhaps that's why I could never settle for —for less."

"I know, darling, I know," Ellie said softly. "Go to Beirut, Caroline. Perhaps you'll find him. Perhaps he'll be safe, and waiting there for you."

They turned and walked from the room, hands clasped tightly at their sides.

Talk of war, terrorism, the new peace treaty between Israel and Egypt, and the tenuous truce between Lebanon's Christian rightists and Muslim leftists dominated the conversation at the Bayard table.

442

Whenever more than two members of the large household in Beirut sat down to a meal the conversation inevitably took that turn.

Donald Bayard, chief Mideast correspondent for International News Organization, of which Kendall Newspapers was the largest member, maintained a swinging door policy at his villa in the fashionable Ras Beirut section of the city. The wives of Alec Harwood and Carmine Bonelli had been there and gone. A correspondent from the Rome bureau was staying at the villa for a few days, and Bayard's wife, Mona, and her sister, Ann, were packing all of the household goods.

"I was delighted to hear you had bought the *Morning Journal* in New York," Donald said as they drove from the airport, where he had met Caroline's plane.

"News travels fast," she said with a smile.

"That's the business we're in." He glanced at her for a moment, matching her smile, then swerved as two large lumbering trucks filled with Lebanese soldiers sped past. "Everything set to go?"

"Yes, set to go. It took some negotiating, but everything's signed." She was watching the passing scene with curious eyes, the odd mixture of normal civilian life and the truckloads of soldiers, the gaping wounds of a bombed-out building, and the barriers and blockades at various points.

She had arrived in the late afternoon, and after a shower and change to something a little dressier than the casual slacks she had traveled in, she felt refreshed.

"We're moving to Tel Aviv," Bayard said to Caroline as he led her into the dining room. "I'll keep two men here, but on a rotating basis so that no two faces or names become too familiar."

Caroline had smiled fleetingly. "I got here just in time, didn't I?" She was staying at the Bayards' villa, a plan that had seemed the safest and, in fact, the only feasible plan. The glossy Hotel St. Georges overlooking the Mediterranean was a burned-out ruin. Shops and restaurants and sleek bars along the Avenue des Français and Rue Hamra had mostly disappeared. Beirut, the Paris of the Middle East, was now a scarred and mutilated city with cannon- and gun-pocked buildings, looted stores, the danger of stray bullets, food shortages, and a feeling of doom beyond the frantic urgency that hung over everything like blowing gray smoke.

"Another week and we would have been gone," said Mona with her charming smile. She was an attractive Englishwoman whom Donald had met in London, as blonde and vivacious as her sister was dark

443

and quiet. They were sitting over coffee and liqueurs in the glass-walled dining room that looked out over a walled garden. Candlelight flickered in tall silver holders, but the walls were stripped of mirrors and paintings.

"There's too much risk in staying on here," Donald, a slender, handsome man with silvery hair, said as he relit his pipe. "It can only get worse. And we can operate much more efficiently and safely from Tel Aviv, with two-man teams moving in and out every few weeks or so." A somewhat long silence had followed, as though everyone knew what Caroline was thinking.

She sipped at her coffee, sitting almost rigidly erect in the tall-backed carved chair, her black dress accentuating the creamy white of her throat, the haunting blue-violet of her eyes. "Please tell me . . . what you think has happened . . . or will happen to Steve McCallum."

Bayard had heard rumors about Caroline Kendall and Steve McCallum, but no indication of it crept into his eyes. As far as he was concerned, they were employer and employee, publisher and correspondent.

"I honestly don't know what to think," he said while puffing his pipe to life. "It has been three weeks now, and"—he looked up at her —"Beirut is like one large bomb, ready to go off. Violent death is a constant occurrence here. And life is very cheap. The lives of three journalists here are worth as much as the mood of the moment. There is absolutely no rationale in much that happens. Their kidnapping seems to have been effected with little purpose in mind. But then, who can read the mind of a terrorist?"

She returned to the States on the day the Bayards drove under heavy guard to Tel Aviv, the small convoy of vehicles first taking her to the airport, where she boarded a plane for a transfer in Rome and then in New York. "There is nothing you could do here" were Bayard's final words to her, "and it is far too dangerous for you to stay on."

Why did I even go there? she asked herself as TransGlobal flight 401 winged over the Atlantic toward New York in the dead of night. What would she have done if the terrorists had suddenly released the three men? Would she have been Caroline Kendall, publisher of Kendall Newspapers? Or would she have been Caroline Kendall, the woman still in love with a big, rumpled man with eyes as blue and changeable as the sea?

444

She closed her eyes and tried to sleep, but the questions kept whirling round and round in her head. When she finally slept, she saw him coming toward her, the brown hair blowing in the wind, but just as he came close, he suddenly turned and walked away, off on the far side of a deep, dark gap that had spread between them. It was always the same, always the same dream, the chasm growing wider and wider, a light coming from somewhere to blind her eyes.

The day began like any other. She rose at six, showered and dressed, and went down to the dining room, where Morgan brought her breakfast in to her, coffee first, then the half grapefruit, with the sections loosened and just lightly dusted with powdered sugar. Getting older, she thought with a wry smile. Everything has to be as it was the day before, the grapefruit, two slices of toast with marmalade, the second cup of coffee . . .

"Snow again today, Miss Caroline," Morgan said, pulling a heavy drape back with a trembling, gnarled hand and peering first up to the sky and then far down to the avenue below.

"Well, get out the snow shovel, Morgan," Caroline said, with the same small laugh. It was their long-standing joke, that he would then go down the twenty-two stories to Fifth Avenue below to help Paul Baker, the doorman, clear a path to the street.

But he hadn't heard her. He simply kept gazing up at the sky.

Will I go on and on with my life, until I am as old as Morgan? she wondered. All of the long years . . . without Steve . . . until I am stooped like Morgan, when my bones will ache and the flesh will be tired, but the pain and loneliness will be as fresh and hurting as it is now?

She picked at the grapefruit, then lifted one piece and slid it into her mouth. Six weeks had passed and still no additional word from the State Department.

During her stay in Beirut, she had talked to military men and officials there, most importantly a Maronite commander in the Lebanese army whom Donald Bayard had led her to.

"In most probability, Madame, the men who took the journalists were from the Fath movement, from the centrist backbone of the PLO, angered, no doubt, by what they saw as complete sympathy for the Israelis," he told her.

She had stayed for less than a week and returned to New York, knowing she could accomplish nothing by staying there any longer.

But back in the United States, she traveled to Washington almost weekly to call at the State Department, determined not to let the American government even hesitate in their search for the three men. Even though she knew that whatever she and Steve had had together was over.

"Yes," Morgan said, finally turning from the window, the pale blue silk drape falling back into place, "along about ten o'clock, I'd say, so don't forget to wear your boots, Miss Caroline."

"Thank you, Morgan," she said with a smile, then lifted her cup to her mouth and took a sip of coffee.

Just as Morgan reached the door to the butler's pantry, Katy came bustling through, a telephone in her hand. She quickly plugged it in the socket and brought it across to Caroline.

"From Boston, Miss Caroline. It's Mr. Pinckney."

Caroline glanced at her watch. It was just eight o'clock. Something fluttered faintly inside, dread or hope, she wasn't sure which.

"Yes, Ed?" she said into the phone, her other hand clutching her napkin in her lap and twisting it into a ball. A sharp stab of fear throbbed in her breast. She could hear Ed talking to someone on his end of the line, his hand half over the mouthpiece, giving instructions of some kind. "Ed?" she said. "Ed?"

Then he suddenly spoke. "Caroline?"

"I'm here," she said, feeling a terrible tension strain at her throat, creep into her voice.

"He's on his way, Caroline."

"What?" she shouted into the phone, holding it with both hands and half rising to her feet. Katy and Morgan were staring at her.

"He and the other two men were dumped into the street at three o'clock in the morning, Beirut time, in the old part of the city. Six hours later, Steve was on a plane heading for the States."

Tears were streaming down her face and her legs almost gave way. Katy and Morgan were at either side of her, holding her arms as she slid down onto the chair again. "On his way! I don't believe it. Oh, Ed—Ed—"

"He'll be at Dulles at eight P.M. Pan Am. Changing planes in Rome. I"—his voice grew lame—"I—just thought you'd want to know."

"Oh, yes," she half whispered. "Oh, yes, Ed. *Yes.*"

"And, Caroline." He hesitated. "In case you go to Washington— our man at INO in Beirut said he'll be at the Mayflower Hotel."

*   *   *

He walked through Customs, led by the State Department man, oblivious to the arms and bodies that jostled him from all sides, smiling as he realized for the first time that he was really free and back on the soil of his native country.

He turned and clapped the State Department man on the shoulder and, with a grin, said, "I'll take it from here." They shook hands, and Steve pushed through one of the doors leading out of the Customs section, his valpack slung over one shoulder and a leather duffle bag in the other hand.

He saw the reporters and photographers surging toward him as a shout went up. *Christ!* he thought with a sinking feeling, *so this is how people feel when we come at them like this!* And with not a little shame he was glad to see the State Department man had stuck close and was shouldering his way ahead of him, as cameras flashed and voices shouted, "Steve! Steve McCallum. Over here, Steve."

"It's okay," he said, sheepishly to the State Department man. "I'll give them five minutes."

And with that, the crowd of reporters swirled around him and shouted questions while the cameras flashed more and more. He loosened his collar and exploded, *"Jesus Christ!* Give a guy a chance!"

She slowly paced the length of the library, back and forth, back and forth, while firelight played on the reddish lights in her dark hair as it swung from side to side at her shoulders. Twice, she paused at the desk by the long windows where the telephone was, then she walked on.

With a tense, shuddering little sigh, she stopped in front of the fireplace and looked up. Lawrence Robertson Kendall gazed down at her. The small enigmatic smile at one corner of his mouth seemed more pronounced than ever. He seemed to be softly saying, "Well, what are you waiting for?" She watched the portrait, searching the face for something more. And then, she remembered . . .

"You might as well know, sweetheart," he had said to her once, when she was very small and a little girl she had spoken to on the beach at Newport had snubbed her, "that there are a lot of things in this world, if you want them, that you have to go out and get for yourself."

She looked at the portrait several moments longer, then smiled up at it. A log snapped on the fire and in the far corner of the library a

447

record was softly playing the "Figlio Che Fai" from *Turandot*. She turned and walked to the desk, picked up the telephone, and dialed a long-distance number, one she had already memorized.

"Would you please ring Mr. McCallum's room?"

She waited while it rang and rang and was just about to hang up when she suddenly clenched the phone with both hands.

"Steve?" she finally said, her voice faltering.

"Yes?" His voice sounded very far away, and sleepy.

"I—I'm sorry it's so late. It's Caroline . . ."

"Yes, I know." The timbre of his voice had grown stronger, but there was still a distance in it.

"It—I was so glad—so relieved—when I heard the news." There was a silence. "That you had been released and were safe."

"Yes—well, there were times"—he laughed, but it was a stranger's laugh—"times when we thought we'd had it. These characters who had us were pretty psyched up most of the time. Trigger-happy and nuts!"

She clenched the phone harder and felt her heart thudding. "I—I've heard—been told they can be brutal, and—and unpredictable."

"Unpredictable!" He laughed, and the laugh was like a shard of ice. "That's being complimentary." She could tell he was lighting a cigarette and, with a sudden stab of jealousy, she wondered if a woman lay beside him, warm and murmuring softly in the dark of the hotel room, touching his shoulder as he sat hunched up against the pillows, his cigarette glowing in the darkness.

"Please," she cried out, "don't make it so hard for me!" With her other hand, she roughly pushed the tears off her cheek.

"Caroline—"

"I have to talk to you, see you—I have to." She was crying harder. "Oh, God, Steve."

"All right," she heard him say. "But I can't get out of Washington for several more days. I have to talk to people at the State Department and—"

"I'll come there. Tomorrow morning."

"Good. Why don't I plan on being back here at the hotel by noon?"

"I'll be there at noon."

"Good night," he said, and she heard the soft click of the phone.

"Good night," she whispered. "Oh, darling, good night."

The lobby of the Mayflower Hotel was crowded, but Caroline pushed her way through, quickly. And alone. She smiled a wry smile.

448

Since her father's death less than a year earlier, she had stopped the bodyguards. Her mother had weakly pleaded with her, but she had insisted.

"I just can't go on that way the rest of my life. It's like wearing chains on your feet. Even if it's a risk, I have to finally feel some kind of freedom."

And Elizabeth had smiled, trying to understand.

At the elevators, Caroline felt a sudden rush of fright. She leaned for a moment against the wall and closed her eyes. She had hardly slept the night before, rising before it was light to bathe and dress. For the first time since she had ordered the two private jets sold, she wished one were still at her disposal as she boarded the shuttle to Washington.

On arriving at the Mayflower, she had told the desk clerk to have her suitcases taken up to her suite, then asked for the number of Steve's room.

She finally walked into the elevator and stood in one corner as it filled up with a noisy group of conventioneers. It was ten minutes past twelve and her heart was beating wildly. She slowly unbuttoned her cocoa suede coat and pushed back the fur collar as the elevator rose, stopping stubbornly at each floor while one or two of the convention-eers pushed out into the corridors, calling back over their shoulders about how they'd all meet in Charley's suite in half an hour for drinks. When she finally reached Steve's floor, she was alone in the elevator. She walked out and down the corridor to his door, hesitated, and then knocked softly.

When he opened the door, they simply stood and stared at each other for a long moment.

"I *had* to see you," she half whispered, as though it were part of their telephone conversation the night before. Her heart seemed to have stopped and she thought her knees would buckle beneath her. She put out a hand to grasp at the doorjamb, but suddenly she was in his arms and miraculously his lips were against her ear, and mur-muring, "My God, how could I let you go? How could I have let it happen?"

She was laughing and crying all at once, as he picked her up in his arms, kicked the door shut, and carried her over to the bed. And as he quickly undressed her, she knew, in a flash of insight, that it would always be this way, long separations and wildly passionate reunions, anger and hurt and tears and love and always the separations that would make their coming together again moments like these—his hands and mouth and the wide sloping shoulders in the shadowy light of the room coming down to her . . . coming down to her . . . and closing out the lights.

She lay with her eyes closed, the warm silence cradling her. Their bodies were close, but not touching. For the moment that it was in their lives, it was a time for no words, for breathing again, for listening to sounds of distant traffic, for feeling the coolness of air against their damp skin, for knowing that they were within touching distance, that there were words that must be said, decisions that must be made.

But for the moment it was enough just to know they could reach out and feel, lean close and touch with their mouths, turn heads and whisper.

She heard the click of the lighter and against her closed lids saw the glimmer of light and slowly breathed in the drifting trail of his cigarette smoke.

"All I could think of that day . . . that day, that moment when they threw us into the back of the van . . . was you."

She didn't move. She didn't breathe. She strained to listen, her heart silently crying out.

"Suddenly I knew that nothing that had happened mattered. That it was unimportant . . . *who* you were. *What* you were. The fact that we agree on almost nothing. All I knew was that I *had* to get back to you—"

"Steve—"

"—that no matter what happened, I had to see you again, had to hold you in my arms again. When you look into the mouth of a submachine gun, things like money and importance and power and tinted-glass limousines don't mean very much. Everything suddenly melts away and there's only one thing left, and either you have it or you don't have it. *Life.*" He slowly turned his head and looked at her in the shadowed light. She let her eyes open and saw that he had risen on one elbow above her and was looking down into her eyes. "And life isn't really worth very much if you don't have what's most important in it." His mouth was slowly moving down to hers. "And that was you," he whispered, just as his lips touched her lips.

Magically, they were again making love, their bodies familiar and precious to each other. Like two threads of music, it was point and counterpoint, the first long, slow, and sensual ritual of love, growing in intensity, building with exquisite pleasure to where bone and flesh

450

and muscle melt into one another, seeming to flow from one body to the other and back again.

"I need you so desperately," she whispered as she kissed his throat, all of the pent-up desire again rushing from her and into him. His mouth and hands were giving her body life again, and she gave it in return, wildly, losing herself in their growing passion, until he thrust again and again, deeply inside of her—the last of the fears and loneliness sliding away and disappearing with the years of her life when she thought she had lost him forever.

They danced, slowly and sensuously, their bodies hard against each other, her hips following his, his fingers tracing the fine little ridges in the vertebrae down her back. The lights were low and the music throbbed softly. It was a small nightclub, small but sleek, with smoke drifting in the blue spotlights on the band. They had ordered dinner and let it grow cold. The wine buzzed pleasantly in her head, sang in her veins, and as they returned to the table, she leaned close to the crystal bowl, where three gardenias floated, and breathed their fragrance.

"It won't be easy," he suddenly said, as he watched her. He had grasped her hand and was slowly twisting the plain gold band on her third finger. She raised her head and looked at him.

"I know that." Her face was close. "I knew that the first moment I met you. Because I think I fell in love with you that first moment I saw you."

He kissed her lightly on the tip of the nose, then chuckled softly, remembering the old *World Inquirer* in Boston and its city room, the clutter and dirt and discarded coffee cartons, the rattling wire machines, grimy windows, and a beautiful young girl pounding on a typewriter. "I think . . . it was the same for me," he said, half whispering, his mouth close to her ear.

She tucked her hand in his. "Take me home, darling."

"Home?" He smiled quizzically. And then he nodded, still smiling, as they rose. "Just the first of many homes, I rather imagine," he said. "The Mayflower Hotel."

They stood behind the massive glass walls in the terminal and watched a plane as it taxied toward a far runway. He turned slowly and, leaning against the glass, looked down at her. He liked the fine lines at the corners of her eyes, the more mature set of her features, and when the dark lashes swept upward and she returned his gaze with those deep violet eyes, he felt his breath catch in his throat.

"You could always have ordered me back," he said, wonderingly. "But you never did."

She slowly shook her head. "If I had . . . I would have lost everything. You would never have come back to me." She smiled, and the smile had sadness in it. "This way, I at least had hope."

He looked off at the other travelers, sitting in the long rows of colored plastic chairs or walking about impatiently and gazing out upon the vast airport, which was caught in darkness, lights of moving planes and service vehicles glittering through the night. He pulled her to him and held her close against him.

"Come to me . . . whenever you can."

She looked up into his face. "El Salvador isn't that far."

"Anywhere is far, now that I've found you again."

"I'll come there soon, darling," she whispered. "Very, very soon."

They heard his plane being announced and from the corner of his eye, he saw the gate being opened and travelers swarming toward it. His arms tightened around her and he kissed her. And then he held her hard against him again. "You understand . . . why it will be like this . . . why I have to do it this way?"

"Yes," she said, not trusting herself to say any more.

He kissed her again, then, suddenly thrusting her away from him, he swooped the leather duffle bag up in his hand and strode away. She watched him, a tall, broad-shouldered man in a worn and rumpled trench coat, hat pulled low over his eyes, pausing to turn and look at her, then disappearing through the gate to his plane.

452